D0013540

Kris Longknife
MUTINEER

Mike Shepherd

ACE BOOKS, NEW YORK

THE BERKLEY PUBLISHING GROUP
Published by the Penguin Group
Penguin Group (USA) Inc.
375 Hudson Street, New York, New York 10014, USA
Penguin Group (Canada), 90 Eglinton Avenue East, Suite 700, Toronto, Ontario M4P 2Y3, Canada
(a division of Pearson Penguin Canada Inc.)
Penguin Books Ltd., 80 Strand, London WC2R 0RL, England
Penguin Group Ireland, 25 St. Stephen's Green, Dublin 2, Ireland (a division of Penguin Books Ltd.)
Penguin Group (Australia), 250 Camberwell Road, Camberwell, Victoria 3124, Australia
(a division of Pearson Australia Group Pty. Ltd.)
Penguin Books India Pvt. Ltd., 11 Community Centre, Panchsheel Park, New Delhi—110 017, India
Penguin Group (NZ), 67 Apollo Drive, Rosedale, North Shore 0632, New Zealand
(a division of Pearson New Zealand Ltd.)
Penguin Books (South Africa) (Pty.) Ltd., 24 Sturdee Avenue, Rosebank, Johannesburg 2196,
South Africa

Penguin Books Ltd., Registered Offices: 80 Strand, London WC2R 0RL, England

This is a work of fiction. Names, characters, places, and incidents either are the product of the author's imagination or are used fictitiously, and any resemblance to actual persons, living or dead, business establishments, events, or locales is entirely coincidental. The publisher does not have any control over and does not assume any responsibility for author or third-party websites or their content.

KRIS LONGKNIFE: MUTINEER

An Ace Book / published by arrangement with the author

PRINTING HISTORY
Ace mass-market edition / February 2004

Copyright © 2004 by Mike Moscoe.
Cover art by Scott Grimando.
Cover design by Rita Frangie.
Interior text design by Kristin del Rosario.

ISBN: 978-0-441-01142-1

ACE
Ace Books are published by The Berkley Publishing Group,
a division of Penguin Group (USA) Inc.,
375 Hudson Street, New York, New York 10014.
ACE and the "A" design are trademarks of Penguin Group (USA) Inc.

PRINTED IN THE UNITED STATES OF AMERICA

17   16   15   14   13   12

1

"There's a terrified child down there."

Captain Thorpe's baritone reverberated off the hard metal walls of the *Typhoon*'s drop bay. Marines, a moment before intent on checking their battle suits, their weapons, their souls for this rescue mission, hung on his every word. Ensign Kris Longknife divided her attention; part of her stood back, studying the impact of his speech on the men and women she would soon lead. In her short twenty-two-year life, she'd heard a lot of fancy oratory. Another part of her listened to her commander's words, felt them roll over her, into her. It had been a long time since mere words had raised the hackles on her neck, made her want to rip some bastard limb from limb.

"The civilians tried to get her back." Kris measured his pause. He came in right on the downbeat. "They failed. Now they've called for the dogs."

The marines around Kris growled for their skipper. She'd only worked with them for four days; the *Typhoon* had sortied on two hours' notice! Captain Thorpe had gotten them away from space dock, short half the crew and without a marine lieutenant to command the drop platoon. Now a boot ensign named Longknife was surrounded by marines with three to twelve years in the Corps, champing at the bit to do something definite and dangerous.

"You've trained. You've sweated." The captain's words had the staccato of a machine gun. "You've drilled for this moment since you joined the Corps. You could rescue that kidnapped girl with your eyes closed." In the dim light of the drop bay, eyes gleamed with inner fire. Jaws tensed; hands closed in tight fists. Kris glanced down; so were hers. Yes, these troops were ready, all except one boot ensign. *Dear God, don't let me screw up,* Kris prayed silently.

"Now drop, Marines. Kick some terrorist butt, and put that little girl back in her mother's arms where she belongs."

"Ooh-rah," came back from twelve hyped men and women as the captain slow marched for the exit. *Well, eleven hyped marines and one scared ensign.* Kris put the same angry confidence into her shout as she heard from the rest. Here was none of the calm, the cool of Father's political speeches. Here was why Kris had joined the Navy. Here was something real; something she could get her hands on and make happen. Enough of endless talk and nothing done. She grinned. *If you could see me now, Father. You said the Navy was a useless waste of time, Mother. Not today!*

Kris took a deep breath as her platoon turned back to their preparations. The smell of armor, ammunition, oil, and honest human sweat gave her a rush. This was her mission and her squad, and she would see that one little girl got home safe and sound. This child would live.

As the memory of another child rose to fill her mind's eye, Kris stomped on the thought. She dared not go there.

Captain Thorpe paused in his exit march right in front of her. Eye to eye, he leaned into her face. "Keep out of your head, Ensign," he growled in a whisper. "Trust your gut. Trust your platoon and Gunny. They're good. The commodore thinks you have what it takes, even if you are one of those Longknifes. Show me what you've got. Take those bastards down hard. But if you're as empty as your old man, let Gunny know before you funk out on us, and he'll finish the mission. And I'll drop you back in your momma's lap in time for the next debutantes' ball."

Kris stared back at him, her face frozen, her gut a throbbing knot. He'd been riding her since she came aboard, never happy with her, always picking at her. She would show him. "Yes, sir," she shouted in his face.

Around her, the troops grinned, figuring the skipper had a few choice words for the boot ensign, none knowing just how choice. The captain snickered. A scowl or a snicker or a growl was all she'd ever seen on his face since coming aboard. Was there a different crinkle to his eyes, a new uptwist to his lips? He turned before she could read him better.

It wasn't her fault Father had signed all Wardhaven's legislation for the last eight years. She had nothing to do with her great-grandparents splashing the family name all over the history books. Let the captain try growing up in shadows like those. He'd be just as desperate as Kris was to make *her* own name, find *her* own place. That was why she joined the Navy.

With a shiver Kris tried to shake off the fear of failure. She turned to face her locker and tried again to adjust the standard-issue, size three battle spacesuit to fit. Six feet tall and too small everywhere else was her usual requirements for a suit. She'd never had a civilian suit that didn't leave her plenty of room for her pet computer to conform around her shoulders and down her arms, but those suits weren't semirigid plasta-steel a centimeter thick. Nelly, worth more than all the computers on the *Typhoon* and probably fifty times as capable, was a problem in battle armor. Marines were expected to be lean as well as mean; nothing extra was allowed anywhere. Kris tried slipping the main bulk of the computer down to her chest. She didn't carry much there, and most marine males seemed to be a bit bulky in that spot. Resealing herself in, she rotated her shoulders, bent, then stooped. Yes, that worked. She put on the helmet, rotated it until she got a firm click. With the faceplate down, the suit was a bit warm, but she'd been hot before.

> *"Krissie, can I have an ice cream?"* Eddy wheedled. *It was a hot spring day on Wardhaven, and they'd run to the park, leaving Nanna well behind them.*
>
> *Kris fumbled in her pocket. She was the big sister; she was expected to plan ahead now, just like big brother Honovi had done for her when she was just a little kid. Kris had enough coins for two ice creams. But Father insisted that planning ahead included making things last. "Not now," Kris insisted. "Let's go see the ducks."*
>
> *"But I want an ice cream now," came in as much of a wail as an out-of-breath six-year-old could muster.*
>
> *"Come on, Nanna's almost here. Race you to the duck pond." Which got Eddy's feet moving even before Kris finished the challenge. She beat him, of course, but only by as much as a ten-year-old big sister should beat a six-year-old kid brother.*
>
> *"Look, the swans are back." Kris pointed at the four huge birds. So they walked along the pond, not too far behind the old man with the corn who always fed the birds. Kris was careful to keep Eddy from getting too near to the water. She must have done a good job because when Nanna finally caught up with them, she didn't give Kris a lecture about how deep the pond was.*
>
> *"I want an ice cream," Eddy demanded again with the single-mindedness of his few years.*
>
> *"I don't have any money," Nanna insisted.*
>
> *"I do," Kris put in proudly. She had planned ahead, just like Father said smart people should.*
>
> *"Then you go buy the ice cream," Nanna grumbled.*
>
> *Kris skipped off, so sure she would be seeing them again that she didn't even look back.*

There was a tap at her shoulder. With a shiver, she turned to see a freckled face and raised her faceplate in time to be met with a "Need help, short fork?"

The drop bay was busy and noisy, and her shiver went unnoticed. She managed the cheery "No way, wooden spoon," reply the infectious grin and challenge demanded. Ensign Tommy Li Chin Lien had been born to a family of Santa Maria asteroid miners. Rather than hang around that isolated world, he'd joined the Navy to see the galaxy, thereby greatly disappointing his folks and, per his great-grandmother, his ancestors.

At Officer Candidate School, they'd passed hours swapping stories about how their parents had stormed and ranted against their career choice. Kris was surprised by how fast they became friends, one from supersophisticated Wardhaven, the other that crazy blend of Irish and Chinese that so much of Santa Maria's working class still held to.

Right now, Tommy waved his universal tester in Kris's face. Raised in vacuum, he distrusted air and gravity and viewed mud-raised people like Kris as hopeless optimists, dependent on him for the proper paranoia toward space. Kris raised her left arm for Tommy to plug his black box into the battle suit she'd been issued. While he ran his checks, Kris worked with Nelly, running her personal computer through interface tests with the command net. Auntie Tru, now retired from her job as Wardhaven's Info War Chief, had helped Kris with Nelly's interface, as she'd done with most of Kris's math and computer homework for as long as Kris could remember. Nelly lit up Kris's heads-up display with every report or screen authorized to a boot ensign on a mission . . . and a few it was better the skipper did not know Kris had access to. Kris and Nelly finished about the same time Tommy detached his tester from Kris. She flipped up her faceplate.

"Your camouflage adjustment is about five nanoseconds below optimum, but it meets Navy standards," Tommy grumbled. The Navy rarely met his expectations for perfection. "Your coolant system isn't all that far into the green, either."

"I'm more worried about my heater. It's arctic tundra where I'm headed, haven't you heard?" She grinned.

He refused to swallow his scowl for her attempt at a Santa Maria brogue. "And there's a bad gasket in there somewhere." They'd been over that one before; one of the battle suit's jelly seals was a slow leaker, but every suit aboard had at least one bum seal. It was a bitter joke among the troops; good seals went to the civilian market, weak ones went to lowest-bid government contracts.

"I'm not working the asteroids, Tommy. I won't be living in this suit for a month." Kris gave the standard reply the procurement chiefs gave her father. The prime minister of Wardhaven always accepted it. But then, he didn't do drop missions. Today, his daughter was. "I'll only be in vacuum an hour, two at the most. Sequim's atmosphere is good."

"Mud hen," Tommy answered in disgust.

"Space head," Kris shot back, giving Tommy one of his own trademark grins, then turned to the Light Assault Craft that would be carrying her and her squad. It was the minimum vehicle that could get you from orbit to the deck, not much more than a heat shield that doubled as a wing and a flip-on top that was just there for stealth. Then again, Kris had raced in smaller skiffs. "This check out?" she asked, serious once more.

"Didn't I test it four times?" Tommy grinned. "Didn't it pass four times? Your humble servant will get you there." Which only left Kris struggling to keep hold of her temper. The Navy trusted the marines to put their asses on the line, but not with the car keys. It would be Tommy's job to fly the two LACs from the *Typhoon* in orbit to the ground, all except for two or three minutes when ionization took the two LACs out of radio touch—and they'd be on autopilot for that. All the while, Kris and her eleven marines were supposed to sit there dumb and bored. That was just one part of the approved plan she would like to change. But a boot ensign does not change plans that her skipper and his Gunny Sergeant like.

"Help me on with my kit," she told Tommy. Along the bay, the platoon members were paired up, checking each other's suits, loading them up with weapons and drop gear. Corporal Santo went down Gunny's squad, Corporal Li checked Kris's. Gunny would double-check them; then Kris would triple-check.

Kris's load was a tad lighter than her teammates' since Nelly weighed in at half of a standard-issue Navy personal computer while holding all the command, control, communications, and intelligence—C^3I in military speak—that an ensign could ask for. Still, hanging from her armor or carefully stowed in her pack were rocket-propelled grenades of many flavors; six spare magazines for her M-6, half of them rounds of nonlethal intent, the others real ones; as well as water, first aid, and food. Marines never left home without lugging a ton of stuff. Fully loaded, again Kris rotated her shoulders, twisted her hips, checked the load if not for comfort at least for problems. She'd carried more backpacking through the Blue Mountains on Wardhaven during college vacations. Those carefree months of outdoor living was one of the reasons she was here.

Tommy eyed her as she did a deep knee squat and bounced back up. "You good for this?"

"Everything's in place. Not too heavy."

"You good for this business? Rescuing a kidnapped kid." The grin was gone; she saw what the Santa Marian looked like serious.

"I'm good for this, Tom. I'm the best Navy small arms weapons qualifications on this boat. I've got the best Navy physical training scores, too. The skipper's right. I'm the best he's got. And Tommy, I want this."

"Ensign Lien to the bridge," came over the ship's MC-1, ending any further questions. Tommy clapped her on the back. "The luck of the little people and God go with you," he said as he headed for the hatch.

"No spare seat for Him in an LAC," Kris shot back over her shoulder, another salvo in their long-running debate. But Kris was already trailing Gunny, rechecking the fall of gear, reverifying weapons loads. She finished a second behind him.

He went over her kit, and she went over his. He tightened one of her straps and growled, "You'll do, ma'am." She found nothing to modify on him; she hadn't expected to. Gunny had practiced for this moment for sixteen years. That this was his first live-fire mission in all that time didn't seem to bother him or Captain Thorpe.

"Let's drop, team!" Kris called to her loaned platoon.

With a shout of "Ooh-rah" the two squads turned in unison to face opposite bulkheads and board their two Light Assault Crafts. Kris went down the line of her squad one more time, checking their restraining harnesses and the arrangement of their gear as they settled into their low seats in the LAC. All readouts showed green. Still, Kris gave each a good hard tug. That webbing was the only thing holding her troopers in. Satisfied, she settled her own rump onto the low composite seat in this minimum spacecraft and stretched her legs out ahead of her, careful to avoid the control pedals. The legs of the tech seated behind her surrounded her. Kris had once tried a toboggan. Mother had refused in horror when Kris asked to take a ride downhill. That toboggan was roomy compared to an LAC.

She rechecked to make sure her harness was firmly attached to the LAC's narrow keel, checked again to make sure none of her gear was out of place, then pulled the canopy down and felt it click into place. Like so much of the LAC, the canopy was paper thin; it added nothing more than stealth to the craft. Only their drop suits would protect Kris and her troops from the vacuum of space or the heat of reentry.

The control stick began to rotate between Kris's legs. That would be Tommy running tests. Still, the sight of it moving brought back good memories of some damn fine stick time of her own. She wiggled in her seat and felt the light craft respond to her movements. Bigger than a racing skiff but just as sweet.

Kris banished those distractions by replaying the drop plan in her mind as she waited. These kidnaping sons-a-bitches had a simple plan. They'd snapped up the Sequim General Manager's sole child during a school outing, then dragged the poor kid off to the northern wilderness before anyone knew what had happened. *Ignore the child's name . . . much too familiar. Only pain there.* Quickly Kris returned to tonight's problem. The approaches to the kidnappers' hideout were long, difficult, dangerous—and booby-trapped! So far, the bad guys had outsmarted—and killed—too many good people.

Kris ground her teeth; how had cruds like these gotten their hands on some of the most sophisticated traps and countermeasures in human space? She could understand the traps; humans now frequented planets with very nasty critters. And while she had never hunted big game herself, she was looking forward to this hunt for the most danger-ous game. What frosted her was the legal bunk used by specialty stores to excuse their sale of measures and countermeasures that were only going to make her job damn dangerous tonight. Normal people didn't need elec-trocardiogram jammers. Why would any good citizen need a decoy device to simulate a human heat signature? Blast it, her suit was warm; sweat was already running down her back.

The day was so hot, the ice cream melted even as Kris trotted toward the duck pond. Kris paused just long enough to give both ice cream cones a quick lick, then felt guilty. "Eddy, I've got your ice cream," she called as she hurried on. She hurried so much that she was well out of the trees and halfway across the vale to the pond before the wrongness of it got through to her. Kris came to a slow halt.

Eddy wasn't there!

The man with the corn had fallen, half in the water. The ducks gathered around him to pluck at the fallen grain.

*Two lumps of clothes doted the vale. In her night-
mares that night, Kris would recognize them for
agents who had been with her for years. But right
then, her eyes were riveted on Nanna. She had fallen
down. Her arms and legs splayed around like a rag
doll. Even at ten, Kris knew that was all wrong for a
real person.*

*Kris began to scream. She dropped her ice cream
cones as she tried to cram her hands in her mouth,
bite down hard on knuckles hoping the pain would
wake her from this bad dream. Somewhere behind
her, a voice shouted into a commlink. "Agents down.
Agents down. Dandelion is nowhere in sight. I
repeat, Dandelion is missing."*

A flashing red light grabbed Kris's attention. "You did it
again," she growled at herself as she yanked her thoughts
back to the problem at hand. Around her, the drop bay ran
through decompression. Air gone, Kris and her troopers
breathed only what their drop suits provided. Kris checked
all her readouts. Her suit was good, as good as Navy issue
got. So were all of her troopers. "Good to go," she reported.

With a thump to Kris's rear, the LAC fell into silent,
black space. Tommy let them drift for only the moment it
took Kris to get a good look at the *Typhoon*, her smart-
metal hide stretched thin to give the crew individual rooms
and spin gravity while in orbit. Her bow and stern was
proudly painted with the blue and green flag of the Society
of Humanity. Then the LAC came alive; the stick moved as
Tommy guided both LACs into reentry.

Well, if Tommy was doing the work, Kris could use the
time to check the ground situation once more. "Nelly,
show me the real time target feed," Kris subvocalized. The
hunting lodge filled Kris's heads-up display. Several dozen
human shadows showed on the infrared detection. Six or
eight moved around the building . . . all in pairs. Per the
guarantee provided with every human heat decoy sold,
there was no way Kris was supposed to know that only five

real humans were moving. Thank God the manufacturers had so far stuck to the pledge of silence the government had extracted from them.

For ten years, no bad guys had tumbled to the fact that 98.6 degrees was only the *average* human temperature. This late at night most people's body heat was slipping down into the 97s and 96s. In the six upstairs rooms of the lodge, the heat signatures of six little girls lay chained to their beds. Two gunmen sat at opposite ends of the hall, ready at the first sign of rescue to dash into the one room that held the kidnapped girl and kill her. Thanks to the sensors on the fifty-gram Stoolpigeon hovering 1,000 meters above the log cabin, Kris knew there was only one gunman—and which room held the terrified girl.

Terrified! Kris ground her teeth, then looked out of the LAC to rest her eyes on the planet revolving slowly below her. She tried to do anything but touch the nerve that took her again into her little brother's grave. At least these kidnappers had not buried their victim under tons of manure with a damaged air pipe the only lifeline to the world for a six-year-old kid.

At school, Kris had overheard other students talking, saying that Eddy was dead hours before her parents paid the ransom. She didn't know the truth of that. There were some reports she just couldn't read, some media coverage she could never sit through.

What could never be ignored for a moment were the what-ifs. What if Kris hadn't gone for ice cream? What if the bad guys had had to take down Nanna and Eddy *and Kris?* What would a wild ten-year-old girl have done to their plans?

Kris shook her head, willed away the images. Stay there too long, and tears came. A spacesuit was no place for tears.

Kris focused on the planet below. The day terminator lay ahead, changing the green and blue cloud-shrouded globe to dark—darkness and storms. A surprise night drop needed thunder to cover the sonic booms, darkness to hide their approach, night to make guards inattentive.

Kris smiled, remembering other planets she'd watched from orbit, a fast racing skiff under her. And her smile slid into a scowl as the memories she'd been struggling to hold at arm's length for a week came flooding back.

Father vanished from Kris's life the day after Eddy's funeral. Off to the office before she awoke, he was rarely home before her bedtime.

Mother was something else. "You've been a little savage long enough. Time to make a proper young lady out of you." That didn't get Kris off the hook for winning soccer games for Father or showing up for his political parties. But Kris quickly discovered "proper young ladies" not only went to ballet but also accompanied Mother to teas. As the youngest at any tea by twenty years, Kris was bored silly. Then she noticed that some women's teas smelled funny. It wasn't long before Kris got a chance to taste them. They tasted funny, too . . . but they made Kris feel better, the parties go faster. It wasn't long before Kris found what was being added to their tea . . . and how to raid her father's liquor cabinet or mother's wine closet.

Somehow, the drinking made the days endurable. Kris didn't even care when her grades took a nose-dive. It didn't matter; Mother and Father only frowned. Other kids at school had fun things like skiff racing from orbit; Kris had her bottle. Of course, the bottle and the pills Mother's doctor prescribed to help Kris be more ladylike did not help her soccer game. The coach shook his head and sidelined her as much as he could. Harvey, the chauffeur who took her to all the games, just seemed kind of sad.

But Harvey was grinning the afternoon he picked Kris up from school late. "Your dad's invited your Great-grampa Trouble to dinner tonight. General Tordon is on Wardhaven for meetings," Harvey added before she asked. Kris spent the drive home wondering what she'd say to someone straight out of her history books.

Mother was in a snit, overseeing dinner preparations herself and mumbling that legends should stay in the books where they belonged. Kris was sent upstairs to do homework, but she staked out the balcony, reading with one eye and watching the front door with the other. Kris wasn't sure what to expect. Probably someone ancient, like old Ms. Bracket who taught history and seemed dry and wrinkled enough to have lived it. All of it!

Then Grampa Trouble walked through the front door. Tall and trim, gleaming in undress greens, he looked like he could destroy an Iteeche fleet just by scowling at them. Only he wasn't scowling. The grin on his face was infectious; Mother was right, he was totally inappropriate for a "proper legend." And at dinner, the stories he told. After dinner, Kris couldn't remember a single one of them, at least not completely. But during supper they were all funny, even those that should have been horrifying. Somehow, no matter how bad the odds were or how impossible the situation had been, Grampa Trouble made it sound terribly funny. Even Mother laughed, despite herself. And when supper was over, Kris managed to dodge Mother until she excused herself for her whist club. Kris wanted to hang around this wondrous apparition forever. And when they were alone and he turned his full attention to Kris, she knew why kittens curled up in the sun.

"Your dad tells me you like soccer?" he said, settling into a chair.

"Yeah, pretty much," Kris answered seating herself ladylike across from her grampa and feeling very grown-up.

"Your mom says you're very good at ballet."

"Yeah, pretty much." Even at twelve, Kris knew she was not holding up her end of the conversation.

But what could she say to someone like her grampa?

"I like orbital skiff racing. Ever do any racing?"

"Naw. Some kids at school do." Kris tasted excitement. Then she remembered herself. "But Mother says it is much too dangerous. And nothing for a proper young lady."

"That's interesting," Grampa Trouble said, leaning back in his chair and stretching his hands upward. "A girl won the junior championship for Savannah last year. She wasn't much older than you."

"She wasn't!" Kris stared, wide-eyed. Even from Grampa, she couldn't believe that.

"I've rented a skiff tomorrow. Want to take a few drops with me?"

Kris fidgeted in her chair. "Mother would never let me."

Grampa brought his hands to rest on the table, only inches away from Kris's. "Harvey tells me your mom usually sleeps in on Saturday. I could pick you up at six." Later, Kris would realize that Grampa Trouble and the family chauffeur were in cahoots on this. But Kris had been too excited by the offer just then to put two and two together.

"Could you?" Kris yelped. She couldn't remember the last time she'd been up early on her own. She also couldn't remember the last time she'd done something that wasn't on Mother or Father's To-Do List. She couldn't remember because to do that would be to remember what life was like with Eddy. "I'd love to," she said.

"One thing," Grampa Trouble said, reaching across the table to take her small, soft hands in his tanned, calloused ones. His touch was almost electric in its shock. His eyes looked into hers, stripping away the little girl that faked it for so many. Kris sat there, with nothing but herself to hang on to. "Your mother is right. Skiff racing can be dangerous. I only take people riding with me who are *stone cold sober. That won't be a problem for you, will it?"*

Kris swallowed hard. She'd been laughing so hard at Grampa Trouble's stories that she hadn't stolen a drink at supper. She hadn't had one since lunch at school. Could she go through the night? "It won't be a problem," Kris assured him.

And somehow she made it. It wasn't easy; she woke up twice crying for Eddy. But she thought about Grampa and all the stories she had overheard from the school kids about how fun it was to see the stars above you and ride a falling star to Earth, and somehow Kris didn't tiptoe downstairs to Father's bar.

Kris made it through that night to stand at the top of the stairs and look down at Grampa Trouble so magnificent in his green uniform, waiting patiently for her on the black and white tiles of the foyer. Balanced careful as ever she did in ballet class, Kris went down the stairs, showing Grampa just how sober she was. His smile was a small, tight thing, not at all the open-faced one Father flashed all his political friends. Grampa's tight little smile meant more to Kris than all she'd gotten from her father or mother.

Three hours later, Kris was suited up and strapped into the front seat of a skiff when Grampa Trouble hit the release and they dropped away from the space station. Oh, what a ride! Kris saw stars so close she could almost touch them. The temptation came to pop her belt, to drift away into the dark, to fall like a shooting star and make whatever amends she could to dead little Eddy. But she couldn't do that to Grampa Trouble after all the trouble he'd gone through to get her here. And the beauty of the unblinking stars grabbed Kris, enveloping her in their cold, silent hug. The pure, lean curves of skiffs on reentry were mathematics in motion. She'd lost her heart . . . and maybe some of her survivor's self-loathing.

Mother was actually pacing the foyer when they came in late that evening. "Where have you been?" was more an accusation than a question.

"Skiff racing," Grampa Trouble answered as evenly as he told jokes.

"Skiff racing!" Mother shrieked.

"Honey," Grampa Trouble said softly to Kris, "I think you better go to your room."

"Grampa?" Kris started, but Harvey was taking Kris's elbow.

"And don't you come down before I send for you." Mother enforced Grampa's suggestion. "And what did you think you were doing with my daughter, General Tordon?" Mother said coldly, turning on Grampa.

But Grampa Trouble was already heading toward the great library. "I think it best we finish this conversation out of earshot of little pitchers with big ears," he said with all the calm Mother lacked.

"Harvey, I don't want to go to my room," Kris argued as she and the chauffeur went up the stairs.

"It's best you do, little friend," he said. "Your mother's been stretched quite a ways today. There's nothing to be gained by you pushing her any further."

Kris never saw Grampa Trouble again.

But a week later, Judith came into her life, a woman Grampa Trouble would probably have enjoyed meeting. Judith was a psychologist.

"I don't need a shrink," Kris told the woman flat out.

"Why'd you throw the soccer game last month?" Judith shot right back.

"I didn't." Kris mumbled.

"Your coach thinks you did. Your dad thinks so, too."

"How would Father know?" Kris asked with all the sarcasm a twelve-year-old could muster.

"Harvey recorded the entire game," Judith said.

"Oh."

So they talked, and Kris found that Judith could be a friend. Like when Kris shared that she wanted to do more skiff racing, but Mother would have kittens at the very thought. Instead of agreeing with Mother, Judith asked Kris why Mother shouldn't have a kitten or two? The thought of Mother with a kitten made Kris laugh, which needed an explanation, and before they were done, Kris had come to realize that what Mother wanted wasn't always the best, and that the mother of a twelve-year-old girl should have kittens occasionally. Kris went on to win Wardhaven's junior championship to the prime minister's delight and Mother's horror.

"Get out of your head," Kris growled in Captain Thorpe's voice and yanked tight on her restraining harness, a life-affirming act that now came naturally to her.

Then Kris's stomach shot into her throat as her lander turned dervish, spinning to the right as the bottom dropped out from underneath her and the still-blasting thrusters rose above.

"What the hell?" "Who's driving this bus?" rattled in her ears as Kris grabbed for the wildly gyrating control stick. Aft, Corporal Li restored discipline with a "Pipe down."

The stick fought Kris, refusing to obey. She punched her commlink to the *Typhoon*. "Tommy, what the hell is going on?" Her words echoed empty in her helmet; her commlink was as dead as she and her crew would be if she didn't do something—fast.

Mashing the manual override, Kris took command of her craft. With hardly a thought, her hands went though the motions needed to dampen down the spin and pitch. The LAC was heavier, slower to respond than a skiff. But Kris fought it . . . and it obeyed.

"That's better," came from one of the grateful marines behind her. Unless Kris figured out fast where they were and where they were going, this momentary "better" just meant they'd be less shook up when they burned on reentry.

"Nelly, I need skiff navigation, and I need it now." In a blink, the familiar skiff routines took form on her heads-up. "Nelly, interrogate GPS system. Where am I?" The LAC became a dot on her heads-up, vector lines extended from it. She'd been accelerating rather than decelerating!

"Corporal, get a line-of-sight link to Gunny's LAC."

"I've been trying, ma'am, but I don't know where he is."

Her computer could probably tell Kris where the sergeant should be with respect to them, but Nelly was doing her best to plot a course that would win Kris another championship.

They didn't hand out skiff trophies just for hitting that dinky ground target. They expected winners to do it in style: be on the dot, use less fuel, take less time. Kris gulped as her heads-up display filled with the harsh challenge ahead. The LAC was out of position and lower on fuel than any skiff she'd ever flown in competition. It would take every ounce of skill Kris had to land her marines anywhere within a hundred kilometers of one terrified little girl.

Kris had raced for trophies. Tightening her grip on the stick, she began a race for a little girl's life.

2

Kris acted more on trained instinct than rational thought. Her right hand firmly on the stick, she first stabilized the craft. That done, she spared a second for Nelly's search to get Kris and her marines down safely. Thank God she'd kept Nelly and refused the standard-issue computer with all its Navy limits. "Nelly, get our present coordinates from GPS. Use the hunting lodge for a target. Now, give me a low-risk flight plan." Nelly did it in hardly a second; it would get them down safely—but on fumes and fifty klicks past the lodge.

Even as Kris adjusted her deceleration burn to fit that trajectory, she snapped, "Alternate flight plan. Assume I can bleed off an extra twenty percent of my energy aerodynamically. How much fuel would that leave me?" Kris had to have a cushion. In competitions, each skiff had a two-minute separation between the one ahead and the one behind. Today, Gunny's LAC was somewhere off to her right, no more than ten kilometers, probably less. That might be an acceptable safety margin if Tommy was flying both of them to their drop point, but not now, not with Kris careening all over low orbit.

"Nelly, add in the assumption that I need a hundred kilometers north separation from Gunny's LAC." In a blink, Nelly modified the latest flight plan, but the result flashed red. Even assuming Kris cut her orbital burn to the bone, there was no way she could aerodynamically dissipate enough energy. She'd have to overshoot the target by a good hundred klicks.

"Assume twenty kilometers displacement," Kris re-ordered; her first S curve would have to be away from Gunny's LAC. Nelly quickly generated the requested flight plan; Kris could make it. However, a yellow button on the heads-up flashed a warning. Her fuel reserve would be below competitive standards; she would be disqualified.

With a rueful shrug for the machine's concern, Kris said, "Do it, Nelly," and settled in for the ride of her life. Very early, Kris had learned that every computer-generated course could be improved upon by a human. To take home those trophies scattered around her room, she'd saved a lit-tle fuel here, a little more there, always on her own.

"Sir, I mean ma'am, I think I see the sergeant." Corporal Li's voice was a series of nervous squeaks and cracks.

Kris was rooted to her machine. Her hand had merged with the control stick; her rear was part of the heat shield and wing's fabric. Kris's eyes might as well have been the angle of attack, g meter, and speed gages. To break con-centration now would be agony. "Where, Corporal?"

"Off the starboard bow, two, no, two-thirty, ma'am, low one, one-thirty. I think that's him. Ma'am."

Kris risked a glance. Yes there was an LAC, a bit ahead and below her, still breaking just as she was now. "Try to raise Gunny," she ordered and went back to flying a miracle.

"What I'm getting is all broken up and crackling, ma'am."

"Right." Kris kicked herself. "His engine ionization is between us." A moment later it was time to terminate the burn. She rotated her craft, placing its heat-shielded nose to the atmosphere, and got ready to ride it down. Li made several more attempts to contact Gunny, but LAC Two was still breaking, pointing its ionized exhaust at them. Kris told him to stow it as the nose of her LAC began to wrap itself in dancing light.

Now came the hard part. Here a good skiff driver made up for the fuel she'd saved—if she did it right—and dropped her boat on the dot. Diving, Kris plunged her craft quickly—and hot—into the atmosphere. Then she put the LAC into gentle—or maybe not so gentle—S curves to bleed off that extra energy. Kris gauged them through narrow eye slits. She had to keep the heat shield between the searing ionized airflow and her very burnable body. Cut the curve too tight, and hot gases would take her—and her marines'—heads off. Cut it too loose, and she'd overshoot by kilometers. Kris had learned these moves when it was only a game and when she flew one of the best skiffs built on Wardhaven. Now Kris honked her craft over on first one side, then the other—a craft she knew nothing about.

Kris had preflighted this rig. No trained pilot put her butt into an air vehicle without first giving it a thorough checkout. But she had never flown it! She recognized the manufacturer's name emblazoned on the cockpit. They had a reputation for building good boats, but once in a while their quality control hiccuped. Kris's stomach twisted into knots as tight as her grip on the stick. Was this LAC one of their good ones, or was there a hidden flaw buried somewhere in the keel, on the wing support? If Kris pulled too many g's, risked too much heat, would she break its back—send them all tumbling to a fiery death?

Kris forced herself to complete calm, the better to feel every groan, every moan from the craft's tortured structure as she pushed it to its limits. Behind her a marine broke into unfamiliar prayer, thanking his creator for the food he was about to receive. "Someday we'll all laugh about this," Kris muttered on hot mike. *If we live,* she added only for herself.

The LAC was hot. Despite the shielding, Kris could feel the heat through her suit, rising up to warm, then scorch her rear. The gauge confirmed it; she was well into the manufacturer's red warning zone. Out of the corner of her eyes, Kris measured the extra bend in the overstressed wing and growing flutter along its superheated trailing edges. The LAC's flight had turned into a sluggish waddle through defiant atmosphere, worse than any skiff she'd flown.

Still, Kris demanded more. She was above her approach path. Kris nosed her craft over, picking up speed—and heat—as she dropped like the proverbial lead brick. On path, but now too fast, she muscled her heavy lander into S curves as tight as she had ever dared on a skiff, bleeding off energy, adding to her heat. Kris fidgeted in her seat as her skin cooked. The temperature readout, confirming the complaints of her own flesh, passed deeper into the red. But not too far, not if there were no surprises hidden in the structure of the craft beneath her.

"Ah, ma'am," Corporal Li whispered softly in Kris's earphone, "my check-back says your suit is awfully hot. You want to switch the blower and chiller to high, ma'am?"

Kris came back to herself just long enough to make the adjustments. Damn it, her suit back home would have done that automatically. But service suits were intentionally dumb, as a Gunny Sergeant at OCS had drawled. "You don't want them doing nothing without your permission when unfriendly folks are shooting and all hell's broken loose around you."

"Can you still see Gunny?" Kris asked Li.

"I think he's still out there ma'am, but it's kind of hard seeing with all these fireworks going on around us."

"Anybody sees Gunny, give a holler," Kris said, concentrating on her controls.

"Yes, ma'am," came back in several-part harmony.

It seemed like forever before the temperature gauge started to edge down. Kris tried to get a GPS report on her location, but she was still surrounded by too much ionization. The LAC's inertial guidance system insisted they were about where she wanted to be, and Nelly agreed. With a deep breath, Kris leaned back, tried to unknot every muscle in her body, and discovered it was a real kick flying this thing.

"I see him." "There he is," chorused behind her. "There's Gunny, ma'am," the corporal confirmed.

A quick glance showed a falling star off to their right maybe thirty kilometers, if Kris could trust her own judgment. With LAC Two in sight, Kris let out a sigh of relief and put her stick over to bank closer. As she planned, Kris was subsonic and about three minutes out from the target. She had enough fuel for a few seconds of cruise if she needed it, but with a self-congratulatory grin, she knew she wouldn't. A moment later, Kris spared enough attention from the flight controls to aim her helmet and its line-of-sight antenna at Gunny's craft.

"Gunny, please advise the *Typhoon* that LAC One has successfully reentered." Kris waited a slow five count for a reply, then began to repeat her message.

"Roger, One. I have you on visual. Report your status," was Gunny's reply.

"I lost my uplink to the *Typhoon*. Can you patch me through to Captain Thorpe?"

"I'd better. Ship's been screaming for you."

Kris gritted her teeth and prepared for another nice talk with her least favorite military person. She hadn't long to wait. "So glad you could fit us into your busy social schedule," Captain Thorpe's voice was the ice of space. "Report your situation."

"I lost my uplink, sir. Lowest bidder, I presume." That was the skipper's perpetual beef, that and budget cuts. "Gunny is patching me through to you. We are in position to execute the recovery, sir."

There was a long pause. Kris could imagine Captain Thorpe reviewing the reports pouring into his bridge, weighing each one carefully to see what would make a certain Ensign Longknife's life the most miserable.

"I see that you are, Ensign." There was a shorter pause. "Ensign Lien, can you acquire control of LAC One?"

"Negative, sir," came back quickly. "Our downlink to LAC One is toast. I cannot fly that vehicle."

"Then we go with plan B," the captain said tersely.

And Kris broke into a grin.

*Kris had showed up at the planning session with the
captain and Gunny loaded with options to find the
skipper grinning from ear to ear. "I knew those tight-
wad civilians would holler for the dogs. I pulled in
every chit I had to make sure we were the ship they
got. Now we do this job right."*

*"No problem, sir, we'll show the fleet and those ter-
rorists that the Typhoon is the best," Gunny chortled.*

*Kris was no respecter of kidnappers. She'd at-
tended part of the trial of her brother's murderers.
Add the IQ of all three of them together, and you still
needed a negative number. However: "Sir, those terrorists have plenty of specialty gear," Kris pointed
out. "They've wiped out three rescue attempts."*

*"Those were civilians. Now they face marines."
Gunny's voice was deadly cold.*

*"A bunch of unshaven terrorists can't stand
against what the Typhoon is bringing to this party,"
Captain Thorpe said with confidence and laid out his
plan. A stealthy night approach would let the marines
do a drop right in the kidnappers' front yard. The
trigger pullers could pop their chutes and go straight
to work. Kris swallowed hard and pointed out that a
similar approach had been used in the last hostage
rescue. She thought she left hanging clear in the air
the question,* Do we dare try the same on guys with
this much tech? *She might as well have saved her
breath.*

*"It worked, didn't it?" Gunny snapped. "Five
bucks says we beat the time, drop to last shot, of the
Cardinal's landing party for that hostage incident on
Payallup last year."*

*"I already bet the Cardinal's skipper a case of
scotch we do," Thorpe grinned. Faced with that kind
of confidence, Kris swallowed her own reservations.
The three did a thorough review of all the recon feed.*

It showed no problems for a close-in jump; the skipper approved Gunny's close jump. And Kris said, "Aye aye, sir," like a good boot ensign . . . and went hunting for Tommy.

But if Kris jumped now, her bird would make a very noisy hole in the tundra, sure to wake the sleeping beauties below. Kris had half expected orders to keep flying the LAC and let Gunny lead the platoon. Apparently, the Navy truly was averse to heavily armed marines wandering around without an officer present.

"Plan B it is, Captain," Gunny replied on net. Kris echoed him, all grin out of her voice.

Captain Thorpe cleared his throat. "One last thing before we break this link. I am required to remind you marines that this is not a slapdash search-and-smash mission. We have been invited by Sequim to assist their police forces. As such, you will operate under local law enforcement procedures. I expect you to take prisoners, not come back with a load of bodies."

Kris keyed her mike. "You heard the skipper. Those bastards have the right to face a jury of their peers. Then the people of Sequim can hang 'em." The troopers growled happily at that bit of information. Kris had done the search; Sequim had yet to ratify the capital punishment clause in the Society of Humanity's Human Rights Declaration. Kris's father had almost lost his chance at the prime minister's job because of the tactics he used to delay Wardhaven's ratification of that same clause just long enough for Eddy's murderers to hang. Strange, Kris could never think of little Eddy suffocating. But she had no trouble with his murderers dangling at the end of a rope.

Done with talk, Kris did a quick check on the hunting lodge. The Stoolpigeon still circled. Its sensors reported all quiet. "Sergeant, does Ensign Lien have me on sensors?"

"Yes, ma'am."

"Tell him to tuck you in close behind me. I'm heading for the pond five klicks north of the target."

The pause was short. "Ensign Lien says LAC Two will conform to your movements."

That would take some good flying. This was, after all, a dark and very stormy night. Kris aimed to set the LACs down in the shallows of a pond near the hunting lodge. From where she was at 20,000 meters, she could make out two or three nasty-looking storm cells between her and there. "Nelly, connect to the local weather satellite." Interesting, the LAC's uplink to the *Typhoon* was hashed, but Kris's own civilian commlink worked fine.

The weather feed let Kris plot a series of descending curves around the most dangerous of the storm cells. Still, the last 15,000 meters was bumpy. Rain lashed at the canopy, blurring Kris's vision; her racing helmet would have been crystal clear. All the complaints about standard-issue equipment served up by the lowest bidder took on hard meaning as she peered into the darkness, trying to make out something before that something made a very big hole in her. *Father, we have to talk.* From behind her, marines provided a chorus of groans, grumbles, and, in general, wishes to get this damn thing on the deck.

Kris's altimeter claimed 1,000 meters between her and sea level when she broke out of the slope. More importantly, the arctic tundra was supposed to be no higher than 650 meters around here, leaving Kris to do the happy math. However, the topo maps of the area reported enough hills, trees, and other exciting terrain features to make Kris wish she could dare a couple of radar sweeps. With bad guys as well-equipped as this bunch seemed to be, she doubted they lacked a radar detector or even a few radar-homing missiles. No, using radar anywhere above their horizon was a dead giveaway. Death in this case was spelled with a little girl's name.

Kris put her craft into gentle circles, each one lower, keeping her LAC just above stall speed. Corporal Li reported LAC Two out of the last squall and right behind them, three maybe four kilometers back. Kris grinned. At least if she put her squad into a hill, Gunny would avoid their funeral pyre.

Half of them would still arrive to take on the kidnappers.

Right on schedule, Kris's low-light system detected the snag she'd chosen for the start of her landing way. Her LAC touched water, hissing from residual heat, tossing spray as it bled off the last of its speed. She put the stick over as the craft started to settle. A moment later, she came to a jerking halt on a narrow, sandy beach.

"Corporal, pop a night light for Gunny." Kris said. As the canopy rose above her, she hit her restraint release. Throwing her legs over the LAC's side, she vaulted to the ground. Wow, was she pumped, a rush beyond any race. She opened her faceplate and drew in a deep breath, laden with the perfumes of water, night, and living things. It felt wonderful to be alive and breathing. She studied her squad as they stamped their feet, checked their weapons, brought their systems up.

"Okay, crew, we're down. I know a little girl who could use a hug about now and some bastards who need a hard kick in the ass. Let's do it."

The five marines returned grim, determined nods.

I'm coming Eddy, I'm coming.

3

Gunny's LAC slid to a stop on the sandy beach ten meters from Kris. As Gunny and his squad readied themselves, Kris hiked over to them, stepping over driftwood and a half-eaten fish thing, and had Nelly beam Approach March B to Gunny.

Long before the call came for the *Typhoon* to drop everything and jump for Sequim, Kris had been following the kidnapping; it was the number-one media event this month among the rim worlds. The betting in the wardroom had been two to one that Sequim would holler for the Navy when the second attempt went bust. Kris had put the bets down more to hope than expectation. Then the third local effort to storm the cabin ended with two of their best trackers taking a dive off a 100-meter cliff into raging white water. That, fifteen clicks from the cabin, was the closest the local police got. Kris figured the Navy would get a call, but she never expected the *Typhoon* to answer it or that she'd lead the platoon. But as an old commander growled at OCS, "Ours's not to reason why, ours's but to do and then fill out the paperwork."

So Kris had spent every waking moment for the last four days either preparing her platoon or planning this assault. Gunny and Captain Thorpe wanted a fast drop and grab, so Kris prepared for a fast drop and grab. Still, one of Father's Rule Ones was always to have a backup in your hip pocket. With little spare time on her hands, she drafted Tommy to help look for plan B.

"That tundra looks mighty rough," Tommy said, *studying the Stoolpigeon feed of the front yard they were to drop in.*

"It's summertime. Tundra gets messy. The computer says it's within standards. Don't you trust the computer's standards?" Kris asked with a nudge in Tommy's ribs.

"Nope," Tom answered without looking up. *"If I or someone I trust haven't fed the computer the numbers, why trust it?"*

"So you trust God, but not computers."

"And didn't my Grandma Chin tell me to?" he answered without so much as a blink.

"Find me a back door to this place," Kris said.

"I could set the LACs down on this pond, and you could walk in from there," Tommy pointed out.

Kris had been studying the pond and the ground between it and the hunting lodge housing the kidnappers. *"These woods show as much electronic noise as these other places where the civilians got themselves dead."* Kris had memorized the electronic signatures of the three different spots civilian rescue teams had died. Their bodies were still there; no one would risk bringing them out.

"But isn't the swamp kind of quiet, I ask you?"

Kris pursed her lip, studying the mud and muck. Unlike some city kids, Kris had no illusions about how nice Mother Nature was in the raw. She'd split her last summer at university between running brother Honovi's election campaign and hiking the

*rugged Blue Mountains of Wardhaven. "Just the kind
of place some lazy hoods might not bother with."*

*"But marines and certain dumb boot ensigns like
to play in the mud." Tommy grinned and got elbowed
in the ribs . . . hard this time. But the point was
made; there was an exit from the landing site. It took
Kris another half hour to put all of plan B in Nelly's
memory.*

Now she laid out a soggy line of march to Gunny. He
nodded. "Tough, but nobody joined the Corps for easy."

Kris signaled her tech specialist. "Hanson, sniff the
route I fed to your heads-up." It was 10:00 P.M. by Sequim's
25.33-hour clock, and going from gray, stormy day to dark,
even this far north, when Kris's two squads headed into
muck up to their waists. The going was slow. Battle suits
kept the icy water out, even as the camouflage systems
struggled to match the suits against the ever-changing
backdrop. One poor marine's suit gave up; head to toe, he
was sand yellow, no matter what background he waded
through. The suits kept the water out, but armor was thin
insulation against a chill as cold as Gunny's heart. And
whether the water was up to their waist or below their
knees, each step still buried their boots in mud up to their
ankles. To make matters worse, gnats or some local equivalent developed a taste for them. Kris slapped her faceplate
down as her troops followed suit. Breathing became slow
as they sucked against filters designed for nasty things a lot
smaller than a gnat.

As 2300 hours approached, Kris's tiny command was
back on hard ground. She signaled a break while she, Gunny,
and her tech examined the woods ahead. The trees here
stood thirty meters tall, their greenery perched high on
bare, scaly trunks much like the Earth evergreen forests
that had so quickly spread across the Blue Mountains of
Wardhaven's temperate region. But unlike Earth stock,
these evergreens' needles ended in barbs. Kris's briefing
didn't say how allergic her troops were to whatever was in

those barbs, and she didn't want to find out. "Keep buttoned up," she ordered.

While the others rested, Hanson searched the woods for any sign of human life, booby trap, or general discomfort. The Stoolpigeon swept low, adding its contribution. "There're a few big things here and there," Hanson advised, overlaying his sensor reports onto Kris's map. "Probably nothing we can't handle, but it would make for a more exciting night than my recruiter ever promised, and mixing it up with party animals is bound to get the neighbors talking."

Kris marked them on her team's charts with a "No Go," and asked what else. That got a shrug. "Plenty of medium to little stuff. For the local furry residents, this is the time of year to make hay."

Kris dismissed him with a "Thanks." *I'm coming Eddy.*

The break seemed to have refreshed her troops; Kris's legs had gone from screaming to just hurting. *I got to spend more time in the workout room if I'm going to hang with marines.*

Around her, the night was deepening into solid dark. She was right on her schedule. Kris and her troops moved silently among the shadows of the sparse undergrowth. The techs kept a lookout for human presence, but it was nature that got them. The rain had left everything with a sheen in the fading light—and slippery. Twice, a marine went down. One was just embarrassed by her fall; the other ended up activating the pressure bandage at his suit's ankle. He continued with a limp and teeth gritted against the pain.

Half an hour later, Kris hand-signaled another halt about 100 meters before the trees petered out. While her troops settled in, she and Gunny inched forward carefully to get a personal look at the doors they'd come to kick in.

The hunting cabin was a two-story log structure; the few small windows gave a good idea of just how cold the winter months were around here. A steep-roofed veranda covered the front and the back of the house. Infrared showed a half-dozen man-sized heat sources scattered front and back. However, night-vision scopes showed only two of the six supposed guards to have a real human body to go with the heat.

Kris brought the Stoolpigeon in as low as she dared, five hundred meters above the house. Get too close, and even stealth gave a radar return. With two gunmen outside, Kris wanted a solid lock on inside target locations. Four in-house heat targets showed temperature variations. Kris opened her faceplate and whispered, "Six targets."

Gunny nodded.

For fifteen minutes Kris studied the six as they slept. Only one, the guy on the back veranda, showed any action, and that was merely to clomp inside to visit the head. In the house, three men seemed pretty solidly asleep in beds. A fourth man, on the upstairs landing, the appointed executioner if any effort was made to rescue the girl, never moved from his chair.

"Pretty unprofessional," Kris observed. Negotiations had dragged out for a week, the main sticking point a starship willing to take them wherever they wanted to go. No captain wanted to have anything to do with these bozos.

"If we'd followed my plan, my squad would have taken these duds before they even knew we were here," Gunny growled.

With a shrug for what might have been, Kris waved Hanson forward to examine the 300 meters of cleared ground circling the lodge. From 500 meters, the lowest they dared risk the Stoolpigeon, it had identified nothing interesting about that plot of land. Up this close and personal, Hanson quickly spotted the hum of several low-powered batteries.

"What they powering?" Gunny demanded.

"Working on that, Sarge."

Not fast enough for Gunny, he ordered his own tech forward. Both took a few more minutes of fiddling with their sensor suite before Hanson let out a low whistle. "Hyperlow-power lasers," he whispered. A moment later, he had the frequencies. Kris adjusted her laser defense system and found herself looking at a cat's cradle of beams, crisscrossing the field but only rising twenty-five or thirty meters. Nothing on the Stoolpigeon would have spotted these things unless it buzzed the field—and that was against policy. *Damn! These fellows knew too much and were way overequipped. Who the hell staked them for the up-front costs of this job and was telling them what to do?*

Then again, Sequim was a rich planet, and its manager had a wide range of investments in its wealth. Kris wondered who he was meeting with tomorrow to borrow the millions demanded to ransom his young daughter's life. Kris, raised the daughter of a cynical politician herself, expected there would be many offering help . . . for "minor" considerations. Kris frowned; she'd never thought about who offered to loan money for Eddy's ransom and what collateral was demanded. Interesting thoughts . . . for later.

Hanson was still busy; he grinned when one of his sensors started blinking in several multicolored sequences. "I got residue from the out-gassing of C-12 and soft plastics," he whispered.

"Let me see that," Gunny barked softly and grabbed the instrument from the tech's hands. He frowned at the gadget, batting it on the side once, then studied it some more. Finally, he glared at the field. "I don't see any digging out there. Didn't see any from orbit. Don't see any now."

"Mark 41 Chameleon land mines?" Kris suggested.

"They aren't issue yet," Gunny snapped. "They just started up production!" His words slowed as what he knew was possible fought with what he saw. "Damn, if these sons-a-bitches have that kind of pull?" He left the rest unsaid.

"There's mines out there, Sarge," Hanson said with surety.

"Rigged to the lasers or just pressure?" Kris asked.

"Your guess is as good as mine, ma'am, but I'd bet both."

Kris took a good smell of the marshy tundra ahead of her. Rubbing her eyes, she studied the sky. Cloud cover was thick, but there was a graying light to the south. Dawn was an hour away. True, these fellows had a tendency to sleep until well after the sun was up, understandable when the sun was only down for three or four hours. Still, the guards were more restless come daylight. And a single noise would change a sleeping watchman to a shooting one—with enough daylight to see what he was shooting at. Kris needed to get herself and ten fit marines across that last 300 meters and get them across fast.

Kris backed into the woods to face her team. "Whose laser spotters are bust?" she asked. A few moments later, four very embarrassed troopers acknowledged that the gear they'd so carefully nursed into operation in the loading bay was now dead weight. Kris's one bit of luck was that both her limper and her sand-yellow were among the laser blind; she'd only have to leave four behind.

"You four are my fire support team." That, however, was only the start of Kris's problems. The two-millimeter darts of the M-6 came in two flavors. One left you dead. The other was Colt Physer's best efforts at a sleepy bullet, a round with nonlethal intent. The M-6 did not have cartridges. Once the range finder established the distance to the target, it automatically squirted an appropriate charge into the chamber. Still, there was a problem with sleepy bullets. If you put too much energy behind a dart, it shattered bone, artery, and brain. At 300 meters, the low-power sleepy dart was very subject to wind drift. The odds of it hitting anything were way past bad.

"Gunny, have the two best marksmen among those four load sleepy darts. The other two load live ammo." Gunny handed out firing orders with deft hand signals. "If things get interesting, Gunny or I will say who and what gets fired." Kris told them softly, then decided it was time to make her own prefight statement. "Remember, Marines, we're here as cops. These kidnappers have a right to face a jury of their peers. But Sequim still has the death penalty. We bag 'em. They hang 'em."

With a happy growl, the marines mounted up. Gunny's fire team led, reduced to him and his tech. Behind him followed in single file his corporal and a shooter. Kris led her squad off, Hanson with his gadgets ahead of her. Corporal Li and a trigger puller brought up the rear.

Gunny's tech went first, using her satchel of magic tricks to tell those following when to step high to avoid laser beams, when to edge right or left away from mines. Kris eyed one mine as she passed it. Its surface was a perfect match of the tundra surrounding it. At fifteen centimeters across and rising slowly to maybe one centimeter high, it left no shadow. It was, however, developing one telltale. The summer sun had warmed it. It now sank two or three millimeters into the tundra. Kris looked around. Now that she knew what to look for, she could spot a half dozen. No footprints, though. That was what she'd looked for from orbit; footprints on the fragile tundra. They must have dropped these from a chopper. Again, more expenses. *Who was footing the bill for this?*

Kris badly felt the need for a shower, some coffee, and someone to talk over what had been thrown at her in the last few hours. There were patterns here, patterns that eluded her.

Eddy didn't need patterns solved. Eddy needed rescuing.

Kris concentrated on the problem at hand. Hunched down, halfway across a 300-meter minefield, she discovered a whole new meaning for naked and vulnerable. She watched her step. She watched the Stoolpigeon's feed for action in the house. She watched the sleeping guards for any hint of wakefulness. Occasionally, she remembered to breathe.

Reentry had taken what seemed like a year. Kris aged centuries crossing the tundra in front of the lodge. When finally she was close, Kris signaled Gunny to take his squad around back; the front door was hers. It gave her a direct run at the central staircase and the upstairs gunman. Kris wanted her battle armor over that terrified child's body ten minutes ago. Whatever happened in the house after Kris got to the kid, harm would come to that little girl through Kris's dead body.

Kris's luck ran out ten meters shy of the lodge. One of the sleeping beauties roused himself for a head visit. In his ambling, he wandered in front of the lodge's one picture window.

"Marines, we got action in the house," Kris whispered into her mike as the guy stopped in front of the window to scratch.

"We start this show on my count. Gunny, you take down the back and pacify the downstairs. My squad will take care of the front and the upstairs." She paused for questions—just as the thug in the picture window yanked up his gun and went fully automatic at them. "Fire support, get that guy in the window. Corporal Li, you get the sleeping guard on the front porch before he wakes up. Hanson, blow us a hole."

"Doing it," Hanson whispered, stuffing the end of a line charge into his grenade thrower and taking aim at the front door.

Behind Kris, Corporal Li's private took rounds, full in the chest. The force threw her a good five feet. She landed on a mine and got more air time.

"Fire in the hole," Hanson shouted. Kris hit the deck while her tech's grenade launcher went off with a whoosh, lobbing a charge at the front door and draping a line charge between her and said door. The door blew in; then, like failing Christmas tree lights, the charges on the line behind it went off. Most just went pop; three set off mines. Waiting just long enough for the explosives to blow, Kris dashed for the door. She was on it before it finished falling in.

Kris struggled to catch her balance as she hurtled into the living room. The stairs were ahead of her. She could not see the upstairs gunman. Off to her right, one man collapsed under a hail of fire from across the yard, even while another man rolled off the couch, gun coming up.

Kris wanted the upstairs gunman, not this one. The nice thing about keeping company with marines was that one of them was always behind you, always on backup. Ignoring the gunner, Kris raced for the stairs, gun up, magazine switching to sleepy darts. *Eddy, I'm here!*

Halfway up, the sleeping gunman came in view. The racket was bringing him awake. His eyes popped open wide as he saw Kris's gun aimed right at him. His hands came up. Maybe he was going for his gun. Maybe he was just trying to fend off her fire. It didn't matter. Kris shot.

Darts stitched up the man's chest, throat, and face, knocking him over backward. Kris reached the top of the stairs, did a hard left, and headed for the middle bedroom. Scream after scream came from that room; there was no question where the hostage was.

Kris hit the door and bounced off.

Hanson was right behind her. He slid to his knees at the door, jammed a wad of explosives in the lock, covered it with a flap of armored cloth, and ducked his head.

The door blew open.

Kris was moving before the explosion finished. That wasn't possible, but later she'd swear she did. She flew in with the door, did a quick scan with her rifle to the right and left, then dashed for a tiny figure in torn jeans and a filthy green sweater. The girl was sitting half up in bed, yanking at her restraints and screaming at the top of her six-year-old lungs. All Kris wanted to do was hug the child to her chest, but there were rules in situations like these. She dropped to the floor. Something small and nasty looking was attached by wires to the bottom of the bed. "Hanson, we got a bomb here."

Her tech slid to a stop on his knees while Kris did a further check on the room. What looked like a school backpack had been reloaded with clothes and other junk. Kris decided it could be ignored for a moment. Otherwise, the room was as bare as its wooden floor, light green walls, and tan ceiling permitted. No closet. Kris turned back to the howling child just as Hanson finished his examination of the monster under the bed.

"Bomb, rigged to the restraint. I pop them, it goes boom."

"Disarm it," came from Corporal Li as he entered the room, trailed by his trigger puller, much the dirtier but apparently no worse for wear from her encounter with live rounds and mines.

"You okay?" Kris asked the private.

"She's fine," the corporal answered for his gunner. "Landed on the mine flat on her back. It she'd stepped on it, it would have blown her foot off. As it was, it only tossed her around."

"Remind me to tell HQ their mines suck." Kris grinned.

"I'm ready to clip the leads on this thing," Hanson said, bringing them back to a child who hadn't quit screaming. "If this doesn't go well, it would be nice if we had some armor between the kid and this bomb."

Nothing would harm this girl. Kris gauged how much the little girl was bouncing around under restraints and slid herself onto the bed between the ragged blanket and the child. As Kris wrapped her arms around the girl, she stopped crying, though her breath came in short, choked gasps. "Nobody's going to hurt you now, honey," Kris whispered in her ear.

"Nobody?" the child said with a hiccup.

"Nobody," Hanson assured her. "Now, everyone back in the hall." Once the corporal and private were gone, Hanson sighed. "I think I got this right." He pulled his faceplate down and slid under the bed.

For a long moment, nothing happened. Kris waited. Nothing still happened. Then Hanson was getting back to his feet, raising his faceplace, and grinning like the man who broke the bank at Harrah's. "Don't just stand there," Kris snapped, "cut the girl loose."

"Yes, ma'am." Hanson said, producing clippers.

Li and his gunner were back, forming a wall between the outside world and their little girl. Kris raised her faceplate. "The Marines are here, honey. You're safe. Nobody's going to hurt you." The girl took it all in, her face sheet white and frozen, her eyes darting from one marine to another. As Hanson freed the child's arms, the tension in her tiny muscles began to loosen under Kris's hug as she tried, really tried, to believe what this stranger said. Finally free, the girl rolled over and wrapped herself around Kris, buried her face in the hard battle armor, and gave herself over to deep, racking sobs. Ensign Longknife held her, protected her, and mingled in some tears of her own. Tears from a Navy ensign who'd saved a stranger's child. Tears from a ten-year-old who'd failed to save a brother.

Above Kris, three marines kept guard, guns out, grins proud.

"Way to go," Corporal Li cheered.

"Way to go," Hanson echoed.

"God almighty, God almighty," the private repeated.

"House secure," Gunny reported on net. "Tech verifies no deadman switch. One bad guy dead. Five are cuffed and sleeping soundly. A few of the sleepy darts were at mighty close range. Some of these guys could use medical attention."

Kris sniffed, then managed to stand without the kid losing a square centimeter of body contact. "Very good, Gunny."

Kris blinked her commlink to full local net. "This is Ensign Longknife. The hostage is safe. Repeat, the kid is unharmed. Five bad guys are in custody, some injured. Request emergency medical backup. Warning, the ground around the target is mined. Do not land until we disarm them." Kris got acknowledgments from a half-dozen police nets and the *Typhoon*.

Kris looked down into red-rimmed eyes looking up at her. She hugged the girl tight. *You are wrong, Mother. The Navy's not a waste of my time. Some days are worth more than anyone could ever pay.*

4

In a game simulation, Kris would have popped the Game Over button about now and gone out for pizza. In the real world, it's not over until it's over, and this one was far from over.

The girl, so fragile and light in Kris's arms, mumbled, "Edith," when asked her name. Right, that had been somewhere in Kris's briefing, but it was too close to Eddy for Kris to dare remember it. From the way Edith clung to Kris, you'd think they shared a heart. At the moment, Kris wouldn't deny that. The private threw the upstairs gunman over his shoulder. Corporal Li and Hanson kept close to Kris and Edith as they worked their way downstairs. No one wanted to lose the girl to some surprise now. The private plopped his sleeper down in the living room next to two others. All showed blood where darts had hit them; two bled freely. One shivered in apparent shock. Two awake prisoners huddled on the couch, hands taped behind them. A pool of blood in front of them showed where one body had been taken out back.

"Who's in charge?" Kris demanded.

The two conscious ones glanced around as if just noticing the room. "Martin," one muttered. The other pointed at the shivering sleeper. Gunny retrieved a wallet from that one and opened it. Martin had an Earth driver's license and social ID. Earth! What was an Earth crook doing out here? This situation was way past strange.

But Kris had pressing housekeeping problems. "Folks," she told her prisoners, "there're land mines out there. I want them turned off. Who has the key?" They just stared blankly at Kris.

"Get me their IDs. I want to know who we've got. Specialist, can you wake up our sleeping beauties?"

Hanson stepped over to the supine forms, gave each a shot, then started rocking the first one with his foot, a rifle in his face. "Wake up, dude. You're in a world of hurt." Hanson smiled down cheerfully. His subject came awake with a cough, opened his eyes, took in the gun muzzle, and did his damndest to roll away. That only put him hard up against the next terrorist's back. The tech got down and in his face. "Who controls those mines?"

"Martin. He has the codes," he answered, eager to please.

Efforts to wake Martin only sent the heavyset man from drugged sleep into out cold. "This one's got a bad heart," Hanson reported. "He needs a hospital, or we'll lose him."

Gunny stooped to go face-to-face with one of the recently awakend sleepers. "Where does Martin have his codes?"

"In his 'puter. I swear they are."

The tech patted down Martin and pulled a banged-up and aging wrist computer off him, liberally covered with blood. The tech tried to wipe it clean on his battle suit, but armor was meant to keep blood in, not wipe it away. He ended up wiping it on the couch before trying to turn it on. No activity there.

"He was fingering it when I darted him," Gunny growled.

"I think he wiped it," Hanson concluded. Kris had learned long ago that nothing in storage was ever quite gone, not if the right people went after it with patience. She took the computer and slid it into her pouch as she studied the field through the gaping door. Four of her marines were on the other side of a too-live minefield. Kris would risk no one now that Edith was safe. In theory, her techs could clear the field, but mines had no friends, and Kris was not about to see one of her crew hurt, even if a mom and dad were airborne, headed this way.

"This is Ensign Longknife. I have no way of turning off the land mines. Anyone on net have any assets for clearing mines?" Several police nets gave her a negative. As Kris mulled her unacceptable options, her net boomed.

"This is Captain Thorpe of the *Typhoon*. We're inbound, thirty seconds out from the hunting lodge. We'll take care of that minefield. I suggest everyone dirtside get under cover."

The troops around Kris exchanged puzzled glances. Hanson shook his head. "The captain ain't gonna do that. Please, somebody tell me he ain't gone and done that. My gear's gonna be all over the place."

"He's thirty seconds out. I think he's already done it."

Kris shook her head. "He wouldn't. Not with me dirtside."

"I think he has, ma'am," Corporal Li chuckled.

"Let's do what the skipper said," Gunny growled. "It's gonna get noisy and messy hereabouts in a few seconds."

While her troops got their prisoners headed for the back room, Kris made a quick call to her fire team and ordered them back . . . way back. Then she eyed the brightening sky through the front window, eager to see what was coming. The manual said the smart metal of the Kamikaze-class ships could restructure themselves in several different ways. She herself had changed the *Typhoon* from general travel to orbital mission, but that was done all the time. To change a starship into an air-capable vehicle . . . now, that would take some rearranging.

The clear blue sky let go with a high-pitched scream. Kris spotted a white contrail off to the southwest, headed her way in the morning light. She wondered how you made a house safe when a starship landed next to it; not an evolution covered by any book she'd read at OCS. "Gunny, pop the windows out, break the glass before it shatters."

"Right, ma'am."

While her team went rapidly through the house, Kris scrounged several blankets and wrapped Edith in them. "There's going to be a big noise. Don't worry. I've got you. Nothing can hurt you now." The child looked up at Kris with wide, accepting eyes; then, if it was possible, she snuggled closer.

Kris stationed herself next to a window to keep an eye on things both inside and out. The roar outside went from loud to painful; Kris lowered her faceplate. Looking like a winged bird from hell, the *Typhoon* was aiming for the field in front of the lodge, coming in at about 400 knots. Half its engines were pointed down now. The overpressure out there was going to be nothing short of hellish. Kris held Edith tightly against the wall, assuming that her cowboy of a captain had calculated the full impact of the ship and mines on the house. What if he hadn't? Kris had a vision of the cabin's giant logs reduced to kindling and prayed the skipper knew what he was doing.

"See, didn't I tell you?" One of her marines pointed. "Don't it look like a Klingon Bird-of-Prey? Right out of the comic."

The *Typhoon* wasn't a hundred meters up when the first mine blew. Its explosion would have gone unnoticed in the racket, but Kris spotted the splash of water and mud that didn't fit the regular air flow from the *Typhoon*'s engine blast. Then another and another mine added its pop to the display. Water, mud, bits of vegetation, and rocks went flying every which way, none even close to the *Typhoon*. Kris had seen enough. "Everybody down."

Reluctantly, her troops obeyed. With her back to the log wall, all Kris could think of was the mess the heat was making of the tundra. Summer had softened the top dozen centimeters or so. Now, hot rocket exhaust was digging two or three meters into the frozen earth, melting everything, turning it into a slurry and throwing it far and wide.

Kris hoped whoever owned this place wouldn't mind. If someone got stuck doing an after-the-fact environmental impact statement and mitigation plan, Kris knew who was high on Captain Thorpe's list for the duty.

Outside, the scream of rockets changed to a settling whine; Kris risked a glance. The ground steamed and roiled in a broad slash as the *Typhoon* settled onto a dozen thick landing gears well away from the last mine. Police choppers would be wanting to land next. Kris turned to her team. "Gunny, have the techs police up the area. If there are any mines left, explode them. Start with the veranda."

The two specialists had their satchel of techno tricks out, checking the door before they opened it.

"Here's one."

"Here's another," came back to her before they'd gone two paces.

"Crew"—she waved at her marines—"let's gather for a prayer vigil in the back room while our friends bless our dear departing mines out front."

"Yeah," a corporal grinned, "a mine is a terrible thing to waste."

"Keep that up, and these prisoners are gonna sue us for marine brutality."

"Where's my mommy?" Edith put in.

"She's coming, honey. Just a few more minutes." Kris sat Edith on the kitchen counter, while Gunny kept the prisoners in another room. Kris pulled her ration pack out, rummaged through it for a candy bar, and gave it to the girl.

Edith studied it, her mouth twisted in a reflection of the conflict within. "My mommy told me never to take candy from strangers."

"Honey, I'm not a stranger." Kris laughed. "I'm a marine."

"Hard Corps," Corporal Li agreed.

"All the way," the other trigger pullers chimed in.

Edith must have agreed. She attacked the candy bar with zeal. Kris rummaged through the rest of her ration pouch, hunting for anything else the girl might like. The work out front was regularly punctuated by booms as exposed mines were set off by charges. Kris took several calls from police helicopters asking when a landing pad might be ready. The eighty-member crew of the *Typhoon* had no explosives experts to contribute to the two marine specialists, much to Captain Thorpe's disgust, so everyone waited while Kris's two worked.

As the booms got farther from the house, Kris took Edith back to the front room. From the door they watched the marines at work. Sniffers picked up the scent of explosives in the swirling mist of steam and exhaust. The marines would toss a package of explosives at the exposed mine, back off, and detonate their charge. That usually was enough to explode the mine as well. The few that didn't respond to the treatment were marked and left for later handling by a real bomb squad. This informal approach to field clearing finally yielded a large enough space that Kris ordered one specialist to drop back and set up a transponder for the first chopper.

Two minutes later, three rotorcraft orbited the clearing; Kris ordered the mine hunt to pause. One chopper swooped in to quickly deposit a team of explosives experts before lifting off again. These volunteers from a local mining consortium turned to helping the marines. As soon as the pad was clear, a second helicopter flared in for a landing without asking permission.

There was no question who it brought. A woman and man bolted from it. Edith let out a whoop, and Kris almost lost her. Kris held on, trying not to fight, and amazed at how strong a six-year-old was when she wanted to be. The woman Edith's scream identified as "Mommy, Mommy," raced across the field, slipping and sliding until she was covered with mud, and dashed up the steps to the lodge, the man not two steps behind her. The child that before had seemed bolted to Kris's hip flowed into her mother's arms. There were tears and hugs and all kinds of blubbering as the three of them lost themselves in each other.

Kris had cried her tears; she turned back to the lodge,

quickly found her prisoners under Gunny's less-than-gentle care, and got them organized to move out. When next Kris stepped onto the veranda, the rejoined family was where she'd left them. A large chopper now occupied the single helipad, its engines spooling down as it disgorged a dozen men whose uniforms and hard eyes identified them as cops. Kris edged the family to the far corner of the veranda, then brought her prisoners out under heavy guard. The three, still locked in a hug, spared no notice for the kidnappers. The leader of the police force took in the handcuffed walking four and the half-carried fifth with a hard glare, as if already measuring them for coffins.

"There's a dead one on the back porch. We need to exchange any paperwork," Kris asked, "or do I just turn them over to you?"

"I'll take them off your hands, ma'am. You want paperwork, I can scare you up some. We're kind of light on that stuff out here," he said, not taking his eyes from the prisoners as they were quickly marched off. "I understand one of them needs a doc."

"The wobbly one," Kris pointed out.

"He'll make it," the cop growled.

"Well, they say he's the boss man," Kris said with a wave at the other prisoners. "I'd like to hear what he has to say."

"He'll be talking real soon." Now the cop grinned. "I suspect we can get them all talking. Get them glad to talk."

That left Kris wondering what other parts of the Society's Declaration on Human Rights Sequim hadn't gotten around to ratifying yet. Kris had other problems. "Gunny, have your squad police up our gear. Otherwise, don't disturb the crime scene."

"Yes, ma'am," he saluted.

Kris turned to Corporal Li. "Our squad will retrieve the LACs. I want to personally do the breakdown on our boat's commlink. Nobody touches it before me. Got it?"

"In spades, ma'am. No bloody squid's gonna get by with sloppy work that damn near fries me and mine." It was nice when leaders took a personal interest in their people's work.

Kris did a slow look around, found everything under somebody else's control, and followed her corporal.

It took Kris a while to collect the troopers who had
provided fire support from the woods; they'd gotten *way*
back when the ship came over. With them, she headed for
the *Typhoon*. At the gangway, a corpsman was waiting to
take over the limper. Right beside the medic stood Captain
Thorpe himself, grinning like a pirate as he surveyed the
results of his landing approach.

"Damn good, if I do say so myself."

"Yes, sir," Kris agreed. "I need to pick up the LACs. Can
I sign for a hovercraft?"

"Your marines too lazy, Ensign, for another walk in that
swamp you took them through?"

"No, sir. Just thought you might want everyone back
aboard before the sun gets too high," she answered. If she
had gone straight for the landers, he'd be damning her for
wasting time making mud pies. Kris was getting used to
being damned if she did and damned when she didn't.

"Take number two hover, and make it quick," Thorpe
ordered, then added as if as an afterthought, "Well done,
Ensign."

Kris saluted and led her squad back aboard. No surprise, turning the *Typhoon* into a landing ship had shuffled
a lot around inside. However, Nelly quickly showed Kris
where Hovercraft Two was docked. Kris used a second
gangway to slip back out; no need going through Thorpe's
idea of motivation twice. She found the right patch of skin,
gave the order over the ship's net, and watched as a hatch
slowly opened, lowering the hovercraft from its travel bay.
In another three minutes, Kris had checked it out and
mounted up her team. The corporal drove, Kris seated next
to him. In the backseats, the marines let loose with whoops
and shouts as they shot away from the *Typhoon*.

As the corporal dodged trees and bounced over rocks,
and the celebration in back got louder, he leaned toward
Kris. "Thanks for getting us down, ma'am. I figured us for
fried. I don't know many officers who could have done

what you did. Getting us down was about all I was hoping for. Getting us down where we could help that little girl. Well, ma'am, you may not be a marine, but I'll *Semper Fi* with you anytime."

"Thanks," was all Kris could manage. *Father, you are wrong. A won election isn't the greatest feeling in the world.* Kris doubted she'd ever feel more pride than she felt at this moment from her subordinate's praise. Better than medals any day.

The LACs were where they'd left them. While three marines loaded Gunny's in the bay of the hovercraft, Kris and Li gave their own lander a once-over. The commlink was still as dead as horse cavalry. "Go easy," Kris said as the three troopers lifted this one much more gently and deposited it in Hover Two.

"Yeah, be a bleeding shame to knock what's wrong with it back right," one private observed. Kris chuckled; just because they were marines didn't mean they were dumb . . . just, well, marines. The trip back was slower. By the time they reached the *Typhoon,* a cargo hatch was open in the ship's skin, so they drove right into the loading bay. Tommy was waiting, test kit in hand.

"Ready to tear into this piece of crap?" Kris asked, as she dismounted.

"Nope," he said, relaxing against the bay door, "thought I'd get some air." He waved his tester. "Which LAC was yours?"

Kris had the marines unload it, then dismissed them. Tommy went straight to work. Kris found her locker and doffed her drop suit. She would have loved a shower but had no idea where one was in the reorganized ship. She settled for putting on yesterday's khakis. As she finished changing, Tommy waved her over to gaze with him into the innards of her cockpit. "What can you tell me about my bum commlink?" she asked.

"That my heart quit beating when you went off-line," he said.

Kris wasn't sure if that was just Santa Maria's Irish

talking, or if Tommy was actually flirting. She dodged the question by ignoring him.

He went on, "There's a recall out on the commlink. Subcontractor got ahold of a batch of nonspec parts, but they initially passed inspection, both his and the contractor . . . or so the paperwork says. Let me check this one."

With the cover off, the inner workings of the cockpit stood bare. Kris didn't need Tommy's magic tester to find the problem; the circuit board he pulled showed scorched plastic. "Any way to know if that's just dumb luck or if someone tinkered with the board?" Kris asked, giving full rein to the paranoia she'd learned at her father's knee.

Tommy squinted one eye as he glanced her way. "Who'd tinker with it? It's depot-level maintenance."

Kris sighed, stood, and leaned against a closed locker. She eyed the parts laid out before her, trying to make sense of what she saw. Had a random distribution of bum parts almost killed her and her marines? And then saved them!

"What're you thinking?" Tommy asked, squatting beside her.

"That I ought to debrief my team," she said to no one in particular. "Didn't one of the books at OCS say something about critiquing an action, that talking things through will soften post-traumatic stress if anything stressful happened? Think almost frying on entry qualifies?"

"Grandma Chin and the ancestors would," Tommy agreed.

"Thing is, I'm feeling a tad stressed myself. Real soon, my father and I need to have a long talk about the procurement practices of his government," she said. Then something hit her. "If that damn part was on recall, why hadn't it been replaced?"

"We didn't have a spare. Squadron Six's supply officer promised me a replacement in three days. We sortied on day two."

"Luck? Right. You know, Tommy, I think I need to do something to change my luck. Any suggestions?"

"Have you tried leaving milk out for the little people?"

"I think I'll have a beer myself," she muttered. "They can have any I spill."

"Good by me," the leprechaun beside her grinned.

Before Kris could say anything more, both their comm-links went off, doing their level best to beep their way through the bugle notes of Officer's Call. Captain Thorpe had a very old notion of military decorum and motivation. Kris and Tommy hit both their commlinks at the same moment, so they were treated to the same message, in stereo.

"Sequim's general manager requests the presence of all ship's officers at a reception being given at his residence at nineteen thirty local time. The *Typhoon* will lift for Sequim's main space port at seventeen hundred local. Uniform of the day will be dress white."

Kris took a whiff of herself, decided she didn't like it, and went hunting for her quarters. With a little luck, her dress whites wouldn't look too bad after being trundled all over as the ship remade itself. Somehow, Kris suspected, her luck had been busy elsewhere this morning.

Kris was right. Though her locker and wardrobe had managed to move themselves into the stateroom that Kris now shared with Chief Bo, Kris had no idea where the contents of her desk and lockbox were. Hopefully, they'd show up tomorrow when the ship got back into orbit. As expected, Kris's uniforms looked like they'd been put through a wringer. "The girls have an iron in the main room," Chief Bo said as Kris surveyed the wreckage.

Under the ship's normal configuration, Kris and Bo occupied separate staterooms at the opposite end of "the temple," that space where the Navy housed its "vestigial virgins." This was someone's bright idea of how to keep men out of the enlisted women's sleeping quarters. Kris assumed it worked; she'd never bothered to catch any males making the run in or out of the spaces the enlisted women shared two to a room, or, more often, one to a room thanks to the *Typhoon* being below even the skimpy peacetime crew authorization. Since it was work hours, Kris didn't feel the need for a coughing fit before entering the enlisted women's area. The iron and its board were easy to spot, and despite theatrical levels of shock and dismay among her fellow cadets at OCS that a Longknife would iron her own uniforms, Kris had gotten the hang of it quickly.

At 1630, Kris joined the nine other ship's officers in the hulking shadow of the *Typhoon* as a line of vehicles arrived to take them to the reception. The captain and XO shared a limo; Kris and Tommy piled into a reasonably clean all-terrain rig.

At the general manager's residency, the officers arranged themselves in rank order before entering a crowded, wood-paneled ballroom lit by several crystal chandeliers that would have been right at home on Wardhaven but seemed a bit out of place on a start-up world. Captain Thorpe in dress whites resplendent with rows of medals led his officers toward a formal reception line, civilian men in brightly colored formal wear, women in floor-length gowns from last year's Paris designers. As the most junior members of the *Typhoon*'s crew, Kris and Tommy made sure no one got behind them. That didn't last very long.

"Longknife. Kris Longknife? That *was* you in that skiff this morning!" Kris looked around for the voice; she didn't recognize it. A young man in a maroon tux and a drink in both hands headed for her. He looked vaguely familiar.

"Recognize me?" he beamed.

Raised on politics where everyone was your best friend, at least until the door closed behind them, Kris had plenty of experience watching Mother or Father fake eternal friendship. "Long time, no see," she said, taking the offered drink.

"Hey, Anita, Jim, you have to meet this girl. Come on over. This has to be the woman Edith says saved her." At that shout, the receiving line disintegrated just as Captain Thorpe extended his hand to the general manager. Leaving the skipper's hand waving in empty air, the man and woman at the front of the line headed for Kris, with everyone else only a step behind.

"Are you the woman who rescued my Edith?" Behind the sequined gold lamé dress and expensive coif, Kris saw the woman who had slogged through muck to her child this morning.

"I led the ground assault team," Kris answered, trying to avoid letting her small area of responsibility impinge in any way on Captain Thorpe's overall command.

"I told you there was a Longknife flying that skiff, didn't I?" Kris's unidentified friend went on. "She beat the pants off me two years running at college. I'd recognize those smooth curves anywhere. Ought to, I studied them damn near every night. Can't tell you how glad I am to see you again."

Beneath that umbrella of continuous chatter, the mother introduced herself as Anita Swanson, wife of Jim Swanson, Sequim's general manager and sister to the magpie. A servant was dispatched to wake Edith, who had gone to bed early under protest at not being allowed to come to the party. Through all this, Captain Thorpe stood ignored at the elbow of Jim Swanson's powder-blue tux. Watching the red rise on her skipper's neck, Kris did what she'd better do if the entire crew was to be saved from a miserable week, month, and year. "General Manager Swanson, may I present to you the commander of the ship that saved your daughter, Captain Thorpe."

Jim Swanson turned to shake the captain's offered hand. "I want you to know that as the planetary leader of this colony, I have recommended Ms. Longknife for the Distinguished Flying Cross. I may not be the afficionado of skiff flying that my wife's brother Bob here is, but I want you to know that I've never seen the skills that this girl put into her skiff flying this morning." Kris started backing up, looking for a convenient place to hide. Mr. Swanson sounded like one of those politicians who knew just enough about the military to make it really miserable for anyone he took an interest in. "We were watching on the secure hookup you provided us, Captain. I was hardly breathing when your skiffs started their drop. Then this kid's skiff takes off doing loop-the-loops, and even I can tell it's burning reaction mass in all the wrong directions. How much did she have left when she got down?"

"I will have my executive officer look up what the fuel situation was on *Ensign* Longknife's *Landing Craft Assault*," the captain said, emphasizing that it was no racing skiff Kris flew that morning. "The skill Ensign Longknife displayed today," the skipper continued with a nod in Kris's direction, "was in the highest tradition of the service. However, Mr. Swanson, the DFC is out of the question. That is a combat medal, sir."

"And those kidnappers weren't more heavily armed than anyone the Navy's come up against in years?" Mr. Swanson observed dryly.

"So it seems, sir, but we were here in support of a police matter, not a military combat drop."

Even Kris, just getting used to being a subordinate, could read the captain's cutoff as clearly as a brick wall. However, Kris had witnessed several of her father's failed conversations with military types. This had all the markings of a massive one.

"I should think, Captain Thorpe, that as the skipper of the good ship *Summer Morning Breeze,* you would be happy to have one of your crew recommended for a distinguished medal by the senior political official on a rapidly growing colony planet."

Oh boy. Kris glanced around for a place to hide. As the daughter of a prime minister, this might be fun to watch. As a very junior officer at the center of all this attention, she'd gladly forgo the honor. The ship out at the spaceport might be the Fast-*Response* Corvette *Summer Morning Breeze* to the politicians who paid for her, but she was the Fast-*Attack* Corvette *Typhoon* to the officer who commanded her. Kris had heard several variations on both names among the enlisted, but they didn't count. She'd heard her father say, after a long, bitter budget battle, that he'd call a ship any damn thing he needed to get the votes to fund it, and if the votes were for *Warm, Cuddly Koala Bear,* by damn, he'd have a nice little old lady commission it that. What the Navy officers chose to call it once they took possession was their own damn business.

It had only taken two nasty incidents before the prime minister learned to keep careful track of who he was talking to and call the ship by the appropriate name for the listener. Mr. Swanson was about to have such a learning experience.

"Is that her? Is that the 'arine that came for me?"

Said learning experience was forestalled as a tiny form in a white nightdress with pink ribbons dashed into the room. Kris found herself gazing down into familiar wide blue eyes. This time, there was no red rim from tears. The face had been washed and was about as angelic as a six-year-old ever got. Edith now had a cuddly teddy bear in tow. Her mom bent to pick up Edith, but the girl made a beeline for Kris.

Handing her untouched drink off to Tommy, Kris stooped, starched uniform crinkling, to swoop up the child. Edith gave Kris a hug that had to be worth all the medals the Navy ever minted. "You have a beautiful little girl, here," Kris said to mother and father. "It was my pleasure to return her safe and sound to you. I know I speak for my marines, and the entire ship, when I say it was our honor and joy to see her in your arms."

That drew a unanimous round of applause.

Made unsure by all the noise, Edith decided she wanted her mother's arms around her. As Anita took the girl from Kris, she muttered, "If only all such horrible things ended so happily." Then the mother blanched. "You're Kristine Longknife. You lost your . . . Oh, I'm sorry!"

Breath went out of Kris like she'd been kneed in the belly. It was so easy to handle people and their fights. Thanks to Father, she had plenty of experience there. But solicitous people, people who thought they knew the pain she'd been through, that was more than daunting. Steeling herself to put on the required face, Kris nodded. "Yes, ma'am. I'm that Kristine Longknife. And I am very glad that your family's ordeal ended very different from mine."

Anita seemed at a loss for words; her husband stepped

in. "I think we're about ready to serve dinner. If Edith is ready for Miss Lilly White's party, Nurse can put her to bed and the rest of us can discuss matters further over dinner."

Edith left with backward waves for all. Kris excused herself, claiming rest room necessity. There was an exit just past the ladies' room; Kris took it. Outside, the air was warm, but an evening breeze cooled the expansive grounds of the general manager's mansion. Hands stiff at her sides, Kris fought to organize the emotions ripping at her gut. That was what Judith said. Know the dragons coming at you out of your darkness. Name them if you wish, but get familiar with each and every one of them. Some were easy. The captain she knew.

He needed his ship and the authority it gave him. He needed control of his domain. If he hadn't chosen the Navy, he'd be a senior manager by now, maybe running his own business. But he'd chosen the Navy because it did Important Things That Mattered!

Kris understood Swanson as well. He was Building Things! People looked up to him for what he did. Someday, they'd put a statue of him in the planet's capital, when it had an elected legislature and full membership in the Society of Humanity.

The captain and the general manager were Very Important People, and Kris had watched her father take the likes of them apart, leaving them bleeding career-wise and begging for help. Yes, Kris knew big men like these could be made very small.

So why was she in the Navy where Thorpe could order her to risk her life using two-bit equipment to rescue Jim Swanson's daughter because he hadn't funded his own police well enough to do the job?

Because today I did what I couldn't do when I was ten. Today I saved Edith. If only I had been there to save Eddy. There it was. Still the survivor's guilt. No matter what she did, she'd always be alive and the little boy she was supposed to take care of would always be dead.

A knock at the door yanked Kris out of this all-too-familiar round of self-flagellation; Tommy stuck his head out. "Thought I'd find you here. You should get back. They're about to officially seat us, and you don't want to make a grand entrance."

"Already made one today. Think I'll save the next one for tomorrow."

"By my ancestors' count it's already two today. And yes, even the wee people would be saving up the next one for several tomorrows from now."

Kris gave Tommy the grin his mixed-up mythology deserved and slipped back into the dining room before the movement to the tables was so pronounced as to make her absence noticeable. Kris was seated well away from the head table, although Bob, the magpie brother-in-law, somehow managed to seat himself next to her; that settled the table's conversation on skiffs. Kris found that if she played it right, she did little of the talking. Magpies did have their benefits.

Late in the meal, a marine brought message traffic for the captain. The officers grew silent at something so important it required the old formality of the captain reading a flimsy, though talk among the civilians continued undimmed. Captain Thorpe signed the receipt, then pocketed the message. The officers would learn about it in the captain's good time.

When Mr. Swanson stood to lay more profuse praise on them, the captain asked if he might say a word. As the skipper rose, he pulled the message flimsy from his pocket. "The *Typhoon* has been ordered back to base," he said curtly, glancing around the room. "Due to the failure of the President and the Senate to arrive at a budget resolution, all ships of Fast Attack Squadron Six will stand down for a three-month storage period. Officers will be placed on half pay. Enlistments that will be up in the next ninety days will be processed immediately. I regret to say that all requests for reenlistments have been declined at the highest level. We will be raising ship at oh six hundred tomorrow." That said, the captain sat down.

"That's impossible," Mr. Swanson sputtered. "The Senate and the President agreed on the full Navy bill. That's what my contacts on Earth informed me."

The captain did not stand, but his command voice carried to the farthest corner of the room. "You are correct, sir, as far as your information goes. However, to fund the full appropriation required an increase in taxes. The rim got the Senate to pass it. The Earth-born president vetoed it. While we are authorized to write enough checks to operate the Navy, Treasury lacks the money to cash them all. Rather than kite checks into next year, the Navy Department is ordering a stand-down." Thorpe paused for a moment before adding, "Be glad your daughter was kidnapped *this* month. Next month there wouldn't be a ship to respond."

Mr. Swanson stumbled back a step, as if hit by a wayward asteroid. The captain wasn't exactly correct. Supplemental appropriations were available for emergency activity. Indeed, this entire response might be debited to that account, leaving more money to cover naval operations, but Kris was not about to correct her captain. On that note, conversation around the room limped on. Ten minutes later, Captain Thorpe asked the hostess's leave to depart, and the ship's officers left as a group. As the door closed behind Kris, the civilians' conversation took off like thunder. She could easily imagine the topic.

The Executive Officer was waiting for Kris as she crossed the quarterdeck. "Ensign, a moment."

Kris stayed with him as the other officers went to their quarters; he said nothing until they had the space to themselves. "Captain Thorpe has forwarded a recommendation that you receive the Navy Marine Corps medal for your lifesaving effort today. Swanson was kind enough to provide us with a copy of his write-up." Kris nodded, but the XO wasn't finished. He stared off across the port to the city lights of Port Swanston, Sequim's largest city. "I hear Sequim is trying to get Wardhaven to finance some new mines along their asteroid belt. Got to look nice, him putting the daughter of Wardhaven's prime minister in for a fucking medal," he spat.

Stunned at the hatred in the XO's voice, "Yes, sir," was all Kris managed to sputter. She'd risked her neck to save a kid's life, not for a medal, and all anyone could see was that she was one of *those* Longknifes. Dismissed, she stumbled through the unfamiliar passages to her room, slammed the door behind her, then pounded on it a few times for good measure.

"Don't think that door will be bothering anyone for a while, ma'am," a quiet voice drawled in the darkness.

Kris whirled: the dark of her room showed nothing. "Lights, dim," she ordered, trying to keep the emotions strangling her throat from turning her voice into a series of squeaks. The overhead came to life, casting low light around the rearranged quarters. *Right, I'm sharing a damn room with Chief Bo.*

"I'm sorry, Chief, I forgot. I'll be quieter. Lights, out," Kris ordered, to hide herself.

"Lights on," the chief said as she threw her covers aside and sat up in bed. Worn pajamas were missing the two top buttons, and the pants were cut off at the knees, revealing more wrinkled yellow skin than Kris wanted to see as the old chief settled cross-legged on the lower bunk.

"Honey, you look like you been rode hard and put away wet," drawled the small, Oriental-looking woman. The question, *Don't you want to talk to your Auntie Bo?* was left hanging. As far as Kris was concerned, it could hang there until it strangled. She turned to her locker to get her pj's and to hide her face.

Her locker wasn't there.

"Damn it, where is everything?" Kris exploded.

"Scattered around the ship, as best I can tell," the chief answered easily. "You know, ma'am, I don't think they quite have the hang of rearranging the ship in flight. At least this time, we didn't space anyone."

Kris was kicking her way along the panels under her

bunk, hoping a door would pop open. Mainly just kicking. "They haven't actually spaced anyone during a reconfiguration," she said, then added, "have they?"

"The Navy has its stories, and old chiefs do love passing them along to the young'uns. Like today. It'll make quite a story; boot ensign goes out, saves a squad of jarheads with some fancy flying, then saves the whole damn platoon when she flies them over the minefield Gunny and the skipper were enthusiastically planning on dropping them into. Great story. So tell me, why you look like somebody stole your puppy?"

"XO says the skipper is putting me in for the Navy Marine Corps medal."

"Hell, dearie, everyone on the boat knows that. Skipper ordered it about ten hundred this morning."

"He's not doing it because Sequim's general manager wanted to put me in for a medal?"

"No ma'am."

"Then why'd the XO . . ." Kris started to form the question, then stopped. Never ask a question you already know the answer to was the prime minister's Rule One.

"I expect the XO is riding you. Like the skipper is, maybe was. Wants to know what you're made of."

A panel flew open at Kris's last kick. The drawer was upside down; underwear cascaded onto the floor. Kris pulled a pair of gym shorts and a college sweatshirt from the pile, shoved the rest back inside, and stripped quickly. When she turned to the sink, toothbrush in hand, the chief was still eyeing her. "Why you here? If you don't mind the question, ma'am?"

"I wanted to do some good," Kris said, smearing paste on the brush. "Think I did, today," she said, jamming the brush in her mouth to cut off further discussion.

The chief shook her head. "My sister wanted to do good. She joined the Salvation Army. In case you didn't notice today, the good you did for the little girl is gonna mean some things very bad for the guys that grabbed her."

"They're getting what they deserve," Kris spat through the toothbrush.

"Right, you're one of those Longknifes. But trust me, honey, the bad guys ain't always going to be so deserving or so obvious. Navy shoots what it's aimed at, no questions asked, no answers sought. Politicians like your daddy point us. You sure you want to be out here on the tip of the spear with the rest of us folks with smelly feet?"

"I joined," Kris said, rinsing out her mouth.

"So did every mother's daughter snoring out there in the bays. Some joined to get out of that mother's house, or father's. Some joined to dodge a marriage, or the law. There are a couple out there earning money for college. They'll be the first in their family ever to get one of those diploma things. Every girl out there knows why she joined. Why did you?"

"I said I joined so I could do some good," Kris snapped.

"And?" Chief Bo wasn't going to let her off that easy.

"Would you believe I wanted to get away from home, too?"

"Maybe," came with a raised eyebrow.

"No, I'm not some poor little rich kid, damn it, who had to join the Navy to get any attention. I had the prime minister and his lady's attention. God, did I have their attention. So much of them, there was no room for me. That's why I joined the Navy. To find a little space for me. To find a little air of my own to breathe. That a good enough reason to join your damn Navy?"

"Maybe," Chief Bo said, reaching for her covers and stretching out on her bunk. "Good enough reason to join. Not good enough to stay. Let me know when you figure out why you want to *be* Navy."

"Why are you Navy?" Kris snapped.

"So I can have these fun late-night girl talks with you young officers and still get a good night's sleep in my own rack. Lights, out."

In the dark, Kris could hear the chief rolling over, and in

only a moment, she was snoring, leaving Kris to sort out a day that was more full than most months back home. Kris tried to organize all that had hit her in the last thirty hours but quickly found that all her mind wanted to do was spin past the day in a blur. Kris measured her breath, slowed it, and in a moment, exhausted sleep found her.

6

The *Typhoon* lifted on schedule at 0600. At 0700, while most of the crew was at breakfast, the XO converted the boat from Air Vehicle/Planet Lander mode back to Acceleration/NonCombat mode. Kris reached the bridge just as the reports on the Success/Lack There Of began to pour in.

When a Kamikaze-Class Corvette was in noncombat mode, it wasn't a bad ship to be on. The thick hull armor for combat was spread thinly throughout the ship to make spacious passageways and work spaces. The bridge wasn't too claustrophobic, and each officer and many enlisted had their own private room. The XO had followed the book on how to change from one mode to the other and back again. Painful to say, and it was for him, the reconfiguration didn't quite work as the book promised.

Kris got the job of figuring out what the book missed. As Defensive Systems Officer, she was trained to move the ship's skin around in combat to compensate for damage. That left Kris the only one among the *Typhoon*'s ten officers and sixty crew even marginally qualified to answer questions about wayward lockers, storage rooms, tool chests, et al. Kris spent most of the trip back to Squadron Six's base on High Cambria trying to get the *Typhoon*'s insides back where they belonged. Ninety-five percent of everything worked just like the builders' specs said it would.

Kris worked sixteen-hour days on the remaining 5 percent.

It had its compensations. There was new respect in the crews' eyes even as they pestered Kris for this and that. Quite a few put in a good word about the rescue. And all of them thanked her for what she was doing now, even the last, the owner of footlocker 73b2 and tool locker 23's mechs. After five tries, and five failures, neither space would move to its designated location. Kris solved it, finally, by having the spacers involved empty the lockers in their wrong locations, deleting them, then re-creating new ones in the right space. The *Typhoon* seemed to tremble with a quiet sigh of relief and a cheer when Kris finished. "Hope we don't do that again any time soon," Kris muttered to herself . . . and the rest of the bridge crew.

Captain Thorpe raised an eyebrow to the Exec.

"I followed the steps in the manual," the Executive Officer defended himself. "You were looking over my shoulder, sir."

"Yes, I was." The captain chuckled, then turned to Kris and actually let the smile stay on his face. "Right, Ensign, we will avoid this drill in the future. Before you stand down, Ensign, write me an experience report to forward to ComAttackRon Six for Commodore Sampson's review, entertainment, and referral to the yard for an explanation." The bridge team shared a laugh, and Kris stowed away the skipper's smile. It looked like she'd finally made it. She was an ensign, just one of the crew.

Then they arrived back at base and went immediately into stand-down for storage. Except for the captain, all officers went on half pay. They could leave the ship for the next three months, or they could work half-time, rotating with each other. The four department heads planned to do that. The six junior officers like Kris and Tommy were told

they had a choice: get lost for all three months or just for the
first six weeks, then work the last six for chow and a bunk.
Either way, leave a place the Navy could contact them in
case of emergency recall.

Kris found Tommy flipping through the freight lines,
looking for a cheap ticket back home. "We Santa Marians
always knew we were the wrong end of nowhere, but with
these connections, I'll get home just in time to come back."

"There's a direct liner leaving for Wardhaven tomorrow.
We could be there in four days."

"And what would I do on Wardhaven?"

"Keep me company. Tell my mother there was nothing
dangerous about how I won the medal my father is going to
pin on me. You know. Provide moral support."

Tom laughed. "And your ma's going to believe me?"

"More than she will me."

So it was settled. They dashed aboard the luxurious
Swift Achilles a good ten minutes before the air locks were
hatched down. Each ended up sharing quarters with six
other junior officers headed for the beach, but Kris figured
a cruise ship would be good for some serious relaxing. She
was wrong.

At breakfast the next morning, she bumped into, literally,
Commodore Sampson, the commander of Attack Squadron
Six. He eyed her like she was something really hideous that
had just crawled out from under a rock. Kris was getting
used to senior officers giving JOs that treatment. Out of uniform, she braced and said, "Good morning, sir."

"Ensign Longknife, isn't it?" the short officer rumbled.
Kris agreed that she was. "Interesting report on smart metal.
Your grandfather's shipyards should find it informative."

"Yes, sir," Kris answered, then headed for the other end
of the dining room where the lowlifes and JOs hung out.
For the next four days, she did her best to be elsewhere
when her superior officer was anywhere.

Once the *Swift Achilles* docked at High Wardhaven,
Kris had Nelly take charge of seeing that her and Tommy's

luggage was shipped dirtside. She wanted her hands free as she moved about the station, hurrying for the elevator. It couldn't be that she was excited about being home. A sign at the elevator station proudly announced that the contractor had finally gotten the bugs out of the passenger cars on the orbit-to-surface elevator, a reminder that the Navy wasn't the only one with quality-control problems. Viewing cars were now available, and Kris and Tom grabbed tickets for one's fourth level, the one that gave a full view of Wardhaven as they dropped.

Once the car came out of the station, there were ohs and ahs at the view of the planet laid out 44,000 kilometers below them. Kris found tears forming in her eyes. Just four months ago she would have been glad to never see Wardhaven again. Today it was the most beautiful place in the galaxy. Its white clouds spread across blue oceans; its lands were green or brown or even bright yellow when the desert outback came in view.

"It looks just like Santa Maria," Tommy noted beside her, "but not as beautiful." Did everyone in human space feel that way about their home planet?

At midcourse, the car began to decelerate; Kris went from being gently pushed back into her seat by the one-quarter g force to hanging on her restraints. A computer voice suggested they turn their seats around, but Kris was not about to give up this view. Now she could make out the particulars of home. Lander's Bay, a curving hundred klicks of water. Barrier islands had made this spot on the equator the choice for orbital landers until a runway could be built. The Old Miss, wide and reaching far back into South Continent had given the city of Wardhaven a boost for trade both off planet and up-country.

"What's that needle?" Tommy asked.

"Grampa Alex's doing," Kris answered. "Most of Great-I-forget-how-many Grampa Nuu's factories are off planet now. But we still own that chunk of land east of the river and south of town. He's turning it into one monstrous office and apartment complex and returning most of the land to parks. He bragged you'd be able to see the center piece of it from low orbit, and you can."

"You own all that?"

"My family does," Kris corrected, not relishing the awe in Tommy's voice. "We're a big family. I don't own all that much."

"Yeah, right." Tommy didn't sound all that persuaded.

Kris suppressed a sigh; right about now was when she lost a lot of friends. Instead, she pointed. "Those lakes out there beyond town. We used to have a sailboat. Honovi, my older brother, and Eddy and I would go sailing whenever we could. We would have sailed all summer if they'd let us. You ever go sailing?" There, she'd said Eddy's name. She didn't choke on it. Her heart hadn't bled. She'd saved Edith; maybe now she could face Eddy.

"That pool back at OCS was the first time I saw water over my head," Tommy reminded her. Now, only a hundred klicks up, most of Wardhaven City was coming into view. Kris noted how much farther the city had spread around the bay since she'd seen it from Grampa Trouble's racing skiff. Well, Father's eight years had been prosperous ones. Good for Wardhaven. Good for his reelection campaign.

Now the car shuddered as the brakes were applied, and they slowed to a crawl to enter the station. As soon as the car turned level, riders were unhitching their harnesses, reaching under their chairs for their carry-on luggage even before the car announced such goings-on were safe. Kris was in no hurry. Even though Nelly had messaged ahead, there had been no one to meet her at High Wardhaven. She doubted there would be anyone here.

As she and Tommy looked for their luggage, Kris got a surprise tap on her shoulder. She turned and yelped with glee.

"Uncle Harvey." She threw her arms around the old chauffeur and gave him a hug and kiss on his scarred cheek. It took an effort to believe that he'd been younger than she was now when his one battle qualified him for disability and a plush job at Nuu House, as he called his work. To

Kris, he'd always been old Uncle Harvey, and he'd always taken her to the soccer games, the plays, and all the other places a little girl had to go. And he'd stayed there to cheer her on, buy an ice cream to celebrate victory or take the edge off defeat. They'd been through Eddy together. Uncle Harvey was the one person she'd dare share her "If only I had . . ." horror with. And sharing, she'd discovered she wasn't alone with thoughts of what might have been.

"Where's Mother and Father?" she asked.

"Now, you know they're busy, or they wouldn't be the important people they are," he said, taking her luggage. "You're traveling light, only one bag. I haven't seen you manage that since you were shorter than my knee, and the bad one at that."

"I'm an officer now, in case you haven't noticed." Kris did a quick whirl to show off her undress khakis. "You always said you travel light in the Army, well that goes double for Navy."

"And who's this other poor sailor hanging around an old man, looking eager for a ride?"

"Harvey, this is Ensign Tom Lien, the best friend I've made in the last five months. We're both kind of on the beach, and he's from Santa Maria. I thought we might have room for him for a couple of weeks."

"Not at the Residency, they just hired two new special assistants. Damned if I can tell what's special about them. Anyway, there's no spare bedrooms anymore. It'll have to be the old Nuu House," Harvey said, reaching for Tommy's bag.

The young ensign swung it out of Harvey's reach, "Da would tan my hide if I let a gray hair like you lug me bags."

"If you can find a gray hair up there, you're welcome to it, but thanks for not saying old baldy. I suspect your folks raised you better than that." They exchanged grins. "Come on, you two, the car's just a short walk. Let's get moving."

The car brought more happy time. Gary was with it. A six-foot-four linebacker type, Gary was Kris's security detail at games and restaurants and whatever for the last ten years.

"What's Mother's schedule like?" Kris asked as she settled into the backseat of the black limo. "I was hoping for a quiet dinner tonight."

"It's a state dinner tonight for the both of them," Harvey said. "We've got a visiting delegation of firemen from old Earth, out here to talk and jabber and not do a thing. They've scheduled a quiet dinner tomorrow, only a dozen or so besides you and your brother."

"Tell Mother I'll have Ensign Lien with me." She immediately silenced Tom's protestations with a wave. "If you aren't there, the prime minister will have me paired with some old or young lecher whose vote he's chasing. With you, at least we can crack Navy jokes under our breath." That settled, Kris eyed the city around her. Everywhere she looked, something was being built out of stone and concrete. The red brick buildings that seemed so tall when she was just a kid were being replaced by buildings that soared out of her adult sight. Yep. Times were good, traffic was lousy, and Father was at no risk of losing any election he called. Five months ago, that was all she supposedly needed to be happy. How a little time had changed that.

As they approached the old Nuu mansion, Harvey regaled Tommy with the tale of its growth. "Old Ernie Nuu started with that two-story block over there. That's where I and the Mrs. live. He added that long three-story wing when the grandkids started coming. Then, with the General bringing in all kinds of people, not just the likes of me, he added a new kitchen and dining room, a ballroom, and a couple of dozen parlors and studies with the fancy columned portico. The great library was, I think, his wife's idea. Then with great-grandkids, he built another wing. They say old Ernie was building until the day he died. Folks still swear sometimes they can hear him walking the halls at night."

"I never heard him." Kris frowned at her deprived state.

"You were never quiet long enough," Harvey shot back.

Gary smiled.

Now, there was someone quiet enough to hear a ghost. Kris started to ask him. Before she got a word out, the main gate came into view. It was staffed by a dozen marines in battle armor and rifles.

"I thought you said Father was at the formal residency."

"He is; this is for the visiting firemen. The General himself is back from Santa Maria. Your Great-grandpa Trouble is due in today."

"What's going on?" Tom asked.

The driver and security guard exchanged glances. "Need-to-know basis, son," Harvey answered. Kris and Tommy had to produce IDs and retina scans to prove they were who they were. As the car came to a final rest before the front portico, Kris realized that between college and the Navy, it had been a while since she crossed that door. It opened automatically as she approached; Nelly had done her job of answering the door's challenge. The foyer was in shadows, but it was the floor Kris eyed.

Great-great-grandpa Nuu had been in his spiritual phase when he built this section. The floor tiles were a spiral of black and white, starting along the wall and closing into a tight coil in the center. The design was from an ancient Earth cathedral; as a child Kris had walked it as a kind of game, her on the blacks, Eddy on the whites. Always they met in the middle. It had been a long time since she'd walked it.

The ensign who saved Edith Swanson wondered what it would feel like to walk it now.

The great library, off to the right, had more marine guards, these in dress red and blue. They eyed Kris as she crossed the cold marble floor, came to attention. It was clear that if she came an inch closer, they'd very likely shoot. She and Tommy headed directly for the thickly carpeted stairs. Kris got her old third-floor room back. Harvey apologized for putting Tom so far down the hall. "All the rooms in between are taken."

"Who's in them? Could they be moved?" Kris asked.

"General, general, admiral, colonel," Harvey said, pointing at each door.

"I guess we don't move them," Kris agreed.

"Would you have a small corner, maybe up in the attic, where I could lay a sleeping bag?" Tom asked, voice cracking.

"Tom, what's to be afraid of?"

"You're a girl. You don't have to worry about meeting one of them when you're halfway through a shower or sitting on the can. I'll be standing there at attention, myself hanging in the wind. Kris, this is not what I bargained for."

Harvey turned to rest a hand on the young ensign's shoulder. "I know how you feel, boy. Fresh out of the Army with private stripes still on my soul, being around the General and those that ended up around him, it was a shock to the old system. But, son, they get up just like you and me, every morning. And it seems to me that the higher up they go, the more they know that. Not all, but trust me, any around the General and Trouble are good ones. If they weren't, they wouldn't have had the smarts to come here to ask the General how to get out of this mess."

"What mess?" Kris asked.

"Not for the likes of me to know, girl, but if I was a betting man, I wouldn't bet an Earth dollar that the Society flag is flying over Government House next Landing Day."

"Devolution," both Kris and Tom whispered the word. "Is it that close?" Kris finished.

"Ask the prime minister. Better yet, ask your grampas."

Kris wasn't so sure she wanted to meet folks studied in her history books. Besides, she had things to figure out about her last mission and with the whole of human space on the line, this was no time to meet a bunch of family strangers and dump her problems on them. "Harvey, could I borrow a car? I'd like to go see Aunt Tru about some computer stuff."

"Tru will love that," Harvey agreed, "but why borrow a car? Isn't my driving good enough for you?"

"Yes, Uncle Harvey, but aren't you busy?"

"Hang around this place too long, and they'll have me taking care of the cook's wee ones or even my own great-grandkids. Nice little tots, but if I don't keep moving, the women will have me changing diapers. I'd rather be driving."

Fifteen minutes later, Kris and Tom were in the back-seat of a much smaller car. Of course she had time, honorary Aunt Tru assured Kris. She'd just been working on a way to jimmy the new local lottery, but their network was down just now, so there was no rush. Tom gave Kris a questioning look and confessed to no longer being sure when the people around Kris were exaggerating. Kris laughed and told Tommy how Tru had helped her through elementary algebra in first grade and even given Kris her first computer. Then they got to Tru's penthouse apartment; it hadn't changed a bit, though a shiny new complex was going up next door.

"I thought you said she was a retired government worker?" Tommy said.

"She is. She bought this place when she won the lottery fifteen years back."

Tom gave Kris a sidewise glance but didn't say a word. Kris missed a step, rerunning what she'd just said. "Aunt Tru would never cheat. If she could win the lottery every time, why doesn't she?" Kris asked no one in particular.

"Smart woman knows not to push a good thing too far." Harvey winked.

And Kris found herself wondering just how much of what she accepted without question as a kid was in dire need of a second look now that she was a woman.

Then Tru opened the door, and Kris got lost in a hug of mega-huge proportions. Mother never touched, and Father never even came close to Kris, but Aunt Tru hugged. Kris let the breath go out of her as she had so many times before. With it went the tightness in her stomach and the iron-fisted grip at her throat.

It was Tru who broke the hug and ushered them into her living room with its spectacular view of Wardhaven. With Papa Nuu's industrial plants off planet, the capital city was a lovely place of trees, boulevards, and towering buildings watered by the Old Miss's meanderings. Tru had heard of Kris's experience on Sequim . . . it seemed most of the Rim had. There were even pictures of her LAC ride, so that was not something Kris could avoid when she met Mother, though, with luck, the woman would have no idea what she was looking at. Tru briefly swapped stories with Kris about the one or two times she had ended up with the booties, dodging bullets while she tried to find the right algorithm to close down all that noise. Now Kris caught the tightness around her aunt's eyes, the catch in her voice.

Tru dismissed herself to get herbal tea or fresh-squeezed lemonade for her guests. That was one of Tru's rules; no talk before some good, healthy refreshments. Even in Kris's bottle days, a dose of Auntie Tru's lemonade had been better than bourbon. Kris rummaged up the computer she had removed from the crime scene on Sequim. When Tru returned with a tray, it was sitting as innocent as it could on the coffee table.

"A little present for your Auntie Tru?" she said, putting down the tray.

"A little old and beaten up for a present," Kris said. "More like a puzzle. You still like puzzles?"

"Umm," Tru said giving the computer a quick once-over while the others served themselves. The computer was an old wrist unit, fairly thick and heavy, at least 200 grams. It used an old-fashioned display; didn't even jack into eyeglasses. Tru tried and failed to activate it. "Wiped at a pretty low level," she observed.

"Can you get at it?" Kris asked.

"Probably," Tru muttered, eyeing the empty tray. "I thought I had some cookies, but I seem to be out."

"I could bake some," Kris said, jumping up. Tru had been the one who taught Kris all that she knew about kitchens. It wasn't much, but Tru could whip up a wicked bunch of chocolate chip cookies, and Kris had learned from the expert.

"You talked me into it," Tru smiled, her eyes still concentrating on the unit. So, while Tru turned her kitchen table into a hacker/cracker dreamland, Kris led Tom in an assault on Tru's immaculate kitchen. As they had for many years, the pans waited for Kris in the lower right drawer beside the oven. The flour was in the white earthen jar on the back of the kitchen counter. A bag of Ghirardelli chocolate chips stood its usual watch from the top shelf in the pantry. So much in the world had changed, but Aunt Tru's kitchen was a constant Kris could always count on.

There is something to be said for the spiritual healing power of turning a little girl loose in a kitchen to bake cookies . . . or a big girl, for that matter. As the wondrous smells collected around them, she and Tom licked the spoon, snatched scraps of dough, and would have pulled chunks off the main ball if Tru hadn't announced loudly and forcefully her fear that nothing would remain to cook. Harvey curled up in a corner with his reader, checking all the oddities in the news and sharing the strangest with anyone listening. Tru tinkered with the computer; its cover was now off, its innards revealed like entrails to be read.

"This bit of artificial intelligence is part of a kidnapping investigation, ongoing on Sequim, isn't it?" Tru asked, attaching chunks of the offending unit to an analyzer she'd built herself.

"Yes," Kris admitted, pausing from greasing a cookie sheet. "But the local cops didn't seem all that interested in it. At least, no one asked where it went. I figured you'd have a better chance of getting at it than anyone on Sequim. And besides, I came near to dying on a minefield set by those punks, brand-new Mark 41 land mines that aren't even issued to my marines, much less to kidnappers. I want to know where all their tech came from." Kris pursed her lips. "And the up-front money."

"How are they building their case?" Tru said absentmindedly.

"On confessions," Harvey put in. "The four are singing like fine Irish tenors in a well-stocked pub, wouldn't you say?" he asked Tom.

"Loud, if not so sweet," the young ensign answered.

"Four," Kris turned from her kitchen duties. "We captured five."

"One had a heart attack the day after you bagged him," Harvey said without looking up from his reading.

"Hmm," Tru muttered before Kris could ask which dead man was already filling a coffin. "I'm in, but it seems that paranoid here encrypted everything. Looks like a standard commercial package. Should have some interesting stuff in a few minutes. Who are these kidnappers?" Tru asked Harvey.

"They claim to be just petty crooks," Harvey said, flipping through his reader.

"And they were from?"

Harvey paged back. "Earth, New Haven, Columbia, New Jerusalem." That covered a big chunk of the Seven Sisters, the first planets colonized from Earth. The first two, New Eden and New Haven had been wide open. Yamato, Columbia, Europa, and New Canton drew their original populations from specific regions of old Earth. New Jerusalem had been a unique case . . . and still was. Five petty thugs from Earth and three of her seven overpopulated sisters had snatched the child of the general manager of a raw rim colony. That invited a raised eyebrow from Tru.

Harvey snorted. "Damn punks got a government dole to feed them and nothing else to do. Small-time hoods must have figured they could make it big out here hitting on some hardworking rim type and retire to perpetual fun and games back home."

Kris hid her surprise at Harvey's attitude. She knew a lot of rim folks didn't think much of the billions in the central worlds that wouldn't immigrate. Kris had even studied the situation in college. It wasn't that Earth and the Seven Sisters actually were welfare states; their teeming billions

were as fully employed as you'd expect for a mature economy. What they were was self-absorbed, maybe a bit self-
important, and more than a bit decadent. It wasn't a mixture
to appeal to the rim worlds. Add in an incident like this that
only served to solidify misperceptions like Harvey's, and
things could get volatile. "That's the way some folks would
perceive it," Kris skirted confrontation with her old friend.

"Perception is everything," Tru muttered. "And reality . . .
may be subject to change," Tru finished with a smile and sat
back in her chair. "That didn't take so long. Let me copy this
to my newest child. Sam can organize the data while we try
a few of those cookies," Tru said, then mumbled softly to
her personal computer to get it working on the project.

"They need a bit more time to cool," Kris said, but was
already using the spatula to move them to a plate. The
chips were gooey and dripping; the cookies were as delicious as when Kris had needed to stand on the chair to
get at them. So much had changed in her life; Aunty Tru's
cookies had not.

The first dozen cookies were gone, the second batch
just out, as a third batch went in the oven, when Tru grew
distracted by Sam's report. Tru slipped a phone in her ear,
muttered a few things under her breath, and passed up the
next offered cookies. She leaned back, eyes going unfixed
as she listened, a frown growing on her lips. "Seems to be
a perfect match for the news reports. Too perfect."

Kris set down a cookie, wiped her hands, and took a
close look at the wrist unit. It looked old, battered, pretty
much the standard type of unit that anyone could buy for
twenty bucks for the last fifty years. Kris reached up to
move the overhead light. Inside the back of the unit was a
mess. "What's that crud?" she asked.

Harvey looked up from his paper, squinting. "Looks
like the gunk that gets in your wristband. You know, the
stuff you clean out when you're supposed to be doing your
homework."

"But *inside* the unit?"

"Bastard must have sweated a lot and never cleaned it.

Slopped over inside. Surprised it's still working," Harvey shook his head at such slovenliness.

"Let me see that. Oh, Auntie's eyes are getting old," Tru shook her head ruefully. She left the room, returning in a moment with a black box that Tom was immediately making loving eyes at. Tru set it down next to the unit, then began muttering orders to her computer. In a moment, tiny filaments sprouted from her box and weaved their way to the unit under study. Tiny, thin strands glistened in the light as they wandered over the surface of the unit's back. Then two attached themselves to something. Those strands attracted others, and the filaments wove together into a solid pair of wires.

"Found the input and the output." Tru smiled happily.

Kris frowned. "Input and output of what?"

"The real computer this bastard was carrying. Your poor old Aunt Tru has been wasting her time on the stalking horse they put there to distract her. Now we'll get at the real stuff. This may take a while. Do I smell cookies burning?"

That batch went into the trash can. While Kris made the next batch, Tru and Tommy leaned over the wrist unit, studying it with new respect. "What's a two-bit punk doing with this kind of tech?" Harvey asked.

"They've been surprising us with tech all along," Kris called over her shoulder as she put the next cookies in the oven.

"Yes, yes," Tru agreed. "The old girl is getting forgetful."

Kris wiped her hands on a towel and went to stand over her two favorite elders. "What kind of computer is that? I've never seen anything like it."

"You won't for a few more years," Tru assured her. "Self-organizing circuits will revolutionize wearable computers like my Sam and your Nelly, but the cost is out of sight. Some of my friends are using it for covert missions."

"Like this one?" Tommy asked.

Tru leaned back in her chair, eyeing the objects lying on her kitchen table as if seeing them for the first time. "Yes. Like this operation."

The following silence was broken by two beeps. Kris turned her attention to the oven, whose timer she had finally remembered how to work, while Tru returned to the center of their attention. Kris was starting to put the next dozen cookies on the sheet.

"Don't," Tru ordered. "Put the dough in the refrigerator. Turn the oven off, and put the cookies in a napkin. We're going visiting."

"Where?" Harvey asked.

"Nuu House. Kris needs to talk to her Great-grandfathers Ray and Trouble."

"We can't bother *them!*" Kris shouted, gulping hard.

"You can't," Harvey said bluntly, pocketing his reader.

"Her great-grandfathers need to fill Kris in on a bit of family history," Tru said, placing the computer parts carefully in a stasis box she had produced from a drawer under the table. "They are at Nuu House. We are going to Nuu House."

"But they're doing important stuff," Kris pleaded. "We can't bother them."

"More important than your life?"

Harvey cut in before Kris could figure out what kind of response that deserved. "Tru, you won't get into Nuu House. They've got marines crawling all over the place. They're applying the Mark I eyeball to all visitors and their credentials. You and all your electron magic will not get past the first eager marine with an M-6."

"Old-fashioned, are they?" Tru sighed, closing the now-full stasis box.

"Very old-fashioned," Harvey said.

"Then we'll have to go elsewhere. Harvey, take us to the prime minister's residence."

"No," Kris squeaked, but her chauffeur was already moving toward the door, Tru on his heels. "We can't bother the prime minister. He's got a full schedule. You can't just barge in on the man who's running the planet." *Boy, did Kris know that.*

"He will find time in his busy schedule." Tru paused, her mouth moving in subvocal communications with Sam. "He already has. So has your mother."

Kris hurried after Tru, Tom following her. "My mother. Oh, no. She's got a social schedule booked solid 'til New Years. Besides, you don't want to talk to my mother." Kris tried to chuckle. It came out sounding even to herself more like a terrified cackle. "Why do you want to talk to either of them?"

Tru and Harvey were at the elevator. Kris and Tom hurried to squeeze in as the doors closed. A woman, toy poodle in her arms, joined them on the next floor. The ride down was silent.

"What is it you think you have to talk to Mother and Father about?" Kris asked as she hurried to keep up Harvey's fast pace in the cool shade of the underground parking garage.

"Your life." Tru snapped, settling in the front seat beside Harvey. That left Kris and Tom the backseat.

As she belted in, Kris still tried to stop the car. "So the mission could have gone bad. That's part of the risk you take when you put on the uniform. Yeah, I want to talk to the prime minister about the equipment, but I was planning on getting him aside when he was in a good mood. Maybe when he pins that medal on me. There's no rush," she insisted. "God, you don't just barge in on my father, and definitely not my mother." *No way. You check with their personal secretaries first. Check out their moods. Then you make an appointment to slip in. There are basic things you learn when your parents run a planet.*

"Kris, you are wrong. There are things involved here that you are unaware of." Tru turned to Harvey. "Please hurry, I don't want to have to reschedule this meeting. People might notice what I've done." Tru smiled as she turned to Kris. "People are so confident anything a computer tells them is true. It won't do to undermine their illusions." Satisfied that she'd said all that she intended, Tru faced front and began to mumble to her computer. Kris had seen Tru deep in consultation with her alternate self and knew better than to interrupt.

Accepting the inevitable, Kris leaned back in her seat. Tom nudged her. "We're about to meet William Longknife, the prime minister of Wardhaven?"

"Yeah." Kris shrugged. "That's my father."

"I'll stay in the car."

If Tom thought he was scared, Kris wanted to find a deep hole to hide in. She knew what they were in for. She weighed several options, including leaping from the speeding car, and decided that if she couldn't wait in the car, Tommy couldn't either. "You're with me. I deserve some backup. You were on the mission, too. You can tell Mother it wasn't so dangerous."

"It was."

"No, it wasn't. I had everything under control."

"If you say so."

"I do. You back me up on this."

Tom looked none too sure about that. For a long moment, he eyed Kris, mouth half open. When he finally spoke, he surprised her. "It's a bitch, you know, being an adult around the folks who changed your diapers."

Despite everything, Kris found a smile slipping onto her face. Tommy was always good for that. And maybe Santa Maria wasn't so far from Wardhaven. Kris nodded. "The bitchiest. Why can't they ever forget? And they didn't change all that many diapers, what with the hired help."

Kris waited out the rest of the drive, reminding herself that she was a grown woman, had commanded a drop mission, and she was not going to let her mother or father buffalo her. She kept that mantra up as they parked in a reserved place in the basement of Government House, rode up a reserved elevator, and walked down a cold marble No

Admittance hallway, doors opening before they came to them. Kris didn't know there were that many automatic doors in Government House; she'd always needed someone to open them. "Nelly, remind me to ask Tru how she does that."

"Yes," her computer whispered, "I would love that applet."

Then, without going by his secretary's desk, they were in the prime minister's cluttered private office, and William Longknife, Billy to his cronies, was rising from his paper-covered work desk. "So glad you could make it on such short notice," he said, extending his hand. "It's critical we discuss . . ." Father trailed off as his computer failed to fill in the expected words. As Tru shook his hand, his smile morphed into as much of a frown as the politician allowed himself. "Tru, you haven't done this to me again."

"Afraid I have, Billy."

"Who else have you invited?"

"Just your wife," Tru smiled, with teeth showing.

Before the prime minister could react, the door to his front office opened, and Mother sailed in. Petticoats were the rage in Paris this year; Mother must have had on a dozen. "I hope I'm not late. I must talk to my secretary. We went over today's schedule, and she didn't say a word about meeting you, Trudy. If I hadn't glanced at my wrist-watch, I might have missed it entirely. As it was, I had to just throw on anything close at hand and rush over. Do let me catch my breath."

"Darling, you look divine," Tru said, pecking at the offered cheek. "Your breathless rush has gotten you here before we could begin. Woman, you are a wonder." From their private talks, Kris knew just what kind of wonder Tru considered Mother: a relic from the middle ages. How a woman could be born into the twenty-third century and act Mother's part was a wonder to everyone who met her, except that Kris knew several other women of wealth that fit right in with Mother. *No way I'm going to be like her,* Kris swore. No surprise, Mother threw only a nod at Kris.

Never one for informal chitchat, Tru folded her hands and began. "As you know, Kris recently drew a rescue mission."

"Yes." Father nodded.

"No," Mother breathed in shock. "It wasn't dangerous, darling. After all we've been through with . . ." The sentence petered out like all where Eddy's name might be mentioned.

"Mother, of course not," Kris immediately filled in the vacancy left by the sudden hush, trying to put just the right twist on the words to make them beyond doubt.

"I think we should all be seated," the prime minister suggested, pointing to a report-laden low table surrounded by worn couches and chairs where he met with his closest staff. Father took the rocking chair at the head of the table, an affectation he acquired after reading about some other politician who reached the pinnacle of power at a young age. Unlike so many others of his fads that were dropped as quickly as Mother changed fashions, the simple wooden rocker remained. Father's bad back liked it. Mother took the overstuffed leather chair at the opposite end of the table, leaving the two couches in between for the rest. Kris hated it when her mother did that. It left her swiveling her head, trying to keep track of how each of them was reacting to whatever the other was saying.

"What about this rescue mission?" Mother insisted. "If it wasn't dangerous, why was the Navy asked to do it?"

"Honey, the Navy would never put our daughter at risk," Father assured her. "I followed the entire thing on net." He'd told Kris about the family addendum he'd put on his news search after Grandfather Alex did something with Nuu Enterprises that caused Father a lot of political fallout. Grandfather had resigned the prime minister's job and demanded his son give up his seat in the House. Not only had Father not left politics, he'd wrangled all his party connections into making him the next prime minister. The two hadn't shared a word since.

"You knew all about it and didn't tell me!"

Kris tuned out what followed; she'd heard it too many

times. While Mother and Father did their individual theatrics, Tru cleared a space for the captured computer and
attached its working parts to the table's station.

"Unfortunately, I must disagree with you, Mr. Prime
Minister," Tru said softly into a break in Mother and Father's
battle of clichés.

"No!" came from both of them. Tru had everyone's
attention.

"Before I begin, let me point out what I am dealing with
here," Tru said, pointing at the computer parts arranged on
the table. "Outward appearance is that of a very old, cheap,
and battered wrist unit ... and they are totally deceptive.
Sprayed onto the inside of the case is the latest in self-
organizing computer hardware. The cost of this alone is several times the ransom demand." Tru raised an eyebrow to the
prime minister but did not state the obvious. Money was not
the objective of this crime. Kris's father rocked back in his
chair, hand coming up to rub his chin, but he said nothing.

"You must be wrong." Mother filled the silence. "No
one with money would behave like that." That was Kris's
mother's inevitable answer to money. Not born to it herself, she worshiped it now that her marriage made her the
high priestess of lucre on Wardhaven. And since those with
money had servants to do their work, they, of course, never
did anything nasty.

"I've cracked two of the longer messages in his rather
sparse collection of mail," Tru said. "Here is one."

"They've taken the bait. Navy is being called in. Deploy
greetings," appeared on the computer screen recessed into
the tabletop.

"What kind of greeting?" the prime minister asked,
leaning forward. Kris had a strong suspicion that greeting
involved a very invisible minefield.

"Here's the other message," Tru said. "We got the ship
we want. Activate greetings. Assume plan B," scrolled onto
the tabletop.

"What kind of greetings, and what do they mean, the right
ship? I hate it when people don't say what they mean,"

Mother snapped in the voice that had made Kris jump when she was eight or nine. Now she hated it.

Tru, for her part, leaned back into her couch and folded her hands. As she had so many times before when teaching Kris, Tru had laid out the problem; now she left Kris to figure it out. Kris had learned to hate that, too. Where was a role model when a young woman needed one?

Kris leaned forward, looking at the two messages. Assuming the *Typhoon* was the "right ship," the "greetings" were . . .

"The kidnappers," Kris began slowly, "had a field of Mark 41 land mines scattered around their hideout. Had we jumped as planned, we would all have been killed." Kris had intended to corner her father about the shoddy equipment. But the busted uplink to the ship had forced Kris to fly the LAC down, making a jump impossible, thereby spoiling the best laid plans of the bad guys. Kind of hard to bitch about the equipment now.

The prime minister mumbled to his computer link. "Mark 41s haven't been issued yet," he repeated after his datalink.

"Yes, Father, Navy doesn't have any. And a field of them would cost a hell of a lot more than their ransom demands."

"Kristine Anne, a lady does not use such language," Mother contributed to their considerations.

"Between the traps that wiped out the first three rescue attempts, the mines, and this computer," Tru pointed out, "this was a losing financial proposition." The prime minister rubbed his chin some more, raised an eyebrow to Tru, but said nothing.

"But who would do that?" Tommy blurted out.

Mother shot a freezing glower at Tom for interrupting, then an even colder one at Kris for dragging a stranger into something that clearly was a family matter. *Well, it wasn't a family matter when I came here,* Kris shot back wordlessly, then remembered she was a serving naval officer, not just Mother's little darling. Leaning back, she stared at the ceiling.

"I'm staying at Nuu House," she said. "The place is crawl-ing with guards. One of my great-grandfathers wouldn't hap-pen to be in town?" she asked the ceiling, wanting to make official what Harvey had given to her under the table.

"Both of them," Mother spat. Neither were among Mother's favorite people. Mother blamed Trouble for Kris's decision to join the Navy. This despite Trouble staying long and far from Kris with his job as president of Savannah's War College, the post he'd taken after retiring from chair-man of the Joint Staff on Savannah. Ray had spent the last thirty or forty years since leaving public life mostly on Santa Maria, about as far from the rest of humanity as pos-sible, with his youngest daughter, Alnaba, a researcher. Kris kept hearing rumors that they were going to crack the riddle of The Three *real soon,* the three species that built the jump points between planets. Hadn't yet. Maybe Grampa Ray had finally met something he couldn't do.

"If I identified those troops roaming around Nuu House, they were Earth marines." Kris found the hint of a grin start to wiggle across her mouth as she turned to eye her father.

"Who they're meeting with is on a need-to-know basis, young woman. Need I remind you, you're in the Navy. I can have you transferred to the refueling station on Hell-FrozeOver," the prime minister pointed out. "And darling, you should not have mentioned that my grandfathers are here," he added to Mother.

"You invited them to the reception tomorrow." Mother pouted. "It can't be that secret."

"By then they should be done," the prime minister answered, a tinge of sadness creeping into his voice. "Until then, we don't want it blasted all over the news."

"So you are dividing up the fleet." Kris said, surprised she could get her mouth around the words.

Father blanched; if he had any faith, it was in the union, the absolute belief that humanity had to go to the stars as one. And the Society was the embodiment of that union. "It is my policy," Father said, hand going dramatically to his heart, "and the policy of every prime minister of Wardhaven since we were admitted to the Society of Humanity, that Humanity must go to the stars a single people." Father repeated the words Kris had heard hundreds of times. Missing today was the vigor and confidence that the policy would remain.

Kris shivered and was startled by her reaction. In her mind's eye she saw the green and blue flag of Earth and its Society of Humanity come down the flagpole, as it did every day at sunset. The thought that some morning was coming when it would not go back up brought a chill to her. How many times had she and her friends debated a new, more proper role for the Society? Now their bull sessions were becoming reality.

"What would be the reaction if not only had a little girl been kidnapped by cheap, Earthy scum, but that a Longknife had died trying to free her?" The words came ice cold from the logical part of Kris's brain. They were out of her mouth before she remembered Mother was on the other side of Tommy. Mother turned a stony stare at Kris, who ignored it. "Mr. Prime Minister," Kris said to show she had not been cowered.

The hand that had been over his heart now took a worried swipe at his forehead. "There would be an uproar against Earth," he said slowly. "It would make my job much harder."

"And strengthen several different coalitions, would it not?" Tru asked.

"Yes."

"Including the Smythe-Peterwalds of Greenfeld?" Tru said.

Now Father did rock back in his chair.

"Oh, the Peterwalds are such a nice family. Henry dated me in college, proposed to me on a beautiful moonlit night."

"Yes, Mother, we remember," Kris snapped without taking her eyes off her father. "Mr. Prime Minister," Kris repeated, wanting to hear what was going on in his political mind.

"No," he shook his head. "No member of any government would dare do that. No policy is worth such a risk. And if it was traced back to a sitting government, it would crush it. They'd never get elected again," said the head of one government.

"He has a boy about your age, Kristine. You ought to meet him," Mother added.

"I know, Mother, you've only mentioned him a million times."

"Have you told Kris about the Peterwalds and Long-knifes?" Tru put in softly.

"I have told her many times," Mother insisted.

"No." Father answered. Mother cocked a questioning eye his way, but his eyes were locked on Tru. "It has never been proven that the Peterwalds had anything to do with either the war or the drug trade. Just because Greenfeld is usually on the opposite side of a major issue from Wardhaven is no reason to ascribe personal motives to them."

Tru shook her head. "Someone was bankrolling Unity before the war. You've read the histories. There was too much corruption at the lower levels. Hardly a dime of tax money reached Urm, yet he was doing more and more each year. When Wardhaven and the Longknifes broke the back of the drug trafficking, the Peterwalds' fortune vanished, and the family fled to Greenfeld. Ray forced them to give up Elysium after the Treaty of Wardhaven limited human expansion. You agree that the Longknifes have cost the Peterwalds a lot of money."

"Yes." The prime minister was out of his chair and pacing around the room, his feet stomping into the plush blue carpet. "But that proves nothing. There's not a damn piece of evidence that will stand up in a court of law." He whirled on Tru. "And, woman, I am a man who must deal in the law."

Tru looked at the table, read from it. "We've gotten the right ship. That ship was the *Typhoon*, your daughter's ship. It was minus a marine lieutenant. Normally, I would think that would be a very good reason to pick another."

"The skipper really wanted that mission," Tommy put

in. "The word around the station was that he was calling in all his markers with Commodore Sampson to get it."

"Understandable for a warrior," Tru agreed. "Still, I imagine it was also common knowledge that Kris was on that ship and that Thorpe was riding her pretty hard."

"How'd you know?" Kris said.

"Just because I was Info War Chief doesn't mean I spent all my time with computers. I've known some hands-on warriors who like the smell of powder . . . and who'd need to know if you're a warrior or just some politician's daughter run away from home. If he was a politician, he'd have treated you with kid gloves. If he was a warrior, he'd push you."

"He pushed me," Kris grumbled.

Tru turned to Father. "If I could put those pieces together, so could anyone else. The death of a little girl *and* a Longknife in a botched kidnapping would get the entire Rim up in arms. Internal passports limiting travel between Earth and the Seven Sisters would have passed by acclamation. The Society would be shattered in all but name."

"Who said anything about the little girl dying?" Kris tried to slow Tru down. What she was saying took Kris's breath away.

"Excuse me. I forgot. You haven't seen plan B." Tru muttered to herself, and the screen on the table changed. "No surprise, I found no reference to a plan B in the computer. No plan A, either. However, the police inventory of the lodge has two interesting items. First, two kilos of high explosives hidden in the bottom of the pack the girl's clothes were stuffed in, along with a radio squawker and detonator. Second, a tight beam radio, set to the same frequency as the explosives squawker. As I recall, they were negotiating for a shuttle to take them to a starship and the ship to take them wherever they wanted to go."

"If the leader could manage not to be on the shuttle, he'd be in the right position to blow up the shuttle as it was rising," Kris breathed slowly.

"That's certainly the right gear for it," Tommy agreed.

"Blow it up just before it makes orbit, and pieces of shuttle will be coming down over half of Sequim."

"All that is supposition," the prime minister snapped.

"All this means nothing," Mother said, cold and distant.

It meant something to someone. Someone who wanted Kris and a little girl dead. Who would profit from such a losing proposition? Kris didn't know about the recent one on Sequim. She did want to know about the one ten years ago. "Father, who offered to help you get the money to pay Eddy's ransom?" Kris asked into the growing silence.

"Kristine Anne," Mother snapped.

"That's enough, young woman," Father shot to his feet.

"Mr. Prime Minister, your next appointment is waiting," the intercom informed them.

"Send him right in," the prime minister said. Mother rushed for the private exit in a shower of petticoats, searching through her pillbox. She pulled two, no three of the pink ones out and swallowed them down. Kris shook her head; Mother would probably not remember a thing from this meeting. Tru collected her computer parts as Kris and Tom stood. When the door closed behind Kris's mother, Father put his face inches from Tru's nose. "Trudy, you have gone too far this time. I've got six hundred worlds flying apart. I do not need you setting my own family on me as well. I'll be doing good if I get a word out of that woman in the next month," he said glancing at the door his wife had just left by. He turned on Kris, his face cold rage. "You, young woman, are staying here at the Residency tonight. I don't want you hanging around this wild woman."

"Father," Kris cut in, "there aren't any vacant bedrooms, remember. You just converted the last ones into offices for special assistants."

The prime minister muttered to his computer, scowled at the response, then turned on Kris. "How did you get here?"

"Harvey drove us."

"Harvey will take you to Nuu House. You can do whatever a sailor wants to do on leave, but you will not talk to

Tru. I can and will send you to HellFrozeOver if you bring this up again. Woman," he said at Tru, "my chauffeur will take you home."

"This doesn't solve anything, William," Tru said. "You can't run away from reality."

"This will solve it as well as anything can," the prime minister said, turning his back on them. Tru strode for the door Mother had used just as the prime minister's personal driver poked his head through it.

Kris, eager to beat a quick retreat, used the door she had come in, Tom on her heels. Halfway to the door, Kris stopped, causing a minor collision with Tom. "Father, I really need to know how you arranged for Eddy's ransom money."

He was adjusting his coat, putting on his formal face as he turned to the main entrance to his office. "Since you insist, I will tell you. I went to my father, your grandfather, for the money. He didn't ask me for a damn thing. Now get out."

Kris scooted out a split second before Father opened the door to admit his next appointment.

8

"**IS** your da always like that?" Tommy asked.

The drive home had been full of poisoned silence. Kris was grateful for any break, even if there was no answer to his question. Kris had had a lifetime to get used to her family. Tommy had been dumped in the deep end . . . and if Kris was honest, he *had* asked to be left out of the entire thing. "What about my father's way of doing things are you curious about?"

Tommy shrugged. "I don't know. Is he always so legalistic. I mean, if I told my folks someone was out to kill me, they wouldn't ask me if I had proof that would stand up in court."

"My father would." Kris answered easily.

"Then your da really would assign you to HellFroze-Over."

"Oh yes," she answered without a moment's reflection.

"His own daughter. You're kidding."

"I need a drink," she announced, glancing out the car window and seeing her surroundings for the first time since she left her father's office. They were cutting through a corner of the university district. "Harvey, let's stop at the Scriptorum."

Harvey didn't touch the car's controls. "Miss Kristine, I don't think that would be wise."

"And what have I done so far today that was? Will you tell the car to head for the Scriptorum, or shall I have Nelly override you?"

"I've had the car's security upgraded since you graduated from college." Harvey growled at her.

"And I've had Nelly upgraded. Want to see who bought the better upgrade?"

Harvey gave the car new instructions. Even though traffic in the university district was its usual mad scramble, the city computer found them a parking spot less than half a block from the Scriptorum; there are advantages to having personal plates bearing PM-4. The Scriptorum hadn't changed in the four or five months since Kris graduated. A new crop of freshmen had taken over the tables near the door. There was the inevitable bull session going at the seniors-only table; Kris heard "devolution" and was tempted to join. But she wasn't a senior anymore. And besides, it was one thing to argue for or against Earth when it was just a game. Now it was for real, and she was a serving officer who would have to face what the hard changes brought. Somehow the fun was gone.

Kris settled for a table in the professors' section.

Relaxing into her chair, Kris tried to see the place as she had for the four years of her college education. The diffuse lighting showed every crack and flaw in the fake-brick, wattle-and-daub walls. Despite the aroma of pizza and beer, the overriding smell was of students: sweat, readers, and hormones, more like a library than a bar. The thick wooden tables were scarred by students' carved graffiti. Across the room was the table Kris and her entire Twenty-fourth-Century Problems class had carved their initials in on the last Saturday they met here; old Doc Meade had refused to talk about the problems of 600 planets without a beer in his hand, so they eschewed their classroom and met here every Saturday for a semester. That table was occupied; a dozen students had it covered with readers, flimsies, and keypads. Some were actually concentrating on the work, while several couples among them concentrated on each other. Kris smiled at the familiar scene.

"Whaddaya want?" a waiter/student demanded with the usual lack of concern typical of service at the Scriptorum.

Tom passed the question to Kris with a glance. Harvey sat in his chair, back ramrod straight, his face a study in Topkick disapproval. He'd driven Kris to school enough times, twelve years old and hungover as a deacon. Most likely, he'd turned her in to Grampa Trouble. Now he eyed Kris with all the silent disapproval that any Gunny Sergeant ever put into a blank face.

That answered the question of why Kris took so easily to the Chiefs and Gunnies at OCS. Hell, she'd grown up with one of them at her elbow. Of course, she knew what they were thinking behind those blank, formal faces they wore when they addressed the future officers.

"I'll have tonic water, straight up with a twist of lime," Kris said. And Harvey relaxed just that smidge that was all the approval he would ever give her. And it was all Kris ever needed.

"I'll have a soda, caffeinated, whatever they have on this planet," Tom ordered.

"Same for me," Harvey said.

"Right, Navy," the waiter said, and added as he turned back to the bar, "Aren't you burr heads out of bounds?"

Kris blinked twice at the snide remark. Of course they were in civilian clothes, but Tom and Harvey both sported the usual crew cut of the uniform services, and Kris's hair was a good two feet shorter and a lot more organized than it had been when she sat at Doc Meade's elbow arguing for this or against that. Kris almost stood, called the kid back, and gave him a dressing-down. That was what ensigns did to undisciplined ratings.

But the waiter was no spacer, and as Kris took in the Scriptorum with opening eyes, she *was* out of bounds for her kind. This room was chock-full of cloud dreamers who had no idea of the cost of their wild plans or responsibility for paying for them. Now that Kris had put her life on the line for a plan of her own making, this place seemed rather cheap, unreal, a waste of space. Almost, she got to her feet and marched out.

Still, Tom had asked a question, and he deserved an answer. "Yes, if I crossed my father, he would get me assigned to HellFrozeOver, and I'd spend the rest of my Navy career there."

Tom looked blank for a moment, then connected her statement to his question of five minutes ago. "I can't believe that."

Kris noted that Harvey said nothing. Again, that silence was all the verification she needed. She was reading her old man right. "My father is a politician," she told Tom. "I once heard him say that a good politician is one who stays bought. Loyalty is about the only virtue I've ever heard him praise. If you're loyal to him, he'll move heaven and earth for you. Break faith, and he'll damn you to hell without a backward glance. You haven't seen the way he locked up when an ally of twenty years changed sides. He didn't even blink, but that ex-friend never got the time of day from Billy Longknife again."

Kris leaned back in her chair, took a deep breath, and let it out slowly. "The pressures on my father must be hellacious." A quick glance in Harvey's direction showed the merest hint of a nod. "His threat is real, but to hell with that. *I* don't want to add to the burden he's lugging."

Tom pulled out his reader, began flipping through screens. "Maybe I can hitch a ride back to Santa Maria from here. Ensign Longknife, I'm beginning to think that knowing you could be a career-ending relationship."

"If it isn't life threatening," Harvey growled.

Kris reached over and flipped Tom's reader closed. "Get ready to march, crew," she ordered as the waiter approached with their drinks. As the kid slapped them down, slopping sticky liquid on the table, Kris stood. Tom and Harvey were on their feet with her. Scared he was about to be stiffed for the drinks, the waiter opened his mouth in protest, but Kris slapped down a bill equal to twice the cost of three sodas. That silenced him.

"My marines pried a six-year-old girl from terrorists last week," she said in a voice she'd learned at her father's knee and that carried through the place. "But apparently, people who work for a living aren't good enough for this place." As the tables fell silent, she glanced at the one she'd sat at last year. "You might add that to your problems of the twenty-fourth century."

Everything worth saying said, she marched for the door. Tom and Harvey fell in beside her. In step, they quickly covered the distance to the exit. A couple of students were just coming in. They took one look at the phalanx bearing down on them and took two steps back, holding the door wide as Kris led her tiny detachment out into the sun, then they quickly scurried inside and pulled the door closed behind themselves.

"That was fun." Tom grinned.

Kris squinted at the blue sky above her, sun glaring down out of a fine spring day. "We need to get Tommy a pair of sunglasses."

"Sunglasses," the Santa Marian echoed.

"Yes. You're in my gravity well now, spacer," Kris said, turning for the car. "No space helmet visor to protect those baby-blue eyes of yours, no suit between you and my sun. You'll need some sunscreen as well, you pasty-skinned spacer."

"And why might I be needing all that?"

"Harvey, my parents still keep the *Oasis* at the lake?"

"And the dockhands still check her out each week to make sure there's no problems, though the prime minister and his lady haven't been on her for five, six years."

"Their loss." Kris grabbed her fellow ensign by the elbow. "Tommy, me boy, you are about to discover how great it feels to have wind in your hair, a tall ship beneath you, and a good star to guide her by, even if it is just to the other end of a lake."

"A real-live sailing ship!" Tommy enthused with under-whelming excitement. "Any chance I could get Thorpe to let me hide out on the *Typhoon* for the next six weeks? My bunk back there is looking better and better."

"Come now, Tommy, you've sailed the stars. Haven't you ever wondered how the ancients first sailed the seas of old Earth?"

"No. I never wanted to swim, either."

"Have no fear, me boy, I'll hitch you up with a life belt that'll keep you safe should you encounter more water than you can drink."

"Just what I've always wanted, a bit of cork and plastic between me and suffocation."

"And what's a space suit?" Kris laughed.

"Something I'm very familiar with."

"Harvey, to the lake."

As the car slipped into traffic, Kris took a moment to commune with Nelly. "Do a planetwide search on Longknife and Peterwald, every contact they or their businesses have had in the last eighty years. Then expand the search to the entire Society of Humanity. Before you go too far, check Aunty Tru's computer to see anything she might have on the topics."

"Tru's computer has very good security," Nelly noted.

"Yes, but you might find a file or two in a less-secure vestibule on Sam. Father told me not to talk to Tru, but I'm assuming that you and Sam are not covered by that."

"Beginning search."

Kris relaxed back into the car's leather seat. Even if someone did want her more than the usual dead that she'd learned to live with as the prime minister's daughter, here on Wardhaven she'd be her usual safe. She had six weeks to decide if a certain boot ensign had more than the usual problems of a Navy career to worry about. That was plenty of time. Growing up with a politician in the household, that was one thing Kris had learned early. Time could change anything.

* * *

The next day, slightly sunburned but happy as Kris could only be when a tacking wind had blown the cobwebs from her brain, she and Tommy were in starched whites as Harvey drove them into the driveway circle in front of the Museum of Natural History. Its immense ballroom had been dragooned into what Harvey grumbled was going to be the worst of a long line of back-patting jamborees. "May they break their bleeding arms," was the old trooper's fond hope. Tommy had done his best to duck out, but Kris had dragged him along, protesting all the way.

"What's there to worry about? No one's ever been hurt at one of these things." Kris assured her friend.

"Be my luck to be the first."

"Not possible. There's absolutely no way anything can go wrong," Kris said with a confidence that evaporated as Harvey brought them into the drop-off circle. Several limos were already taking up parking spots there, including one identical to Kris's, except for the red and yellow paint dripping down its shiny black exterior.

"Whose is that?" Tommy asked.

Gary, riding shotgun, pointed his wrist unit at the blotched limo and punched a button. "One of ours, number four. Had General Ho of Earth today. I thought we had the anti-Earth demonstrators far enough back."

"I didn't see any demonstrations," Kris said.

"So I guess we had them far enough away for you," Harvey drawled as he pulled up next to an even larger white limo that needed four rear tires to support itself.

"Who owns that monster?" Tommy asked.

Again Gary shot his query at a rig, then smiled. "Thought I recognized it. Not too many like that one. Henry Smythe-Peterwald the Twelfth's private battleship," Kris's security guard announced.

Tommy raised an eyebrow as he opened the door. "And didn't you say no one ever got killed at these shindigs?"

"And didn't you say there's always a first time?" Kris brogued right back as she measured the vast, hulking transport beside them. Body armor was light enough for unpowered battle gear. So what was all the weight that made that white elephant need four huge tires?

"How am I going to explain to me ancestors my coming before them with no descendants to carry on the family name?" Tommy said as he stepped gingerly out and held the door for Kris.

"I'm sure your Blarney-kissing Irish tongue will come up with a fine story to regale them," Kris answered, dismounted, and squared her shoulders. While it was true that real blood was never spilled at these affairs, the political equivalent of the red stuff could run knee deep. Before, she'd just been Father's darling daughter, Mother's eligible debutante. Today, she was Kris Longknife, ensign, serving officer and medal recipient. Maybe she should rethink this.

With a shrug, Kris joined the flow of people moving up the stone steps of the museum and into the rotunda. A six-meter-tall, horned and rampant tusker stood in the center of the room, more a tribute to the taxidermist's art than to the actual creature that had terrified the original landers on Wardhaven. Most tusker habitat had been replaced by Earth-type flora; still a few herds managed to survive up on North Continent. The young Kris always considered this stuffed creature a thing of sadness. At the moment, it reminded her that today's power broker could end up as tomorrow's stuffed rug. *And you wanted to be your own person.* A part of her laughed.

The high-ceilinged reception hall was resplendent in tall marble pillars, rich gray rock run through with bright streaks of reds, oranges, and blues. The vast expanse of plush royal blue carpet beneath her white shoes brought out the colors in the marble and made the cool power of the immense room even more overbearing. What a splendid room for this moment's great to celebrate their instant of glory.

Kris took in the human company and found it rather shrunken by its surroundings. Most of the men were ignorable in white tie and black tails, tights, or trousers as they chose . . . and not always because they fit well in them. Mother had set the women's fashion with a floor-length red dress that took up a good four feet around her, flounced out by at least a score of petticoats, Kris estimated. The top of the arrangement ended way too soon for Kris's tastes in a tight, gleaming bustier that forced up what a woman had for all the world to see, except all the women were wearing them, and the men seemed too busy being seen to notice all the pulchritude around them. All the men except Tommy.

When Kris first put on the dress whites' high-necked choker, she'd figured it for a torture device. Count on Mother to come up with a worse one. Kris, with nothing for the bustier to force up, was quite content behind her starched whites. Unfortunately, the whites did not bug out Tommy's eyes like the bustiers did.

Mother held court on the far south corner of the ballroom with most of the social women, parliamentary wives and the likes. Father, for his own reasons, circled through most of the men of parliament and business in the northern corner. Big brother Honovi, still in his first term in parliament, was right at Father's elbow. He was learning the family trade from the best; Kris wished him well.

The east corner was anchored by a fleet of admirals and generals. Captains and majors formed an outlying picket line that seemed to shelter the big brass from all but the most insistent civilians. Kris considered taking refuge in their ranks, but at the heart of it was another cluster of family, her Great-grandfathers Longknife and Trouble. She had no idea how to handle meeting them for the first time in ten or fifteen years. Does an ensign throw her arms around an old general and give him a hug, or stand stiff at attention and throw out a brisk "Good afternoon, sir." General McMorrison, Chief of the Wardhaven Staff, stood elbow to elbow with General Ho, the Chairman of Earth's General Staff. Around them was an unusually large contingent of other planetary staff chairmen. Somehow Kris doubted she had the security clearances for their small talk.

Resigning herself to the inevitable, Kris turned for the prime minister's contingent to see what official duties were assigned her. Before Kris reached Father, Honovi detached himself from the prime minister's elbow and moved to intercept her. Following in his wake was a new fellow who, judging from dress and crew cut, had to be a security agent. Kris smiled greetings to both. The agent actually nodded in her direction. Honovi launched immediately into the business at hand.

"Little sister, you really have the old man bent out of shape. It's worse than when you ran off to the Navy."

"I do seem to have that effect." They exchanged a mutual shrug they'd mastered long ago for the inevitable.

"Well, I've got him calmed down for the day. What do you say we don't risk you two having a bit of a chat?"

"I could just circulate and smile and say a few nice words."

"Very few, very nice words," Honovi emphasized with that irksome way that he had of making like he'd won Kris over to what she'd already surrendered to.

Kris came to an exaggerated attention. "Yes, sir, no questions asked, sir."

"Somehow, I doubt even the Navy can get that out of my little sister." Honovi smiled. "And, Sis, I do appreciate what you did for my campaign. Even Father says, in his calmer moments, that you pulled my chestnuts out of the fire."

Kris leaned over and gave her big brother, who was now a good two centimeters shorter than her, a peck on the cheek. "Keep up the good work, Brother. Make Father happy."

"I will. Now shoo. The more Longknifes circulating, the more hands get shook." He quoted Father's perennial demand, then glanced at each of the corners of the room not under family domination. "Say something nice to that officer clique over there or to the veterans. You and I both know Father could use all the help he can get on his right wing, and what with your medal and all, it can't but help."

It was nice to know how risking her life was valued by her Father. "On my way," Kris said dutifully, turning away.

"Is that the way it is?" Tommy asked once Honovi was gone.

"You mean politics first, nothing else even a close second?"

"I guess."

"Isn't it business first in your family?"

"Yes, but we have fun, too."

"Tommy," Kris said, glancing around, keeping her smile firmly pasted on her face, "this is a very politically rich target environment. It's times like this that my family *does* its business."

"Think Harvey could run me home?"

"Just smile and listen, and nothing can go wrong," Kris said, tossing Tommy the minimum survival advice her father had offered when she was six. Opposite the active military was a collection of old veterans marked by their medals proudly worn on the lapels and prim necklines of civilian clothes. Since they included no family Kris could recognize, she headed for them, but her progress was slow.

"Kris, I hardly recognized you in that white," one of Mother's socialite friends called loudly. "Girl, it is so *not* your color." Kris sighed and paused as a matron and her daughter sailed down on her and Tommy. The mother simply bulged the latest fashion in all the wrong places. Her daughter's bulges were enough to make Tommy's eyes bulge out worse . . . and she had either rouged her breasts or was showing a few more millimeters than even Kris's mother displayed.

"I was hoping you would organize our summer fashion show the way you did last year," the mother gushed. "You do have such a way with schedules and checklists and things."

"Mother," her daughter said, rolling her eyes at the ceiling, "even you can see she has other things to organize. Or are they letting you do much of anything?" she said, looking Kris up and down. "You are starting at the bottom, aren't you, a pennant or flag or whatever your rank is."

"Ensign," Kris provided. Behind her, a more interesting conversation was going on.

"There'll be no limit on the profit potential, son," assured a high-pitched voice, "once we throw out that bunch of scared old ladies in petticoats back on Earth that have kept a lid on our expansion. They're bleeding us white, making *us* settle every barely habitable planet in *their* expansion zone before they'll let us take another baby step outward. It's embarrassing that the damn treaty strangling growth is named after Wardhaven."

"Well, I know that sweetie McMorrison," the matron went on. "Maybe if I put in a good word for you, he could loan you for this year's fashion show."

Kris muttered something like "Good luck," and turned away as they did the same. She found herself face-to-face with a rotund businessman who went as red as his tie when he realized his last remark had been made in the presence of the great-granddaughter of the man who, as president of the Society of Humanity at the close of the Iteeche War, made the treaty limiting human expansion his last achievement before retirement.

Kris smiled, offered her hand and, as he took it reflexively, she said without missing a beat, "Don't you think expanding the human growth boundary four times in the last sixty years showed a lot of courage on the part of those who fought the Iteeche?"

He sputtered something, and Kris passed on.

"How do you do that?"

"Do what?"

"Keep track of all the conversations and switch from one person to the next like some kind of computer," he said.

"Well, for one thing, I don't forget my name every time a pair of bouncing boobs comes at me."

"It must be great having your own nice pair to look at every time you take a shower." Tommy grinned shamelessly.

"Wouldn't know, myself."

"I'd be glad to offer an opinion," Tommy said solicitously, then swallowed a laugh. "Can you imagine the look on Thorpe's face when he gets orders to TDY you to cover a fashion show?"

"Don't even go there," Kris said, trying not to cringe

visibly. All she'd done to be just a regular ensign would vanish if General McMorrison gave in to that biddy.

"Kris, what are you doing in the Navy? I thought you were headed into politics," came from Kris's left. She paused to give a young woman, who was actually dressed, time to catch up with her. It wasn't enough time, however, for Kris to dredge up her name. Kris smiled and offered a hand.

"I bet you don't remember me," the woman started. "I'm Yuki Fantano, from up north in Tuson. You spent a week putting our campaign headquarters in shape for your dad's last reelection."

"Of course, Yuki," Kris lied. "How are things up north?"

"Hot as the dickens, and this early in the year, no less. I still can't get over how quickly you took that chaos and turned it into a cracking good show."

"Well, I have a bit of experience in that sort of thing."

"I bet you do." Yuki grinned.

"And I didn't know any of you, so I just started sweeping things up, and you were all kind enough to go along with me."

"When is Billy Longknife finally going to admit we have to have import duties to protect our industries from the cheap crap Earth spews out for its bulging slums?" Kris heard behind her. A quick glance showed two older men in concentrated talk. "And look at all these women, gussied up like Brenda Longknife. They look like Earth whores. Maybe now Billy will support travel restrictions. Christ on a crutch, in a few minutes we're going to pin a medal on that Longknife girl for saving one of our kids from a bunch of scum from the Seven Bitches. A good passport system would have kept those crooks where they belonged."

"If a Longknife did it," his friend assured the speaker, "it couldn't have been too hard. After all, the kidnappers were just two-bit thugs. All the inner worlds ever teach their kids in school is how to steal old ladies' purses."

Yuki blanched.

Kris shrugged, smiled, and went on her way.

"Why didn't you say something there?" Tommy asked.

"Ever try to teach a pig to sing?" she answered.

"I guess that would be a waste of time. So tell me, how did you turn the Tuson office on its ear so fast you impressed Yuki?"

"Just about anything is easy, Tom, if you don't care how successful you are or if the people you're switching around are 'so honored' to have you. I learned that the second time I got dumped in the middle of nowhere with orders to make a bunch of strangers work together and help get Father votes." *And joined the Navy so they couldn't keep sending me off to wherever their bacon needed saving. The military stays out of politics so, now, Ensign Kristine Longknife will, too.* "Of course," she finished, "whatever you do, smile while you're doing it."

"Smile, huh?"

"Yes, and keep smiling. I know these two."

"Earth business is robbing me blind because of that ridiculous short patent life," Dr. U'ting, research professor of nanobiology griped. "Just about the time we get one of my ideas into production out here, those thieves on Earth declare my patent expired and start cranking stuff out for themselves. The Rim is doing all the research, and they're not paying us a wooden Earth nickle for it. I say cut them loose and let them rot."

"We need a central patent law, Larry, and the Rim has been trying to lengthen patent durations," Dr. Meade, Kris's old Political Science professor, pointed out.

"And the last time the Senate passed it, that Earth slave of a president vetoed the bill. Hell, Grant, when was the last time the Rim elected a president? Longknife wasn't it. Oh, maybe one or two since, but so long as the president is a popular election, Earth and her Seven Witches will fill that slot, and we can't get a law through. As far as I'm concerned, we're better off on our own. Each planet for itself. We issue our own patents, we lock up our own files. Let those thieves try duplicating my work without my own patent application to rummage through."

"They are the largest market," Doc Meade pointed out, taking a sip from his drink.

"And they have the largest fleet," Kris said, joining the conversation on cue. "Back in the Iteeche War, it was that fleet that saved us. That and Earth's billions to crew them."

"Hello Kris, I see you've done well," Doc Meade beamed.

"Just did my job," Kris answered.

"Who cares about ancient history," the other growled. "The Iteeche Empire has gone back to sleep, and nobody's seen any sign of another alien species."

"Thanks to the Treaty of Wardhaven, we really haven't done much hunting for aliens," Doc Meade pointed out. "It's a big galaxy, and we've only touched its surface."

"You're sounding like some Earthie with his head stuck in the sand."

Kris nodded to Doc Meade and moved on, leaving him to the familiar argument. She was in a contest to shake as many hands as possible. A bar wasn't far ahead. Kris paused just long enough to get a tonic water; Tom finally got a beer.

Close on her right were the vets she had been working her way toward. They were easily recognized by the medals they wore on their lapels: veterans of the Iteeche War. These older women were probably the only ones in the room who had stayed with the coats, blouses, and flowing pants of that older era. Then again, Kris could think of no way to pin their battle ribbons to a bustier. The thought of Mother putting the golden sun blossom of the Order of Earth, or the Military Medal anywhere on her getup made Kris smile. Several of the veterans returned her smile and Kris easily gravitated toward them. As the prime minister's daughter, she had spent little time with these folks. As a serving ensign, they welcomed her. They did not, however, let her arrival interrupt the inner circle's ongoing topic.

"What these kids need is a good war."

"Too soft, too soft by a straight shot, I tell you."

"A good war would give them some grit. Solid grit."

"Look at them, all got up like a bunch of hussies."

"Bunch of blind followers."

"A good war would teach them how to stand on their own two feet."

"And look who's leading them. That damn Longknife and his scandals. Bastard never served a day in uniform in his life."

"A couple of hours with a good DI, and that man would know which direction to lead.

"My DI would have given him a bit of backbone."

"More than a bit," got dry chuckles all around.

A few of the insiders of the circle noted Kris's presence; it was kind of hard to not notice her whites against the garish colors circulating around the room. Gentle nudges were usually followed by glances her way, but there was no slowdown in grumbling about her father. Tommy seemed ready to withdraw, but Kris just let it roll. Once you've faced an Iteeche warrior, a minor thing like a politician's daughter could hardly make you change your mind, let alone your favorite topic.

It was nothing new to Kris; she'd heard it all before. Even some senior officers, Captain Thorpe included, felt kids today were only out to make their first million, and damn the cost to the community. Duty and honor were lost on this generation and the politicians leading them. In some corners there was even a darker twist. The wrong people were running things. A good war would show the world who really deserved to be top dog.

Eye contact and a smile exchanged with everyone, Kris turned away. "You know, I can understand why these old vets are the way they are," she told Tommy. "It's a lot harder to understand why someone under a hundred would sound like them."

"Could it be that you're kind of close to the folks that have it good?" Tommy asked and answered.

"You saying I'm part of the problem?"

"No, just maybe too close to one side to see the other."

"You in favor of charging out into the unknown?"

"Hey, Kris, I'm from Santa Maria. We are out in that

unknown. But even there, some folks see it one way, others the other."

"But we all have to live in the same galaxy. And somehow we have to do it all together. Any suggestions?"

"If I had any, wouldn't I have told your old da the first time I saw him?"

Kris studied the room. Mother and her henhouse was to her right. The military was ahead of her. Kris started across the room to see what she could do there.

And ran into Commodore Sampson and ... "Kristine Longknife, I bet you don't remember me." A slightly gray, middle-aged man, impeccably dressed said, holding out a beefy hand. Behind him, three, no, four security types that made the men around Father look actually anemic took her measurements, then went back to scanning the crowd. Now there were four people who weren't assuming no blood would be spilled here today.

"Hello, Mr. Smythe-Peterwald," Kris said, making sure her smile didn't falter. "What brings you to Wardhaven?"

"Oh, there's so much going on. You can almost smell the future. This is where the real power is, so that's where I go. Once I get your old man past his family's bugaboos about limits on human expansion, there's a whole galaxy out there we can grab with both hands."

"Last time we tried that, we ended up with Iteeche tentacles wrapped around our neck," came from behind Kris. She turned to find her Grampa Trouble, gleaming in dress red and blues, giving Peterwald a rigidly neutral face.

"The Iteeche Empire has been cowed for the last sixty years," Commodore Sampson pointed out.

"Some might say quiescent," Trouble noted, taking a sip from his beer. "Their emperors never were much for expansion."

"But humanity must expand." Mr. Peterwald said low. "Nothing can limit us. Why should we limit ourselves?"

That was the essence of the expansionist party's position. Humanity the Magnificent. Given her druthers, Kris would gladly go along with them. *But the Iteeche almost made us Humanity the Extinct.* Kris kept her mouth shut.

"Yes." Trouble nodded. "Expansion is necessary. But managed expansion can make sure that we're ready for whatever we stumble into next time. At least as ready as we can be. The galaxy is a pretty vast place, Petie, and who knows what's out there."

"What do you think, Kris?" Mr. Peterwald turned his smile on Kris. She tried to measure the sincerity behind it and came away with a plus or minus ten . . . on a five point scale.

"The galaxy's an interesting place, but I'm just starting to learn my way around it," Kris dodged as she'd been taught. Father was not going to see any sound bites from Kris on this evening's opposition media report.

"You sound just like a careful young woman," Peterwald's smile got even blander, if that was possible.

"Not a bad way to sound." Trouble nodded.

"Well, my son is with your mother's entourage. I hope you'll join me there later. I don't think you've met my son."

"No, I haven't had the pleasure."

"Well, maybe today."

"Yes." Kris stayed put while Peterwald made his way, smiling and glad-handing all the way, toward Mother's side of the room. Without a word said, Commodore Sampson turned his back on General Trouble and joined another group of officers. Kris took the time to catch her breath and check her smile.

"I hear you done good," Grampa Trouble said, slipping one hand into a pocket and sipping his beer with the other.

"I got everybody out in one piece, sir."

"You gonna start sir'ing your old grampa?"

"When we're both in uniform and in public, I think so, sir."

"Damn straight," he said.

"How bad is the mess?" she asked him.

That gave the old soldier pause. He studied the bubbles in his beer for a moment, then shook his head and glanced at Tommy. "Not quite bad enough that I wished you weren't wearing that suit, young woman. I think us old farts who still remember what a real war is like should be able to keep the forgetful and misinformed from doing anything stupid." He sipped from the beer. "I hope. What you drinking?"

"Tonic water, Grampa."

"I still think your biggest problem was the pills your mom was pumping into you back then to make you a 'nice girl.' I doubt you're an alki."

"There are many things in life I don't need to know." Kris smiled at how gently he passed over what still brought her awake at night, cringing.

"Ladies and gentlemen, if I may have your attention," caused only a slight lowering in the room's ambient noise.

"You want to join us?" Grampa Trouble offered. "You two are wearing the suit for it, and as I understand, you *are* our poster child today."

"If you don't mind, I think I'll stay where I am," Kris said, with Tommy nodding rapid agreement beside her.

"Afraid of a few old generals?"

"You've got several galaxies of stars over there."

"It's your galaxy, too, kids. Someday you'll probably be wearing your own constellation."

"Grampa, we're serving ensigns. We are not cleared, and we don't need to know the little asides you'll be passing around among yourselves."

"You're chicken? Hey, you've faced mines and rifles. You can't be afraid of a few old men and women. Or is it just the two of us your afraid of? God knows, with your family, you have a right to steer clear of your relatives."

"Not you, Grampa, never you."

He took her arm; reluctantly, she let him guide her around the room. Tommy followed with all the enthusiasm of a ship being towed to the breakers. They passed through the outlying pickets without so much as a bobble. Father was presenting the first couple of medals to artists and bureaucrats as Trouble rousted a pair of three-stars to make room for him and her at the elbow of Earth's Chairman of the Joint Chiefs. Kris stamped a smile on her face and took the vacated seat between the two generals as Tommy took the opportunity to head for a safe, quiet corner.

"General Ho, this is my Great-granddaughter, Ensign Longknife." While Kris struggled to remember she was the prime minister's daughter and had survived situations worse than this, she rapidly went down the protocol requirements. *He's uncovered. I'm uncovered. Do not salute. Wouldn't anyway: this is a social situation. Like hell it is.*

Kris returned his formal nod.

"I understand you did rather well by us."

"I did what any ensign would have done in the same situation, General."

"And don't you forget that. Being a Longknife, that might not be so easy. Right, Ray?"

Damn! Her other Great-grandfather had bounced a five-star from her seat on the other side of Ho. Just what Kris needed: a family reunion. She was still trying to figure out how to function as an ensign in a multistar environment, and now she'd have to do the dysfunctional family thing as well. Oh hell.

"If she survives it, she just might learn a few things," Ray agreed.

The prime minister was going up the list and getting more long-winded as the recipients became more politically important to his party. However, the attitude of the military around Kris saved her from further reaction. They had been invited by their political masters, so they came. Still, as a mass, they sat, arms folded across their chests. Silent as embattled sphinxes, they faced out toward a society that did not understand them, rarely needed them, and pretty much ignored them.

As Father reached the end of his unmercifully long list, he announced that the last award would be given not by him, but by General Ho, thereby passing over Wardhaven's own Chairman, General McMorrison. True, Kris was serving in the Society's Navy, but the *Typhoon* was built and crewed by Wardhaven, and was, for all practical purposes, a Wardhaven ship. The prime minister was cruising for another lesson on the care and feeding of his own warriors . . . a lesson Kris would not give him.

General Ho raised his eyebrows a fraction of an inch, and the disapproving creases around eyes and mouths deepened a similar fraction among the generals and admirals surrounding him. Still, he made his way to the podium without hesitation. The master of ceremonies handed the general the folder with Kris's citation, then passed the medal to Kris's father. Kris had spent the last hour praying to every bureaucratic god in the pantheon that her family would leave this one to the soldiers who knew how to do it. All to no avail. Mother was sashaying onto the stage, her petticoats flouncing. It was rapidly becoming a bloody political circus. General Ho did not suffer political circuses, bloody or otherwise. "Ensign Longknife, front and center," he growled.

The other recipients had glad-handed their way onto the stage, laughing, talking to Father, or even shouting at people in the audience. Kris marched, shoulders back, head up; her DI would have been proud of her.

General Ho read the citation in a clear, gruff voice ending with, "Your actions, in the face of criminal acts and hostile fire, reflect credit on yourself and the Navy in which you serve."

Kris blinked; in the past, such citations always concluded, "and the Society of Humanity's Navy in which you serve." General Ho offered her the award folder. Behind her, in their ghetto, high-ranking officers shuffled their feet, a virtual scream of opposition to what was missing. Kris sneaked a peek at the citation. The traditional phrase was there in black and white. General Ho had omitted it. Was this his way of telling his fellow officers that the green and blue flag was coming down?

The civilians, of course, missed this bit of drama playing out in front of them. They were on their feet as Mother and Father surrounded Kris. Mother, of course pinned on the medal.

"Well, dear, now that you've got your bauble, are you ready to come home?" she whispered as she managed to put the pin into Kris's left breast. "A miniature of it will make a lovely pendent. I know a jeweler who could place a few diamonds on it and make it truly divine."

"Mu-ther," Kris whispered back, intentionally shaping the word to echo her fourteen-year-old self . . . and probably generations of girls. "You don't just walk away from the Navy. They call it desertion, mutiny, things like that."

"Oh, your father was just telling me this morning that the Navy has itself in a budget bind. Aren't they sending their sailors home early?"

"Yes, Mother, but I'm an officer. We're just on half pay, and they want us back for half of it."

"Well, it seems to me that—"

"Ladies, smile for the cameras," Father ordered through a clenched-toothed smile of his own. Kris and Mother obeyed.

The ceremony self-destructed after that as everyone went their own way. Mother and Father had people to meet. General Ho had a lot of raised eyebrows to answer. Kris went looking for an out-of-the-way chair where she could recover her naturally sunny disposition and stanch the need to order a real drink.

She had expected to be mobbed or at least respond to a few well-wishers. She found herself alone with Tommy and free to observe. The chasm between the civilian and military parts of the ceremony was as glaring as the differences between what they'd done to get here. The civilians had built, discovered, made things happen, all for the greater glory of humanity . . . and their own, thank you very much. Kris had damn near got herself killed so a little girl might live.

Kris shook her head. "General Ho muttered something under his breath as he left the stage. Something about them being so far out in left field they didn't even know what game was being played," she said to no one. "I didn't ask him who he meant, the audience or the generals, but I suspect I know what he'd say."

Tommy looked around. "It would fit both." Thus leaving Kris with a mental picture of trying to keep a baseball game going when the two teams never left right or left field.

Kris watched as her great-grandparents circulated, trying to manage an endgame for the Society of Humanity, striving to resolve the tension between two factions: one with an almost religious faith that humanity had to be one, the other insisting everyone had a right to do what they wanted. Still, after the split between them was resolved, there would be two groups in each of the new factions, one playing for profit, power, and the glory it brought, the other going for self-sacrifice, power, and glory. Games within games. Kris looked into the faces around her. How much game playing could the fabric of society survive?

Kris came alert as Grampas Ray and Trouble headed her way at the same time Mother did with a young man in tow. Kris hoped Mother would flinch away; Trouble was Mother's least favorite person in the galaxy. No such luck. Kris resigned herself to more dysfunctional family than anyone should have to survive.

"Kris, I want you to meet Henry Smythe-Peterwald the Thirteenth. You two really should get to know each other. You have so much in common." *Right,* Kris thought, *and if I marry him, my father-in-law will quit trying to kill me.* The hard look on Grampas Trouble's and Ray's faces as they took in the young man left that answer in doubt.

Young Peterwald, however, smiled sunnily and held out a hand. About Kris's age and height, he had the sculptured look that parents with too much money and ego gave children in these days of genetically manipulated offspring. Kris took the offered hand, but before she could say a word, her and Tommy's beeper went off in duet. A quick flick of the wrist treated her to, "Recall. Your leave is canceled. Emergency circumstances on Olympia require your return to duty immediately."

How's that for a reprieve! But Kris managed a frown anyway. "Olympia, where's that?"

Before Nelly could answer, Grampa Trouble chuckled. "Oh, that one. You've drawn a dilly again, kid. New colony, not yet fifty years old. Had a volcano blow on the other side of the world from the main settlement area."

"Lucky for them," Kris drawled.

"Hardly. Massive blow, tossed enough gunk in the air that the planet skipped a summer. Total crop failure. Now, a current in the ocean offshore has gone missing, and they've been treated to the proverbial forty days and nights of rain."

"They should wish they were so lucky," Grampa Ray cut in. "They're at twelve months of rain and no end in sight. Looks like you'll have your work cut out for you, young woman. Starvation, flood, and, oh, yes, complete breakdown of civil authority. Bands of heavily armed and desperate types roving the sodden landscape, fighting over what's left." Ray grinned at Trouble. "Yep, looks like the kid drew a nice one."

"Kind of reminds you of the good old days." Trouble laughed.

Mother frowned. Young Peterwald shrugged, and Kris, despite the bad news, felt like a ton had been lifted from her shoulders as she and Tommy excused themselves.

9

An old lieutenant at OCS had warned the candidates, "Being in transit is the closest thing to being a civilian you can get while in uniform. And don't you smile at me. It's hell. And if you're Senior Officer Present, it's worse." Kris had only been in transit once, between Wardhaven and High Cambria. A commander had been Senior Officer Present. He'd spent most of the passage in a corner of the bar he alternately designated Naval HQ and the O club. Kris had buried her nose in anything Nelly could dig up on the Kamikaze-class and hadn't surfaced until the liner docked. Now she wished she'd taken better notes.

This trip, Kris was Senior Officer Present.

There weren't a lot of officers to choose from, first two, later four boot ensigns. But Kris graduated a seat ahead of Tommy, mainly because of her rifle range scores. The two ensigns who joined at Pitts Hope were a whole week junior to Kris. Kris found that out from their files because the two of them came aboard, went straight to their adjoining rooms, and never came out, except for meals.

"Doubt the door between their rooms gets closed too

often." Tommy scowled. The door between Kris's and his rooms stayed closed . . . except when Kris needed help on official duties, like going over all the vaccination records of *her* personnel. Kris signed for all the Navy personnel that came aboard, as if they were sacks of potatoes. She also had to verify everyone was up to date on their shots and had all they needed for Olympia. Unfortunately, those requirements were subject to change. Conditions on Olympia were bad and getting worse. Not only was the planet incubating all kinds of new bugs, others that healthy humans kept under control were turning pandemic.

"Typhoid," Tommy yelped. "I thought we wiped that out a couple of hundred years ago."

"So did I, but there must have been a carrier on Olympia, 'cause now people are getting sick." That particular problem left Kris pacing the dock at High Pitts Hope, waiting for a hastily ordered shipment of vaccine as the good ship SS *Lady Hesperis* prepared to raise the gangplank and leave. The vials arrived just seconds before the ship's Third Officer's fourth deadline expired, so Kris was not left on the station as the ship pulled away. Kris was none too sure she would have minded that.

Kris doubted the *Hussy,* an ancient wreck of a liner, had ever been a good ship. Although none of the merchant crew advised them to, Kris quickly learned to strap herself into her bunk at night and hold tight to her mess gear. It seemed that *Hussy*'s engineers had trouble maintaining a steady burn. The ship's accelerations and decelerations were subject to wild excursions from a small fraction of a g to three g's and back again, without benefit of warning. The civilian crew's laughs and jeers left the passengers feeling more like zoo exhibits than naval personnel on their way to save a planet.

A glance through their records showed Kris why the rest of her shipmates took so long to learn how to survive the *Hussy*'s wild ways. For many, this was their first time in space. Most were raw recruits fresh from boot camp. Some had not even finished basic training, as their confusion on

even how to wear the uniform showed. Kris flagged down
one of her third-class petty officers and ordered him to
square away a few of the worst offenders. He said, "Aye
aye, ma'am," and headed for the problem child. Yet when
Kris looked back, the PO had taken a hard right into the bar,
and the recruit was still as much a wreck as before.

Now Kris took a deep dive into the personnel folders at
her disposal. She came up shaking her head and knocking
on the door between her and Tommy's room.

"Come on in," he shouted. She found him deep in a
reader.

"Have you seen our troops?" she said, waving her own
reader.

"I believe so. Sad to say."

"No, I mean their records. We've only got two second-
class and four third class POs. All are in their second or
third enlistment and were pulled from advanced schools
for this job. Wardhaven dollars to donut holes, under the
latest policies, they'd never have been shipped over.

"Kind of makes you suspect that a posting to Olympia
is the Navy's way of telling all involved to shape up or get
out," Tommy said, not even looking up from his reader.
"Maybe just get out."

Kris did not ask him what he thought that said about
the two of them. Was Father trying another approach to
getting her back where he wanted her? *No way, Mr. Prime
Minister.*

"Did you know the Olympic system has seven jump
points?" Tommy asked as the pause lengthened.

"No," she said, coming over to glance at his reader. It
showed Olympia and its surroundings.

"Thing is, from those seven jumps you can get to just
about anywhere in human space in two or three more."

"That would make it a great trading point," she mused.

"Would seem so, so why are they sending the dregs of
the fleet here to do a bit of this and a bit of that for it?"

Now Kris did frown. "Nelly, what's the organization on
the ground for this mission?"

Nelly took longer than usual to start populating Kris's reader with an organization chart. "I am sorry," Nelly apologized. "The daily reports do not balance and change from day to day with no explanation."

Tommy raised an eyebrow at that. Even as boot ensigns, they'd learned that the Navy took daily reports—or, for that matter, any reports—very seriously.

"Who's running this show?"

"Lieutenant Colonel James T. Hancock, SHMC," Nelly said.

"Him," Tommy breathed.

"Must be two of them," Kris assured him, but she didn't have Nelly check that out. There were some things better seen first. Instead, she glanced over the Table of Organization. Mercy missions like this one didn't have to follow any definitive structure; commanders were free to improvise on the ground. However, they usually followed the structure of a battalion or regiment, depending on the size of things. Olympia wasn't close to battalion strength, say 200 plus or minus the 30 the daily reports couldn't agree on. But the org chart looked like amoebas doing one of Tommy's Irish jigs around the CO's box.

"Communications, medical, intelligence, finances, supply operations, MPs," Tommy said, "all reporting direct to the CO, and then there's this huge Admin section with most of the personnel."

"Notice what's missing?" Kris said.

Tommy looked up at her, then rolled his eyes at the overhead. "All tail, no teeth."

"Right, all tail, no hands giving a handout."

"Maybe it's all in Admin," Tommy suggested.

"We wait and see." Kris sighed. Father might be right, today's troubles were enough to keep her busy. Maybe tomorrow's troubles would solve each other before they got to her.

Kris wondered if maybe her father really was an optimist.

* * *

TWO days later, Olympia was large in the view port, giving Kris her first look at the mess she'd drawn. The orb reflected brightly, about what Kris expected when an island thirty klicks long and a dozen wide blew itself to dust. Despite the gunk in the atmosphere, she could see another line of storms blowing in from the ocean to add more to a ground already saturated from big, weeping clouds trying to make it over an inland mountain range. The desert behind showed recent signs of flash floods. Even the rain shadow was getting soaked.

"You the woman in charge of those hellions wrecking my boat?" Kris turned to find a potbellied man who hadn't shaved in days lumbering down on her, what might pass for a grimy captain's hat barely hung to his head, a flimsy in his hand.

"I believe I am Senior Officer Present," Kris admitted.

"Sign here."

"And this says . . ."

"I'm delivering ninety-six enlisted and four of you officers to the Olympia Emergency Services Command, per my contract."

"Nelly, do we have ninety-six enlisted personnel?" Kris had studied their files; she'd never done a count.

"Yes."

"Kris, shuttle is loaded," Tom called over the net.

"Do you have ninety-six enlisted personnel on board?"

"I don't know."

"Have 'em count off."

Tommy's voice disappeared for a long minute. Then he was back with a crisp "Ninety-six enlisted personnel present, ma'am. Me and the other two ensigns are waiting on you."

"Be there soonest," Kris said and signed. "I want a copy."

The captain produced a second flimsy from beneath the first. Kris's signature had carried through. "Thank you, Captain. With luck, we won't be sharing a ride again."

Kris hefted her bag. Marine battle dress was the uniform of the day, the night, and next week for this operation. The ancient warrant officer on Wardhaven who briefed them had taken great delight in pointing out that new ensigns *were* permitted to get their hands dirty on this tour. From the looks of things, there would be plenty of chances.

The shuttle ride was bad, made worse as one after another of the new recruits lost his or her lunch. If Kris hadn't strapped herself in so tight, she might have gone up front and relieved the pilot. Then again, flying a skiff was one thing, a hundred-passenger shuttle was quite another. As it was, they were lucky; Port Athens was in between the worst of its daily parade of storms. The landing, however, was a whole new experience. Upon dismount, Kris found a rutted runway dotted with potholes.

"Don't these people have any pride?" a recruit snorted. "Back on Hardly's Heaven, we'd never let concrete get this bad."

"Your runway might not look so sweet after a year of acid rain," a local unloading the cargo bay snapped back.

"Natives appear to lack a sense of humor," Tommy noted.

"I think it washed off with most of those buildings' paint."

Between red streaks, the terminal showed patches of its original paint. It might once have been a gay jumble of blues, greens, oranges, and others. All were dull now.

Two buses rolled up to the shuttle, but their doors stayed closed while Kris's troops collected in the rain. Only when the trickle from the shuttle cut off, did the bus doors open. A couple of dozen troops made a dash for the shuttle through the rain. There was no order in their leaving, no structure in their mad stampede for the freedom ride. Few had any attention for their replacements other than an occasional obscene shout or gesture. Tommy watched them, then gave Kris a shrug.

With the buses empty, the other two ensigns grabbed the front seats on the nearest one. "Are they avoiding me or ignoring me?" Kris muttered, standing in the rain as she oversaw the boarding of her ninety-six enlisted personnel.

"Maybe they've noticed that things can get lethal around you," Tommy said, a lopsided grin taking only part of the sting out of his words.

"And you?" Kris shot back.

"I have the luc' of the little people," he assured her.

"Then you ar J your little people take charge of that last bus. I'll handle the one with our prima donnas. Didn't anyone ever tell them that seniors enter a vehicle last?"

Tommy glanced up, blinking into the pouring rain. "Whoever made that rule didn't spend much time on Olympia." Tommy headed for his bus, and Kris took the other and found herself stuck standing, the fifty-first person aboard a bus intended for forty-eight. A young spacer with a badly broken-out face offered her his seat. Mother or Father would have taken it without a second thought; Kris couldn't picture Grampa Trouble doing the same. She stood for the fifteen-minute ride.

The drive was as dismal as the port. The roads were more potholes than road; all the buildings showed the effect of water's constant assault. Somewhere a sewer main had broken, adding its stink to the misery. People plodded along, heads down, shoulders hunched against the latest downpour. Several windows gaped broken; a store had been burned out. Kris's crew grew quiet as the sights of desolation and despair accumulated.

They pulled into a compound, rusting barbed wire setting it off from the buildings around it. To the right was what might have once been an office building. Society's green and blue flag had been painted on the plywood that filled a broken window. Across a drowned and muddy park, two hotels rose, one to four stories, the other to ten.

The driver demanded Kris hurry her charges off his bus; he had other places to go, other fares to earn. Kris doubted that, but the buses were civilian, and the Navy always kept its people moving. Unfortunately, that just meant her troops hurried off the bus to stand in the rain. The truck that had followed them with their gear pulled up behind them. Its two civilians started tossing duffels into the deepest puddles around.

"Okay troops, let's form a line, single file," Kris ordered, "to draw your baggage. You, you, and you"—she pointed at the biggest men in the ranks—"go help those civilians unload the truck. See that the kits land on dry land." That helped; the duffels started landing on their bottoms, standing where Kris could read the names on them. She rethought having the troops file by. Calling out names might work better.

"Is anybody in charge here?" Tom whispered to her.

Kris's curt answer died in her throat as she caught movement out of the corner of her eye. The Admin building's door opened. A marine officer in battle dress strode out, back ramrod straight, a battle board slapping purposefully against his hip. There was no question who was in charge. From the scowl on his face as he took in this new addition to his command, there was also no doubt about his opinion of them.

"Atten-hut," Kris ordered.

"Who's in charge here?" came from the officer, more a challenge than a question.

"I am, sir," Kris fired back, not hesitating a moment to take on her responsibility.

"And who might you be?"

"Ensign Longknife, sir."

"Right." He eyed her for a moment, didn't seem to care much for what he saw, then turned his back. "Form your personnel into two divisions, Ensign."

An easy command, but one there was no way Kris could obey properly. By all that was good, holy, and Navy, Kris should turn to a chief and order him or her to form divisions. Anything else was unofficer. But all Kris had was a pair of second-class petty officers who'd shown no initiative on board or since arriving. No, what delusions of leadership as was here consisted of her and maybe Tommy.

What had Grampa Trouble said the morning he picked her up for her first skiff ride . . . without clearing it with either of her parents? "If you're going to be damned if you do and damned if you don't, then *do* it—with panache." She turned to Tommy. "Ensign Lien, form a division of your bus team."

He saluted. "Yes, ma'am," did a snappy about-face, and stepped into a deep pothole. Still, he kept his balance as he marched away.

Kris turned to face the milling group of sodden spacers and marines. "My busload, form on me. Petty officers will form files to my left." As a suggestion, she pointed to where she wanted the few crows among them to stand. They took the hint and did so. Kris had one second-class and two third-class; that gave her enough for her first file. "Dress right, dress" got the petty officers' arms out. It began to dawn on the rawest recruit that they should have somebody's fingers touching their right shoulder. It caught on. Twenty meters to Kris's right, Tom's busload went through the same drill. In a surprisingly short time, the mob transformed itself into two divisions of three ranks. They were still getting soaked and growing more miserable, but they looked Navy.

The other two ensigns watched all this from a dry overhang as if this was for their entertainment. Kris followed Hancock's lead and ignored them as she did her own about-face, saluted, and reported. "Divisions are formed, sir. All new arrivals are present."

The lieutenant colonel turned, a scowl still occupying most of his face. "You have a manifest, Ensign?"

Kris dug it out of her pocket. She could just as easily have beamed it from her computer to his battle board, but he was doing this the old-fashioned way, and he had the rank.

The officer took the paperwork. Without a glance, he pocketed it. "Welcome to Port Athens Marine Base. I am Lieutenant Colonel Hancock, and that is all the welcome and thanks you can expect to get here.

"Those of you who joined up to do good, look around. This is as good as it gets. Enlisted will be issued web gear and rifles. Carry them with you at all times on duty or on base. You will not take them off base while off duty. Officers." His glower got worse, if that was possible. "You will also draw web gear and side arms. If you are smart, you will draw a rifle, too. If you don't know how to use one, learn.

"I've shipped three of you ladies home," he growled at the massed troops. "One may actually get to keep that arm. I've shipped three people home and the only return fire so far has been from a young woman who managed to shoot a local with his own gun. She says it was self-defense. He has witnesses to the contrary. She's being tried by a jury of *his* peers, since she did it off base and on her own time. My advice to you boys and girls is to stay on base and consider all your time my time. Do it, and you just might make it home to your mommies."

He turned to her. "Ensign Longknife, is it? You one of those Longknifes?"

Kris turned her head just enough to look him in the eye. "Yes, sir." She didn't add, *General Trouble sends his compliments,* despite the temptation. Trouble would not send any kind of compliment to Colonel Hancock. Not *that* Hancock.

"Figures." He scowled. "Well, Ensign, have your booties report to Admin, then draw their web gear and check into their billet. If they hurry, they just might get some chow before the mess hall closes for the night. Admin will see they get issued ration chits and work assignments. I advise you to turn in any cash you're carrying as well as your personal credit cards. It's worth your life to carry them around here." He redirected his scowl from the troop formation to the two ensigns, then Tom, then Kris. "You officers see me when you're done."

"Yes, sir," Kris saluted. The wave she got in return might have been aimed at an annoying insect.

Kris turned back to her troops. They looked as stunned as she felt. If that was what passed for leadership around here . . . But that was not their problem. The rain was coming down harder, and Kris looked to be the only officer around that gave a damn about them.

"Petty officers, fall out and call the names on those duffel bags," Kris ordered. On that bit of guidance, the troops got organized. Kris set up a smooth flow as troops collected their duffels, lugged them into the office building in front of them where Admin took up the ground floor. From there they moved to the armory to draw their web gear and weapons. With no bunching up, her new arrivals proceeded fairly smoothly to their quarters and from there to chow. Of course, the last to have their name called would be soaked to the bone.

As luck would have it, the two other ensigns' names were called very quickly. They took their gear and headed inside. Kris's bag was also called early. She made a note of where it lay in the mud and stayed with her shrinking command, taking over from a name-caller when he found his own bag. With a pained expression, Tom took the place of the second caller to find her duffel. When the last person's name was called, Tom and Kris followed the sopping-wet spacer into Admin, their own "waterproof" boots squishing and contributing a liter or two to the deep pools flooding the tiled hall.

"Did we have to do that?" Tommy asked.

"Grampa Trouble would have tanned my hide if I'd left them out there alone in the rain."

"No one in my family would have complained. What do you say next time we flip on it? Heads we follow my family, tails we do it your way."

"You two are late. I finished with those other officers an hour ago," a hulking first-class petty officer whined. "You're making me late for dinner."

"You would have had to wait for all these," Kris waved at the rest of the crew checking in.

"Nope, I just had to wait for you officers. Colonel told me to make sure you got your quarters, orders, and chits. Then I'm done for the day."

"Thought the Colonel suggested we work sunup to sundown. It was safer," Tommy pointed out.

"Who wants to live safe? Listen, there's a lot of desperate

women out there. Amazing what a little hard cash can buy." The first-class glanced at the papers he was handing Kris. "Oh, right, you're a Longknife. You can always buy anything."

Kris signed her chit and kept her money to herself. "Where's the leading chief, the armory, and the chow hall?"

"You're looking at the closest thing we got to a leading chief, ma'am. We enlisted swine ain't drawing half pay during this cluster fuck. Nobody comes here 'less they pissed somebody off big time."

"And you?" Kris asked.

He ignored the question. "The armory is across the way in the short quarters. The chow hall's in the tall one. They close in thirty minutes, so I'd shag my ass over there pronto."

"Thanks for the advice." Kris looked at her orders. "I'm reporting direct to Colonel Hancock?"

"Hardcock wants to keep down the overhead. Besides, he ain't got all that many officers. Couple of do-gooders. Most senior officers would rather go on half pay than go here. You'll see soon enough. Now, I'm done, and I'm out of here." He turned for the door. "Somebody turn off the lights when you're done."

Tom stuffed his orders and chits into the pockets of his battle dress. "It's so nice working among happy people. Think it'll get better?"

Kris stowed her paperwork, then hefted her duffel. "Don't know, but I think I'll draw a rifle and side arms first, then risk eating." Kris drew web gear, rifle, and side arm, stowed her gear in her room, locked her rifle down in the floor's weapons bay, and raced into the chow line five minutes before it closed down for the night. What they slapped on her tray would win no awards, except maybe from a pig swill purchaser, but it filled an empty stomach. She and Tom were just getting the first forkful in their mouths when their beepers went off. Kris waved Tommy to keep eating. She had a strong suspicion what this was all about.

"Ensigns Longknife and Lien here. What can we do, sir?"

"What the hell's keeping you two?" Colonel Hancock growled.

"Just enjoying a delicious, nutritious meal, sir, in the dining hall. Exactly what a growing girl needs, Colonel."

"I told you to report to me as soon as you were done." Tommy started to get up. Kris waved him back to his seat.

"Yes sir, I planned to do that, sir. We saw that the new arrivals were processed properly, got our assignments and chits, drew our web gear and weapons, stowed our gear and got our weapons locked down, and were just enjoying the first mouthful of this wonderful meal they're serving in your dining hall, sir. We should be with you in another thirty minutes."

"What are you going to do, take a walk in the moonlight?"

"Might, sir. It's actually stopped raining for the last two minutes." Tommy's eyes were bugging out. Kris just smiled.

"Longknife, get your ass over here in fifteen minutes or keep walking."

"Understood, Colonel. See you in fifteen minutes." Kris said, punched off, and reached for her second bite of dinner.

"We can be there in five." Tommy gulped.

"And add heartburn to our problems? Nope, I'm eating it nice and careful."

"Like a Longknife?"

Kris studied her tray as she chewed unidentifiable and probably indigestible food. "Don't know. Maybe I am letting myself be guided too much by a couple of Grampa Trouble's sea stories. But, Tom, when you draw hell for a billet, you can either run with the demons or run at them. Got an opinion?"

"One who battles with demons needs a dragon at her side."

"Is that some old Irish saying?"

"No, mine, based on spending too much time too close to you."

Kris rapped on Colonel Hancock's door exactly fifteen

minutes after she rang off. He was seated, feet up on his desk, face in a reader. She and Tommy filed in and came to attention in front of his boots. He glanced up, took in a clock on the wall, then went back to his reader. "Took you long enough."

"Yes, sir," Kris answered.

"The warehouse is a shambles," the Colonel said, not looking up from his reader. "Straighten it up. For some reason, we're only issuing bags of rice and beans to the people hereabouts. There's got to be a better diet in that warehouse. Find it."

"Yes, sir," Kris said. Waited. Nothing further happened. She saluted the Colonel's boots; Tom joined her. Colonel Hancock threw her another wave. She led Tom in an about face, and they marched from the office.

"What was that all about?" Tom repeated his earlier question of the evening.

"A game," Kris said.

"Do you know the score?"

"I think we're ahead on points," Kris guessed. "Where's the warehouse?" Nelly had no answer to that question, so Kris went looking for the duty section. Down the hall from the Colonel's office they found what might be one . . . two guys sleeping in their desk chairs. "Where's the warehouse?" Kris asked. Twice.

One woke up, looked around, saw Kris, reached for a sheet of paper, and tossed it her way. Kris eyed it; it did show an arrangement of streets. She rotated it slowly, trying to match the streets to what she had seen on the drive in. The map worked best if you held the paper at a thirty-degree angle. "Looks about two blocks that way," Kris concluded.

"You going there tonight?" the only slightly awake sleeping beauty asked, getting comfortable again in his chair.

"Planned to," Kris answered.

"Take your pistols."

Kris left the two to their dreams.

"A sloppy bunch. Think we should have woken them up?" Tom asked.

"If they feel safe sleeping just down the hall from the Colonel, do you think two boot ensigns could get them excited?"

"What kind of Navy is this?"

"I thought you'd recognize it, Ensign Lien. This is the Navy your preachers talked about. This is hell's Navy." Kris stopped by the locker to collect her M-6. She had to remind Tom how to lock and load his weapon. Together, rifles slung over their shoulders muzzle down to keep the rain out, they walked the two blocks to the warehouse. Actually several warehouses, all surrounded by barbed wire. A civilian guard stood at the gate, his rifle also muzzle down against the beating rain.

"Who are you?" greeted them.

"Ensigns Longknife and Lien. I'm in charge of the warehouse facilities here in Port Athens. I've come to inspect them."

"You can't. It's dark."

"So I noticed," Kris said, taking in the warehouses. The area was bathed in light; several trucks were backed up to the loading docks. "Looks well enough lit to me."

"Listen, I don't know who you are or what you think you're doing here, but you don't belong here. Get lost while you can, or I'll . . ." The rifle started coming Kris's way.

Kris doubted she could outrun a bullet, but at the moment, the rifle looked within reach. Without thought, Kris grabbed for the muzzle. Her hand wrapping around the cold gun metal sent a shock through her. *You're crazy, woman.* Still, it seemed like the kind of thing Trouble would do. The guard looked just as shocked to see her hand on his gun as she was. He struggled for a second, but she yanked the weapon from his grasp and brought the butt up under his chin.

"Looks like we need to have a little talk," Kris growled. Up close, under the lights, Kris got her first good look at the guard. A kid of maybe thirteen, he stared through wide, round eyes at his rifle in her hands.

"What's going on here?" Kris demanded. Running her brother Honovi's campaign, she'd walked into some messes. Course, most of Honovi's campaign crew didn't carry guns and looked a lot less hungry. For an answer, the kid started screaming out names. Kris brought the butt up hard on the erstwhile guard's jaw, just like they did in the vids, and to her surprise, his eyes rolled back and he slumped into a mud puddle. However, heads popped out of trucks and loading dock doors. Kris had the attention of a good twenty or thirty folks. Time for a campaign speech.

"You are trespassing on government property," she shouted—and ducked as a rifle came up. The round was high, but Kris felt a distinct lack of cover. Ducking, she brought her own M-6 up and snapped off a three-round burst, likewise over her targets' heads. People piled from the warehouses into trucks. Motors came to life.

"Is there any *other* way out of this warehouse?" Tom asked from his fighting position at the bottom of the largest pothole available.

"I don't think so."

"So they'll be leaving right over us?" he squeaked.

"Oh God," Kris breathed. She need not have worried. Trucks turned away from her and, with a few more shots over her head, smashed a hole in the fence opposite the formally agreed-upon exit. Kris stood only after the last truck was long gone. She glanced down at the kid.

"What are you going to do?" the terrified youngster asked.

"Send a message," Kris said, using the muzzle of her M-6 to signal the boy to stand. He looked painfully thin. His clothes needed patching. "Who hired you?"

"I'm not gunna tell you nothin', lady."

"What's your pay for this?"

"A sack of rice. My mom, brothers, sister, they're hungry."

"Come by the warehouse tomorrow. You work for me,

I'll see your people get fed. And tell the folks you were working for that if they come back here tomorrow, I'll see what kind of jobs I can find for them. They come back tomorrow night, there'll be armed marines walking the perimeter. Tell them there's a new broom in the warehouse. They can change and eat, or try to do it the old way and starve."

The kid's face changed as she spoke. Terror drained out. Dismay and shock were there for a while, along with a large dash of doubt. But he was nodding his head as she finished. He started backing away, careful like. Kris watched until he disappeared into the dark.

"What do we do now?" Tom asked.

"Well, unless you want to spend the rest of tonight walking fence, I say we go back to our rooms and get some sleep. I strongly suspect tomorrow is going to be a bitch of a day."

"But the fence, it's wide open."

"So I noticed. And likely to stay that way until we get it patched. Kind of inviting to anyone who wants to wander in. Hungry women, kids, anyone at all. Check me out on this, Tommy. We are here to feed people, right?"

"Right."

"Well, if a few people want to help me in the distribution of the food, that's fine by me."

"Then why did you shoot at those trucks?"

"Because they had guns. How much of that food do you think they were planning on sharing?"

"Right," he snorted. "Count on a politician to care more about how they do it than what they do."

Kris thought she was just being practical. With a shrug, she turned and headed back to the main compound, now shouldering two rifles. "What else can you do, Tommy? Nine times out of ten, perspective has more to do with the final result than anything you do. Perspective . . . and getting some results."

At the base, Kris paused in the rain. The Colonel's window was still lit, the only light showing in the Admin building. "What is it with him?" Tommy asked, shaking his head.

"There was trouble on a planet, Darkunder," Kris said. "Farmers didn't think they were getting fair trade for their crops. Happens every once in a while. Hancock led a battalion of marines dispatched to keep order. Some reports say he was too friendly with the money interests. Other say he just had a bunch of battle-sharp troops. Anyway, standard crowd control methods didn't seem to be working, and somebody thought machine guns would be better. Lots of recriminations. Hancock was brought up on charges, but the court-martial found him not guilty."

"So he *is* that Hancock. Yeah, even on Santa Maria we heard about him. Media about went ballistic. How could the man be found not guilty when a hundred unarmed farmers died?"

"You know many farmers on Santa Maria?" Kris asked.

"A few."

"I know a few generals. They felt Hancock did his job. He stopped a bunch of anarchists from murdering, raping, and pillaging in the streets."

"You agree with them?"

"No, but I understand them. I also wonder if the Navy had sent two or three battalions to Darkunder if the crowd wouldn't have seen the wisdom of going home early before anything got out of hand. Anyway, Hancock was exonerated by the court, but you can see what kind of assignment he drew next."

"Yeah, but I don't understand it."

"Brass won't hang him because the civilians want him hung. But they don't want any other officer making the mistake of thinking they can get by with that kind of failure. Since he didn't do the honorable thing and quit, he's here having his nose rubbed in the fact that he's a failure."

Tom glanced around at the compound. "Does look a mess."

"And I suspect it will only get worse. When I was in college, I read an essay on leadership by Grampa Trouble. He had a lot to say, but the thing that struck me was his idea that leadership depended on belief, maybe even illusion."

"Belief? Illusion?" Tom didn't sound like he was buying.

"As the commander, you have to believe that you are the best person to lead, that you can get the mission done with fewer casualties, less grief, better than anyone else can. And your troops have to believe the same. Even if it isn't so, you all have to buy into the illusion that it is."

Tom shook his head. "No illusions here."

"Right," Kris agreed. "And that, more than the rain, is making this place hell."

"What are we going to do?"

"I don't know," Kris said slowly. "Well, yes, I do. We are going to see that these people don't starve. Beyond that, we'll just have to wait and see."

"Why do I find waiting to see what an *Ensign* Long-knife will do very frightening?"

"Oh, you ain't seen frightening yet, Tommy me boy. Now, what do you say we get out of this rain."

Back in her room, Kris did a quick survey. Standard hotel fare: bathroom with shower, bedroom with closet, easy chair, desk, and beautiful-looking bed. So long as the hotel's self-contained energy, water, and sewer continued to work, Kris's own personal matters would be taken care of. Her duffel stood in a puddle of water-soaked carpet. She dragged it into the bathroom; most of its contents were soaked. For a moment, she considered leaving it to the hotel's staff to clean up. However, a glance at the mildew on the tile suggested there was no staff waiting on her every whim, no matter how big the tip.

With a wry smile, Kris fed her battle dress through the washer, dryer, and presser in the bathroom. She wondered how many other debutantes on Wardhaven knew how to do their own laundry. There were things to do while her hands were busy. Having to ask for a map to find her own ware-house was ridiculous. "Nelly, did Sam pass you any new routines before we left?"

"Several."

"Can you get yourself synched with the military system?"

"I have several routines that should do that."

"See if you can hook into the military network here."

"Searching," Nelly responded obediently and maybe just a wee bit enthusiastically, if Kris was reading her AI's inflections. By the time Kris had her undress khakis and one set of dress whites ready to hang up and was wondering why she hadn't taken the warrant officer's advice and left them home, the presser was overheating and threatening to scorch her fingers. Nelly picked that moment to respond. "I now have access."

"Nelly, can you turn off the warehouse compound lights?"

"Yes."

Kris thought for a second. "At oh two hundred local, turn the warehouse lights out. That ought to give the folks in need enough time. Can you lock down the warehouses?" Kris took a moment to pull off her sodden uniform and hang it in the shower, soaked boots, too. She turned the humidity down to the minimum. Taking Nelly off, Kris set her carefully on the desk.

"That information is not in the military net." There was a short pause. "I can access it on the warehouse system."

"The warehouse has its own system?"

"Yes, ma'am."

"Lock them down at oh two thirty," Kris ordered, crawling under the covers and pulling the blanket up. Her feet were cold, but that wouldn't last long. "Nelly, what time is reveille?"

"The Administrative Division's handout welcoming you to Olympia Support Base says reveille is at oh six hundred."

Not Port Athens Marine Base. Kris noted the discrepancy between Hancock's greeting and his Admin Division. Another thing to look into tomorrow. "Nelly, wake me at oh five thirty."

10

Kris woke to a splitting headache and a dry mouth. "Nelly, lights. What's the humidity in here?"

"One moment while I connect to the hotel network," was not what Kris wanted to hear, but it told her another network had not been merged into the overall system. She was no computer whiz like Auntie Tru, but this was poor management all around.

"Humidity is eight percent in your room, and your unit is approaching failure mode."

"Turn it up," Kris ordered as she glanced around at the mess of hanging underwear and socks and took in the stink of fast-dried boots. She headed for the shower to try and get some moisture back into her head, then went back, made up her bed, and dumped everything that had dried out in the bathroom on the bed. Only then did she take some aspirin and a shower. Feeling almost human, she laced on her spare boots, pulled on her poncho, and at oh six hundred met Tommy in the hall on his way to chow.

They stopped in their tracks, rain pouring off them, halfway to the other hotel. The mess hall was dark. Then again, no lights were showing in the hotel windows above them, either.

"What gives?" Tommy gulped.

"One place I want to check before I do something I'm going to regret," Kris said with a shrug and trotted to the HQ. As she expected, the lights were dim; the duty watch slept at their desks. A light still burned in the Colonel's office. Kris walked quietly to his door. The man slept, head thrown back in his chair, snoring. Tom frowned a question. Kris motioned him back down the hall.

"So," Tom said, "that's the way it is. Nothing we can do."

"I'm hungry, and I intend to eat," Kris said as they quick-marched through the rain to the mess hall. "Nelly, give all personnel's rooms a wake-up call. Lights on everywhere. Locate the cooks. Tell them I want them down here now."

"Yes, Kris."

"Can your computer do that?"

"Aunt Tru gave Nelly a couple of new routines. You're the one who said I needed a dragon if I was going to fight demons."

"Yes, but I'm not sure I like the idea of someone else's computer waking me up." Tom's frown deepened. "Ah, Kris, are we ensigns the only other officers here?"

"Oh no!" Kris gasped. "Nelly, are there any senior officers here?"

"Affirmative. In addition to you ensigns there is a Lieutenant Commander Owing, a Lieutenant Commander Thu, who is also a doctor, and a Lieutenant Pearson."

"Did we wake them up?" Kris asked in a voice gone small.

"I hear no noise except snoring in Owing's and Thu's rooms."

"Turn off their lights," Kris and Tom both shouted.

"Done."

"Lieutenant Pearson's room?" Kris asked.

"She is showering."

"Two out of three ain't bad," Kris sighed.

"Senior Boot Ensign, are we going about this right?" Tom asked, very respectfully and very junior.

"Doesn't look like I am," Kris acknowledged as Nelly opened the door to the mess hall without bothering to ask. Kris reviewed her problem for a long minute. A kid sister strong-arming her brother's campaign workers looked cute. How would officers react to her? Some might consider what she was doing a good exercise in initiative. Others could fall back on words like *insubordination* or *mutiny*. Upon further reflection, Kris decided on a new tack. "Nelly, locate yesterday's arrivals. Inform them that they are wanted in the chow hall in fifteen minutes. Show me a list of the ones assigned to the warehouse."

In half a minute, Kris knew most of those she'd brought down would be in her department. Good. If she was going to play power games, it would be best if she started with a base she'd already looked after. Kris eyed the mess hall around her and scowled at her first impression. Upon further review, her scowl got deeper. The floors of the converted restaurant showed mud, and the tables needed cleaning. She headed for the kitchen; it definitely needed a good cleaning.

"Show me the personnel files on the cooks." Nelly did; Kris was not impressed. Two third-class petty officers seemed to alternate being in charge . . . at irregular intervals. Hmm. Right, they had a tendency to divert potatoes to their own, as yet unlocated, still. Had this operation drawn the hind end of everything? *Well, you're here, aren't you?*

"Nelly, do any of our other personnel have some cooking experience?"

"Second-Class Blidon graduated from the New Towson School of Culinary Techniques. Father is a five-star chef. Second-Class Blidon is detached from weapons maintenance school."

Kris and Tom exchanged looks of pure joy. "Another kid trying to avoid the family curse," Kris crowed.

"He's a second-class. That outranks two third-classes any day." Tommy chortled.

"Nelly, tell Mr. Blidon his presence is required in the mess hall immediately, if not sooner. And where are our cooks?"

"Still sleeping."

"Nelly can you find any bugle calls in your files?"

"Yes."

"Full blast into all mess hands' quarters." Even on the ground floor of the converted hotel, Kris heard the bugles. Two minutes later, PO 2/c Blidon appeared. To Kris's surprise, Blidon was a short woman fighting a weight problem, which probably explained her assignment here.

"You wanted to see me?" she said sourly.

"Did you eat here yesterday?"

"Yes, I did, and no, I didn't much like it, but no, I'm not interested in cleaning up this mess." After a long pause, she added, "ma'am."

"What's your price?" Kris asked.

"My price?"

"Yep, everyone has one. Right now, I need you. In case you haven't noticed, this outfit ain't going to hell, we're already fully established in residence. Food can change a lot for a spacer. We need to change things, and you look like the best change agent in town."

Blidon scowled at the praise. "You're a Longknife?"

"Yep, and I don't much like having what my father does thrown up in my face, so I suspect you don't, either."

"How many cooks they have?" Blidon said, glancing around.

"Two that like to drink the potatoes, and three renegades from boot camp." Blidon wrinkled her nose at that. Slowly, she paced her way into the kitchen. That drew a disgusted grunt.

"No wonder the food's so bad." She turned to Kris and offered a hand. "My friends call me Courtney. I'll name my price later, and it won't be cheap. For now, the challenge has hooked me. And I'm hungry. I want six volunteers to start cleaning this kitchen right now."

Kris volunteered the first six from the warehouse that came through the door.

When the cooks finally meandered in, Courtney took

one look at them and declared them unsanitary and unsafe in any kitchen. Kris peeled off another six of her crew, with a third-class in charge and orders to get those two clean if they had to use wire brushes. After last night's meal, Kris had to turn down volunteers for that detail.

Lieutenant Pearson showed up as the cooks were marched for the showers. "When is breakfast?" she asked. The voice was high, the handshake limp, and the dark roots showing in the blond thatch left Kris wondering if anything about the woman was authentic.

"Give me a half hour," Courtney shouted from the kitchen.

Pearson didn't hide her disappointment. As the lieutenant glanced around the mess hall, Kris could hear her grinding her teeth. "I guess I'll be at my desk. I'm still trying to define the correct policy for who we help. There are so many in need, but so many of them have guns. What this place needs is a good gun control law. Really. Ensign, have someone bring over some toast when it's ready, and some fruit, spring melons if there's some left from yesterday. I'll just start my day early at my desk." Her exit, however, was slow, as if she expected Kris to stop her, do the proper junior officer thing of asking the wise senior to tell her all she needed to know.

Kris didn't have time for that; she headed for the kitchen and its scrub teams. That got Pearson moving in the opposite direction. "Nelly, what's Pearson's job?"

"She commands the Admin Division."

"Last night's sleeping watch standers," Tommy remarked.

"Looks like it. Can you imagine her and Hancock in a staff meeting?"

"Why do I suspect we won't have many staff meetings?" Tommy grinned at the prospect. "But did I hear right? She's developing our policies?"

"And probably will be for the next ten years." Kris knew people like Pearson, both in volunteer work and on campaigns. They were usually too fixated on their minutiae to get in Kris's way. "We'll get everybody fed, with or without policies."

Courtney came to stand in the kitchen door, hands on hips. "Scrambled eggs and bacon is the fastest thing I can get out this morning. Any of you smiling faces ever flipped hamburgers or done some industrial-strength cooking?" Kris cringed at Courtney's choice of words; the woman grinned unrepentantly. Several hands went up among the gathering troops. The new head cook waved them into her kitchen with a proprietary grin and a "Scrub your hands, then draw an apron and gloves."

While the place took on the smell of a kitchen in use, Kris circulated. Nelly gave Kris a heads-up about who had what assignments and how long they'd been on Olympia. With Nelly coaching, Kris asked a question here, made a neutral observation there, and managed to get most talking about their jobs.

Then Kris listened. There was a lot of resentment, some at the locals, lots at the brass, but most of it was frustration, pure and simple. Olympia was a lousy place to be, and they were just sitting on their thumbs while it got worse.

"Who is in charge of the warehouse?" she asked the first person who admitted to working there.

"I don't know, ma'am. I think we're in Admin, like most of the rest here. There's a third-class petty officer that shows up sometimes, but most of us just sit over there and stack supplies when a shipment comes in."

"Who built the fence?"

"A local contractor. Why, ma'am?"

" 'Cause there's a hole in it that needs fixing."

"Wasn't there yesterday when we knocked off, ma'am," the able spacer assured her.

"Nope, a truck drove through it last night when I was shooting at it."

"You went there at night!"

"You shot at them!" The woman beside him added.

"Seemed like the thing to do. They were shooting at me. You know about the nightly shipments from the warehouse?"

The two looked at each other, palpably uncomfortable.

The woman answered, "We know things are gone most mornings. Nobody told us to do anything about it."

"I think we'll be doing something about it," Kris said.

As they walked away from those two, Tom shook his head. "I'm starting to think the smartest move I ever made in my life was stopping to tie my shoe during that obstacle course. I can't tell you how glad I am you graduated a seat ahead of me at OCS."

"And all the time I thought it was that final exam on military etiquette," Kris said, nudging him in the ribs.

The cooks returned from the showers to impromptu applause and turned to under Courtney's watchful eyes. Two of the volunteers asked to stay on. Kris started making a list of things she was going to need forgiveness for. She definitely wasn't about to ask permission first. Father always said it was a lot easier to get Parliament to forgive what was working than get those prima donnas to approve what might blow up. Everything she'd seen in the last four months convinced her that, at least in that one respect, Father and the Navy Way were the same.

Her meal done, Kris went through the line again and took a tray and coffee mug across the way to the HQ. Pearson was bent over her workstation, moving a paragraph from one part of her document to another. Hancock was still asleep in his chair. Kris set the tray and mug on his desk and turned to go.

There was a snort behind her as snoring halted, then the sound of boots hitting the deck. She turned. The Colonel looked at her through red-rimmed eyes for a long moment, then reached for the mug. A long swallow later, he put it down. "What you looking at, Ensign?" he growled as he attacked the plate.

Kris flipped a coin. As Billy Longknife's daughter, she'd gotten away with a lot. As an ensign, it might be a good idea to at least let the Colonel know what direction she was headed off in. "Nothing, sir. I was wondering if I might ask for some guidance, or whether I should wait for Officer's Call."

"No way I'm going to . . ." The Colonel decided not to finish that sentence. "Okay, Longknife, what do you want?"

"Am I in charge of the warehouse?"

"Yep."

"I report directly to you."

"I told you so."

"There's a hole in the warehouse fence where a truck drove through it last night. Who do I talk to, to get it fixed?"

"Pearson," he bellowed. "Get in here."

The lieutenant did not rush to her commander's call. Adjusting her khakis, she came to stand beside Kris in the Colonel's doorway. Her "Yes, sir" came out with a mixture of pain and disdain.

"Ensign here wants the warehouse fence mended."

"I'll have to inspect it, sir. The warehouse is under my division."

"Not anymore. The ensign has it all to herself, her and that freckle-faced boot."

"Sir!" Pearson didn't quite squeal. Kris had heard similar bureaucratic shrieks when her father shaved a sliver off someone's empire. She waited to see who wore the boondockers in this command.

"The girl has the warehouse. I gave you the other two ensigns. Maybe the three of you can finish your policies." The Colonel eyed the eggs, took another bite, then bit off a piece of bacon. "This breakfast is damn good. New cook?"

"Yes sir," Kris cut in. "Second-Class Blidon had some culinary training on the outside. She's willing to oversee the kitchen." Kris turned to Pearson. "With the lieutenant's permission."

"My toast tasted as good as always," Pearson sniffed.

"Well my eggs are the best I've tasted in too damn long. Ensign, you want the mess hall assigned to your division?"

"Not if you and the lieutenant don't want it that way, sir." Even a prime minister's daughter learned a little bit about tact.

"I want it that way. Also, see if you can't do something

about the quarters. They're filthy. Pearson, turn the budget for them over to Longknife here, and let her run with it."

"If you say so, sir."

"I think I just did. Now, you two women get out of my face. I need a shave."

Kris saluted and backed out of the way. Pearson stopped her in the hall. "Just remember, *Ensign* Longknife, I'll be the one auditing your expenses, and people can go to jail for misappropriating government funds, no matter what their name is."

"Yes, ma'am. I understand completely," Kris said and marched from the HQ. "Nelly," Kris whispered, "is there anyone unassigned with accounting training?"

"No."

"Anyone have an accountant in the family?" Some other scion was going to hate her for dragging them into a profession they'd learned to hate at their parent's knee. "That's just life, kid," she whispered to whomever her next victim was.

Kris had Nelly inform her warehouse personnel to form division, under arms, at 0800. Uniform of the day was battle dress and rain ponchos. She passed up the temptation to put her five marines in battle armor. Somehow, she doubted heavy stuff had been landed for a mercy mission. Kris delegated the dining hall and quarters to Tom, which left her just enough time to interview a pair of third-class spacers who shared the same views of the accounting profession and their rarely home accountant parents. Tom and she flipped to see who got which. To loud protestations that "I didn't join the Navy to count beans," Kris told Petty Officer Spens he'd be doing just that for her.

At 0800, Spens formed the division and marched them for the warehouse; if he'd ever learned drill commands, he'd forgotten them. Spens made up some pretty creative replacements to get the division moving; the troops got the message, even if they didn't keep in step. "Count cadence, count," Kris shouted.

The "one" was pretty weak, mainly marines in the rear ranks. "Two" got stronger. By the second "four," even the worst offenders had managed to get their feet in step with the others.

"Lift your heads and hold them high," sang out from the rear rank where the marines marched proud and tall, "Space marines are marching by. One, two, three, four."

Her spacers, heads thrown back and shoulders straightened by the cadence call, joined in the count from force of inexperienced habit, unaware that they'd just been had by the marines.

Spens was fully aware. He waited a short four beat before bringing on the same call, ending it with "Your space Navy's marching by." Well, a bit of competition never hurt anyone, and the troops were starting to look a lot less like drowned puppies and a bit more like Navy. A very wet Navy, but Navy. Kris hoped the Colonel had heard them. Even he might smile.

Around Kris, civilians were out, hunched in upon themselves against the latest downpour. At the shouted cadences, their heads came up, too, some with mouths agape, others curious. A few took a good look and took off running, carrying what message to whom, Kris had no idea. But anyone spreading the word that a new day was dawning at the warehouse was fine by her.

There were shouts from the crowd already gathered at the warehouse fence as they approached; people milled around the gate and the hole in the fence. Others raced to join them from *inside* the warehouse yard. Apparently the building lockdown had been successful; the runners came empty-handed. Only as the divisions came to a halt did Kris have Nelly unlock the warehouses.

She turned to face her first real command. Some knew her; she'd done her best to get them out of the rain as fast as was humanly possible last night. Others were old hands, stationed here for up to a month . . . a long time to serve in hell. They looked at her like drowned rats, wondering if she might have a straw for them to cling to. Kris reran some of the pep talks she'd given campaign crews, did a quick edit, and began.

"Crew, I don't know how some of you feel about the work you've been doing. Maybe you're happy about it. Maybe you're not. That doesn't matter. Today, here and now, we start the mission to Olympia. There are hungry people out there. We've got the food. We're gonna see they get fed. Those of you who've been working at this for a while, you take the lead for these new hands. I'll be circulating most of today. You got a problem, see me. You got a solution, see me, too.

"Most of you are new to the Navy. If you'd drawn ship duty, you'd be someplace dry and warm." That drew a rueful laugh. "You'd also be a small cog in a very big wheel, doing what you were told to do. Here, you're critical to saving people's lives.

"We are all in this together. I need ideas. You come up with a good one, you'll find I'm a good listener.

"Any questions?" Kris spoke the inevitable end to these kinds of talks. Just as inevitably, there were none.

"Petty Officer, dismiss the division to workstations. See that those needing assignments get them."

Oh, that sounded so easy. Maybe with a few good chiefs it would have worked. Her third-class petty officer was just as over his head as she was. Still, she left him to do a by-guess-and-by-God bit of detailing while she did her first of many walk-arounds in the mud and rain.

The warehouse area opened on a large bay; muddy, choppy water lapped at the seawall. A marine railroad on the left had hauled a large unmanned drop ship out of the water. It lay like a beached whale, open and half empty. Bags of rice and beans were getting soaked. A young spacer led a group of recruits in dropping hundred-pound food bags on waiting shoulders and lugging them to the nearest warehouse. Backbreaking labor; that couldn't be the way it was usually done.

At the break in the fence, people stood in the downpour. They needed food, work, too. She needed laborers to get the food to them. "Nelly, can I hire local workers?"

"No, ma'am. There are not funds in this mission for

local employees." Of course, Navy all the way. The more debited to the emergency appropriation, the more left over for the rest of the fleet. Kris had heard that some commands even kept an extra ship in commission, betting that enough expenses would be soaked up by emergencies to fund it.

"Ma'am," a quiet voice called to Kris as she walked toward the torn fence. Kris turned to face a thin, gray-haired woman in a slicker and kerchief. "Are you the new person in charge?"

"Yes," Kris said; then, when the woman seemed unable to respond, Kris softened. "What can I do for you?"

"My name is Ester Saddik. My church runs a soup kitchen. Lots of men lost their jobs when the crops failed. Families are going hungry. We're seeing they get one warm meal a day."

"That's very nice of you," Kris offered to the woman when she seemed unsure how to go on. None too sure how to help, Kris at least could give the woman a listening ear.

"We're out of food." Kris knew that was coming; she nodded. The woman's words stumbled on. "We've been buying food from this Navy man, but we're out of money."

"Third-class petty officer?" Kris asked, remembering what she'd heard about the warehouse leadership. The woman shrugged; rates were a mystery to civilians. Kris wondered if she could arrange a lineup but suspected the culprit would be long gone, if he hadn't managed to ship out on the *Hussy* yesterday. No, Kris's problem was how to go forward, not look back. She wiped the rain from her face as she puzzled her problem. She was here to feed people, but she couldn't just hand out food. Obviously someone had been, for a price. *But I'm a Longknife.* Oh joy.

"Nelly, who can hire local civilians on missions like this?"

"Nongovernmental organizations are the usual employers of the local labor forces." The woman listened, dripping in the rain, as Kris continued her conversation with her assisting AI.

"Do we have any here?"

"No."

Not a surprise. This place was the inglorious hind end of everything. But Kris had volunteered as a counselor for a handicapped kids' summer camp her freshman year in college. She'd gotten them their tax-exempt status. "Nelly, what does it take to set up an NGO?"

"I have just completed the paperwork to set one up. Before I send them off world for registration, what should I name it?"

"Nelly, you're wonderful," Kris grinned, and the woman across from her actually cracked a chip of a smile. "Make it the Ruth Edris Fund for Displaced Farmers," Kris said. Now, that would make her great-grandmother's day.

"I went to school with a girl named Ruth Edris," the woman muttered, "a long time ago on Hurtford. We were fun kids, then."

"I hear Granny Ruth still is. She was from Hurtford, a long time before I was born. Nelly, are those papers served?"

"Done. How large do I endow this fund?"

"What would I have to pay you to do what you're already doing?" Kris asked Ester.

"If you feel you must pay me, I am willing to work for an Earth dollar a month," the woman answered. Kris tried not to show a reaction to that. With just a week's earnings from her trust fund she could probably hire every person on this planet for a year. Nelly's last upgrade had taken two months' worth of income, and that in Wardhaven dollars.

"I can get volunteers to work for free," the woman went on, mistaking Kris's silence for disapproval. "If you arrange the release of food to the soup kitchens, a lot of men will work for you. Not just my church's kitchen. There are many others in town."

"I think we have a deal," Kris said quickly to reassure the woman. Then she added subvocally to Nelly, "Put a hundred thousand in it for starters." To the woman, Kris continued, "Let me run this by my boss. Nelly, page the Colonel."

"Hancock," came from Kris's commlink a moment later.

"Colonel, Ensign Longknife here. I need some more advice."

"And you expect good advice from me?"

Kris ignored the question and quickly ran down what she'd done.

"This displaced farmer fund is a legitimate NGO?" he asked as she finished.

"I have it on the best legal advice," she said, grinning at Ester. The old woman did smile this time.

"Yeah, we can release food to soup kitchens, food banks, and the likes, so long as we've got some NGO vouching for their legitimacy. This gig ain't the most popular show on Earth, so you may have noted the lack of media coverage and NGOs. If you got one, do it, Ensign," and he tapped out.

Kris pulled a Wardhaven dollar coin from her pocket and handed it to Ester. "I guess that makes you the fund's first employee. You know anyone else who might help me?"

Ester glanced around; a man stepped forward. His boots had holes in the top of them; his pants were soaked. "Name's Jebadiah Salinski. Jeb to most. I was a foreman at this transfer station before the rains came and management hightailed it off planet. I see your guys lugging bags of beans around. I know the folks who used to work here. We know where the lifts and carts are, though they don't work so good since the rains came. Acid rain damaged them, the boss said before he ran."

"You're hired," Kris said and fished in her pocket for another dollar. Like the prime minister, Kris always carried a couple of dollar coins. You could never tell when you'd want a soda and the net would be down. As she hired her second employee, she asked, "Either of you know anyone who used to work at the hotel that's our barracks?"

"Millie uZigoto was the head housekeeper there," Ester said. "When people quit coming, the hotel folded, managers left."

"Sounds like a lot of people left?"

"Not a lot. Only all who could."

"Well, for those still here, this is the drill." Kris rushed out her words before anyone could change their mind. "The pay's a dollar a month." Kris handed her third and last dollar to Ester. "Give that one to Millie. The rest will have to wait a while for pay. Also, they get all they and their family can eat at the nearest soup kitchen. That sound like a fair deal?"

Ester and Jeb glanced around at the others standing farther back in the rain. Here a head nodded a bit, a finger twitched, a hand raised a little. They came forward when Jeb motioned them in. Under Ester and Jeb's direction they began hand-unloading the just-landed supplies. A check of the three trucks in the yard turned up only one that worked.

Kris tapped her commlink. "Tom, how's the barracks?"

"Lousy. Kris, I couldn't keep my room clean in an environmental- and humidity-controlled asteroid station. How am I supposed to clean up this place?"

"I think our local nongovernmental agency just hired someone to take over the barracks for you."

"I didn't know there were any NGOs here."

"Wasn't this morning. Is one now."

"Why do I so not want to know how that happened?"

"Just pray to your ancestors and Saint Patrick that Hancock is happy not knowing, too. Now, I've got three trucks out here, and only one will turn over. I've got lifters and loaders damaged by the acid rain. You got any ideas about how to cure them?"

"Probably damaged their solar panels. Don't have much sun to start with, got to make good use of what you got. I could probably reprogram the nanos I've got keeping my brightwork shiny to rework the solar panels."

"You're using nanos to polish your uniform brass?"

"Of course, doesn't everyone?" came back pure startlement. Kris rolled her eyes at the sky . . . and got rain in them for her dramatics. Blinking, she turned back to her commlink.

"Tomorrow morning, Tom, you turn over the barracks to someone who knows them, and you get your tail over here and put your leprechauns to work on my broken gear."

"I'll bring the ancestors' kami along, too."

"Believe me, we need all the miracles you can spare."

The lone truck was loaded. Kris peeled off three armed, able spacers to guard the cargo while they dropped off food at the kitchens Ester listed. Ester promised to get the guards back unharmed and before dark. The spacers might be the ones carrying M-6s, but they looked much relieved by the woman's assurance of safety. With all her pocket change gone, Kris had Nelly arrange to ship in a box of Wardhaven dollars with each relief ship, inconspicuous like, and finished the day feeling pretty good.

The next morning started bad and got worse. First, for Millie uZigoto to take over managing the hotel required a meeting with both the Colonel and Lieutenant Pearson. The Colonel immediately went on record as not caring who did it, so long as barracks got cleaned. Pearson insisted on a signed contract and only withdrew her long list of objections when it became clear that this service was being provided under the Society's Apprentice Training Volunteer Program and no Navy appropriation would be tapped. Nelly's fast law search found that bit of legal fiction while Kris stalled. The Colonel seemed to be enjoying himself immensely as Kris tap-danced around Pearson's opposition.

Once free of the HQ red tape, Kris got Tommy doing an inventory of what they had mechanical and what they needed to convert it from wet and rusting junk into something useful. Kris assigned herself the miserable job of getting a full, complete, and honest inventory of supplies on hand, separating Navy issue from relief goods. She had barely touched the surface that afternoon when a breathless runner skidded to a halt beside her. Armed thugs had held up a soup kitchen, cleaned it out of food—and pistol-whipped Ester Saddik for reasons that escaped Kris.

Kris stopped herself two steps into running down to Ester's kitchen. That would do no good. In this rain no one left tracks, and if things were usual, no one saw anything. While Kris struggled with lousy options, Jeb took over the inventory. Free, Kris stepped outside to let the pouring rain cool her off.

There was no use rushing across town; the boy said Ester was already being bandaged by the best doctor available. It was tempting to take a dozen armed spacers to chase down the culprits. Fat chance she'd have. That left her with the less pleasant problem of how to make sure it didn't happen again. She spent a good hour pacing up and down in the rain. The problem wasn't all that different from trying to clean up a sour campaign office. Of course, it often was wiser when all hell broke loose to have hit up the nearest so-called adult leadership before she did too much on her own. And getting that adult leadership to agree to what Kris wanted often took a bit of finagling.

That evening at supper, she set her tray down across from Colonel Hancock, shrugged out of her poncho, and settled into the seat. "I need your advice, sir."

"I'm starting to get scared when you start misusing that word, Ensign. What bridge you trying to sell me this time?"

Kris updated him on the warehouse. He nodded, satisfied, as he buttered a croissant that looked fit to melt in his hand. Then she hit him with the problem of food being ripped off by guys who beat up old ladies. His bread went down uneaten as he looked at her. "And you expect me to do something about that?"

"Sir?" Kris left the question hanging there.

He leaned back. "I don't doubt you are aware that I'm not the most popular field-grade officer in the Corps, charged with using machine guns for crowd control."

"I am aware, sir."

"You're also aware of the quality of the recruits we've got, Ensign Longknife." The two of them eyed the room full of new, half-trained Navy and Marine personnel.

"Not really, sir, but—"

"But what?" he interrupted her. "The people who settled this mud ball chose to have every home incomplete without a weapon, preferably automatic, in the closet. A nice trigger lock to keep the kiddies from hurting themselves. Good God, do these idiots really think their pop guns could stop a fleet of raving bug-eyed monsters if one charged through their jump point?" He snorted. "Well, there's all hell to pay and the devil fully armed to beat the band, and I'll be damned if I'll put my troopers out there for anybody who wants to take a potshot at them." He looked hard at Kris, then went on more softly.

"They said those farmers were only throwing rocks. I swear to God I heard automatic fire. But we didn't find guns in the wreckage, and no one believes marines. Except marines. But I'm still in this hellhole, and I'll be damned if I'll put anyone else in a worse spot." He balled up his napkin, threw it down on his half-eaten supper. Scowled at it. Then looked up at Kris.

"So, Ensign Longknife, what are you going to do about thugs that steal food from soup kitchens and beat up old ladies?"

"I intend to post a constant guard on the warehouses."

"Put our poor booties out slogging in the rain and mud. Makes them easy targets, too."

"No, sir. One warehouse has a business tower, four stories high. Its roof should give our duty watch clear fields of vision all along the fence." And fire lanes. "I've recycled rice bags into sandbags and built a bunker up there. That should give our personnel protection. I'll need a searchlight."

"I can scare one up for you."

"I'm also asking locals—ministers, officials, small business types—to share the night watches."

"So they can give the order to fire?"

"No, sir. To serve as witnesses in any local court when and if one of our petty officers does give the order to fire."

The Colonel eyed Kris for a long moment. "Not bad, Ensign. You know, they're starving on the farm stations."

"Yes sir. We're due for a dozen trucks sometime this week. I'll start spreading out then."

"First convoy is bound to get shot at, maybe even raided."

"I'll be leading that one, sir. Unless you want to."

He snorted. "Sorry, kid. I've been in that barrel. Once you've been hung out to dry by the chain of command, you learn to take what minor advantages delegation offers you."

"Thank you, sir," seemed the only answer to that. The Colonel stood, abandoning his unfinished meal. "One more thing, sir," Kris quickly added. "That NGO that's helping me. I hear it's hiring locals with guns to guard the kitchens."

That got her a long, measuring stare before the Colonel finally picked up his tray. "What the locals do to each other is their own damn business," he said slowly. "Just don't you go spending too much time on it."

"Of course not, sir."

11

First thing next morning, Kris checked in at the warehouse; Jeb and a dozen of his team had worked through most of the night. They expected to complete the inventory by noon; Kris left them to it. Tommy showed up a few minutes later. Millie had appeared at the barracks front door that morning with a small army of ex-hotel employees. "We can handle things from here, Kind Sir, if you will just get out of our way, Kind Sir, we should have everything spick-and-span by supper, Kind Sir, now, Kind Sir, please, get lost." Tommy had several ideas about how to get the rolling gear rolling, so Kris left the "Kind Sir," to himself and concentrated on what she wanted to do.

Ester was back at her soup kitchen, a spick-and-span building in need of paint on the outside but as homey as could be on the inside. The woman sported a bandaged head but didn't let it slow her down one bit. Nelly had discovered a local bank with rolls of Wardhaven dollars in its vault. Kris plopped four rolls, a hundred dollars, on the table in front of Ester. "How long will it take to get armed guards on each kitchen?"

"They're already here," Ester answered. Behind the serving table, two young women smiled and produced rifles from under the table. "My daughters," Ester explained. "Their husbands are out front."

"And the other kitchens?"

"All have guards today. No man wants his wife put through this," she said with a wave at her head.

Kris pointed at the rolls of dollars. "See that every one gets his or her pay. And Ester, it will be a problem for me if my Colonel is embarrassed by something done by our guards. Could you see that they understand that while they take our dollar and eat our food, they are . . .?"

"On their best behavior," Ester smiled. "Yes, I will let them know that Grandma Ester expects only the best from her men."

That was not exactly Kris's words, and it certainly wasn't the way a Marine Colonel would express his expectations for discipline within the ranks. Still, it was probably the best this lash-up would allow. Kris hiked back to the base.

Somehow word had gotten out that Tom needed machinists and mechanics; the warehouse fence was already lined with men and women with automotive skills seeking employment. For a repair shop, Tommy identified a large building next to the warehouse that could be easily included in their perimeter fence. One of the hires was the owner of a failing truck firm halfway across town. He was painfully eager to sell his inventory for ten cents on the dollar. Kris was uncomfortable at the idea until the man admitted his off-world bank was selling him off just that cheap. If Kris would buy him out, he could pay off his debt and be in a position to buy it back from the Navy when they left. Under those conditions, the Displaced Farmers' Fund happily wrote a check and got the gear moved inside the fence.

While the actual work was quickly done on a handshake, the paperwork required Kris to coordinate with both Supply, Finance, and Administration. Kris quickly discovered why Supply and Finance wanted nothing to do with Admin. She had no problem getting the petty officers in the two sections that usually would have reported to Admin to sign off on all the required paperwork. Getting Pearson to approve anything turned into a Herculean task.

"Why do we need all this stuff?" the lieutenant sniffed.

"If it's broke, we have to fix it." Kris had to go to the Colonel to get that answer declared acceptable. Still, five times the Admin chief bounced Kris's paperwork for minor corrections. Five times Kris resubmitted it.

"Why are you putting up with this?" Tommy asked.

"I wouldn't, if we had some trucks to work on, but the ones due yesterday still aren't even in orbit," Kris sighed and played the lieutenant's game. When the dozen trucks finally did arrive, Kris was glad for her prework. Donated rigs, the newest truck had a hundred thousand miles on it. The mechanics took one look at them, shook their heads, then turned to and totally rebuilt them, using every machine and tool Kris had laid her hands on.

Kris didn't let Pearson and her runarounds eat up all her time. Mornings she quickly did her Navy duties. Afternoons, she devoted most of her time to the Ruth Edris Fund. If she failed to hitch a ride with a supply truck, she hoofed it, making the rounds of soup kitchens, checking how everything was going. There were no more robberies, no more beatings. The rain still came down in sheets as Kris traveled the flooded streets of Port Athens, the people still hunched against it as they splashed from puddle to pothole, but now they seemed less beaten.

Whether she hitched a ride or walked, she wound up soaking wet by sundown from the top of her hat to the soggy soles of her boots. The only thing between Kris and utter misery was the humidity controls in the barracks, and when Millie reported the entire unit ready to give up the ghost, Kris paid extra to hire the only man on planet able to nurse the collapsing system along. A dry, warm room each night was cheap at any price.

Pearson was still developing policy when the mechanics wiped grease from their hands and declared six of the trucks as ready as they were ever going to get for the roads up-country. Kris didn't intend to wait any longer for policy; the farm stations were starving. She collected the people she'd met on her rounds and put the question to them: "Where do we start?"

"I think down south is having it harder," a farm implements sales manager advised. "Up north, the land runs to hills and gullies. The gullies are taking up a lot of the water. Down south, it's flatter. Water doesn't have anyplace to go. It's going back to swamp."

Across the table from her, a priest and minister nodded their heads. "That's what we hear, too," said the priest. "But young woman, the gangs are also worse down south. A lot of gunmen are running down there. And with the swamps, there's no way anyone can trace them."

"We've got some pretty smart gear, Padre," Kris answered.

"I know you do, but I haven't seen any of it flying around here," the red-faced priest answered back. "Is it only my imagination, or is this whole effort being done on the cheap?"

"Father!" Ester Saddik swatted his wrist. "My mother taught me to say 'thank you' when someone offered a helping hand, not count the fingers."

"Sorry."

"Nothing I haven't thought, Father," Kris acknowledged. "Tomorrow, I'll take a half-dozen trucks south. Should be back in a day. Thanks for your help."

"Do you want a few of our armed men with you?" Ester asked.

Kris had been thinking a lot about that. Armed civilians riding shotgun for the Navy didn't feel right. A few witnesses? No. "This is a Navy show, ma'am. We'll do it the Navy Way."

THE trucks were eight-wheelers. Each wheel was supposed to be good for both traction and steering; Kris was just happy if they turned. Each cab had a front and backseat.

The days of troops riding on the truck bed were gone . . . no safety belts back there. Kris assigned three gunners to the backseat of each truck. That left room for a driver and a boss in the front seat. Kris would command the first truck. She should have assigned Tommy to command the last truck, but he asked to be her driver; there might be an advantage to having both officers up front. With her pair of third-class POs, that only put a supervisor in three of the six trucks. Her accountant insisted on commanding one truck. "I get out of the office, or the auditors are going to find really weird things," was a threat Kris respected.

Unfortunately, when you give in to one threat, you only get more. "Burnt toast if I don't get a truck." Courtney smiled. So she got a day away from the mess hall.

The sixth truck was all marines.

Her convoy on the move, Kris found herself with time on her hands and a puzzle that would not go away. Everyone here was supposed to be armed to the teeth; the city folks certainly were. So, how come the farm stations were off net with rumors they'd been beat up? The orbital photos showed most of them were in the middle of wide fields, clear lanes of fire as far as any shooter could sight. Anybody trying to rob a farm station should have been very dead five hundred meters out. Maybe someone could sneak up on one or two, but Kris was scheduled to stop at five. Five! Something was wrong here.

To the three recruits riding shotgun in the back, there was definitely something wrong, but nothing like what worried Kris. "I didn't join the Navy to be no errand boy," one young spacer said, not caring if Kris heard.

"Hell," the next one agreed, "if I wanted to do deliveries, I could have stayed home and worked for my dad's shop. At least there, after you put in your eight hours, your day is your own. No offense meant, ma'am. It's not your fault we have to take night watch once a week."

"None taken," Kris assured him, knowing full well that all the troops knew she was the reason for the night duty.

"Wouldn't do you any good to have spare time," the third,

a woman, chimed in. "No place to go, and if you do, it's raining, raining, raining. Join the Navy and see the mud holes."

The first one was ready to come back in. "I joined up to be a gunner. I got the highest score on Tuckwillow in SpaceFighter. Nobody can zap those bug-eyed monsters like I can."

"We haven't found any more aliens," Kris pointed out. "Getting chow to starving people is a bit more pressing than getting ready for hostiles we haven't met."

"Yeah, I know. You're an officer, ma'am, and you have to think like that. But me, just give me a four-inch laser and a squadron of incoming badasses, and you'd see what I can do. This stuff, it's just making the do-gooders back in their overstuffed couches on Earth feel like they did something good when they paid their taxes. They ought to come out here and play around in this mud."

Kris didn't tell him Wardhaven had do-gooders, too, and that was why she joined the Navy.

The first station on their list was big: owners, their kids and wives, grandkids—maybe a few of those getting up marriage high—filled several dozen family-size houses. A number of families from small stations had also taken refuge there. Before it went off net, they reported groups of horse- and truck-mounted bandits roaming the area. Kris shook her head; they ought to have been able to field a continuous watch. They ought not to have gone off the air.

Approaching the station, Kris matched the map on her reader against reality. The muddy road was wide enough for two trucks but in need of repair; Tom slipped and slid from side to side looking for the shallower potholes. The fields on either side of the road were muddy from a crop that never grew and rain that never stopped. She had an unhindered line of sight across those sodden fields to a creek that had overflowed its banks, swallowed the trees around it, and flooded hundreds of meters more. An abandoned tractor was up to its hubs in water. This muck would have channelized any attack; the raiders had to hit them from the road. They should have been mowed down.

What were Kris and her tiny convoy driving into?

"Lock and load," Kris ordered as they came in sight of the station. That made a few troopers' day. Tom left his rifle in the scabbard hanging from the door.

"Can't use it and drive."

It had been a successful farm, if three large barns said anything about its prevolcanic wealth. A big house held pride of place facing a central yard. Other houses and outbuildings turned the station into a small village. There was no one in view.

Kris ordered the other trucks to halt and go on over watch, then explained that meant them watching, rifles ready, while she had Tom drive slowly in. Maybe she spotted motion behind a window. Maybe the barrel of a gun protruding out a door. With a fatalistic grimace, Kris ordered Tom to stop at the gate, dismounted, and started to walk the rest of the way in.

Activating her mike, Kris announced, "I am Ensign Longknife of the Society Navy," when she was a hundred meters from the nearest outbuilding. Her voice boomed from her truck's loudspeaker. "My rigs have food. You went off net several months ago. Do you require aid?"

A barn door opened; three men slipped out before closing it, then started walking toward Kris. At the big house, several women appeared on the porch, two with babies in arms. They also made for the center of the commons. Kris did, too.

They met in the middle. A tall, bald man held out a hand to Kris. "I'm Jason McDowell. My father started this station." He waved at the thin, graying woman leading the other women. "This is my wife, Latishia."

Kris shook his hand, then the woman's when she joined the group. "I have food packages for you. I was hoping to leave about a month's supply. How many people do you have here?"

The man shook his head. "A hundred or so, but a month's worth of food is too much. They'll just come back and take it," he said bitterly.

"We could hide some, Jason," his wife whispered.

"They'd make us tell. Someone would give it out. They'd *make* us."

The wife looked away but nodded agreement.

"I guess we can come out here once a week," Kris offered, not really wanting the workload. Others now came from the barns, houses, and outbuildings; the number kept growing. Kris had expected to see guns. There weren't any.

"Before I can leave the food, I'll need every person's Identacard to verify the delivery."

"Don't have any. They took 'em." Jason dropped the words like lumps of hot iron.

"Does that mean you can't help us?" Latishia asked, her hands knotting her apron. The two silent women beside her clutched their children.

"We didn't drive all this way to tell hungry folks we can't feed them because of a paperwork snafu," Kris said. *And Lieutenant Pearson can finish her policies in hell.*

She chinned her mike. "Tommy, bring 'em in."

Still, losing Identacards was no minor matter. For the last month, these people could have had their bank accounts emptied, their personalities misused on the interplanetary web. Anything could have happened to them while they were off net and unable to say a word in their defense. This did not sound like the work of local hooligans. "With no IDs, I'll need photographs of everyone," Kris said, then ordered Tom to break out a camera.

"Brother, if they've got a commlink, I could check our bank account," one of the men with Jason said.

"You do that, Jerry."

"Tom, see that this man gets a link to the net." Tom took the flood of orders with a grin and a "You got it, ma'am."

"Can you get everyone out here?" Kris asked.

"My mother is bedridden," Jason said. "I guess we could bring her down here, but . . ."

"I'll go see her. I'm just trying to keep the damn auditors from flaying me too badly when this is over."

"I understand. We're in business . . ." Jason stopped, glanced around, ended up staring at the muddy yard. "We were."

"We will be again," his wife said, offering a hand that he flinched away from. As a commissioned officer, Kris ought to leave this well enough alone. Still, Judith would never have let Kris get away in therapy with dodging what these two were running from, and Kris owed Judith her life. In the mud room of the house, Kris shucked her poncho before taking the stairs slowly to the third floor. The house was made of wood, finely polished by work and use. In a bedroom hung with the needlework of years, a woman lay alone on an oversize bed. She moaned in pain. With three quick steps, Kris knelt by the bed, lifted the covers from the old woman. Her weathered skin showed the blue and yellow discoloration of a several-weeks-old beating.

"I've got a corpsman in the convoy. Can I have her take a look at your mother?"

"We've done what we could for Mother," the man said, eyes flinching from the woman.

"Do you have painkillers? They took ours," his wife said.

"Tom, send up the corpsman. Have her home on my commlink."

"Yes, ma'am."

Kris turned from where she knelt, looked up at the couple. "Are you going to tell me what happened here? Everybody told me when I got orders to Olympia, watch your back. Everybody carries a gun. Our Colonel doesn't want us on the streets at night. Too many guns. Well, I haven't seen a gun in this compound." Kris pointed at a gun rack hanging on the wall beside a window—empty. "Where are your guns?"

"Gone," the man said. "They're just gone. Leave it at that, Navy."

"My husband went to the fields," the woman began softly.

The man turned on his wife, his eyes begging her for silence. She met his eyes with her own, level, unflinching.

When she didn't turn away, he fled to the farthest corner of the room.

"A farm isn't something that you take care of when you feel like it, not if you're like Jason and his family. His pa carved this station out of a grant. It was swamp when they came here fifty years ago. They drained it. The pumps have to be checked. Now especially. And the pumps are close to the swamps."

"There were five of us," Jason said to the floor. "All armed. We knew that"—he failed to find a word—"those men were out there. We figured we'd see them coming." Jason looked up at Kris. "We're good shots. Pa had us practice every week, and there are things we locals call a buffalo in the swamp that can trample a crop into the mud. We're good at hunting them.

"They came out of a ditch. Must have been breathing through hollow reeds or something. They had the drop on us before we even knew they were there. If we'd gone for our guns, they'd have slaughtered us." The man looked up at his wife. His voice choked. "Honey, I wish to hell we'd fought."

Now the woman went to her husband's side, gave him a shoulder as he sobbed. Kris had rarely seen men cry. On the bed, the old woman struggled to find a comfortable place, moaned. Kris stood, her hand going to the butt of her pistol. There were things she'd joined the Navy to take care of. At the moment, the local bad guys were two up on her. She didn't like the score.

As her man wept, the wife continued the story, her voice a low monotone that screamed, *Wrong*, by its very softness. "The trucks stopped four hundred yards out. About a dozen got out. Any of them that weren't one of ours, we had them in our sights. Then someone shouted. "Woman, I got a pistol at your husband's head. You have your men and womenfolk drop their guns, and everyone's gonna come out of this alive. People start shooting, and he dies first."

"I told you to shoot." The man's voice was begging for understanding, forgiveness. "I shouted at you, screamed for you to shoot."

Kris wondered what she would have done, as wife, as husband.

"More men got out of the trucks," the wife continued, "spread out in the mud, went to ground. There must have been thirty or forty riflemen. We had children," she looked up at Kris, pleading for understanding. Kris nodded, tried to give what the woman wanted. The wife shook her head and went on. "Some of the men were for fighting it out, let the devil take the last one standing."

The woman looked Kris hard in the eye. "We have our children here. We women voted to put the guns down." The woman glanced down at her husband. "Maybe if we'd known what came next, we'd have fought. Some of us say we wish we had. Most of us don't."

Almost Kris told the woman that she didn't have to finish the story; already Kris knew the ending. But the wife had come this far; the rest tumbled from her mouth. "They took our guns first, then our food, IDents, anything that seemed important or that they wanted. Then they had the men tie each others' hands. There, in the mud, in front of our husbands and children, they raped us. That seemed to add something to it for them. Jason's father, her husband," she nodded at the old woman in bed. "He fought them, tied up, he fought them."

"Why didn't I? Why didn't I, too?" Jason moaned.

"Because I told you not to. Because if you had, they'd have killed you like they did him. Probably beaten me like they did her." A large sigh racked the woman. "We're alive. Over at the Sullivan place, they're dead. They slaughtered the kids like pigs because they tried to fight them off. We are alive, Jason," she took her husband's face in her hands. "We are alive. We will come through this."

"And we will hang those bastards," Jason whispered.

"If we can. It's all in God's hands."

The medic arrived; Kris left the wife to work with the corpsman and headed downstairs. Outside, she paused; her mission plan called for delivering food. The rules of engagement only allowed her to return fire if fired upon.

"Come on you sons-a-bitches," she whispered to the leaden air. "I got thirty trigger pullers and no kids in this convoy. You know we're here. You know you want what we got. Come get it. *Please.*"

As Kris marched across the yard, the man who'd asked to check on finances came walking back, shaking his head. "They sold the farm. Right out from under us, they sold it."

Kris stopped him. "I'm recording what I'm saying for a legal deposition," she told Nelly and the man.

"You can do that?"

"That and more." Quickly Kris recounted how she'd found the farm station, stripped of IDents and communications. "Any financial and legal actions taken between the time this station went off net and now are not legal and binding. I, Kristine Anne Longknife, do testify to that in any court of law," she finished.

"Thank you," the young man said.

"We'll see what else I can do," Kris said, spotted Tom, and shouted, "We done?"

"Think so. I've got photos of everyone. Even Pearson should be happy."

"Good. Let's pack it in and get moving. We got a lot more to do."

"Yes ma'am." Tom stepped close. "Kris, is something wrong? You look like . . . well, like you want somebody dead."

"Nothing wrong with that," Kris snapped. "We're armed, and there are bad guys out there. Everybody, let's saddle up. We got things to do, places to go."

The troops began to collect by their rigs. They seemed in no hurry to be gone. Several of them were still holding small children, helping them to stuff their faces.

"Ma'am?" one of Kris's backseat guards started. "The bad guys are just going to come back. Take what we left them. Could we, maybe, at least take the kids back to town? They've been starving for the last month. That mom told me the little kids don't have the stomach to digest the grass and other stuff keeping the grown-ups alive."

"Next week maybe we will. Not now." Kris cut him off. "I said move it, troops. I expect to see you moving," she shouted. Navy and Marines got moving. Jason came out of the large house, spotted her, and began a slow jog toward Kris. As emaciated as the man was, still he put one foot in front of the other until he came to hang on Kris's truck door.

"Listen, those guys use the swamps for their hideout. If you keep away from the worst of the swamps, you might avoid them." Kris called up her planned track on her battle board and shared it with Jason. He shook his head. "There, four, five miles down the road, you're headed into Dead Cow Swamp. You've got to go around."

"Can't," Kris found that she was grinning. "Everything around that road is flooded. It's the only elevated road left. We're going right up it."

"They'll be waiting for you."

"I kind of hope so," Kris said, letting her grin take over her entire face. *Grampa Trouble would be proud.*

"Just so you know what you're getting into," Jason said.

Kris turned around, glancing down the line of trucks. "Got no children. Only Navy and Marines. This is what we get paid for."

"Be careful, Lieutenant, or Ensign, or whatever you are. I thought I could take anything that came. God, I was wrong."

"I may have some photos for you and your wife to ID next week when we come through. You may not have to wait until this mess is over before you watch a few of them swing." *Damn, I'm starting to like this.*

"Oh God, be careful."

"Not what they pay me for," Kris said, leaning out the window, looking back. All her troops were mounted up. "Tom, move us out."

"Yes, ma'am."

In the rearview, Kris watched as Jason went from group to group, saying something. Some of the women fell to their knees in the mud, hands clasped in prayer.

"Say your prayers for the bastards ahead of us. Not for me and mine," Kris whispered through tightly drawn lips.

"Would you mind telling me what the hell is going on here?" Tom asked, eyes locked straight ahead, hands in a white-knuckled grip on the steering wheel. "I *am* your second-in-command, and I am *supposed* to take over if something happens to you."

Kris popped her mike. "Troops, you just saw why we're here. Those folks are starving because a bunch of thugs stole what they raised. They killed an old man and beat up his wife. They raped most of the women you saw back there."

"Raped" echoed through the backseat like an electric shock. So, not everyone had gotten full disclosure. Well, they had it now.

"Even the little girls," Kris snapped. "Some of you are tired of being glorified delivery boys. Maybe you could have stayed home and delivered pizza for what we've done so far. Well, I'm told that our road is going to get a bit dangerous in a few minutes. These cruds like to steal things, and our trucks are the only things on the road worth stealing today. Lock and load, crew. Payback time is here, and we'll do the collecting."

Kris turned to Tom; while she talked, he had called up the route on the truck's display. Overlaying that with a photo, he stabbed a finger at Dead Cow Swamp. "There?"

"Looks it."

Tom studied the map. "We could double back about five klicks. There's that other road that stays to high ground."

"Looks flooded to me," Kris cut him off. "We've got food to deliver. If we go wandering all over the place, we'll never make it back to base tonight."

"We could camp at one of the farm stations. Those folks are friendly. They'd be glad to have us stay a night."

"We've got other deliveries to make tomorrow. Tom, we are going up this road. I suggest you check your weapon. I've never seen you fire one."

"I qualified at OCS. I had to, to graduate."

"What did you shoot?"

"The minimum required," Tom said, not looking at her.

"For God's sake, Tom, you're a Navy officer. You knew this was part of the job when you took it."

"You may have noticed, I'm driving a truck, delivering food to starving people. Didn't the priest back home preach "Thou shalt not kill," every time there'd be a barroom fight in town and someone'd be cut up. I joined the Navy to get my college loans forgiven, not to kill."

"Even men who rape and kill and steal food from starving kids?" Kris spat.

Tommy looked out over the sodden land. "This wasn't what I had in mind."

"But it is what you've got now."

Behind Kris, while she and Tom talked, the backseat got very quiet. What were they thinking? Did it matter? They had their orders. They would follow her. Why was she wasting time arguing with Tom? She had things to do. Again, she tapped her mike.

"Longknife here. Roll the windows down. We don't want flying glass in the cabs." Kris looked up, examining the front window. She spotted a release, hit it. The window on her side of the cab swung down to rest on the hood as the rain began to soak her. She told the rest of the convoy to do the same. For a long moment, they rode in silence, swaying from side to side as Tom hunted for more road and less pothole.

"Ma'am," came quietly from the backseat.

"Yes," it was not the expectant hero. He looked white as a sheet as he stared out the window. It was the young woman behind Kris. She'd been in the middle on the ride in.

"We can shoot these people?"

"They'll be shooting at us. Yes, we shoot back."

"My momma and the preacher, they always said death belonged to God, God and the doctors. That's why the gangs were wrong. Now you're saying it's okay to kill. You sure, ma'am?"

Kris had grown up a politician's daughter where you did

anything you had to do to win the next election. Grampa
Trouble had come in like some knight in shining armor
when she was so far down there was no up. She'd loved to
read the history books about what he'd done in the war. He
and Grampa Ray. Even Great-grannys Ruth and Rita were
in the history books, fighting for what was right. Of course,
Kris had learned "Thou shalt not kill." But for her, it had
never been absolute. True, rather than kill a spider, Harvey
would take it outdoors to keep his wife happy, but he'd
fought side by side with Grampa Ray at the Battle at the
Gap and was damn proud of it.

"As I hear it," Kris began slowly, hunting for the words
that would release the safety on her troopers' souls, "there's
a time to build and a time to tear down. A time to live and a
time to die. I say if those men up there shoot at us, it's their
time to die. Or they can throw their weapons down and their
hands up. And hang after the courts get done with them."

Kris turned in her seat to study the three young recruits
behind her; they were pale. The guy in the middle licked
his lips nervously. The girl fingered her weapon as if to see
if it was real. The hero-to-be glanced at Kris, then went
back to staring out the window. "What those men did back
there took them outside the bounds of humanity. If they
shoot at us, we kill them like the wild dogs they've become.
Those are your orders. You will execute them. If I'm wrong,
I'll be the one that stands trial, not you."

"But they'll be just as dead whether a court says you
were right or wrong," the middle said.

"Kind of like the Colonel," the woman agreed.

This was not going the way Kris had expected. In the
history books, there were no reluctant soldiers. Then again,
these were Navy types, hardly out of boot camp. Maybe
Kris ought to have the marines pull their truck up closer to
the front.

Maybe I ought to rethink this whole thing.

Kris swung around in her seat. While she'd talked, the
open fields had given way to mangled trees and scrub.
Some trees were down, big root balls standing in the still

waters. Kris eyed the road ahead of them and what stretched out behind them. Just road and water. Probably a ditch alongside the road. How could she turn this parade around? Couldn't even if she wanted to. Licking her lips, she put that option aside. For better or worse, this convoy went forward.

Kris concentrated on what lay ahead in the next few minutes. Had she done everything? What had she forgotten? That was supposed to be the perpetual question of the commander. What's left undone? She felt a rising panic. What had she missed? She didn't remember that being mentioned in the history books.

Kris checked her gun, eyed the trees growing closer and closer to the road. She activated her mike again. "Crew, we can expect our targets to be hiding behind trees. Your rifles have range finders that automatically set the charge for your darts. They'll set them too low to shoot through tree trunks. Turn your selector to maximum."

"Ma'am," came a shaky voice. "Which switch is that?"

"The forward one," Kris answered, then thought better. "The one closest to the end of the barrel. Ahead of the selector for sleepy darts."

"Thank you," the automatic civility seemed out of place at the moment. Anything smacking of civilization seemed wrong just now. Kris started to say that, then swallowed hard as the truck came around a curve. The trees that had blocked her view ahead now fell away to Kris's right. Ahead, two, maybe three hundred meters, a tree lay across the road.

Kris took the scene in quickly. There was no root ball on this downed tree; a freshly cut stump stood beside the road. Kris switched the sights on her rifle to thermal. Yes, three people lay behind the downed log. Kris quickly scanned the woods to the left and right. Yes, more thermal images: a dozen, twenty. A lot. Kris remembered the man's story, people rising up out of the water. She tried to scan the ditch alongside the road. Some of the water seemed warmer than that around it, but the current in the ditch formed it into a long blur.

Beside her, Tom was slowing. "How close do you want to get, Longknife?" he asked through gritted teeth.

Kris went through her options fast. Drive into the trap and stop, let the bad guys shoot first, then take them. She had more people . . . Correction: she had recruits. Her targets were desperate killers. Kris eyed the water ahead; riflemen coming from the water had gotten the drop on the farmer.

"Stop here," she ordered. Tom braked slowly to a stop in the middle of the muddy road a good two hundred meters from the downed tree. For a long minute, Kris watched the roadblock as nothing happened.

"Throw down your guns and nobody gets hurt," blared over the swamp, sending birds squawking and flapping into the leaden sky. Kris scowled; she was about to say the very same thing.

Well, that settled the question of intent. Kris sighted her rifle at the right-most thermal shadow behind the downed tree. She chinned her mike. "Open fire, crew."

Obeying her own command, Kris sent a long burst into the tree, walking the darts from right to left. Someone tried to get up, run away. He didn't get very far.

Kris switched her concentration to the ditch to the left of the road and sent a long burst into any water that looked warm. A man stood in a shower of bubbles and spray, started to aim at Kris. He fell backward as her rounds took him in the chest.

Forms were slithering from the ditch to crawl up on the road to Kris's right. She slapped the door. As it came open, she dropped through it to settle into a squat beside the forward tire. She fired a quick burst at the closest of the gunmen, lying prone on the side of the road. He slumped over his rifle.

She took aim at the next one. He tossed his gun away, rolled over on his back, and held his hands up in the air. "Throw away your guns, and you live," Kris heard her voice boom over the swamp, amid the rattle of guns. "Keep them, and you're dead."

Five, six people along the road edge were on their knees, hands up. Kris swept her rifle sights along the trees to her right. People were standing, hands waiving high in the air. She glanced over her shoulder. The left-hand side of the convoy looked the same.

"You," Kris snapped at the woman recruit still in the backseat of the truck. "Put those prisoners under guard."

"Yes, ma'am," the woman voice was a ragged whisper. She stumbled as she got out of the truck. Kris flinched away from her rifle, then realized that was the least of her fears. The woman still had the safety on her weapons.

"Unsafety your rifle," Kris whispered. She got a blank look in reply. Kris reached across, flipped the safety off. "Now it will shoot."

The spacer recruit glanced down. "Oh," and went back to waving her weapon unsteadily at their prisoners.

"You in the swamp, walk to the road slowly," Kris ordered. "No sudden moves. Those of you on the road, get up here in the middle of it and lie down."

Kris glanced in the truck. Tom was just getting his rifle out of its holster on the door. The would-be hero and his friend were frozen in place, eyes and weapons covering the left side but doing nothing.

"Are you okay?" Kris asked. When they didn't respond, she repeated, "Are you okay back there?" The hero-to-be blinked twice . . . and was violently ill.

From the back of the convoy, two marines advanced with their weapons at the ready. At least their boot camp seemed to have taught them to take the safety off their weapons. "Cover this side," she shouted to them. They waved fists in agreement.

Switching around to the left of her convoy, Kris found three marines coming forward, keeping their weapons leveled at the slowly moving prisoners.

"I got that one," a marine chortled.

"No, I got him," the one beside him disagreed.

"No, I was shooting at that bunch in the tree." The marine indicated a clump of trees. One body was flung backward over a low snag.

"So was I, buddy boy. I got him."

"You both got him." Kris cut off further debate. "Keep the others covered. I don't want any getting away."

One of the prisoners picked that moment to trip. He went over with a splash. Kris waited for him to get back up, but he didn't. Switching to thermal sights, Kris searched the water, but it was too mixed up to give any kind of target.

"I think one of them is getting away," Tom observed as he dismounted the truck.

Kris scowled. "You prisoners, be careful. The next one of you that trips gets shot on the way down."

"But they're unarmed," the woman spacer behind Kris said.

"They're escaping," Kris pointed out. "And until we check them out, we don't know who's unarmed. You spacers in the trucks get out here. I need some hands to pat down the prisoners for weapons." The rest of the trucks began to empty. The recruits brought their weapons, but about half of them still had their safety on. Most of the other guns didn't look like they'd need cleaning. Now Kris realized why the fight had seemed so quiet around her. She and the marines had been the only ones shooting. Them and the bad guys.

Pairs of Navy recruits went down the slowly forming line of prisoners. While one kept a rifle on a prone figure, an unarmed recruit frisked the captive, making sure they were no longer armed. "Hey, this one's a girl," a spacer said, taking two steps back from the muddy figure he had started to pat down. The woman's response was in no way ladylike.

Kris waved a female spacer over to frisk that prisoner and paused to watch as the pile of gear taken from the prisoners slowly grew. No communications gear, no computers; plenty of knives and usually one gun each. Little ammo, though. The prisoners, stripped to their shorts in most cases, showed thin and hungry. Not the starvation level of the farm people, but even the bad guys had been on short rations. Bad girls, too. Four of the fourteen were women.

Kris turned from the live ones to study the dead. Behind the roadblock, two lay, insects already settling to feast. Kris swallowed hard to keep her own stomach where it belonged. One face was contorted in death. Rage, anger, agony, Kris could not tell, and the dead were not likely to answer her question. The one next to him seemed asleep on his side, quietly drawn up like a child; he provided the only commlink among them. The third rifleman was gone, just a pool of blood showing he'd been shot. Back in the trucks, a medic was caring for his wound. He'd be in fine shape for the hanging.

Kris walked back up the road. Two more bodies lay between the ditch and the roadbed. "You and you," she pointed at two prisoners, the youngest among them, hardly more than boys of fifteen, fourteen. "Pick up these bodies. Hang them by their feet from those trees," she said, pointing to the four standing next to the freshly cut stump.

Tom was at her side in a moment. "It's not right to dishonor the dead."

"And leaving them down here to be gnawed by whatever wanders by is better than hanging them up there as a warning to the rest? I am not taking time to dig a hole here and bury them." She glanced up and down the road. "No place to dig, anyway."

Still, Tom shook his head. "Kris, this is out of bounds."

"You two, start doing what I told you. Marine, see that these two do what they're ordered." The assigned marine nudged the two boys to their feet with his rifle. They'd been dead-fish-belly pale before. Now they were almost ghostly white. Terrified ghosts.

Kris turned to Tom. "Tape the live prisoners' hands and load 'em on the trucks. Once they're down, tape their feet to something on the truck. I'm not losing any prisoners."

"Yes ma'am." Tom snapped to a caricature of attention, threw her a parody of a salute, and stomped off to comply.

"And send me any wrapping tape or rope you've got free." Kris called after him. If it was possible, Tom stomped harder. Half an hour later, the convoy moved slowly past Kris's stark message to the denizens of the swamp. A new team was in town. Get out before you join these.

At least, that was the message Kris wanted them to hear.

The next farm on their list was empty of life. A few bodies still lay where they'd fallen or been cast aside. "Guess this is what happened to a farm that fought," Kris observed dryly to Tom as they slowly drove through the farmyard.

"Maybe she isn't such a bitch?" someone muttered on a live mike. Kris chose not to hear.

The next farm was a repeat of the first. Kris distributed the food quickly, neither asking how they had come to be in this fix nor offering to listen to the silent screams behind dry eyes. She did refuse to let any of her troopers turn their backs on their prisoners long enough for the farmers to get quick vengeance. "They are Navy prisoners. I will turn them over to local officials at Port Athens. You can get your justice there," she snapped when the knife-wielding wife of the farm owner had to be forcibly hauled from one of the trucks.

"You think you can get them back there?" her husband asked.

"I captured them. I keep them."

"Good luck. You know, they're not the only band out here."

"How many?"

"Couple of hundred."

"Who are they?" Tom asked. "What turned them rogue?"

"Ask them," the owner spat.

Two farms later, the trucks were sitting higher on their axles, but Kris was no closer to understanding the dynamics of what made someone a killer and another the starving victim. She didn't like that.

She also was getting a bad feeling about her route back to Port Athens.

The last farm was the smallest on her list, but it had three times the people of the others. They seemed less brutalized; at least, there was no effort to knife her prisoners. Two women even went from prisoner to prisoner, giving them a drink of water, a taste of the rations.

The owner was a lanky, middle-aged man who stood aside and let his people organize themselves to quickly unload the trucks into bunkhouses and several small houses, including one he shared with two other couples and a dozen children. By now, Kris's team had their drill down, so Kris and Tommy joined him watching.

"Much appreciate the food. We've been down to eating grass and leaves."

"You've got an awful lot of people," Kris asked, not quite knowing what the question was.

"Yeah, I didn't let go of my indentured workers when the crop failed. Where would the poor bastards go?"

"Indentured workers?" That was the great thing about being a boot ensign, all the time you were learning new stuff.

"Yeah, New Eden slashed its welfare budget a few years back. Get a job or get a ticket to Olympia or a couple other new colonies where the fields aren't big enough for agribusiness."

"And they'd work for you," Tommy said.

"No, they'd work to pay off their ticket. For one year's work, I'd pay for a seventh of the ticket. Seven years and you're free and clear." The man squatted down to pluck a blade of grass. He eyed it like someone might a vintage wine before sticking the end of it in his mouth. "Of course, the poor damn workfare types got no grubstake, no cash. The lucky ones end up working in town at the processing plants."

"We're feeding them out of soup kitchens," Kris told him.

"I wondered how they were making out," the man said.

Kris did a quick count around the farmyard. Lots of kids, lots of old, lots of in between. "You had a lot of fire-power when the gunmen came."

"Gunman didn't come here."

"Smart of them." Kris grinned.

Tommy frowned. "Then how come you went off the net?"

"Windmills died. No power." The man shrugged.

"We'll leave you some batteries," Kris said. Tom nodded. "But why were you the only farm not attacked?"

The guy looked at Kris like she was a very slow learner.

"Woman, you still don't know who the swamp runners are, do you?"

"You kept your indentured workers," Kris repeated slowly, then saw where that led. "The other farms didn't."

"Yep."

"The folks in the swamps are unemployed field hands."

"Yep." He kind of smiled.

Tommy blinked rapidly for a long moment as his mouth slowly opened. "So the raping, the stealing, the killing was all done by folks that had worked for the farm owners?"

The guy looked up at Tommy. "Maybe. Maybe not."

Kris stooped down beside the farmer; he offered her a strand of grass. She sucked on it; there wasn't much taste. Probably not much food value. Then, she'd eaten a full ration in the truck jostling along between farms. Lack of food was not her problem. People were.

As Tommy sat down, his eyes wide with puzzlement, Kris shook her head. "You can't tell me that a bunch of ex-welfare types who've been doing grunt work out in the fields here stole the IDents, fenced them off world, and in some cases sold entire farms."

"For a Navy type, you're not too dumb, kid." The farmer smiled. "Cops on Eden sweeping up welfare flakes maybe pick up a few extras. Punks, thugs, mafioso wanna-bes, troublemakers they'd like to be rid of. Problem child wakes up on the ship, already under boost. That's one that won't bother those cops again. Bright boy lands here, we put him to work along with the others. Maybe he works, maybe he sets up a floating crap game. Somebody always has something to risk. Then he brings in the alcohol, maybe some drugs, too. No matter how poor folks are, they seem to find money for that." The man shook his head.

"And when all hell comes calling," Kris took up the story, "the likes of him can see their ticket out of here."

"Right. Collect some tough henchmen, some guns, go find the folks starving in the swamp, promise them a meal if they'll help you get back at the folks that put them down in the mud. You know the rest of the story."

Tommy shook his head. "But the raping."

"Not always just the big men and the henchmen. Some of the hands have a lot of anger. But there's a few women I've taken in whose brothers or husbands tried to stop it. They got a bullet or beat up for the trying."

Kris eyed her prisoners. Somehow, they seemed less loathsome. "Think I have any kingpins or henchmen here?"

"I don't know. Some of my folks still have family in the swamps. Maria, who was giving your prisoners water, has a boyfriend out there." Kris frowned at the farmer. He shook his head. "Milo has a job here anytime he wants it. Sad part is he also has a kid brother who thinks being a gunman is what being a man is all about. Milo's trying to keep the kid out of trouble until he can talk him down."

"What about these?" Tom waved at the prisoners. "What will happen when we turn them in to the authorities at Port Athens?"

"Don't know. Even if they aren't murderers or rapists, they were running with them. The people that'll be sitting on the juries are gonna be desperate, scared, and mad. Doesn't make for a good combination where justice is concerned."

"So much for the search for truth." Tommy sighed.

Kris nodded, but she was replaying her little skirmish in the swamp. "I shot the gunmen behind the roadblock tree first off, including the man with the megaphone. I got the first ones out of the water on both sides."

"And after that the rest didn't fight much." Tommy nodded. "Most seemed ready to break and run. What's that make our prisoners guilty of? Being as hungry as their victims. Looking the other way when the toughs get their jollies. Damn. On Santa Maria, no man touches a woman that doesn't want it. A man gets that wrong, and any man or woman in hearing will help him learn that lesson fast." Pain ran across Tommy's face as he shook his head. "My priest taught me a poor man has a right to steal a rich man's bread to feed a starving family. He didn't have much of an answer when I asked about poor stealing from the poor. Damn, Kris, this is a hell of a mess. But nobody touches a woman. No man doesn't answer a woman's call for help." He glanced at the trucks now loaded only with prisoners. "Damn, this is a mess you've gotten me in, Longknife."

Kris only half listened to Tommy's moaning about who was right and who was guilty. She had a bigger problem. She'd pissed off a lot of bad guys with guns. *Now what do you do, smart girl?*

"How you getting back to town?" the man asked.

"Up the road," Kris waved absentmindedly.

"Through Wildebeest Wallow?"

Kris pulled out her reader and shared her map with him. The road went fairly straight through a grove of trees. Surprisingly well-kept trees, now that Kris looked at them. The farmer pointed at them with pride. "That used to be a bit of a swamp. We planted walnut trees in there to build up the land, change the acidity of the soil. In another couple of years, I can cut them down and double my acreage."

"Since there didn't seem to be a lot of standing water, I thought it would be a safe route home."

The farmer shook his head. "Been a lot of trucks going that way this afternoon. I think you kicked over a hornets' nest. If people like you and your food convoy can run around free hereabouts, won't be long before the police come looking for the likes of them. Maybe they can buy a ticket off planet, maybe they don't want to. Maybe some of them think they got enough money to buy this mud ball. I hear that squatters are already moving onto some of the farms, the ones that got shot up when they fought back."

"We didn't see anybody at the Sullivan place," Kris told him, mouth running while her thinking was still elsewhere. "One of the McDowells found that their farm had been sold off planet to someone using their IDents."

"Seems the history books are full of this year's bandit being next year's revolutionary and an established politician the year after that," Tommy observed dryly.

"Yeah, nobody's very demanding of a rebel leader's

credentials," Kris agreed. But that was next year's problem; right now Kris had to survive today. "How many riflemen would you say were headed for that grove of trees?"

"Maybe two hundred," the farmer said. "Everyone they got."

"How many of those do you think are ringleaders and their bully boys?"

"Thirty, maybe forty."

"Problem will be separating the two," Kris muttered. The rain started getting heavy again; the last few hours had been just gray and misty. She tapped her commlink. "HQ, this is Ensign Longknife. I need to talk to the Colonel."

"Wait one," was the reply.

The wait was a lot less than a full minute. "Let me guess, Ensign, you want some more advice."

"Seems that way, sir."

"What's your situation?"

Kris reported on her earlier skirmish and what looked to be building up ahead of her. She emphasized the divided nature of the opposing force.

"I'd been hearing stories that some of the worst problems might be just hungry folks the local establishment here didn't view as deserving poor," the Colonel drawled. "You came up with some pretty cagey ideas here in town for feeding everyone, no questions asked. The level of violence went down as the number of full bellies went up. Think we can do the same out there?"

"Doubt it, sir. The murder and rapes out here have people polarized but good. A lot of them just want payback." *Like me.*

"You got yourself a tough tactical problem, Ensign," was his crisp reply.

It was nice not to face one of Father's rants about responding with her emotions rather than thinking with her head. "Doesn't help that I won't know where it is until it starts shooting at me," Kris answered, staying on the present problem, not rehashing a past that couldn't be helped. "I'd give my right arm just now for a Stoolpigeon."

"I figured you might be asking my advice at a time like this. Stoolbirds are too fragile for weather like this, but a big old Spy Eye can fly in a damn near hurricane. I ordered one out of storage on Wardhaven, almost a museum piece. It arrived last night. I'll have it over you in an hour."

"Thank you, Colonel," Kris breathed in half a prayer.

"Don't thank me until you've got yourself home."

"Any suggestions, sir?"

"None that you haven't already thought of. Try not to get any of your people killed. Try not to kill any more civilians than you have to. You know, the usual crap. Now, if you'll excuse me, I got a Spy Eye to launch, and I may be the only one here old enough to remember how to wind up the rubber band. Hancock, out."

Kris glanced around slowly, reviewing her assets and none too happy. Sleepy darts gave her the option to shoot them all and sort them out later, but the wind was kicking up. Low-powered sleepy darts would be blown all over the place and hit nothing. *Face it, Princess, this is going to be a live fire exercise.*

Hunching her shoulders against the rain, Kris stood. "Tom, let's mount 'em up."

Tom got to his feet, shook himself, glanced around. "I think I'm glad this problem is yours," he muttered. As he strode toward the trucks, he began the usual patter. "You heard the boss gal. We're out of here. Truck leaders, mount your teams." It didn't take long. The civilians gathered for a celebration. Some of the recruits looked to have gotten invited, but when their leaders hollered, they came. Tom was standing beside the lead truck, watching as the other ones filled up when Kris joined him. "So, what's it going to be? We going to use the Colonel's Spy Eye to go around these guys, or are we going to kill some more rapists?"

"What would you think of a fight?"

Tom blew out a long breath. "There's two hundred of them. There's only thirty of us, and we showed what a great bunch of berserkers we are this morning. Still, my da would whip my butt if I didn't come when a woman hollered for help. But my grandmother would be most disappointed if I didn't come home. Tell me, Ensign Longknife. What are we going to do?"

"The only thing we can do. Fight the ones that want a fight. Let the rest run if they will."

"Even if they're rapists? Even if they looked the other way?"

"We need to break the back of the bad guys. I want to get us home safe. I can't afford to worry about anything else."

"If we wanted to get home safe, we'd go around this bunch," Tom pointed out.

"We've got to break them." Kris would not give on that. "It will be easier doing it when they're all together."

Tom shook his head. "They'll massacre us. Half of us didn't get our damn safeties off. Most of the rest didn't have the stomach to shoot. At least this morning, it was thirty of us against twenty of them. Now there's two hundred of them!"

"That was this morning. We've been there once. Now we're veterans."

Tom looked at her like she was crazy.

"Or maybe I've just learned a few tough lessons. Listen, Tom, we have to do this."

Tommy looked at her for a long moment; then, with a rattling sigh, he said, "Didn't me da warn me. 'You take the king's coin, he gets you body and soul. And you do what you're told.'" Tom turned and went to his side of the truck.

Kris pulled herself up onto the running board, tried to shake as much water as she could from her poncho, and settled into her place with a smile of encouragement for the three recruits in the back. They were wriggling out of their ponchos, getting ready for a long ride back to base. The woman glanced at Kris, noticed that she was not doffing her slicker. The recruit's eyes grew wide. The friendly chatter that had started in the backseat fell to silence as the men followed her glance to Kris.

"Oh shit," the failed hero snorted.

"Marines, I want truck six up behind me." Kris spoke softly into her mike.

"That mean you're gonna have some targets for us, ma'am?"

"We'll be stopping a few klicks down the road to talk about that," Kris advised everyone on net. Silence came back to her.

The five trees stood alone beside the road, open fields giving Kris a good view of anyone approaching. Their bedraggled canopy gave some protection from the rain. Kris gathered her crew around her by truck teams; they came quietly. She waited until they stood around her, then she told them to take a seat. She wanted them comfortable. Besides, it was harder to run when you were sitting down.

"Between us and the port are about two hundred bandits," Kris said bluntly. There were low whistles and bitter swearing at her announcement.

"The good news is that not all of them are armed and most of the rest aren't really interested in opposing us. Thirty, maybe forty of them are looking for a fight. The others are just part of the crowd that's hungry and wants to eat. You saw this morning how hard our prisoners fought once their leaders were down." That got Kris several thoughtful nods. Kris quickly filled her team in on the makeup of their opposition.

"So most of them are just hungry farmhands the farm owners here tossed out when things got hard," Courtney said.

"Most. Not all. The guys who sold the IDents off planet, the toughs that are their enforcers, those guys can't have us moving freely here. If we show everyone that we can, they lose, and civilization starts to win again on Olympia." Kris paused to let that sink in. Then she took a deep breath.

"I made a mistake this morning. I threw you into the middle of a firefight without preparing you for it. Some of you may have heard about the hostage rescue op I ran a few weeks ago." That got nods. "Me and my team had four days to prepare for that." And most of her marines were four- or six-year vets. No need to mention that. "I should have given you more time to get ready, to familiarize yourself with your weapon. It's one thing to be issued a rifle. It's another thing to be comfortable with the idea of using it. That's why we stopped here. I'm assigning a marine to each truck team of Navy recruits. I want the marine and your petty officer to take you through all the switches and doodads on your rifle. Yeah, they did that in boot camp, but how many of you ever thought you'd need to use a piece of obsolete technology like this?" she said, grinning as she hefted her rifle. "I don't know about you, but I did some quick studying when I pulled the short straw and found myself stuck with a night drop and hostage rescue." That drew nervous laughs.

"Finally, I want each of you to fire a full clip of darts. There's nothing like the feel of a rifle actually kicking back against your shoulder, the sight of darts hitting what you aimed at. It lets you know you really can do this." Kris paced off two steps, made them move their heads to follow her.

"One last thing. I'm assigning the marines and petty officers the responsibility for putting down the boss men among the bandits and their thugs. The job for the rest of you is to put rounds in the air, in the ground, knocking splinters out of trees, show anyone willing to cut and run that now would be a good time to do just that. Put the fear of the Navy in them. You send the hungry ones running, and the marines and your petty officers will put down the ones that need it real bad."

"If we see someone not running, can we shoot 'em, too?"

"Have at them. Just anyone who shows you their back, let them run."

"Where can they run to, ma'am?"

"I think the last farm would be glad to take them in."

The troops glanced around at their other team members. Some actually had nervous smiles for one another. Quiet. "We can do that." "Yeah, that's not too hard." "If they run, let 'em. That's okay."

Kris let that sink in for a moment, then sent each truck team to its own corner of the small wood. Tom seemed actually happy to take the lead for Truck One. Kris moved from one team to another, observing, encouraging, stomping firmly on one marine who exuded the impression that his survival of the Corps basic training gave him the right to lord it over his navy students. The next marine had a better handle on training. Weapons skill was a light to be shared, not a hammer to belabor the student.

Kris stood beside her hero wanna-be as he sent rounds into a clump of weeds two hundred yards out. "Good shooting," she said.

"Not bad for a coward," he spat into the rain.

"I don't see a coward."

"I locked up this morning. Didn't do a damn thing."

"How long did that shoot last, nine, ten seconds?"

"I don't know. Seemed like forever," the guy said, staring at his rifle.

"I checked my rifle's computer. Nine point seven seconds from first shot to last. Didn't give a hero or coward much time to react. This time, I'll see that you get more time going in. Then you tell me which you are, coward or hero."

"You think so?"

"I wouldn't have you wasting my ammunition if I didn't. How many rounds you shoot in boot camp?"

"I was only halfway through, ma'am, when they pulled me off for this. Never did get to shoot."

Damn! Kris suppressed a snarl at herself. *I should have rechecked this crew's records before I took them on the road.* "Now you have fired a rifle. What do you think of it?"

"It's sweeter than any sim."

"Then keep shooting," Kris said and continued her walk. By the time each recruit, including the marines, had fired off a clip, there was an air of confidence mixing with the rain.

As rifle practice finished up, the first Spy Eye coverage of the problem woods came in. It showed a lot of thermal images and human heartbeats. At least this bunch of robber barons hadn't thought to invest in high tech. Thank God the Colonel had arranged for the Spy Eye. While the last rounds were fired, Kris and Tom studied the enemy's array. "Sloppy," Kris concluded. "They're expecting us to come right up the road."

"Yes," Tom agreed. "But this bunch seems a bit smarter than the last. They haven't cut down a tree. They want us to drive into the trap before they start shooting."

Kris shrugged. "So we make their trap into our trap." As she turned back to the trucks, her eyes fell on one of their dejected prisoners, leaning half out of the back, trying to catch water on his tongue.

"Tom, we're going into a fight. POWs cannot be subjected to hostile fire. Tie them to the trees here. If things work out, we'll come back and get them. Otherwise, I'll call that last farm, tell him to come pick them up. Any he wants to offer a job to, we'll call it even. Any he wouldn't hire, I'll pick up next week."

Tommy eyed the prisoners for a moment, then brought his hand up in salute. "Yes ma'am."

"Now let's put it to some real bastards," Kris said, returning the salute.

12

Kris halted the convoy as they approached the walnut orchard. The trees were orderly, row on row, when seen from above. Ragged with leaves, none showed fruit. The road made a slight jog as it entered what had once been a swamp, setting the rows at an angle, hiding the trucks as they stopped in line.

Kris had her battle planned.

The bandits were about a klick into the woods, arranged loosely in two lines, one to the right, the other to the left of the road. The first two rows of trees closest to the road were empty. Most of the hostiles were bunched in the third, fourth, or fifth line of trees. This uncomplicated array had been invented by hill tribes thousands of years ago and used again and again for the simple reason that it worked.

If the target didn't know you were waiting for them.

Kris did.

"Tom, take half the team and advance slowly on both sides of the road. I'll take the marines and two other truck teams on a fast walk behind their right. We'll open fire, driving them left and back. You can't tell it through the rain, but there're some hills off to the left. If we can get them running that way, they won't stop until they're long gone."

"We can do that," Tom agreed.

Dismounted, the troops spread out, the rain and wind lashing at their ponchos. Courtney's truck team and half of another took the far left flank. Tom took the right side of the road with another seven troopers. That left Kris with fourteen, herself included, to begin the flanking maneuver. She had them count off by twos to form fire teams. "You ones are Fire Team A. Twos are Fire Team B. Remember that, and move when I order you to."

She gave her nervous hero-to-be a reassuring pat as she went down the line and took her place at its front before ordering them to follow her. With luck, she wasn't leaving Tom to face all the bad guys. But then, that was what Custer thought when he left Reno attacking the front and went off searching for a flank and found only oblivion. Kris shook away that thought; she had the Sky Eye. It showed her where every one of the bad guys and not-so-bad guys was. She didn't have to worry about blundering into them before she wanted to. Technology was good.

The reader with the Sky Eye feed went blank as Kris passed the twentieth row of trees and was preparing to turn into the orchard. She made the turn, with thirteen troopers following right behind her, as she called headquarters.

"I know, I know, we lost the picture, too," the Colonel answered. "It's ancient software, and we're having to emulate the hardware here to even get it talking this much to our net. We're rebooting everything. Give us five minutes. By the way, I like your deployment. Flank them, get them running, good psychology."

"I'm kind of counting on the Spy Eye to let me know about any surprises."

"You'll know when it's back as soon as I do."

"Thanks, sir. Things are getting kind of busy here. Call me when the Sky Eye's back."

"Good luck, Ensign."

With her airborne intelligence gone, Kris reverted to the

old-fashioned approach. Two of her marines looked like
they might have had some outdoors experience; she designated them her scouts and sent them ahead of her. She let
them get five trees up, and one over before she moved her
tiny main force forward again. They were supposed to be
fifteen trees behind the ambush. Still, all it took was someone looking for a private place to take a crap, and Kris's
surprise was blown.

The rain fell in sheets. The trees shivered in the gusty
wind. The orchard stank of mud and swamp. Kris could
hardly see her scouts; a herd of elephants could have
stampeded by just out of sight, and she would never have
heard them. Deaf and blind, Kris's troops plodded along
behind her. There was no time to waste. Sooner or later, the
bad guys would start wondering what was holding up the
trucks.

"Spy Eye's back," was all the Colonel said.

"Thanks," was Kris's own short response. She shaded
the reader against the rain and didn't much like what it told
her. She'd gone too far into the orchard. She was about
halfway down the ambush. If she hit them from where she
was, there was a good chance some of the bandits would
flee right into Tom's troops. That, of course, assumed whoever was leading the opposition didn't get his hundred
moving *at* her. If he did, Kris was open to envelopment on
either flank. Should she fall back a bit?

"Scout One here."

"Yes," Kris whispered. Scout one was ahead of her, and
closest to the ambush.

"I got two very chummy bad guys headed my way.
Make that bad guy and bad girl."

"Get down," Kris said, probably unnecessarily.

"That's what he just did to her."

Kris signaled everyone down, then went to ground herself behind a too damn thin tree trunk. She checked her Spy
Eye, found her scout, found two more rapidly beating hearts,
and took a sight in that direction. Movement drew her eye.
Yep, there was the couple. That was the problem with an

orchard. Little underbrush. At this level, all that impeded the eye was a few tree trunks. And rain. Lots of rain.

Kris hunched down where she was, trying to make herself invisible. Behind her, the column did the same, as much as city-raised kids could. Kris concentrated on the pair ahead of her. She'd read in some women's magazine the percent of men that kept their eyes open versus the ones that shut them at moments like these. She forgot which type was supposed to be the better lover. She just hoped this guy was one of the eyes-shut types.

Then the wind died down, and someone behind Kris sneezed.

With the rain and wet, colds were epidemic on Olympia. And about the time they got the right vaccination for one flavor of virus, Olympia sprouted another. The corpsmen were going crazy generating new vaccines. Everyone had to put up with a cold for a couple of days each month. Kris hoped that bad boy up ahead figured it was one of his own.

Bad boy did lose interest, but his first glance was back at the ambush. The girl said something. He shushed her. Still mounted, he picked up his gun, and this time his scan was in Kris's direction. Kris thumbed the safety off her rifle but didn't dare move it. She waited.

The man shouted something, rolled off the girl, and fired two rounds in a direction Kris had no troops. "Keep it cool, crew," Kris whispered on net. "He's firing at ghosts. Let's not give him something real to shoot at."

The girl didn't get up, seemed to be encouraging him to finish what he started. But the man was on his feet now, pants down around his boots, gun out, he advanced a few short paces toward Kris, eyes roving the woods. When his head quit moving, his eyes were locked on her. His rifle was half up; now he brought it to his shoulder, aiming at Kris.

For a second, they stared at each other as Kris brought her rifle up. She knew he'd beat her, but she had to try.

Then his head vanished as a scout took him down in a blaze of darts.

That brought the girl up on her knees, one hand grabbing for her pants, the other stuffed in her mouth to stifle a scream. She whirled in place and started half running, half crawling back to the ambush.

Kris flipped her rifle to sleepy darts and sent a shower at the girl. Wind blew them all to hell, but three of them ended up sticking out of the girl's bare rump. She collapsed into the mud and slid into a tree.

"Flank group, advance with me, in waves. Fire Team B, prepare to provide cover fire from this tree line on my command. Fire Team A, advance with me. Now!" Kris was up and running as she finished the last word. Her team was a bit slower, but they were up by the time she was down.

"Hold your fire, you damn idiots," a voice bellowed against the wind. "The trucks aren't here yet. Who's shooting?"

"I think it's Kars. He and a squeeze headed back of the line a minute ago," another voice shouted.

"Well, tell him to get his ass back up here."

Kris took advantage of the confusion to advance Fire Team B to the tree row ahead and was taking A Team on a double jump before a startled bandit loomed in front of her.

She shot him.

"Weapons free. I repeat, this is Ensign Longknife. Shoot 'em if you got 'em." Unfortunately, there weren't many targets. She was still a dozen rows to the rear of the ambush, more than 300 meters. Too far in this visibility. Sporadic fire came from beside her and ahead of her, but the only thing taking hits were the trees. Waving Fire Team B forward, Kris contributed a few rounds, more to keep heads down than hit any target.

"They're behind us, you idiots," the first voice was shouting off to Kris's right. "Turn around. Shoot."

"Scouts, whoever is doing the shouting is close on your front. Drop him if you can."

Five trees to Kris's right, two uniformed figures glided forward, bodies low, guns level. "We're looking for him, ma'am."

Now it was Kris's turn to advance her line. She waved them forward. "Spens, watch our left for encirclement."

"Been looking for that, ma'am, stretched us out that way. We're kind of thin." Kris's left flank, and her connection to Tom's center, reported.

Kris went to earth beside a trunk maybe eight rows back from the ambush. On her front, people were moving toward her. She scanned along the line, sending a burst into a tree here, the ground there. People anywhere near her hits were dropping to the ground as splinters showered them, mud sprayed them. One man, behind the rest, shouted at them, waved his gun. Kris drew a solid sight picture on him. He went over backward as three rounds took him full in the chest.

Five people took one look at him and ran. More hugged the ground, tried to burrow into the mud. Kris sent a long burst into the trees above them, and a half dozen took to their heels. Kris ignored them and checked to her right. More movement.

"Fire Team B, join us. Let's hold this row of trees."

She waved the second half of her command forward, signaling the two closest to her to go to her right. Her troops were spread too damn thin. Kris pulled up her reader to check the Sky Eye view. The hostiles seemed disorganized in front of her, some moving forward, others back. She shifted the view to check things out in front of Tom.

The screen went blank.

"Colonel," she squeaked.

"We're rebooting."

"It'll be over by then," Kris snarled, shoving her reader back in her pocket.

"I have a lot of fire and movement on my front," Courtney hollered on net. "Lots of people shooting and moving my way. I think they're trying to go around me."

"Discourage them," Kris ordered.

"I saw a couple try to run. One of their own shot 'em. I got him, but there's a lot of them, and I'm not sure I can hold." Courtney's words were punctuated by fire.

"Damn, why can't a plan ever hold together?" Kris snapped. She glanced to her right. The two marine scouts were holding there, supported by two navy types. Yep, one of them was her hero wanna-be. "Navy and Marines to my right, you will hold this flank as we advance. Understood?"

She got four yeses. No shakes in the voices now.

"Fire Teams A and B, we've got to herd these bastards a bit faster than planned. We will advance by fire and movement to the road. Team A, prepare to advance. On my order, A Team advance. Now."

Kris was up, shouting, firing at anything that moved. Behind her, half her team fired as well. Ahead of her, the advancing hostiles stopped in place, apparently startled by the sudden appearance of so many—or so few—shooters on their front. Kris went to ground well away from a tree trunk; she wanted a clear field of fire.

"B Team, prepare to advance. Advance. Now!"

They came out of their positions, shouting, shooting. Kris swept her sights over her front. A short burst sent four running, rifles tossed. A man turned to gun them down. Kris got him first. Another man was shouting, waving his hands as others fled by him. Kris drew a bead on him, but he went down as someone else beat her to the trigger. Kris kept searching.

Two people huddled on either side of a tree trunk. Both were shooting as fast as they could pull the trigger. Kris sent a burst into the trunk, shattering bark and splinters over them. They ducked. One was on his feet in a second, running, his rifle left behind. The other one shouted something, then went back to shooting. Kris put a burst between his eyes as her magazine ran dry. Reloaded, Kris shouted, "A Team," as she got to her knees, "prepare to advance." The next tree row would put them damn close to the hostiles. "Advance. Now!"

Kris fired a long, high burst as she raced forward, past the tree row occupied by her troops and into the space beyond. A pair in front of her threw up their hands and fell to their knees. Kris would have sleepy darted them, but there was no time for that now. "Run! Damn you!" she shouted.

Instead, they fell on their faces in the mud as bullets smashed into the tree near them. Kris spotted the shooter and sent him sprawling backward with a long burst.

Kris slid to ground behind a tree trunk. "B Team, prepare to advance. Advance. Tom, what's it look like on your front?"

"Damned if I know," was an unusual reply from the ensign. "We have people all over the place. Some running. Some advancing. Kris, I have no idea what is happening."

"Courtney, can you hold?"

"I've pulled half of us back so that they have a longer walk to get around us. I think more of them are running than fighting. Maybe. Just a second." Lots of rapid small arms fire over Courtney's live mike. "Yeah, more are running."

"Scouts, how is the right flank?"

"Plenty of targets, ma'am. Someone's pushing them at us, and I can't seem to find the bastard. We could use any spare help you got."

Kris stood up, trying to listen to the sounds of the battle around her. Damn! What she'd give for thirty seconds of Sky Eye feed. The wind whipped the rain in her face as she turned to her right flank, bringing with it the crackle of small arms fire. She'd robbed Peter to pay Paul, helping out Courtney on her left. Now it sounded like her right was going all to hell. "Spens, you take charge of this line, link up with Ensign Lien, and keep pushing the bandits toward the hills."

"Yes ma'am."

"I'm taking the three Navy I can see," Kris said, signaling the only trigger pullers in sight; one was a marine. "Wherever the other two marines are, fall out of line and join me on the right."

Yes, ma'ams answered her.

Kris dropped back through the orchard rows, collecting her handful around her. The sound of fire grew louder. She kept her crew moving but did not return fire, even though an occasional stray fusillade came their way. This was her last reserve.

Whoever was hitting her right still could roll up her flank; the day was not over. Her one hope was to hit them so suddenly that they broke and ran before they knew what faced them. Through rain-dripping goggles, Kris struggled to make out forms ahead of her, heat images, movement, fire. Her front came to her in a kaleidoscope of light and darkness with no possible pattern.

"Ma'am, this is Petro, I'm in the lead. I think I can see one of our guys ahead of me."

"Scout One, can you see us yet?"

After a pause, "Negative, ma'am."

"Let's go another tree row," Kris ordered.

"Petro, ma'am, that sure looks like Navy ahead of me. He's firing to my left, and I'm taking a lot of incoming from there."

"I see you now," Scout One announced.

"Okay, everyone, load a full magazine," Kris ordered, "and get a second one handy. Anyone dry?"

That got no answer.

"On my mark, hose them down, empty a full clip. Then we reload and charge. Any questions?"

None.

Kris loaded her own new magazine. That left her one last clip of 200 rounds and whatever was left in the one she'd taken out. It was going to be close.

"On my mark. Three, two, one, mark." Around Kris the woods came alive with one continuous explosion. Like a jackhammer from hell, each rifle stitched the air, woods, flesh, with one continuos sweep. Kris had read about mad minutes. The M-6 didn't need a minute to empty a 200-dart clip. The fire from Kris's ten troopers raised the mad minute to new levels of insanity and gave back a good thirty seconds.

Kris's rifle closed on an empty chamber. She yanked out the old clip and drove home a fresh one. "Charge," she shouted, coming to her feet. "Up and at them," she screamed. "Go, go! Charge 'em," and a roar that said nothing and meant only insanity came over the net as her command was obeyed.

Here and there survivors of the slashing volley hugged the ground, trembling, trying to raise their hands. A man stood, screaming at the others to follow him. Kris got him in her sights, but he was hit from so many different angles that he couldn't fall but danced a macabre jig, dead but not allowed to drop. The bandits farther back were running. Most had already thrown away their weapons. Not all. Kris hit her mike.

"Those with a weapon will be shot," rang through the woods, overpowering rain and wind. "Throw down your weapon, and you will not be harmed. Keep it, and you will die."

Most of the runners with guns took only a second to correct their error. A few did not. Maybe they were too confused to notice what was still in their hands. Maybe they were the bully boys and could not think of facing the world unarmed. There was no time to ask. Kris and other sharpshooters put them down quickly. A few of the armed runners who were not among the first to die took the extra moment that chance gave them to correct their blunder. Others didn't. More died.

"The Sky Eye is back," came quietly in Kris's ear, reminding her that she was supposed to be the commander here. Reluctantly, she lowered her rifle, mastered the blood thirst raging in her gut, and fought to regain the calm that a commander needed. She took two deep breaths as she pulled her reader from her pocket. Rain and mud splattered it; Kris stepped beneath a tree and stooped beside its thin trunk for cover.

The bandits were running from her troops all along the line, fleeing for the hills to the west of the orchard. It looked like they were making a beeline for a stream and the cover of its wooded ravine. She could head them off, easily. Then she remembered; this wasn't a battle for a body count. Most if not all of those running were harmless. "Colonel, can you get me a scan that shows if any of those are armed?

"They using old-fashioned metallic hunting rifles?"

Kris glanced around, saw five or six dropped weapons. "They look to be."

"Magnetic mass is very low," the Colonel answered. "My call would be they're down to their bootlaces and belt buckles."

"Thanks, Colonel, I'd rather not pursue. Casualty report," Kris changed the subject with hardly a moment's thought.

"I have two wounded, one kind of bad," Courtney reported. "Corpsman is already here."

"Roger. Anyone else?"

"One flesh wound," Tom reported.

"Oh shit, this is Scout One. I've got . . . I've got . . ."

"Where are you?" Kris turned. The riflewoman to her right was waving and pointing out of sight. Dread growing, Kris called up her last reserve of energy to jog where she was pointed.

She found the three she had left to hold the right flank standing over a body. One, the woman that had been behind Kris for the drive, sat on her knees, tears mixing with the rain. The marine that had been Scout One looked up as Kris joined them. "He was okay. I swear to God, he was okay. I saw him start to stand up when you ordered the charge. I figured he was right with us. I thought he was."

Kris stared down at the recruit she had only known as the wanna-be hero. The bullet had taken him in the forehead. He'd fallen on his back, so his blue eyes were open, staring expectantly into the gray rain. His belt clips were gone; the magazine in his rifle must have been his last. He'd more than made up for this morning's freeze. *How will I explain to his mother, his father, what he won and what he lost this day?*

There were a thousand feelings, questions, demands tumbling in Kris's brain. But not now. Now she had a battle to clean up. "Tom, get the trucks moving in here. See that the wounded are collected by the road for pickup. All hands, we've got a lot of firearms lying around. Form a picket line, police up this mess. I want all guns left behind rendered inoperable."

"Ma'am, I've got a real bleeder on my hands," Courtney said.

"I know, Petty Officer. We will police the area until the wounded are loaded. What we bust, we bust. What we don't get to, we'll leave to rust. Good enough."

"Sorry, ma'am," Courtney whispered.

"You three," Kris indicated the survivors of her right wing, "you bring in . . . him." She didn't even know his name.

"Willie, ma'am," the woman looked up. "Willie Hunter."

Kris left them wrapping him in his poncho. She moved with the others through the woods, picking up rifles, stripping them of firing pins. She slammed a gun against a tree, hard. It felt good as the action gave way, the butt flew off. Kris got in some very good whacks before Tom called from the road. "Longknife, I have all the wounded loaded. We need to move out."

"Okay, crew, we've done good, now let's go. Everybody, back to the bus," she shouted. Around her, tired troops finished what they were doing and turned to the road.

"Tom, as soon as you have five people in the next two trucks, you get them and the truck with the wounded moving."

"Are you staying behind?"

"No, I'll get everyone moving right behind you. But the wounded, they go first, and they go fast.

"Yes ma'am."

Kris was just in sight of the road as the first three trucks took off. If she knew Tom, he'd be driving the truck with the wounded. It would have been interesting to be in it, to see how much Tom went for speed and how much he swerved to make the ride more comfortable to those in back. Poor Tommy, he was spending a lot of time torn between two goods.

Kris made a call to the last farm as she waited for her fire teams to trail out of the woods. Yes, the owner would

pick up her prisoners from the first fight. Kris signed off as
the scouts came out of the woods with their heavy burden;
she waved them to the last truck. They settled Willie in the
back, then refused to ride in the cab, preferring to share the
wet, cold truck bed with their fallen friend. Kris started
to join them, then realized that there was no one to keep
Spens company. It had been a long day; the drive back
would not be easy. Someone had to keep him awake.

Kris climbed into the cab. She wriggled out of her poncho as Spens joined the tag end of the line moving out.
"Think we turned a profit today?" her accountant asked her.

"Think you'll be happy keeping to your computer
ledgers after today?" she asked back.

"I don't know. It was kind of nice, getting out here, seeing the look on the kids', women's faces when we arrived
with the first food they'd had in a long, long time."

"And this?" Kris asked, nodding to the woods as they
drove out of them.

"We hurt the bad guys, didn't we? They won't mess
with the Navy next time we come out, will they?"

Kris thought for a long moment. They'd come out here to
feed the starving . . . and they had. They'd had a chance
offered them to make things better . . . and they had. The
price seemed high to Kris at this moment. "Yes," she agreed.
"They won't mess with the Navy."

13

The truck drove slowly into the compound like the hearse it was. Kris dismounted and moved to help those in back remove the body of her one casualty. Colonel Hancock, however, was in her way. "How'd it go?" he said.

"Not bad, I guess," Kris answered, leaning around the Colonel to watch as three spacers from the base helped with the poncho-wrapped burden.

"Let them take care of that," the Colonel told her.

"Him," Kris corrected. Since the Colonel showed no intent of getting out of her way, she turned toward the headquarters. "I'd better look in on my wounded."

"They're being taken care of. I want to talk to you in my office."

"I'll be there in a few minutes."

"Like last time?" the Colonel asked with an arched eyebrow.

Kris turned right and headed for sick bay. The Colonel's office was left; he followed her. As she expected, Tom was applying his asteroid miner first aid training, helping one corpsman while the doc and other corpsman struggled to

keep Courtney's bleeder alive. Kris paused at each of the
wounded, told them they'd done good. One picked that
moment to go into shock. As Tom rushed in to start treatment; the Colonel edged Kris out of sick bay with an iron
grip on her elbow.

A moment later she was seated in his office, a large
tumbler in her hand. The Colonel produced a bottle of fine,
single malt whiskey and popped the cork. The aroma filled
the room even before he began pouring Kris's tumbler to
the lip. He then did the same for himself, raised the amber-
filled glass in a toast, and said, "You did a very good job
out there."

Kris eyed the glass for a moment. How many times had
she almost gotten killed today? Did it matter if she finished
it stone cold sober or not? She took a long sip. It was
fine whiskey, flowing smoothly down to warm her stomach, massage out the knots. She sighed and relaxed into her
chair. "I guess so."

"No, Ensign, *you* did good."

Kris took another sip. If she'd done so good, why did
she feel so . . .? That was the problem; she didn't know
how she felt. Maybe Grampa Trouble would, but she didn't.
All of it was too new, too strange, too scary. She did know
what Grampa Trouble would say though. "A lot of people
did good today. How do I write them up for medals, sir?
Everyone on those trucks deserves something."

The Colonel took a long pull on his drink. "And they'll
all get the Humanitarian Aid Medal."

Kris almost threw her glass. "Hell, sir, they give that
medal for sitting on your backside counting the aid boxes
on Wardhaven. My people were out in the mud, getting
shot at, outnumbered eight to one, in the finest tradition of
this bloody service . . . sir." She finished her bit of tirade
with a bigger gulp than she'd intended. White fire seared
her belly. At least the pain felt good. After today, she ought
to hurt somewhere.

The Colonel took another sip. "I know, Kris, but was it
combat?"

"I don't know what the hell else it was, sir. If that was a noncombat situation, someone forgot to tell the damn bullets."

He nodded. "I know. So are you, then, prepared to declare that those citizens are in armed rebellion against the lawful government of Olympia?"

Kris blinked twice at that sentence, tried to parse its meaning, and gave it up as a lost cause. She retreated into a sip of her own drink. "I haven't seen much 'lawful government.'" She made the words bitter. "Where are they?"

"Around here somewhere," the Colonel waved his tumbler at everything and nothing. "All they have is a legislature. By their constitution it can only meet for one six-week session every three years. They had the last one before the volcano blew. They can't have another for a year and a half unless they hold a new election. You want to run an election in this mess?"

"There must be some option on the books to cover a mess like this." Kris remembered how her father had finagled Wardhaven's laws to get what he wanted. That brought her to a quick stop. She eyed the Colonel.

"'They govern best by governing least,'" he scowled. "It's the first sentence of their Constitution. They are permitted to have exactly one hundred pages of laws. Size of pages, margins, and font size specified to prevent cheating. The founders of this colony were quite adamant that they were not going to have any big government here. No chief executive, no prime minister, just a legislature and its laws."

"Then who asked the Society for help?"

"As I got it, one of the big farmers up north knows someone on Wardhaven who's in the government. Wardhaven sponsored this mission in the Senate. Might be one of your relatives?"

"On my mother's side," Kris growled and washed her mouth with whiskey. "Father's side would have thought this through better. So, let me see if I've got this right. We are here to help a government that for all practical purposes doesn't exist, and these people shooting at us can't be considered rebels 'cause there isn't enough of a government for them to rebel against."

"Begin to understand why I was falling asleep at my desk, trying to figure out how to get a handle on this bag of snakes?"

Kris had never had a senior officer come so close to a bald admission of failure. To hide her embarrassment, she took a long pull on her drink and changed the subject. "We'll need to get more convoys moving, sir. They are starving out there. Adults are eating grass, but kids don't have the tummies for it." There, that was something she could tackle with both hands.

"Already checked. Lien's mechs will have fifteen trucks usable tomorrow. I figure three convoys."

"Which one do you want me to lead?" Kris asked, watching the whiskey swirl in her glass.

"None. I'm restricting you to base."

Kris bristled. "Sir, I fired when fired upon. We were engaged by the bandits. And I did my damnedest to keep civilian casualties to a minimum." Kris didn't know how to count her lone dead. Even one seemed more than Olympia was worth. Yet, against those odds, how could she have done better? *Why do I feel so lousy about it?*

The Colonel waved his drink to calm her. "I know. I told you, you did good today. Still, I'm ordering you and Ensign Lien to limit your activities to the base."

"Why, sir?"

"You have become a very high-value target, Ensign Longknife. You beat the bad guys like a drum. There's a lot of them that want you dead. I send out convoys now, the bandits know not to mess with them. I send you out, and some dude will try to get you to make himself a bad reputation. Whether you like it or not, you *are* that Longknife. The one that beat them at Wildebeest Wallow. I've got a battalion of highlanders due in from LornaDo in a few days. When they get here, I'm sending you and Lien back to Wardhaven, and I intend to send you back alive."

"You're relieving me, sir!"

"Ensign, I'm rotating you. You weren't planning on making Olympia your career, were you?"

"No sir, I just didn't expect to be out of here so quickly."

"It happens on these emergency ops, Kris, especially when there's a budget mess tied in. Nobody stays for more than a month. Don't you think your time's about up?"

Kris tried to think of how long it had been. She couldn't. "Nelly, how long have I been here?"

"One week, six days, eight hours . . ."

"Enough," the Colonel growled and took a drink. "It's bad enough getting that from troopers, now I get it from their personal computers. The Corps ain't what it used to be."

Kris took a slow pull on her near-empty glass. "Who will take out the convoys?"

"Those other ensigns have had it too easy. I think I'll take one. Done enough paperwork. I don't know if I dare send Pearson. People might refuse the food."

They shared a smile. "Send Pearson," Kris said. "She needs to see what reality is like. Might help her with her policies. With the Identacards stolen, there's no way to validate who's getting the food. Can't we just declare everyone on this planet starving and call it quits?"

"Can't. Everyone isn't starving," the Colonel pointed out.

"Outside our mess," Kris narrowed it down.

"There are some civilians who haven't missed a meal, Kris. Some folks have been eating pretty high on the hog. Maybe not as well now that you've got the Navy rations locked down." Again the Colonel raised his glass in salute. Both drained their tumblers. "Another," the Colonel said, offering the bottle.

Kris eyed the swirling liquid. The drinker takes the first drink, the second drink takes the drunk. She remembered how hard it had been to dry out. How humiliated she'd been when Harvey or one of the maids had to clean up after her. Did she want the Colonel to see *that* Longknife? "Thank you, sir, but I think I'll go for a walk."

The Colonel refilled his glass. "Watch your back, Ensign."

"I will," Kris said. *Problem is, I don't know which back is most at risk, my ass or my pride, or my . . . What?*

Kris found herself outside the HQ, standing in the rain. Since she'd left her poncho in the truck, her clothes quickly got soaked, but the whiskey kept her warm. She could go for a walk. She'd done a lot of walking lately. She'd seen a few men vomiting in back alleyways, staggering down streets. What with food for the belly so scarce, most of Olympia was on the wagon. But there was always a bit of the drink when someone really needed it. Kris really needed it tonight; she started walking. "Nelly, I don't want to talk to anyone. Take me off net."

Kris was half a block out before the rain got harder, and her conscience got ahold of her, and she turned back to her room. Dripping wet, she threw herself on her bed, stared up at the ceiling, and tried to get hold of herself. She'd done good. She'd lost a trooper, maybe two. She'd fed some very hungry kids. She'd mowed down people whose only crime was hunger. She'd beat the bad guys. Her head spun, lubricated by the Colonel's whiskey. She remembered chattering squirrels back in the garden at Nuu House, chasing each other's tails. So long as all these thoughts tumbled over and over in her mind, she didn't have to face any one of them. There was a water mark on the ceiling of her room. She wondered where it came from. She closed her eyes, but she couldn't sleep. She'd done good today. She'd killed and almost gotten herself killed. She'd . . .

"Kris, can we talk?" came after a slight tap at her door.

"I don't want to talk to anyone," Kris shouted.

"Tom would really like to talk to you," Nelly said softly.

"So you told him where I was."

"No, ma'am, I took you off net as you requested. However, he interrogated your room's motion detector. I assume he concluded you were in here." Kris scowled down at where Nelly hung from her shoulders. Apparently, her personal computer had not exercised its full initiative to protect her privacy.

"Kris, I'd really like to talk to you," Tommy repeated.

"And I'd really like for everyone to just go away."

"Do Longknifes always get what they want?"

"No, but this Longknife is in a lousy mood and forgot to lock up her side arm. I'd go away if I was you."

"Haven't you noticed? I'm not you." Kris could almost see that lopsided grin of his. "I brought a bottle," he added.

That did complicate matters. Damn, she wanted another drink. "Open," she growled at the door.

There was Tommy, big grin and all. As he stepped through the door, he tossed a bottle at her. She caught it, then made a face as she read the label. "Sparkling water."

"Don't knock it. That's probably the only bottle of the stuff on this mud ball."

Kris aimed the bottle for Tommy's head, but he caught it anyway. "You mind if I tell the Colonel where you are?"

"Why would he care?" Kris spat.

"Because I kind of panicked him when he gave me a big drink and told me he'd shared one with you. A second later, he discovered just how much Nelly there can do. Which did not improve his attitude about rich girls in his Corps."

"I'm in the Navy, not his precious Corps."

"Can I call in?"

"Make your damn call."

Tom did. The Colonel sounded relieved and cut the call short so he could cancel the all-points alarm he'd sent out on her. "What's he so scared about?"

"You didn't jingle today."

"What's that got to do with it."

"If you didn't have any of those Wardhaven dollars, how were you going to pay for your drinks off base?"

"Which is why I'm not off base. You didn't think I was dumb enough to flash my credit card, did you?"

"I had an uncle who wasn't too thoughtful once he got a touch of the drink taken. I didn't know what you'd do."

"I came up here to get some dollars, then decided it wasn't worth going back out in the rain. There, you happy?"

Tommy settled onto the floor next to the door. Kris rolled over on her stomach, propped her chin on her hands, and stared back at him. "Shit of a day," Tommy said.

Kris was ready to mutter a nice nothing, like, "Wasn't it," but that wasn't what she felt. "How would you know?" she snapped. "You just did what you were told."

Tommy eyed her without flinching. "I guess I wasn't much of a backup."

"Didn't feel like much of one out there."

"Doc says Shirri will live." Tom changed the subject.

"That her name?"

"Jeb thinks we'll have fifteen trucks ready for tomorrow's run. Colonel says we can't do any more runs. We've got to share the fun with those other ensigns."

"Yeah." Kris wished she had more of the Colonel's whiskey.

"So when you going to share the pain?"

Kris blinked twice. "What pain?"

"I was trying to give Courtney all the support I could," Tom said, eyes locked on Kris, "but they just kept running at her side. Ignored mine, but all of them seemed to hit her. I slipped folks over to help, but there was just so many of them and so few of us."

"God, there were a lot of them," Kris said, eyes seeing the mud, the rain, the bodies. "How many did we kill?"

"I don't know."

"Nelly, how many did we kill?"

"I do not know, Kris. I have not analyzed the final Sky Eye take for bodies. Should I?"

Kris took in a deep breath, stared at a paint blemish above Tommy's head where the cleaning crew had scrubbed away paint as well as mildew. She shrugged. "It doesn't matter, does it, Tom? They'll still be dead and I'll still be alive and I'll never know if they did something that deserved dead or were just poor dumb slobs who were hungry."

A sigh rattled out of Tommy that would make any Irish mother proud. "No, we'll never know."

"I always end up alive. Someone else always ends up dead."

"Like Eddy," Tom didn't flinch as he used the banned word.

"Like Eddy," Kris whispered.

"So you're alive and wondering if you should get drunk, and they're dead and not all the whiskey you can drink will give Eddy a moment more of life," Tom lowered his gaze to the floor. "Won't help one of them out there rotting in the rain either."

"My, aren't you full of poetry tonight," Kris said.

"It's the truth, Kris. You're alive. I'm alive. They're dead. It happens that way. When a shaft blows out to vacuum, it kills some, and others live. The guy who stayed home sick lives. The gal who went for a new drill bit lives. The kid who slapped his faceplate down lives. The old-timer who took his helmet off 'cause he was sweating and knew it was safe . . . he dies. And there's nothing that anyone can do about it. Maybe we raise a glass to them tonight, but we're all glad that we're alive. That it was them who died and not us. And if it had been the other way around, they'd be raising glasses to us."

Tom shrugged and looked Kris in the eye. "It's always better to be raising a glass than not."

"Is it? Is it better to be alive? What makes you so sure? You ever tried dead? I think I will have that drink," Kris said, throwing her feet over the side of the bed.

Tom didn't stand, but shook his head. "You've had enough."

"There's no such thing as enough."

"The dead have had all they need. And the living have had enough."

Kris stared at him, sitting across the room from her. He didn't tense, didn't make any show of getting up. Still, she knew if she made for the door, he'd be there to stop her.

For a moment, she wondered if she could take him. Would he really fight to keep her sober tonight? She sat back down. "What are you feeling, Tom?"

"I don't know what I'm feeling. I'm wishing I'd stayed back home on Santa Maria. I'm wishing I'd never come someplace where people shot at me and I had to shoot back. Where there were people that I really wanted to shoot back at. You Longknifes make for a very confusing world."

Now it was Kris's turn to sigh. It was a genteel one. Ladylike. Mother would be proud. "I've read so many of the histories, so many books. They always tell of Grampa Ray and Trouble's battles. They never tell what it felt like afterward."

"How did they handle it?" Tom asked.

"I don't know. I just don't know." Kris rubbed her eyes, found herself suppressing a yawn. Maybe the drink was finally kicking in. "Now, why don't you just go away and let me sleep."

Without so much as a backward glance, he left her.

14

Kris awoke to no memory of dreams and only a slightly bad taste in her mouth; there were advantages to staying sober. Showered, dressed, and feeling painfully alive, she made her way to the mess hall. Maybe it was just her, but the troops seemed to have more spring to their step. Were their heads really held a bit higher? A glance out the window showed the same gray rain; that hadn't changed. The Colonel waved her to his table.

"You sleep well?" he asked. Kris took inventory and nodded. The Colonel measured her nod and found it satisfactory. "I checked on your wounded. All three are doing well."

"I'll drop by sick bay after breakfast," Kris said as she found herself hungry and dug into her meal.

The Colonel leaned back. "I hate to tell you, but I've got another difficult mission for you today." So why was he smiling?

"It can't be harder than yesterday."

"Much harder, but safer." If possible, the grin got wider.

"Colonel, has anyone ever complimented you on your wonderful sense of humor?"

He managed a bent frown for a moment. "No, don't recall any."

"Something you might want to think about," Kris paused for a protracted moment, then added the required "sir."

"Just for that, you get no more sympathy from me, Ensign. We've got a visiting do-gooder today, come a long, long way to see all the nice things we are doing with his donations. I want you to escort him around the place, show him what's going on, while I take a nice drive in the country."

Sounded like a thoroughly boring way to waste a day. "Who is this old nanny?"

"Not so old. You might find him cute. A Mr. Henry Smythe-Peterwald, the thirteenth of that name," the Colonel said. "Bad enough to saddle a kid with the same old same old, but to make him the thirteenth." The Colonel shook his head.

Kris managed to swallow what was in her mouth and to smile at the Colonel's attempted joke. *Oh Mother! All my dodging of this nice young man you're throwing at me, and now I've got to spend a day with him.* The fact that his father was at the top of Aunt Tru's list of people wanting Kris dead really shouldn't complicate the relationship, should it?

And you thought today would be safe, Colonel.

Kris saw to the trucks' load out, while Tom did a final check on their ready status. As the three convoys got ready to roll, she kept a smile on her face at the prospect of being chained to a desk while most of those who had been with her yesterday faced more muddy roads, swamps, and bandits. Kris stretched the laugh of offering to trade jobs with anyone about as far as the lame joke could go.

When the trucks headed out, she turned to her office. Jeb was waiting; they quickly went over today's schedule of drops to be unloaded, stored, and made ready for tomorrow's road runs. Spens was at his workstation outside her office; one trip out had been enough for her accountant. As an operations specialist, he brought order out of the information flooding battle boards. He was doing the same for her. He shook his head as she walked by.

"Something bothering you?" Kris asked.

"It's this junk they're shipping us. Twenty-year-old combat meals are just a bit harder to chew. But I have half a warehouse full of medical supplies past their expiration date. Look at this," he waved a printout. "Raw vaccine feed a month past its due date. Can we use that stuff?"

"Check with the pharmacy," Kris said, coming to look over his shoulder. Yep, half of Warehouse 3 was out-of-date junk. "Probably was expired when it was donated."

"By what, a week? Someone's using us for a dump!"

"No, someone's using us for a tax break for their generous donation," Kris spat.

"My old man probably suggested the scam," Spens growled. "And he wonders why I don't want his job."

Kris scowled at the printout with its indictment of the world she'd joined the Navy to get away from.

"Hey, look what the cat drug in," came cheerfully from behind her.

"I'd hoped for a somewhat better introduction than that."

Kris turned to see Tommy grinning and Henry Smythe-Peterwald the Thirteenth, arms folded, standing in her doorway. The finely sculptured handsomeness of him was a lot easier to take without Mother hanging on his elbow. Today he wore field dress, finely tailored and expensive. Kris remembered being similarly decked out by her mother for her hikes in the Blue Mountains back home.

She quickly swallowed a scowl at the memory, lest her visitor think it intended for him. "You don't have a visitor's badge. I'll take you over to the HQ and get you checked in," Kris said, falling back on standard procedures to give her brain a chance to catch up. "You'll want to see Commander Owen. He's in charge, since Colonel Hancock's out on a relief run."

"Can't we avoid all that? I can see paper pushing without leaving home," he said with just a hint of a scowl.

"What do you want to see?" Tommy asked, giving Kris a sidewise glance that yelled, *Besides a certain boot ensign.*

"Anything but my old man. What are you doing out here, Kris?" Henry quickly sidestepped Tommy.

"Whatever the Navy wants me to do, Henry. Joining the Navy looked like the best way to give Mother an early heart attack."

"Ah, our dedication to our parents' coronary health." He chuckled dryly. "So, we do have much in common. And call me Hank. Dad has a pretty solid lock on Henry."

"Sounds fine by me. Mother will love to hear of it."

"Your mom throwing you at me like my dad is throwing me?"

"With all the force of an asteroid catapult."

"Then I probably owe you an apology." Hank smiled softly.

"Given, taken, and returned," Kris said, offering her hand. He took it; for a moment she thought he might kiss it, but no, he just shook it firmly. No first impressions, Kris shouted to herself. She would let this man define himself, not take him on his parents' past history, Mother's illusions, or, for that matter, Auntie Tru's suspicions.

"So, what can we do for you?" Tommy said, bringing the handshake to an early halt.

"I think the idea is for me to do something for you. At least, that was how I talked Dad out of sending me off to run a plant start-up on Grozen. 'If we get our faces in the media for doing good, let's do it right,' I told him. So I have this ship full of various things we thought might come in handy."

"And when it's unloaded . . . ?" Kris asked.

"Then I go on to Grozen."

"How long do you think it will take to unload?" Tommy asked.

"How long do you think it will take me to figure out what's aboard it that is useful here?"

"A few hours," Tom said as Kris answered, "A few days."
Tom threw her a quizzical glance.

Well, no one said this young man was out to kill me.
"Spens here came across some interesting stuff this morning." Kris watched Hank's face while her accountant filled him in on the scam of the morning.

When Spens was done, the visitor tapped his commlink. "Ulric, we have any medical supplies in our cargo?"

"Several tons, sir."

"Send the data on them down here, including expiration dates to, what's your name?"

"Spens, sir."

"I have that address, sir."

"Good, Ulric. Make the Smythe-Peterwalds proud." He turned to Kris. "That should handle that."

Kris nodded. If there was a scam, that should put an end to it for at least today. "So, what would you like to see?"

"What your average day is like."

"That could get messy," Kris said.

"Or dangerous," Tom put in.

"I heard about yesterday. A real Wild West shoot-out."

"Something like that," Kris evaded.

"Why don't I show you where we rebuild trucks?" Tom put in.

"Not a bad place," Kris agreed. It would give her a chance to get her thoughts in order while Tom and Hank did that male bonding thing. More like male bashing, as Tom did his best to show the rich kid how little he knew.

"You've never stripped an engine?" Tom said fifteen minutes later, wiping oil from his hands.

"Never been close to one with its top off."

"Even a car engine?"

Hank stared out the garage door at nothing. "My chauffeur took care of that. Didn't yours, Kris?"

Kris read the *Help me,* there but wasn't about to throw Hank a line. "I helped our chauffeur change the oil, tune up the limos all the time." *Well, twice when Mother wasn't looking.*

"It helps when you get shipped trucks just this side of the junkyard," Tom put in.

With a huge sigh, Hank tapped his commlink. "Ulric, what's the usage on those trucks we have aboard?"

"Highest is fifteen point three kilometers, sir."

Hank tapped off with a satisfied smile. "I doubt if any of the thirty trucks I'm delivering will see the inside of this shop for a while. What else is on my tour of the seamy underside of relief work?"

Tom looked sorely distressed at being bested. His grin actually faltered for a full three seconds before it popped back to full force. Kris stepped in before someone got hurt. "Let me show you my ware yard." That moved the center of attention from Tom to her and gave her a chance to show off what she'd done. As Kris walked Hank around, she found him easy to talk to. Well, it was easy talking about what she was proud of, how she'd blended the warehouse workers she'd inherited, volunteers she'd acquired, and the handful of Navy guards she used to keep the place safe. In her life, she'd straightened up plenty of other people's campaigns or volunteer programs that one of Mother's friends had dreamed up but couldn't organize to save her life. This yard and the people it fed was her show.

It also gave her plenty of chances to point things out to Hank. And while he looked, she studied him. There was a wariness about the eyes in his perfectly sculptured face, but they were wide and expectant as he took in her work.

The walk-around also gave Kris a chance to compare the two men presently in her life: one boyish in his eagerness to make sure the other was no threat, the other self-contained and seemingly oblivious to anything but Kris's words, listening intently, never interrupting, always asking good questions that got her talking again when she ran out of things to say. A guy like this was easy to have around.

They finished up at the seawall, watching an unmanned drop ship on final approach. It splashed down, sending froth and spray flying into the pouring rain. A tug glided away from the marine railroad as soon as the supply ship came to a bobbing rest. "That's one of mine," Hank pointed out, "loaded with a something called famine biscuits. Each two hundred gram bar has a day's allotment of protein, vitamins, and minerals. Nice thing about them is that with water they expand in the stomach to make you feel like you've had a real meal."

"That will be a nice break from rice and beans," Tom agreed.

"What you doing with the landers when they're empty?"

That was a question for Kris. "We're recycling the air jell hulls," she pointed to where bales of the shredded stuff was stacked. "The engines we're reducing to carbon powder. In most rescue missions they'd be recycled into the economy, but Olympia hasn't got any economy to talk of, so I guess we'll just leave them here until something comes up." She shrugged.

"But you can use my trucks?" he fixed Kris in his gaze for the first time.

"In a flash," Kris agreed. "Nelly, show us a map of a hundred miles around here." A holograph appeared before them; Kris concentrating on the map to avoid the intensity of the young man's eyes. She hadn't heard a thing she didn't like in the last hour. What was not to like about a generous young man who took time to come out and see what was needed? She'd joined the Navy to do just that. From the sounds of the business empire Hank was half bossing with his father, this was about the closest the young man could get to the real world.

"We've got food going to the soup kitchens in town," Kris said, waving at the center of the map and getting the boys' attention, "so no one here goes hungry. It's the hinterland that's the problem. Even with Tom's crews working around the clock, we only have fifteen working trucks. Two out of three are down with something wrong. Local mechanics strip one to get another working, but with the roads in such lousy shape, one gets fixed and two get broke." She sighed.

"My thirty trucks should help with that," Hank said, following Kris's gaze to the map. "But up north is going to bring its own set of problems. Lots of hills and river valleys. I don't see many bridges."

"Aren't any," Tom said. Kris quickly filled both of them in on what she'd learned from the Colonel about the goal of minimum government. "Unless a local farmer built a bridge, there isn't one." She overlaid a prevolcano map on the present situation. There had been four bridges; they were all washed out.

"What you need are boats or portable bridges," Hank mused. Then his smile widened. "Let me tell you what I've got for you," he said, sounding like a man ready to sell vacuum to asteroid miners. "Dad just bought out a company that's making boats out of Smart Metal. Like the stuff your *Typhoon* is made from. The boats fold into a standard container-size box, a perfect load for any handy truck. Just put it in the water, select a form, and stand back. In five minutes you've got a boat, a barge, or a bridge, ready to load up or drive over. And the price is something you can't beat, little lady; free for you."

"How much do they weigh?" Tom cut in, no smile at Hank's snake oil routine. "Those roads are muddy. And how do you get them off the truck and into the water? They walk, too?"

"No," Hank sobered. "They are heavy. We usually use a crane. Metal may be smart, but no one, even on Santa Maria, has figured out how to make metal light."

Kris did her best to suppress a grin at this testosterone-powered battle beside her. "Any of those trucks in orbit happen to have a crane on them?" she asked.

"Might be a few. I'm hungry. Will you have lunch with me?"

Now Kris did laugh. "For mobile bridges, I think I can afford to sign for your meal at the mess hall. But I warn you, it's only slightly unfrozen cold cuts. Half our personnel went with today's convoys."

"I was thinking of something a bit more intimate," Hank

countered. "There's this restaurant in town that serves the most delicious steaks."

Tom looked like someone was stealing his teddy. "It can't be still in business."

"My sources assure me it is."

Kris had serious doubts it still was. She had a dozen other reason to say no, from *My boss won't let me go outside the gate,* to *Should we be eating steaks when everyone else is starving?* "Sounds great," was what she said. "You want to come, Tom?"

"Somebody better keep an eye on the fort," he said. Kris had never seen the freckled leprechaun in such full defeat.

Checking her side arm, Kris let Hank lead her toward the gate, where a luxurious all-terrain vehicle awaited them with two good-looking men that might be ex-marines standing by. "Dad won't let me go anywhere without these two mugs. Where's your bodyguard?"

"Military doesn't authorize 'em to ensigns, no matter how much of a pain in the neck you are," Kris answered. "Back home, my chauffeur was ex-military, but I thought of him more as a friend than anything else. I mean, it's hard to think of a guy who roots for you at your soccer games as anything but a buddy."

"You got to play soccer! That must have been wild."

"Didn't you?"

"Nope. Dad didn't think it was healthy, all those other kids out there in an uncontrolled mob. Too risky, he insisted. But then, I was an only child. You're not."

Kris thought she had had an overprotected childhood, especially after Eddy. She'd never considered that big brother Honovi had been a windbreak against excessive parental concern; she usually just thought of him as a pain. "No, I was the second kid," she said without letting the thought of the third one make her flinch.

"It would have been nice to have a kid sister with freckles," Hank said, giving her a sly sideways look. Before Kris had to answer that, they were at their destination.

The restaurant was on a side street off Kris's normal

path. No sign announced its presence, though Kris spotted one set of armed men loitering across the street from it, another on the roof. If she needed riflemen around her soup kitchens, she could imagine the protection a really decent place to eat would need.

The door opened before Hank's bodyguard touched it. The portly man in black tie and tails stood in the shadow of the door, menus in hand. He quickly led Kris and Hank to a quiet corner and a table covered with crystal, silver, and linens. Kris had to make an effort to notice where the guards went to ground, taking over separate tables on opposite sides of the dining room, their gray suits somehow merging into the restaurant's motif of wood, crystal lightings, and thick red carpeting. There were three other sets of customers, but tastefully placed plants made it impossible to make out faces. So the Colonel was right; not everyone was starving on Olympia. Where there was money, there was still fancy food to be had. More education for a boot ensign, a prime minister's daughter, and the recipient of Ernie Nuu's multitrillions.

The menu promised several delicious cuts of steak, even seafood. Ominously, it listed no prices.

"I don't know what to order," Kris said after a quick glance down the menu.

"Let me order for you," Hank answered.

Kris did not appreciate men who assumed that reading complicated menus were beyond a woman's shallow grasp. "I know what the menu says, Hank. The Colonel had us turn in our credit cards," she didn't quite lie. "Not sure I can cover the check."

"I was told that local credit cards were showing up on the black market. Your Colonel is a wise man," Hank agreed. "This is my treat." Since their net worth had to be within a decimal place of each other, Kris decided it would be nice to be pampered by a young man of her own age for a change. After the calls she'd made yesterday, why not let this fellow puzzle over the choice of salads?

"So," Kris started the dinner conversation, "you let your

dad take you into the family business right out of college."

"Hardly. Dad's not one to waste time on useless book learning. I started in the business when I was fourteen. If you can believe it, he had me spend my summer in the mail room. I've advanced my career considerably, don't you think?" he said, waving a hand up the imaginary corporate ladder.

"No college?"

"Well, actually, Dad brought out professors from Earth or wherever to do it on the job. My high school graduation project was a major pharmacy plant start-up, shadowing one of Dad's best men, learning all he knew, and writing it up for Dad and Professor Maxwell. I think that was the guy's name. Maxwell gave me an A. Dad went through the paper point by point, showing me why it deserved no better than a B. I never saw that professor again."

The wine waiter arrived with a sauvignon whose label would have been expensive on Wardhaven. Hank expertly went through the ritual of sampling the vintage. "Very good," he nodded after a sip. "You'll enjoy this," he assured Kris.

Kris waited while her glass was filled, then performed the mandatory sampling, praised it extravagantly, then set it next to her water glass and promised herself not to touch it again. After last night, she wasn't going down that road twice.

"Doesn't sound like there've been a lot of permanent fixtures in your life." Kris said to move the topic away from wine.

Hank thought on that one. "No," he finally grinned. "Haven't you heard, the only permanent thing in life is change."

"Read it somewhere." Kris agreed wryly. "I could usually count on a few things. Harvey was always there to take me to soccer games and cheer me on. His wife was always ready with a treat in the kitchen. And there were always aunts and uncles, some actually blood relatives. Didn't you have family?"

"Uncle Steven died in a racing accident when I was a

kid. Aunt Eve had one of her many love affairs go sour in a rather major way. If she hadn't insisted on traipsing off to the most out-of-the-way places, she'd still be with us. By the way, the trunk of that rig outside has a full emergency medical station in it. The driver isn't certified for brain surgery, but I bet he'd love to give it a try."

Kris put her elbows on the table, rested her chin on her two hands, and batted her eyelashes dramatically. "Listening to you makes my childhood seem rather, well, delightful, on review."

"Oh, come now, it couldn't have been all that great. Nobody has a good childhood. It says so in all the books."

And so the lunch went, each of them cheerfully trying to better the worst the other claimed for their upbringing. It was a game Kris had never had a chance to play; it is hard to get a fair hearing when even those closest to you are envious. At university, Kris had quickly learned that even those she let down her guard around could not believe a Longknife ever had reason to complain.

The meal went surprisingly quickly, and when Kris excused herself to the little girls' room, she was startled to find that two hours had passed. Washing her hands, she stared at herself in the mirror. Her nose hadn't gotten any smaller, and what the weather was doing to her skin would have had her mother galloping for the nearest spa. Her close-cropped hair wasn't quite as bad as that on some scarecrows. Still, Hank was clearly warming to her. He was one man who wouldn't be after her money if Auntie Tru's financial statements could be trusted. Of course, Auntie Tru was sure he, or at least his family, wanted her dead.

Kris tossed the used paper in the basket, eyed the lotions, sprays, and other personal necessities offered for use beside the sink, gave up on a quick remake of the ensign into some kind of glamour girl, and returned to the table. Hank was talking into the commlink merged into his suit's cuffs. "Drop the next three as quickly as you can," he said, then stood to greet Kris. "If you take time for dessert, I think you will find some very nice presents waiting for you at the port."

"What would you suggest?"

Their server had already brought over a cart, covered with chocolate, fruit, and baked confections to make the soul water as much as the mouth. A sniff told Kris these were not plastic stand-ins but truly savory offerings. The imp bit her, as Harvey's wife would say. "Thank you, just park the cart here. Come back in an hour to pick up the crumbs," she grinned.

"You heard the lady," Hank said, waving the young man away.

"No, no, no," Kris said. "I'm already too stuffed to be worth much on the job this afternoon. Do you have any sorbet?"

"Raspberry, strawberry, or citrus medley," the server said.

"Citrus medley," Kris said.

"Same for me," Hank finished, though he looked longingly at the cart as it was rolled away.

"Just because I'm passing doesn't mean a growing boy like you has to," Kris pointed out.

"Discipline, Dad says. 'Discipline yourself, because nobody else will, or can.'" Hank quoted. "I suspect you have already discovered that when rebelling against successful parents, one must be selective. Not all of what they handed us was bunk."

"Ah, yes," Kris answered sincerely, "but separating all that manure from the pony can be the challenge of a lifetime."

"Is that why you're in the Navy?"

"Is that why you're on Olympia?"

"I'm here to see for myself what needed doing."

"Yes, but why are you doing it in the first place? Your father can't be too happy that you're taking this detour on your way to that start-up," Kris said, turning all the generalities they'd tossed about over lunch into a very specific *Why are you here?* that would make Auntie Tru proud.

"Yes, but the straight route would be pleasing Dad a bit too much. I have to get a little of what I want."

"But why do *you* want this?"

"Ah, now that would be telling a bit much for a first date, don't you think?"

Maybe, but then again, it would be nice to know what was really going on behind that dancing smile, those hooded eyes. But before Kris could come up with further probes, her commlink went off. "Ensign Longknife," she snapped.

"There's been a rocket attack at the warehouse."

Kris's stomach went into free fall, and that fine steak started demanding revisitation rights to her mouth. "Casualties?"

"Don't know yet," Tom shot back.

"I'll be right there," Kris said, standing and about knocking over the waiter bringing their sorbet. Hank rose just as quickly and went through the formalities of covering the check. His gunmen assured that the way to the car was clear, even as Hank signed off on a bill that made even Kris gulp. Outside, it was hardly raining, but there was no one else on the street, no one on the roofs, no one peering out any window.

The locals had learned to hide when things went boom in broad daylight.

Five minutes later, Kris was back at her warehouse compound. A gaping hole showed in the south side of her nightly watchtower. Smoke came from her own office area.

"I'm going to have to leave you here," Hank said. "There is only so much stretch in my dad's orders before these two get me in a hammerlock."

"I know what you mean. You had no way of knowing the hornets' nest your lunch date had stirred up."

"Watch the next three drop ships. I really wanted to be here when you opened them. They'll have trucks and those boats I told you about."

"Wanted to see what I look like excited, maybe steal a kiss?"

"The thought had occurred to me."

She gave him a peck. "Now you know what it's like

having a sister. Now I've got to run. See you next time I see you."

He laughed, maybe a bit startled by the kiss. "Yes, I definitely will see you again." And then he was gone.

Kris didn't look back; it was time to be Navy again. Where were the casualties? Where were the attackers? How safe was this place? She tapped her commlink. "Ensign Longknife in the warehouse compound. Any report on casualties?"

"We've collected all three of the wounded at Warehouse 2." That was where Kris's office was. "All present or accounted for. We got lucky. No one killed," Tom reported.

That was good to hear. Kris double-timed it for the wounded. Ester Saddik was wrapping a bandage around one civilian's arm. Spens, Kris's accountant, was lying down, his uniform torn and bloody. A medic was going over him.

"Ouch," Spens said as a bloody section of shirt got lifted.

"Can't be too bad if you can still complain," the corpsman chided.

"Bad enough. Damn it, why didn't Dad ever have a day like this at the office?"

"Probably 'cause Dad never pissed off the bad guys like we did yesterday," Kris suggested.

"Nah, Dad always ran with the bad guys, respectable ones, not like the ones we took on yesterday, but just as nasty. Ensign, glad to see you back."

"Sorry I wasn't here for all the fun." Kris said, kicking herself for a two-hour lunch.

"No, ma'am. Glad you weren't. You think I look bad. It was your desk the rocket took apart. Now you'll have to spend *all* your time walking around the yard."

"Guess I will at that," Kris agreed. "He going to be okay?" Kris asked the medic.

"He will be, if he doesn't complain so much I slit his throat to shut him up," the corpsman answered.

"How about I entertain you with a few of my accountant jokes?" Spens suggested.

"Where's that knife when I need it?"

Everything here as much under control as it was likely to get, Kris headed for her office. Ester joined her. "I didn't know your folks had rockets," Kris said.

"The government arsenal kept a supply; they were not considered proper personal property."

"And the arsenal?"

"It burned down about a month after the rain started."

"Let me guess. There was no big explosion."

The older woman nodded. "The fire was surprisingly low energy for what the building was supposed to have."

"Anyone used rockets since then?"

"No."

"So there's a lot more out there."

"I would imagine so, but have you taken note of what was done here? Only two rockets were fired. They hit your office and your guard tower. None hit where the warehouses had food. None hit the yard where people were working."

"Selective shooting, and very accurate," Kris concluded.

"I believe so."

At her office Tom was overseeing a hose team putting out the small fire that had finished what the rocket started. As Spens said, nothing remained of her desk; Kris now had a new window to look out. If she'd been here, nothing would have been left of her. *Well, Auntie Tru, Hank Peterwald was the main reason I wasn't here. That prove anything to you?*

It did to Kris.

"Any problems at the main compound?" she asked Tom.

"Not a peep. Commander Owing is still sleeping off his five-martini lunch."

Kris surveyed the fire team, more local than Navy. Jeb detached himself from a fire hose team.

"Most of us did volunteer time with the fire department." her foreman told her. "We know what to do."

"Do you know who did it?"

"Got the same guesses you do, ma'am."

"Well, thank you for stepping in." Kris turned to Ester. "Any of your folks feel the warehouse has gotten a bit too dangerous, I'll see what I can do to find them work elsewhere."

Ester turned back to the foreman. "Jeb, any of your folks want to take her up on that?"

"I'll ask around, but if they wanted to go, they'd be gone already. Most of us like what you did yesterday." He glanced at the fire. "Obviously, not everyone."

"They could have killed me," Kris pointed out.

"I know, ma'am. And if I find out who, I'll mention their names to you. But, at the moment, I don't know nothing, so there's nothing I can do."

"Fair enough for now," Kris said. "I'm expecting a lot of drop ships this afternoon. Some of them will have trucks and other heavy equipment. You know any drivers we can trust?"

"I'll send a boy into town to get a couple," Jeb answered.

So Kris went about the rest of her day as if it was routine to have her work spaces blasted to rubble over her lunch break.

True to his promise, Peterwald's next two drop ships deposited thirty large all-terrain trucks in Kris's yard. A third provided a crane truck and a half-dozen boxes whose instructions promised they'd open up into several water-defeating forms. Kris gave Hank a thank-you call. He seemed delighted by her delight but made no offer to come down and share it up close and personal. His ship had a schedule change; Father was cutting short Hank's trip. There was some kind of trouble in the start-up.

Later that afternoon, Colonel Hancock gave a low whistle as he dismounted from his truck, moments after his supply convoy drove through the warehouse gate. "Woman, you do insist on having all the fun, don't you."

"Sorry about the mess, sir."

"Casualties?"

"Three injured. One Navy, my accountant, Spens. My

office was wrecked. The watchtower's sandbags seem to have cut down on the damage. A local engineering tech swears there's no structural damage."

"So. You going to post guards up there tonight?"

"Yes, sir. I'll take the watch, with a couple of marines."

"The marines will take the watch. You will not."

"Sir."

"Don't sir me, young woman. You may have forgotten, but I haven't. You are one of those Longknifes, and I have no intention of getting called on the carpet to explain to the prime minister, your father, how I got you killed."

"You won't have gotten me killed, sir."

"If it happens, it will be on my watch. In case you haven't noticed it, in the Navy, if it happens on your watch, you are responsible for it. I know that, in spades, Ensign. Now, how'd your time go with that what's his name?"

"Mr. Peterwald has been kind enough to provide us with thirty trucks and six convertible boats or bridges. He also took me off base for a two-hour lunch, which explains why I wasn't at my desk when it went to pieces."

"Thank the gods for minor favors. You and he hit it off."

"Better than I did with some of the locals, it appears."

"Ensign, you will soon discover that it is a rare day when everyone is happy. You have one of those days, savor it."

Kris chuckled. "If I get one, sir, I'll take your advice."

Colonel Hancock stayed with her as she checked in each of the convoys. He also checked out the new trucks. Local mechanics had already gone over them and pronounced them fit. Kris doubled the night shift so all the available rigs would be loaded up for tomorrow's run. The Colonel frowned as he took in the rolling stock. "I hate to admit that I'm embarrassed by my riches. Until the Highlanders get here, I'm going to have more trucks than I've got troops to keep them rolling."

"The Highlanders are due tomorrow, aren't they? I've already got four buses under contract," Kris said.

"I got word just before I left this morning that their transport blew two engines. They're having to limp across the last system and down here on half power. Expect them two, maybe three days late."

"So we'll have food and transport but no one to move it where it's needed." Kris didn't like the taste of that in her mouth. There were an awful lot of hungry kids out there.

"Ensign, that NGO you're funding?"

"I didn't say I was funding it, sir."

"No, you managed to overlook that bit of information when you were briefing your superior officer. Don't you think I can do a computer search as well as you can?"

"No, sir, I mean yes, sir. I mean . . . you know what I mean, sir."

"I probably do. I was an only moderately subordinate second lieutenant once. Fortunately, I dodged the mutiny charge as well as I expect you will. Now, could you wrestle me up a dozen civilians who could keep any NGO gunmen in line and follow any orders they get from the likes of Owing and Pearson?"

"Ester and Jeb are pretty levelheaded folks. I've met a priest, preacher, a couple of salesmen I think have the respect of the locals and could get along with any decent Navy types."

"I didn't say decent, I said Owing and Pearson."

"Maybe Ester and Jeb should be assigned to them."

"Then you'll have the base to yourself tomorrow, and I'll have just about everything in uniform on the road."

A quick touch-base with Ester got Kris a list of folks who could ride herd on a batch of riflemen, as well as get along with their Navy coordinator. Jeb was out; he was a Quaker and would not carry a gun. Kris wasn't willing to put him out there without a weapon. Instead, he volunteered to work the warehouse all night to get the rigs loaded. A good day's work done, Kris headed back to base, Ester and two gun-toting women at her side.

"I can take care of myself," Kris told the older woman.

"I know you can. I'm just enjoying a nice stroll."

"Ester, it hasn't quit raining all day."

"I know. Maybe I'm getting used to it." After several

more sallies by Kris, just as cheerfully and absurdly parried by Ester, the women left Kris at the base gate. Kris was just in time for the last of the chow, which under Courtney's hand was just as tasty as the first off the griddle. The Colonel came in for a cup of coffee as she settled at a table. He joined her.

"Your quarters have been moved."

"Sir, don't you think that's taking it a bit far?"

"Blame your friend Lien. He wanted to bunk the Highlanders in a block so their NCOs could keep them out of trouble. He had Millie roust you into new quarters."

"I thought the Highlanders were delayed."

"They are, but that boot ensign didn't get the word."

Or was in cahoots with a certain sly colonel. "My old quarters empty tonight?"

"And the ones all around it. Made sure the cleaning people knew you were moving, just not where."

Kris couldn't argue so long as no one else would be on the receiving end of any rockets intended for her. Tommy was at the check-in desk, waiting for her when she got to the quarters. "Colonel told me what you did. Thanks."

"I didn't do anything," Tom lied through a freckled grin. "Here's your key. You're on the second floor. Far enough up not to be easy to get at and low enough down not to give anyone in town a clear line of flight."

So, despite herself, Kris had a good night's sleep.

15

Kris felt like an unregistered voter on election day as she gulped down her breakfast at Oh Dark Early next morning. Boxed rations were handed out to all for lunch, even those not going out, which Kris discovered was less than a dozen, even counting Spens and the three still in sick bay from Kris's first drive in the country. The Colonel was stripping the HQ for the day.

Kris hurried off to the warehouse to resolve any last-minute glitches, of which there were few, and to wave good-bye to just about everyone she knew on the planet. Even Courtney had a convoy; Tommy, with local cooks, would see to chow for tonight.

The yard empty, Kris checked in with Jeb. Her lead foreman assured her he and his civilians would get the drop ships hauled out of the bay, their cargos transferred to the warehouses, and shipments made up for tomorrow's deliveries. Kris glanced up into the worst rain she'd seen since landing and told him to keep his crews safe. "That's what I got the rifle crew for." Quaker he might be, but he was not averse to having armed men and women walking the warehouse perimeter.

As Kris headed back to the HQ, she noted that she had a tail, the same two women who had come back with Ester last night. They didn't follow her through the gate, which had one lone Navy guard today, but joined the half-dozen gun-toting civilians walking the HQ's perimeter fence.

Kris checked in at sick bay; Doc and one corpsman had the wounded well in hand. As she wandered the halls of the HQ, Kris heard the echos of her footsteps; the place was totally closed down. At the end of the hall, radio static drew her attention. The radio section had even been drafted into the food convoys, but their gear still monitored the net. One was on the main net; she could listen to any of the convoys. That only made her feel more left behind. She had Nelly turn that one down and put a watch on alert words like *Mayday, fire,* and *ambush.*

The other radio was monitoring civilian channels. With a flick of her wrist, Kris sent it on a scan. It went up the band, hit on a line of static, and hung there. Kris hit Scan again, and it did a long search before hitting on another band of static. Kris settled into the duty chair, put her feet up, and tapped the Scan button at regular intervals as the radio's search hung up on something. It took a couple of minutes before she realized it was hanging on about the same frequency every time. She sat up, hit Scan, and watched as the search went up the band, hit the top, then began at the bottom before settling at the same spot.

She did it again and got the same results.

"Would you like me to isolate the signal from all the noise?" Nelly asked.

"Is there a signal in that static?"

"Yes."

"Do it."

The speakers went silent, then gave out a loud burst of static. "Sorry," Nelly said as it cut off. Then the static came back, low this time. Kris thought she spotted words among the crackling: "Flu," "flood," "starvation." Then again, floods and starvation were the expected around here. Finally Nelly hit on the right algorithm, and the message came in weak but clear.

"You've got to help us. We haven't asked for anything before, but we're at the end of our rope. Can anyone hear us?"

Kris grabbed the radio mike. "This is Ensign Longknife. You are coming through weak but clear," she shouted. "Repeat your message." She keyed off and waited. The static was there. Only static. "Nelly," Kris demanded.

"No signal."

Kris leaned back in her chair and counted slowly to ten. At ten, she changed her mind and headed for one hundred. If she talked, she'd override an incoming message. As Kris started to despair of ever hearing from them again, the radio came to life. "Batteries are about dead, but I'm going to keep repeating this as long as I can. This is the Anderson Ranch up the north fork of the South Willie. We've got an outbreak of Grearson fever. Two deaths so far. A dozen or so are showing signs. We burned the bodies to keep this stuff out of the groundwater. We're sick, we're hungry, and now the river's rising. We can't make it up the canyon wall. If you know what's good for you, you better come help us, 'cause if we die from this stuff and the water takes our bodies, this crud will be all over Olympia."

"Nelly, what's Grearson fever?"

"Flulike symptoms, it resides in the body like typhoid, causing the carrier no discomfort until their resistance falls below a certain level. It has a fifty percent death rate for adults who are not treated, higher for children and the elderly. First discovered on Grearson—"

"Enough. Does our warehouse have any vaccine against it?"

"Yes. Approximately a thousand units."

Kris squeezed her eyes closed. A thousand would be a drop in the bucket for Port Athens alone. "Nelly, show me where the Anderson Ranch is." Being the north fork of a south river meant it must be way up in the hills. It was that, and then some.

"Update river information with latest photography."

Up north, the river grew out of its banks and close to canyon walls. "This photography is a week old. We have had continuous cloud cover since then," Nelly told her. They'd also had continuous rain. If it was bad last week, it was worse now.

Kris was on her feet. At the door she remembered she ought to call this in to the Colonel. But he was headed south, and the problem was up north. She pulled two blank flimsies from a stack next to the radios, scrawled a quick note telling where she was going and why, left one in the radio room and the other on the Colonel's desk as she raced down to sick bay. "We got a breakout of Grearson fever about forty miles up the river on a place about to be flooded," she announced.

The doc had his feet up on his desk, reading a medical journal. "Oh shit," he said, feet slamming to the floor. "That would be ten times worse than the typhoid last month. There hasn't been an outbreak of Grearson in thirty years."

"Well, we have one now. Who's coming with me?" Kris asked.

"Hendrixson still might be bleeding," the corpsman said. "I guess that means I go." He started filling a bag.

"If they're coming down with Grearson, Danny, there's going to be all kinds of opportunistic diseases," the doc sighed and started adding to the corpsman's load.

"Meet me at the boat dock at the warehouse. I'll pick up the vaccine," Kris said as she started double-timing for the exit. "How many people live in that valley?" Kris asked Nelly.

"Two hundred thirty-seven."

"We'll take two hundred and fifty doses of vaccine. Get someone at the warehouse to start hunting for them."

"I have located them. I will have Jeb get them."

"Ensign Lien," Kris called over the net, "what you up to?"

"My neck in busted truck parts," Tommy answered.

"Meet me at the warehouse gate. We have a problem."

"And hadn't I better bring my rifle?" He sighed.

Kris picked up her armed escort as she double-timed out the gate. She ignored them as they trotted along a couple of dozen meters behind her. Jeb met her in an electric cart, three small boxes of medical supplies on its flatbed. "That's three hundred units, but unless I'm reading it wrong, it expired last month."

Kris hopped on the cart. "Boat dock," she ordered, then tapped her commlink for sick bay. "Doc, our Grearson fever vaccine expired last month. Can we use it?"

"Damn!" was followed by a pause. "It might do. Maybe use a bit more than normal. Damn, I can't believe I'm saying this."

"We have three hundred doses for two hundred and fifty people. You might want to start making some new stuff."

"No way we can manufacture enough if it gets in the water."

"Understood, Doc, we've got to keep it out of the river." Now, if only the river would keep out of the ranch.

The crane truck was gone, along with two of the boat rigs. Kris headed for the boxed boat closest to the water and tapped the small keypad awake. Instructions appeared on a tiny screen. After reading through several windows, Kris punched 6 on the controls. As promised, that produced a river dory/motorized. Ten meters long, two wide, it had a high prow, flat bottom, and a control station amidships with a wheel on one side of a square pillar, the keypad and screen on the other. Kris studied what she'd done and decided it looked good. Jeb interrupted a dozen men stacking sandbags along the seawall against the rising bay long enough for them to heave the boat into the water, just a few centimeters below the concrete wall. Jeb divided his work crew, half going back to raising the seawall, half dispatched to the warehouse for supplies.

"Who's going?" Jeb asked.

"Me, a corpsman will be along in a minute, Tommy. I need some men, people who know the river."

"Ester said you weren't supposed to leave town."

"I'm not supposed to make a truck run. This is different."

"Only if you're a sprout like you, young woman. Keep this up, and you're going to get yourself killed."

"Lot of people trying. So far, nobody's succeeded."

"So you're pushing your luck."

"Load the boat, old-timer."

"I'll load the boat. Mick, you been bitching about loafing around town. You shag your freckles over to the *Andrea Doria* and tell Addie we want José. This lady's going to ride the river, and she's gonna need the best river runner we got."

"You bet, Pops," said a young man of maybe eighteen as he took off running.

"I'll throw in Olaf, that big bear of a guy over there. You're going into canyon country, so you may need a bit of climbing before you're done. Nabil, Akuba, I need you over here." Two tall, thin men, one dark, the other darker, started jogging toward them.

The corpsman arrived, along with Tommy. He looked around, as if expecting to see smoke rising through the rain. "What's happening?" he asked Kris. She explained. For emphasis, the corpsman started giving shots to everyone tagged for the trip. "Kris, you're supposed to stay here," was Tom's reaction when she finished.

"Already told her," Jeb drawled. "Girl don't listen, so save your breath." Jeb was studying the boat; it drew about ten centimeters now as boxes of food and medical supplies were loaded. "I'll let José have the last say about your load. Some weight might help. Too much, and I don't need to tell you the river is a killer these days. You ever been on water?"

"My folks own a boat. I've sailed a lake on Wardhaven."

"This ain't going to be anything like that."

"I didn't figure it would be."

José arrived with Mick not far behind him. The brown-skinned man of maybe thirty eyed the craft, hopped aboard, studied it some more, then ordered, "Lash everything down.

The river, she's going to be a bitch, and I don't need no more trouble than she's gonna give me. Mick, you get me some paddles and poles." Again, freckles was off a-running.

The men loading the boat had brought plenty of rope; they began lashing it around the cargo liberally. José picked up the three small, flat boxes of vaccine. "These why we're doing this stupid thing?"

"Yes," Kris said. "You understand what happens if we don't get this vaccine upriver."

"People die, and when the river takes them, we all die. You think I'd be doing a thing this stupid for any other reason? Jeb, get everyone a life vest. And get three packs. We'll have Navy here wear the medicine."

Kris didn't like being reduced to a pack animal. She opened her mouth, but José cut her off before she got a word out. "Listen, woman, I am the captain of this boat. If I was up there"—he pointed at the gray sky—"and wanted to stay alive in your space, maybe I'd listen to you. Maybe, if you sounded like you knew what you were doing. Down here, José knows everything there is to know about this river. You want to get this stuff to those people, you listen to José. You do what he tells you and you just may live."

The river man eyed the inlet in front of them with a scowl on his face. "The bay, she bad, with snags and stumps and eddies that will spin you around. The river, she going to be a whole lot worse. But I think, maybe, José can get you up there."

"Maybe," Kris said.

"José's maybe is a lot better than the dead you'd be without me, girl."

"Do it his way, spacer. Otherwise, I don't send my people out," Jeb added.

"I wasn't arguing. You think it's best we wear the medicine?" she asked Jeb.

"You go in the water, you'll float, and the guys will do their best to fish you out. Those boxes go in and they'll sink. I guess we could try to do something about that, but I think José just did."

"Looks that way," Kris had to agree.

Ten minutes later, supplies loaded, they pulled away from the dock. "I should be back before the Colonel is, but if I'm not, tell him where I am," Kris hollered at Jeb.

"Why don't you use that thing on your wrist to tell him yourself?"

"He's got his job cut out for him today. Why worry him?"

"Right. What else should I expect from a Longknife?" Kris shrugged that off, then started bailing. In the time since she'd unfolded the boat, there'd been over a centimeter of rain. It now sloshed around the bottom of the boat; anyone not busy, bailed.

"You know that luck of the little people we've been talking about?" Tommy said from where he bailed across from Kris. "Well, I just saw them waving from the pier. Even they don't have enough luck for this blasted river."

"Tommy, we've got to get this upriver," Kris said, pointing a thumb at the pack on her back."

"*Someone* has to get it upriver. Nobody's died and left *you* the job. Me, I'm starting to wonder how much of the Longknife stuff in the history books is there because somebody just didn't know how to let somebody else do their job." Kris didn't have an answer for Tommy.

José quickly brought the boat up to full speed, about twelve knots. It handled the waves on the bay well, breasting each swell with a cloud of spray that ended mostly back in the water, only some in the boat. Things were fine right up until they hit a snag with a thud and a bump and a sudden falloff in speed, even as the engine raced.

"Damn sinker," José growled as he brought the boat around and idled the engine. Off to their left, just a few centimeters below a wave trough, a log, maybe a quarter of a meter in diameter and spiked from shorn-off tree limbs, spun from their contact. José pulled something the size of a stylus from his shirt pocket, extended it into a meter-long pole, waited until the log settled down to a stable rocking motion, then hurled it at the log. It stuck, a red flare igniting at its high end. In a moment, Kris's boat captain was on the radio.

"Addie, I got a sinker out here near the landing run. It's marked. You better come get it."

"Spotted your flare already," a woman's voice came back. "We're under way. You in trouble?"

"Maybe. I think we dinged our prop. I may need a tow."

"Can do two as well as one."

Kris was not ready to go back. She dropped her bailing bucket and headed for the control station. "You think you can do better?" José said, his face a mixture of macho defiance and rank embarrassment.

"Maybe I can," Kris said, punching the keypad opposite the wheel. The small view screen came to life. "On the *Typhoon*, my job is controlling what the liquid metal does in battle. There's got to be a way to make this metal repair itself."

"You think so?"

"Don't know until I've tried." The view screen was small, and the keypad just numeric; Kris found herself keying through a complex series of option screens, diving deeper and deeper into some kind of tree. It didn't help that the screens had been written by someone for whom English was a very foreign language.

"You aren't going to dump us in the water, are you?" Tom asked. Kris took the question for serious, particularly after the nods his comment got from long Nabil and big Olaf.

"I'll try not to, but you might want to tighten your life vests. Never can tell what a spacer will do, out on deep water."

"Very funny." Tom didn't laugh. "She gets it wrong in space, we're breathing vacuum," he pointed out. But Olaf gave his vest harness a good pull, and Nabil eyed the waves around them dolefully. Kris found something that claimed to be propulsion repair, located her dory, then Water Screw, which she took for prop, and hit Repair. The screen blinked, then went blank.

"Did that fix it?" José asked.

"Try it," Kris answered, not at all sure.

José eased the throttle up; the boat took on way. "Feels right," he said. "Yeah! Think you can take the dents out of the bow?" He pointed forward where the metal was pushed in.

"I'll try . . . when we're on dry land," Kris agreed. That got a laugh from captain and crew. José brought the boat up to something less than its full speed, posted two lookouts with long poles forward, and ordered the rest back to bailing. He motioned Kris to the command station.

"You have a map of the bay?"

Kris pulled out her reader, brought up the latest picture of the sprawling inlet, then overlaid a map from predisaster. "Will that help?"

"Yeah. There's a swamp over there with three rivers feeding in and a dozen ways out. Now they're all just one big mess. We could be quite a ways up the wrong one before we knew it."

Kris tapped the Global Positioning Satellite button, and a plus appeared on the screen.

"You have one of those, too. I had to hock mine."

"This will work," Kris assured him, gave him the unit, and went back to bailing. She didn't have to ask when they hit the river. Even with José putting the engine back to full power, they slowed down. Bare tree trunks stood starkly out of the water, marking where the shore had been. Even after this planet dried out, it would need a lot to recover.

Kris stood, stretched her back, and turned to José. "Will we stay to the center of the river?"

"Not if we want to get there before next week. Current out there is a good six, maybe eight knots. We stay away from that. Course, hitting trees is very bad. Nabil, Akuba up front, keep your eyes open. We don't want to wrap the woman's boat around a tree or rock." The rain picked that moment to get thicker, and visibility dropped to hardly a boat length. José cut back on the throttle a little, and their headway fell to almost nothing.

Progress was slow as the lookouts on the bow poled them away from rocks, shrubs, the odd building, and tree after tree. Kris glanced a few times at the main channel, but there was no going there. Maybe it had once been as placid as her lake back home. Now the water fought itself, roiling up, then crashing down in a shower of white water. Water gone mad with the power to turn trees to matchsticks and rocks to gravel. As dangerous as it was along the flooded bank, the main stream was suicide.

Progress upriver was slow, punctuated with terror. Poling them off a tree, a stray current grabbed them, sending them downriver sideways and slamming them into a rock they'd just passed so carefully. Even big Olaf needed help pushing off. All hands applied poles, oars, and hands to the rock, only to unbalance the boat. Water poured in over the dented gunwale.

"Navy to port, the other side, left," José yelled as Tom went right. Kris fought her way hand over hand up the cargo lashings to hang as far over the left side as she dared, raising the bent but unpierced right side. Nabil and Akuba pushed the boat's nose off, and José let the current carry them downstream a hundred meters while he made sure all was well before putting the engine back in gear and renewing the fight with the wild river.

Kris glanced at her watch; they'd be doing good to make the Anderson Ranch before dark at this rate. She considered calling the Colonel but dropped the idea. She was committed; he could hang her for mutiny or insubordination later. There was little he could do now. Kris concentrated on riding the river.

The rain came down in sheets. Tommy suggested they look for pillowcases to match. Mick answered he was ready for bed, with or without sheets. Which raised the question from Olaf as to who would share a bed with whom. Tired and wet, they could still laugh. If she had to ride a river gone mad, this was the crew to do it with.

As hours went by, Kris grew wet and cold. Her muscles ached in places she hadn't known she had. She couldn't just ride this boat but had to work every moment to keep from being bashed against the liquid metal sides or slammed into the crates of food, maybe shattering the glass vials of vaccine. So Kris stayed on her feet, stooping over to bail, flexing her knees as the boat rose up to slap her or dropped out from underneath her. This was nothing like the cruise she and Tommy shared on the *Oasis*. Would she ever want to be on a body of water bigger than a Jacuzzi again?

"That's the Harmosa place," José called to Kris, pointing at a rooftop between them and the roiling river. "Andersons are next, about three miles farther upriver. Everything is going fine."

As the captain said that, they rounded a bend in the river. Out of nowhere, an eddy from the main channel caught them. José held on to the wheel with both hands, his legs wrapped around the wheel post, fighting the swirling current. The boat whirled as it rose and fell; the worst bucking they'd had all day. Tommy lost his hold and was half overboard before Kris got a hand on his belt. The next pitch and drop would have thrown them both over the side if Mick hadn't gotten a hand on them, his feet entwined in the cargo lashings. Finally, Olaf managed to make his way across the cargo. He grabbed Tommy and Kris by their packs with his big paws and tossed them into the bottom of the boat like they were kittens.

Kris lay on her belly for a long minute, gasping for breath, letting the rain pour down on her, the sloshing water soak into her. She had really gotten herself and Tommy into a mess this time. It was almost over. Just a bit more, she told herself as she struggled to her feet, both hands wrapped around cargo lashings and a leg through a third to boot.

"Thanks, Kris," Tommy said.

"Thanks to all of you," Kris added peering at each of her crew through the gathering darkness.

"We thank you." José laughed. "Think of the stories we will tell when we get back." Olaf and Mick seemed to like that. Nabil just shook his head. Akuba never looked up from his place on the bow, looking for snags.

Now it was getting seriously dark. A glance at her wrist told Kris this was a lot earlier than it should have been. Part of the gloom was the incessant downpour. But they were also in the shadows of the cliffs rising a good 300 meters high on the south side of the gorge the river ran through. "There's rapids three, four miles past the Anderson place," José called to all hands. "Let's keep our eyes open, crew. We'll be in a mess if we go too far."

Kris tried a call on net and got only static. "Nelly, do a radio search. Call anyone on net."

Nelly reported a null search. "Their batteries may be dead," Kris told José and the crew. "Silence means nothing," she assured them. Why didn't it reassure her?

Now Nabil and Akuba on the bow brought out handheld lights. The rain seemed to slacken; in the growing gloom it could easily have been more a wish than reality. Still, they were a good hundred meters off when Nabil's beam settled on the waterlogged wreckage of a multistory building. José throttled back, and they approached it carefully. The top floor had been burned; a few of the larger timbers showed black above the water. Where the river's water lapped along the top floor, two skulls eyed them through empty sockets.

"Mother of God." José crossed himself and steered away.

"They said they'd burned the dead," Kris said. "I guess that was where."

"That's the old house, where the Andersons started fifty years ago. The main place should be over there," José said, pointing off to the left. Slowly, the boat headed in that direction. The rain came back; they almost rammed the first flooded outbuilding before they saw it. Water was halfway up its low walls. "That's a cattle barn. Start looking for a fence," José ordered. Kris decided it was time to call home.

"Colonel Hancock, this is Ensign Longknife." Only static. Kris repeated herself with the same results. "Nelly?"

"I estimate we are in the shadow of the cliffs," Nelly

said. "I cannot get a line of sight on the communications satellite from where we are."

"In this dark, I am not taking us out where the current can get us," José said before Kris could say a word.

"I wasn't going to ask," Kris assured him.

"We're at the fence," Mick called from the bow.

José steered right. "I think there's a gate somewhere around here. I'm cutting the engine. Get ready to pole." They found a hole in the fence before they found any gate. Once through, José headed into the dark. The lights picked up more flooded buildings. The boat bumped against things hidden in the water; again, José cut the motor, and they poled. When the next break in the rain gave them a good look around, they were in the middle of the farmyard. Houses, barns, other outbuildings surrounded them, all flooded. No lights showed.

"They've got to be around here somewhere," Kris frowned.

José frowned, too. "There's a couple of hay barns, closer to the cliffs. One or two houses there, too." He pointed to the right, and they poled in that direction. Once past the last barn, and the fence that began at its edge, the current picked up, and the poling got harder. José reached to start the motor.

"Wait a second," Kris called. "You hear that?" The sound of rain and the river made it hard to hear anything. But as the silence stretched and the crew held its collective breath, the dull roar became more insistent.

"The falls." José sighed. "It must be real bad to make that much noise. But we aren't going to get anywhere against this current by poling." He flipped the engine on, but kept his speed very slow. The land they passed over must have been rolling at better times. Here and there a few bedraggled cows stood on small islands or wallowed in mud up to their utters. They passed a tiny herd that must have taken shelter on a lower island. As miserable as the cows appeared, they must have been the pampered survivors, some optimist's hope that he could save enough to start a new herd when the rains stopped. Now the water was up to the shoulders of this remnant; they lowed pitifully as the helpless humans passed them.

"There's not going to be anything left of us," Nabil muttered to Akuba.

"There's something up ahead. Looks like a fire," Olaf shouted from his station on the bow. José cut the engine. It took them a while to separate out the sounds of the rain and roar of the river, but there are few things sweeter than the sound of a human voice. Olaf cupped his hands to his mouth and shouted in his booming baritone, "Ahoy the ranch."

On the third shout he got an answer. "What bloody ranch? And who are you? I got a rifle."

"José," their captain shouted back, "with a boat full of medicine and food. You want me to land or keep going?"

"We can probably find you a place to tie up for the night, if you got the rope."

"I got the rope. You got a tree?"

"Nope, but if you got food, I'll hold the bleeding rope all night." Six figures slowly materialized out of the mist. One held up a hand, and Olaf tossed him a rope. The six pulled with a will, and the boat glided up to a muddy landing.

"God, man, are we glad to see you. There any more boats?"

"Only this one. Where is everyone?" Kris asked as she stepped over the side into mud up to her ankles.

"Some left before it got too bad. Some are sleeping cheek to jowl under what roofs we have. Some are out here, worrying. You heard our message?"

"We know about the Grearson fever. I got a corpsman here with the vaccine." Kris pointed at the medic as he clambered out of the boat, his two stuffed bags showing a Red Cross/Red Crescent/Red Star. Kris held out her hand to the man who'd been doing the talking. "I'm Ensign Kris Longknife of the Society of Humanity Navy at your service."

From somewhere in the fog Kris heard, "We got a bloody Longknife all the hell and gone out here?" but the handshake and smile that greeted her was friendly. "Glad for anything you got," said a man with graying hair, wearing clothes that hung on him like there'd been a lot more to cover a year ago. "I'm Sam Anderson. My pa started this ranch." He glanced around into the foggy dark as if seeing all there was and once had been. "I guess I'll end it. Listen, how many can you get out on this boat? We got a couple of dozen sick, plus our old and kids. I figure before morning we're gonna have to start climbing the cliff. It would be nice to get the weakest out by boat."

"How many do you have?" Kris asked, getting back into the now-empty hull.

"Minus the three that died today, ninety-eight. Why?"

"Because this boat is a bit different from the average. What you see isn't necessarily what you get." Kris got the screen up and went through the original list. "There's an option here for a river scow/motorized. Good for ferrying trucks up to ten thousand kilos. A hundred and ten people ought to fit. Fifteen meters by six meters. Thirty centimeters of free clearance at full load. José, you willing to take that out on the river?"

"Tomorrow. Not in the dark."

"I'll do the conversion now just in case the river gets too high tonight."

"Good idea," Sam said as Kris punched the conversion option. Even in the dark, the metal walls around Kris took on a gleaming appearance. The high prow began to settle, the sides rolled away as the boat widened from three meters to six.

Then the entire structure of the boat collapsed onto the ground. For a second, Kris thought this was just part of the process, but then flat sections of metal began to break up, mingle with the raindrops, and settle to the bottom of puddles. Kris grabbed a handful of control pillar as it began to come apart. Quickly, she stooped and scooped up a mixture of mud and liquid metal from a puddle with her other hand. In her palms, the metal formed globules like liquid mercury.

"What the hell?" Kris gasped, along with similar expletives from those around her. She controlled the temptation to hurl the liquid metal on the ground. "Quick, someone, get two of those vaccine bottles out of my pack. Empty the vaccine. I've got to store this crud."

"But waste vaccine?" Tommy asked, even as he got Kris's pack open.

"We've got vaccine for three hundred and only a hundred here. But I *am* going to know what just happened."

"If we live that long," Sam added sourly.

Kris and Tommy got the samples of their boat into bottles and capped them. One had quite a bit of mud in with the metal. Well, that was Olympia for you. Kris looked around for another sample, but in just the time it took to do that, all evidence that a river dory had ever been here was gone.

"Let's get the supplies out of the rain," Sam drawled. "If we're going to drown before morning, we might as well do it on a full stomach."

"I never took you for an optimist, Sam," José said.

"A year of gray skies, dead cows, crop failure, and cabin fever, then this fever, would make even you throw in the towel."

"Maybe. You heard the man, let's get some food up to these folks. Hungry people don't make good decisions, and the water is rising." The boat crew loaded up what they had, helped by a dozen ranch hands that were there or materialized out of the rain and fog. The new arrivals were quiet. The ranchers seemed to return to an interrupted conversation.

"I say we build some rafts. We still got two houses left. Tear down their walls and use 'em to float downriver."

"They're wood and plaster walls, Ted. They'd never last an hour on the river. Besides, out there is no place for anything less than a full boat. What you say to that, José?"

"It's bad out there. I wouldn't say you couldn't make it. Who knows, miracles happen."

"I'm not trusting my Candi's life to no miracle. I say we climb the cliffs. We used to do that when we was young."

"Yeah. I got all the way up to the top when I was ten."

"When was the last time you tried to climb a fence, Bill?" That ended that part of the conversation with a snort.

"Besides, we all climbed up Lucky's Trail. Water's eight feet deep between here and there," Sam pointed out. "All we got left is Lover's Leap, and nobody's climbed that one."

"Where is it?" Akuba asked quietly.

"Right behind us," Sam said.

Akuba aimed his light beam. Through the rain and mist Kris could just make out a rocky face with an occasional stunted tree. Muddy water ran down it. The light flicked out. "Bitch of a climb," came from Nabil.

"We got some rope. You got any?" Akuba asked.

"Some."

They reached two structures. One was a small cow barn. Four cows, rain streaming off them, looked morosely at the shelter they'd been evicted from. The other was an even smaller one-room house. "Honeymooners stayed here their first year, if they wanted." Sam supplied the answer before Kris asked. "Let's see if we can get some food warming before we wake anyone up."

Maybe two dozen were asleep on the floor, mostly young or elderly folks. Three women lay in the one bed, sheened with fevered sweat, while two others tried to comfort them. The medic headed that way while Kris followed Sam to the kitchen area and began heating standard field rations. The smell of coffee brought people in. They quietly got what they could, then disappeared back out into the rain.

Once things were moving along, Sam tapped Kris on the elbow. "We need to talk."

Kris followed him to the kitchen table. Sam, Karen, his wife, and a big fellow who introduced himself as Brandon and tried to crush Kris's hand, took three of the chairs, leaving the fourth for Kris.

"So, what do we do?" Brandon asked.

Kris paused, waiting for Sam or his wife to say something, but they were all looking at her. "My medic is taking care of your Grearson cases as best as he can. In a few minutes he'll start giving inoculations to all of you. After that . . ." Kris left that hanging.

"After that, we die," Brandon snapped.

"No," Karen insisted.

"Yes we do," Brandon shot back. Around the room others stood against the wall or settled onto the floor. Everyone awake in the house was watching the four at the table, waiting to see what their fate would be. "Face it," Brandon said, turning to face the listeners more than those at the table. "The water's been rising an inch or two an hour. By dawn, it's gonna be in here up to your ankles. There ain't no cavalry coming to the rescue. The damn Navy's already here, and you can see she's in the same mess we are. That was a really cute trick making the boat go away, even for a Longknife."

"As you said, I'm in the same boat, or lack of it, that you are," Kris put in. "But I'm not going to be dead come morning."

Brandon snorted derisively. "There a helicopter gunna come and take you away, baby cakes. Didn't anyone tell you? With all the acid in our rain, they sold all the airplanes and other nice toys off world. Has your Navy brought some back?"

"No," Kris said, unwilling to lie to any of the people watching her. She looked around at them, hoping to see in their eyes that they were counting on her, no matter how heavy the burden, to get them out of this mess. What she saw was blank hopelessness, as if they already saw themselves dead. Kris gulped; these people weren't looking to her for hope, only that last bit of approval so they could quit.

"So, here we are in the twenty-fourth century, and we got nothing but our own two hands to save us, and little sister, we've worked ours to the bone, and we ain't saved ourselves. If we're gonna die, I say we take this whole mud ball with us."

That absurd statement didn't even elicit a shuffling of feet among the onlookers. Kris glanced at Sam and Karen. They were looking at the table, eyes as dead as the drowned cows Kris had pushed off from the boat on the way up here. How could anyone become so hopeless? Helpless?

"Why shouldn't we take this planet down with us?" Brandon continued. "They didn't do anything for us. And you all know about the offer Sam's got. Does little Miss Longknife know? Maybe your grandpa made Sam the offer."

"I know little about my Grandfather Alex's business. In case you missed it, I'm a boot ensign in the Navy and up a muddy river at the moment without a paddle." Come on folks, laugh, smile, show some emotions.

The people around Kris just stared at the floor.

"Sam's been offered a penny on the dollar for this place, Navy. What do you say to that? When all this is over, we're gonna be just a bunch of wage slaves like the factory workers back on Earth. I sure as hell don't want to live that way."

So that was it. Kris swallowed hard; they'd worked all their lives, and now they were losing it. They'd worked under the open sky, and now that sky was falling on them. They'd asked for nothing, got nothing, and now all guys like Brandon had was a mad to hold on to as the river rose. And the fever now gave Brandon someone to aim his mad at. Kris slowly turned in her chair, studying the people standing along the walls, slumped onto the floor. They were beat, at the end of their hope, and waiting for it to end. *Okay, Ensign Longknife, how you going to make them want to fight for what's left of their lives?* Talk about a leadership challenge.

"You want to die?" Kris asked a woman who made eye contact with her for a moment. The woman flinched and dropped her eyes back to the floor.

"Is that it?" Kris said to a man standing along the wall.

"You just want to lie down in the mud and let the river take you?" He shrugged.

A baby, only a few months old, let out a cry. Her mother rocked her gently, then offered a breast to nurse.

"You ready to drown that baby?" Kris asked, hard and unwavering.

"No," the mother answered, tears in her eyes.

"Well you better get ready, because that's what this guy is talking about." Kris stood. "Okay, you've got it bad, probably a lot worse than anyone else in human space right now." She turned slowly in her place, staring hard at each face as she passed it by, demanding that they look at her, listen to her.

"When Sam's dad came here fifty years back, there were lots of corporations ready to stake him . . . for half ownership, for real control over him. He held out, got a loan . . . and paid it back. I bet he paid it back early," she guessed. Apparently right because she got a proud nod from Sam, a scowl from Brandon.

"Well, I got news for you. There's a lot of banks around that still lend money that way. Sure they don't send people out to train wrecks to hunt for folks so down they'll sign anything. They don't have to. But when this mess is over, and the sun comes out, they'll be there for you."

"You gonna loan us the money, Longknife?" Brandon spat.

"Brandon, your hearing's gone bad. Didn't I just say I'm Navy?" Kris pointed at the gold bar on her collar. "Navy doesn't make loans. We're here to get as many of you out of this mess alive as we can. But Brandon, you aren't thinking very straight, either. You want to get Grearson fever into the water supply and kill everyone on this mud ball. Folks, think this one through with me." Kris continued her slow turn.

Eyes were up now. She had their attention.

"You let Grearson into the river, and it's going to poison Port Athens. Folks are sick and hungry down there. They're going to start dying. A lot of them will be people like me, who came here to help. That the thanks you want to give us?"

A few heads shook. *Finally, they were reacting.*

"Everybody south of Athens is starving. We're shipping them food just as fast as we can. And if the fever is in our water, that means we'll be taking them fever, too. Grearson normally kills half the people who get it. Figure you, your wife get it, one of you dies. Your son, your daughter get it, one of them dies. But folks are starving. They're already sick. Three out of four are going to die. Your family gets it, maybe you'll be the one who lives. Maybe just your daughter. Who's going to take care of a six-year-old orphan kid? There are worse ways to die than the fever."

Eyes that had stared back at her empty now showed emotions, fear, terror, anger. Yeah, she had their attention.

"But you want to know the really sick part of this whole idea of Brandon's? After Grearson's wiped out just about every living soul on Olympia, there's still going to be empty houses, tractors, barns. There's still going to be farms that dead people worked all their lives to build. They'll be bought up, for a penny on the dollar. And when the corporations send out their hired hands to make money for them, up in orbit," Kris waved a thumb at the ceiling, "before they land, they'll give them a shot like the one my medic wants to give you, and it won't matter that Grearson's in the water supply here. The vaccine will keep them healthy so they can work their life away for that corporation. Ain't that funny," Kris sneered.

Nobody laughed.

Taking his cue, the medic pulled his shot gun from his bag, put a vial of vaccine in it, dialed up the amount, checked it against the one lantern burning in the house and looked around. "Who wants a shot?"

The woman with the baby shed her coat and offered her bare shoulder. The medic placed the gun against her skin; it went off with a small click. She pulled the child's diaper down to offer its rump. There was a second click. Sam had his coat off, Karen, too. A line began to form.

Kris turned to Sam. "I've got two climbers ready to go up Lover's Leap. How much rope do you have?"

"Plenty."

Kris looked around the room. "Who wants to help my people climb that hill?"

16

"So, Kris, who climbs the cliff and who stays down here?" Tom asked in a tight whisper out of earshot of any rancher. The whisper didn't hide the tremble in his voice.

"You don't have to go if you don't want to," Kris said, ready to admit she'd volunteered Tom enough for one day.

"Cut the crap, Longknife," he snapped, anger hardening his whisper. "One of us has to stay here. Somebody's got to give them a kick in the butt if bright boy over there starts something again. You're probably the best for that. A Longknife staying here shows they haven't been abandoned." Tom gave a resigned shrug at his own logic. "I'm going to climb that cliff. If they can't make it, someone's got to let you folks at the bottom know. And if I get to the top, I can probably raise the net and get us some help," he finished.

"Sounds logical." Kris nodded, keeping her voice even.

"Yeah, so why don't I like it?"

Kris could think of a dozen reasons. "Beats me," was what she said.

"I should have run the first time I saw you. I keep hanging

around Longknifes, and I'm gonna end up with a medal. Last words me ma told we was, 'Don't you go getting any medals. We have all the metal we need hereabouts.' "

"Why don't you go see if there's any little people under that hill that will help you up it?"

"That's not a hill, that's a cliff. Only thing around them is ogres. Don't you know your fey?"

"Father read me to sleep with cabinet minutes and political analyses. Never read any fairy tales."

"What do you mean, fairy tales? Woman, they're as real as any political analysis." Tommy had his lopsided grin back.

"Can't argue that with you. So, you'll go up the hill, and I'll keep the home fires burning." *Until the river floods the fireplace,* Kris left unsaid. They shared a laugh at nothing in particular. The people around them seemed to take heart at that. Together, Kris and Tom stepped out into the pouring rain.

Sam, José, and the two climbers had collected a dozen men and women. A woman brought a thermos of hot tea. As the climbers hefted rope, hammers, and other climbing gear, Sam explained the general plan. "We've got tackle for two hoists. I brought it up from the main barn. Should have used it days ago, folks, but I just couldn't believe it would get this bad. Sorry," he said.

"None of us saw it coming," a ranch hand said.

"Anyway, we'll snub down a couple of ropes here; you let out your rope as you climb. Once you're at the top, you can haul up the tackle and get the hoists going. Then we'll send folks up. Worst cases you'll have to haul. Folks that can do something will climb best they can with you hauling some. That ought to do it," Sam finished lamely.

"How you know when we're up there?" a rancher asked.

Kris tapped her wrist. "Ensign Lien will climb with you. He'll call me when you're ready, as well as put in a call to Port Athens for help."

"They can't help us," José pointed out. "There's three or

four deep ravines between here and there. It's a long drive around. That's why we used the river."

"Tell the Colonel to use the boats as bridges," Kris said.

"The boats?" Tom echoed in disbelief.

"Yes. Ours worked fine the first time, even when I repaired it. Tell Hancock just not to use it a third time."

"If you say so." Tom looked none too sure. Kris was pretty sure Hancock would do just about anything to give them a hand. Well, maybe her. She was one of *those* Longknifes.

"It's either that or the damn boats don't like Longknifes," Kris said, ignoring the question of whether its philanthropic provider wanted a certain Longknife dead. That thought would save for later.

The climbers trudged for Lover's Leap. Kris followed, trying to spot in the rainy dark where the highest ground lay for her last stand. OCS had included an hour of treading water or a mile swim. She'd managed that fine, but she hadn't had a hundred sick and half-starved civilians to keep afloat as well. The ground rose slowly. There were stunted evergreen trees on the rocky ground. The closer she got to the cliff, the more there were of jagged boulders, ragged proof that the rocky face before her was prone to landslides. After all Kris had been through that day, a falling rock looked like just another way to die.

The climbers shared out the rope they were lifting, Nabil and Akuba first, José next, the ranchers following. Tommy was last; Kris surprised him with a hug. "Stay safe, Tom, your ma doesn't want a medal, remember."

"A little late for you to start thinking about that," he grumbled but softened it with a tight smile. Kris had dragged a boy up the river. It looked like she was sending a man up the cliff. "See you in the morning," he said and turned to follow the others. The ends of two thin lines were tied to the biggest stunted trees available. The climbers carried coils of the rope to let out as they went. It should last them to the top.

Kris didn't wait for them to disappear into the mist

overhead but turned back to her own work. "There any bales of hay left?" she asked Sam.

"Not many. We were only a few weeks away from giving up on the last of the herd and eating them. Then the water rose."

"Think we could use it to build a dike around here?" They turned back to the cliff, watched as the leader and his light disappeared into the gloom above their heads. "I just don't know where they'll set up the hoists," Kris concluded. That was their problem; much to do and too many unknowns. The two plodded back down the trail for what Kris would quickly learn was a whole new vestibule of hell. At least that was what Tommy would call it.

Kris had spent four days preparing for the drop mission on Sequim. For that, she'd had data, plenty of data, data overload, except, as it turned out, not the right data. Here she had nothing. There, she'd had gung ho marines. Now her command consisted of everything, from a three-month-old to a ninety-seven-year-old. She had the sick, the depressed, and most of all, the tired and hungry. The tired she let sleep. At least with the supplies they'd boated in, the hungry got their first decent meal in a year. Enough to give strength for the climb without overfilling half-starved stomachs. As the sleepers awoke, they were fed. Some, the very young or elderly, managed to go back to sleep. Others, feeling almost good for the first time in months, hung around, ready to do something but unsure what. Kris started a list of folks she was about ready to send up the hill on their own. Brandon, who'd somehow missed joining the first string, was at the top of her short list.

"Aren't you going to do something?" he insisted for about the forty-eleventh time.

"Nope." Kris answered while helping feed a three-year-old. "We've moved the rope and the hoists to the trailhead. Some guys are moving what hay bales we have up there. You want to help them?" She'd offered that job before, but it didn't suit Brandon's fancy then. It didn't now. The picks and shovels were already there. What Kris wanted was to know how high the water was, but that was one job she'd never give Brandon. The child fed, her mom took her and began singing a lullaby. Kris glanced at her wrist; three hours until sunrise. Probably three and a half before they got any light down here. Waiting.

Waiting was supposed to be what ancient women did while the men were away at the war or earning a living. Kris concluded that men were wimps. Turning her back on Brandon, she headed for the door. Outside, she ran into Sam headed in.

"What's the river like?" she asked as he backed up.

"Rising. There's almost a foot of water at that dip in the ground between here and the trail head. We're pulling a barbed wire fence down, gonna use it to mark the trail."

"Sounds good."

"Could you call that other navy fellow, ask him how things are going?"

"I could, but would you want to answer a phone when you were halfway up that cliff?"

"No, but it's just not knowing that's making everyone edgy."

"Sam, they could get two hundred and fifty meters up that hill and be stuck at the last fifty." Kris didn't like to think about that, but it was the truth. The sun could well be up, and they still might not know for sure.

"Sam, Sam, you better come quick," a runner shouted as he slid up to them.

"What's wrong?"

"Benny just fell off Lover's Leap."

Kris didn't ask for more explanation; she started running. The runner did a quick reverse and led the way; Sam stayed on her heels. As reported, the water was up to mid-calf for a stretch, but a line of fence posts was being hammered in place. The barbs on the wire between posts didn't look too nasty. Close to the cliff, Kris spotted a light and cut toward it.

A half dozen men stood around one. A glance at the body showed Kris all she needed to know. The arms, back, and legs went in far too many directions. Gashes on the man's face showed where he'd bounced off rocks on the way down. A gnarled pine lay across him. But that wasn't what held Kris's attention. The team was alternating lead climber. That climber would cover the next stretch, then pull the rest up by a rope secured to the rock face, trees, whatever was locally handy. What had gone wrong here? Had the rope broken? Were there more fallen climbers out in the dark? Kris ground her teeth as she eyed her comm-link. But before she'd bother Tom, she'd make this dead man tell her everything he could. She stooped by the body, found a loop of rope and followed it. That required moving the body. She rolled it over with a firm shove.

"God, lady, that's Benny."

"She knows what she's doing," Sam cut in as Kris followed more rope. There was blood on it, and blood on her hands, but she followed the rope until she found the end under Benny's lopsided skull.

"The rope's been cut," she said. "Did Benny have a knife?"

"Of course he does."

"You see it?" The body was again moved, this time gingerly by men who knew and loved the man. Benny's knife was missing.

Kris stood, holding the end of the rope, and swallowed hard at the message she read in it. "He cut himself loose when the pine came out." Kris had tasted the courage it took to lead a drop mission, and she'd drunk deep of the courage that let you charge into battle, gun blazing, but she had to wonder if she could have eaten the plate that fate set before Benny. Could she cut herself loose, give herself the long fall, to make sure her fall didn't take her buddies down?

"Kris, you there?" Tom spoke from the commlink.

"Yes, Tom. How is it?"

"Pretty bad there for a while."

"I'm here with Benny."

"Was that his name? God . . ." The link choked to silence.

"Have mercy on him," someone finished beside Kris and knelt to close the dead man's eyes.

"Anyway, we were in a bad place, but we're all through it now. The next hundred meters looks pretty doable, but I still can't see the top. We're all tied back together. I'll call you later. Out."

"Kris, out."

They left Benny where he fell; the body should go up the hill if they had time. Like all the climbers, Benny had been vaccinated, but Kris had no way of knowing if he was coming down with Grearson. If he was, Kris doubted the vaccine could have done much good in the few hours since he got the shot.

The water was already up to Kris's knees as she waded across the low spot back to the cabin. That settled it for her; with two hours until dawn, she'd get everyone bundled up in whatever might keep them warm and start them for the trail head. "How are the sick doing?" Kris asked the medic as she came in the cottage.

He shook his head. "Give me one medevac flight, and I'd bet my last dollar they'd all live. But taking them out into that rain . . . I just don't know."

"I need to move them out there now. If we stay here much longer, I can't be sure they'll get to the trailhead at all."

The medic closed his eyes and breathed out a long, hurting sigh. "And we've got to get them or their bodies up that damn cliff. Yes, Ensign, I know my duty to public health outweighs my obligation to my patients. Damn. I know it. That doesn't mean I like it much."

"Not much to like today, is there?" she said, putting a hand on his shoulder. "I'll get tarps to the trailhead. The wind's kicking up, but we'll do what we can."

Kris sent them out into the rain in groups of five or so. She wasn't surprised an hour later to discover that she and Karen were nearly alone. An elderly woman remained; she'd been fussing about with children and somehow missed each group going out. The woman with the baby had also held back. "She's got a bad cough," she offered by way of explanation.

Kris took a last glance around the one-room house. It was strewn with empty food cartons, vaccine bottles, the general refuse of a hasty exit. The bed was stripped of blankets and sheets, used when the sick were carried out. If it stank, Kris's nose was long past noticing. Collecting the lantern from its place on the dining table, Kris turned to follow the mother and child. The water was ankle deep as they stepped off the porch. Kris followed Karen and the old woman; they seemed to know the way. By the time they got to the start of the barbed wire fence, the water was up to Kris's knees and had a current to it. Kris put one arm around the mother's shoulders, the other to the wire. The mom hugged her baby close with both arms.

When they reached the low spot, it was clear the older woman had a problem. Short to start with, the water was well up to her shoulders. "You stay here," Kris told her charge, then moved up to help Karen. Holding the elderly woman between them, they got her across the hundred meters of what could only be called a running river now. As a gawky teenager, Kris doubted there was any reason for a girl being six feet tall. Tonight, Kris would have gladly added another four inches to her stature.

Once across, Kris handed the lantern to Karen and immediately turned back. "I'll go with you," Karen offered.

"No, you two get to the trailhead. There's still a patch of dry land there. Dry yourselves off."

"In this rain?" the old woman cackled. "You're dreaming." But Karen got her charge moving. Kris took it slow going back, refusing to believe that the current had gotten faster, the water deeper, in just the time since she'd made the last trip.

Again, Kris put one arm around the mother's shoulders, the other on the top wire of the fence. "Watch your step," she told the mother and child. They went slow, planting each forward step firmly before removing weight from the back leg. Kris was lifting her trailing foot when the woman beside her went down.

In a second, Kris knew she was losing her. She grabbed for whatever she could and got a fistful of coat collar. Kris locked her hand down on the wire, grabbing a barb. Metal cut deep into her palm, but Kris squelched a scream that would have robbed her of air as she was dragged under by the burdened mother.

The fence had been meant as a guide, not a support. As Kris and her charge hit it, the poles nearest to them gave up their hold on the muddy ground. Kris fought to get a foothold, to get her head above water, to get a breath, to hold on to the wire, to hold on to the woman. Somehow she managed them all.

By the time Kris got one foot to hold, she was a good twenty meters downstream. Holding on to the wire and the mother, Kris knew a single foot could not hold, but the several one-legged hops she did manage let her get her head above water for a moment and breath into her lungs.

Now Kris concentrated on getting her second leg down. She did a double hop and sank both feet into the mud. Still, the pull of the current on her and the mother was too much. Kris was dragged downstream for another three hops before she got her stance just right to fight the power of the river. In place, Kris got her own head above water, then pulled the mother toward her, raising her head into the night air.

"Can you breathe?" Kris yelled into the woman's ear.

"Yes."

Despite the wild ride, the woman was still holding her child above the water. "The baby?"

"She's coughing."

"Good." Kris turned to face the raging water. Feet firmly planted, leaning into the current at nearly forty-five degrees, Kris worked the barb out of her palm with the fingers of her bleeding hand, then moved her grip on the wire over a hand's width to the left. She risked a side step of a few centimeters. Then another. Moved the hand past the next barb, got a good grip, then moved a few centimeters over. Checked her grip on the woman. Then repeated.

The water was cold. Kris's bleeding hand quit screaming at her. Now her problem was making sure the cold flesh was holding fast to wire and collar. Feet leaden, Kris pulled them from the mud and moved them over. *Careful. Careful. Ignore the knotting in your calves, the ache in your thighs, the numbness spreading throughout your body.*

A month passed, maybe a year, as Kris made her way, step by step, across the raging current. Despite the passing of eons, the sun did not rise to throw even gray light on Kris's struggle.

Only when the water was down to Kris's waist did she risk settling the woman in place behind her. "Thank you," the mother said breathlessly. The baby sneezed. That was thanks enough for this whole damn project.

It took less than a week to get to ankle-deep water. Karen and Sam were waiting for them. "I was worried when you didn't show," Karen shouted in Kris's ear. "Are you all right?"

"Now. I think," Kris answered, and was grateful for an arm from Sam. The rancher took a look at Kris's bleeding hand. "We'll see if we can't use some of those medical supplies you brought."

The medic examined Kris's palm, like a bleary-eyed gypsy fortune-teller. Then he gave her a shot, cleaned it out, and bandaged it. "That's going to give you a problem going hand over hand up a rope," he told her. "I'll see that you get a lift up."

"This little thing?" Kris said, making a fist. "Ouch." It hurt like hell and didn't get very tight.

"You get a lift," the medic said and turned back to his fever patients. They'd rigged a lean-to using the tarps and some wood that had been part of the barn until recently. Eighty people milled around in the space between the cliff and the rising water. Five small kids, now fed, had a game of tag going, chasing each other through the water and around the adults. That brought smiles from even the sick ones.

Kris looked around for what to do next.

Off to her left there was a rattle as rocks came off the cliff. A second later, a dark-clad body followed, hitting the cliff and bouncing into a stunted pine. Kris and Sam headed for it as Kris's commlink came to life. "Kris."

"I know, Tom, you lost another." It was Akuba, the dark-skinned man that Kris had dragged upriver. The fall had crushed the life from his body. Behind Kris, mothers corralled kids and pulled them away from this sign of their mortality, possibly all their mortalities.

"We're about twenty meters from the top," Tom shouted from the commlink. "There's no good way up. Akuba, José, and Nabil were trying three possible routes."

"Akuba's didn't work," Kris finished for him as she turned to face the ranchers. Several men and women knelt in the mud, praying. Kris hoped their god was listening. Sunday around the prime minister's residence was a day for providing a church-based photo op to the media. That was all Father expected and all Kris understood of church. Tommy was probably up there, hanging on to a rock, and praying. Kris hoped Someone was paying attention to all the words.

"I know," Tom went on. "José and Nabil are still climbing. They didn't even look back when Akuba slipped. God, and I thought marines were tough."

"Keep in touch," Kris told Tom and cut the link.

"We'll know in a few minutes," she shouted to all the interested parties and turned back to Akuba's body. From his jacket, a small chain had slipped out, the medallion on it covered with flowing arabic letters. Kris knew that Islam forbade images. "Allah is great," she whispered gently as she closed the man's eyes. Kris wondered if there was some sort of prayer she should have said over Willie, her dead wanna-be hero. Another thing she'd better learn to do if she intended to stay in this line of work.

If she didn't drown today.

"Kris, Kris," came fast from the commlink. "I think Nabil's in trouble. Stay there. Don't move," Tom shouted on-line. "Let José get to the top, for God's sake, man, don't do it."

Kris tried to picture the struggle taking place above her head. When you delegate a job, you've got to live with what happens, she reminded herself. She ordered herself to silence. The last thing Tom or any of them up the cliff needed was someone yakking at them from the safety of the bottom.

Kris concentrated on what she could do. The water was starting to lap at the clearing around the trailhead. Akuba's fall seemed to show that the climbers had edged to the right of the trailhead, the upriver side. "Those of you who want a job can start lugging the hay bales over here," she announced in a calm, carrying voice that cut through the low rumble of ongoing babble. Some hurried to obey; others stayed on their knees. At the moment, Kris wasn't willing to bet who was right.

"Damn you, Nabil," came from the commlink. Kris got ready to dodge more falling bodies. "He made it," Tom continued, his voice half awe, half laughter. "That son of a bitch made it!" That coming from the usually soft-spoken Tommy got a raised eyebrow from Kris as she tapped her wrist unit.

"Made what?" she asked softly.

"Not to the top," Tommy quickly corrected. "But he was hanging on by a hand and a foot, and it didn't look like he was going anywhere. He's back to climbing, now."

"The climber's safe," Kris shouted to the ranchers. Several crossed themselves. Others whispered, "Praise the Lord."

"Kris," came plaintive from Tommy.

"Yes, Tom."

"Ensign Longknife, you down there," came in an all-too-familiar and none-too-happy voice.

"Thank God you're here, Colonel," Kris screamed. "The Navy's here," she yelled, loud enough to be heard at the top of the cliff without benefit of net. "They're here."

"The marines have landed, Ensign, and the situation

better not be out of hand. Drove all night like the devil to make it, but we're here and alive. Ropes are going over the side, so look out below. How many people you got down there?"

"Ropes coming down," Kris yelled; people backed off as six of her hired gunmen from Port Athens rode ropes down the hill. "Eighty to ninety, sir. And sir," she said turning back to the commlink, "we can't trust those boat/bridges."

"So I learned. One went poof on me as I was pulling it back to move on. The other left a convoy on the wrong side of a very deep ravine. Third time ain't no charm with these jokers. Left me with a half-loaded convoy, so I came back to base early to find one of my ensigns had gone off half cocked."

"Yes, sir. Sorry about that, sir."

"You almost sound like you are."

"It's been a rough day, full of learning experiences."

"Ensign, I want you on the first rope up."

"Sir, we've got some pretty sick people," was Kris's answer.

Sam had come up beside her. "She'll be on the first one," he shouted over Kris.

"At least somebody down there has sense. Who'm I talking to?"

"Sam Anderson. I own this ranch."

"Colonel Hancock, here. I own that ensign's ass. Ship it back to me." So Kris found herself on the first rope lift up, half climbing, half being dragged. There was applause as Kris started up the cliff. She put it down to the joy of the rescue starting. It couldn't have been for the little she'd done. The cliff was not straight up. Some sections were rock, gravel, and mud at no more than a forty-five-degree angle. Kris climbed and slid her way up those, helping guide basket stretchers with three of the really sick civilians. Other parts were a rocky face, too damn close to straight up to make any difference. Kris let herself be pulled up those.

As expected, the Colonel was waiting for her at the top. Jeb was there, too, with a good chunk of her warehouse crew. Jeb had the winches well in hand; at least the Colonel didn't seem inclined to oversupervise him. "My truck," was all he growled at Kris. But he handed her a blanket as he growled.

Kris found Tommy in the back of the truck the Colonel waved her to, huddled in a blanket, sipping on a hot cup of coffee with a big, satisfied grin on his face. He pointed at the thermos and Kris poured one for herself, took a sip, and almost choked. This was very Irish coffee. Someone had been quite liberal with the whiskey.

"No wonder you like it." She coughed.

"Good coffee, but not worth what I went through." He held out a hand, raw and bleeding. "I'm never so much as climbing on a chair for the rest of my life."

"The medic should be up next lift. He can look at your hand." Kris held up her bandaged one. "Barbed wire makes a lousy lifeline." Tom sipped his whiskey-laced coffee in silence. Kris held the cup in her numb hands, letting its warmth seep into her. The whiskey she could do without.

A few minutes, or maybe a year later—time seemed quite flexible at the moment—the Colonel settled into the backseat. Kris and Tommy made room for him. Two civilians piled into the front seats. The driver goosed the engine to life, slipped the rig in gear, and headed them into the pouring rain. Wipers struggled against it. Maybe from the front seat they could see something; it wasn't visible to Kris in the back.

"Is that fear I see in your eyes, Ensign Longknife?" the Colonel chided her. Kris leaned back in her seat, concentrated on her coffee. Wouldn't do to have the Colonel think that after all she'd been through she was afraid of a little drive in the country . . . even if the driver were charging blind into the dark. "We've got the worst cases and the medic in the back, so don't get too unwound," the Colonel advised the team up front. They both leaned forward, faces almost in the front windshield.

"Right, boss. We get you there fast. Maybe even alive. No extra charge."

"Civilians," the colonel growled. "Almost as dumb as some ensigns I know. Just what did you think you were doing, Longknife?"

Kris had been expecting this. "Sir, the Anderson ranch had a medical emergency that involved a threat to the public health of this planet. Exercising independent judgment and within calculated risks, sir, I led a boat expedition to their relief. Our efforts were hampered by what I can only assume at this time is a flaw in the design of the liquid metal boats. We were in the process of rescuing the ranch hands when you arrived, sir." There, she'd made her report, and every word of it was true . . . even if the color was off a bit.

Hancock just shook his head. "So you didn't have time to call me, to run your approach through your commanding officer?"

"Sir, you were committed to a convoy mission. There were no roads to the Anderson ranch. A boat was the only way to reach it," Kris said, knowing full well the truck she was riding in raised certain questions about her estimate of the situation. "Until the liquid metal boat just became liquid it wasn't going so bad, sir. The boat formed up like it should. I even repaired the prop when it got bent on a log. Sir, we didn't have any other choice."

Colonel Hancock's face remained a hard mask as Kris tried to explain why she'd done what she did. If anything, the tightness around the eyes got tighter. "You'd activated the boat modification system twice already."

"Yes, sir. But I didn't know it was a problem."

"If you'd touched that keypad one more time on the way up, it would have dumped you and your entire party into the river."

"Yes, sir," Kris agreed lamely.

"I found out the damn system was a piece of crap while using it for a bridge. It broke while no one was on it. In one day I already knew we had a problem, and no lives were put at risk. None but yours, because you didn't have any choice."

Kris didn't have an answer for that.

"Ensign Lien, Tom isn't it."

Kris was grateful to have the Colonel's full attention shift from her, then felt guilty all the same. Tom hadn't done anything she hadn't asked. No, this was the Navy. She'd ordered him to do what he did. She was the senior. She was responsible.

"Yes, sir," Tom answered.

"Did you have no other choice?"

"No, sir. I had choices."

The Colonel already had his mouth open. He closed it and eyed Tom for a moment. "What makes you say that?"

"We always have choices, sir. At least, that's what my grandma always says. No matter how bad it looks, there are always choices."

"What choices did you have today that Ensign *Longknife* didn't seem to notice?" *God, the sarcasm was thick.*

"We could have called you, sir. Asked for your advice. At least kept you informed of what we were doing. I didn't think about driving up here like you did, sir, but maybe if we'd kicked things around a while, we might have thought up that idea. But sir, we didn't have the lift crane for moving the bridges on and off the trucks. I'm not sure we could have done that, sir."

"But you didn't think about it then, did you?"

"No, sir."

"Why?"

"Kris said to take the boat, sir, and I followed her lead."

"You followed her, without question."

"Yes, sir," Tom said.

Kris knew that wasn't quite true. Tom had griped, questioned, complained, but she'd ignored him. Ignored him just like she always did.

"You'd follow her if she led you into hell."

"Yes, sir."

"Or off a cliff."

"Or up one, sir." Tom actually managed a lopsided grin.

"You listening to this, Ensign?" Kris had the Colonel's full attention again, but she was busy digesting what Tom said.

"Yes, sir."

"You hearing it?"

Kris took a moment before she answered. "I think so, sir."

"You are a leader. Probably the best damn leader this lash-up has. You filled a vacuum I let happen. For that I bear a great degree of responsibility. However, young woman, you can never slough the responsibility for the leadership *you* provide. From the moment you set foot on this planet, you've been leading. People who were bitter or lost or struggling on their own found they could trust you to lead them. That's the way it's supposed to be. But damn it, woman, you're in over your head. You are an *ensign* in the Navy. That means a lot, but it doesn't mean anywhere near what you, *Ensign* Longknife are making it mean."

Kris had done her best to follow the Colonel, but somewhere in there, he'd lost her. "Sir, I don't understand."

"You are a *Longknife*. You don't have a choice. That's what Ray Longknife said after he killed President Urm. 'There was no alternative.' That's what your Great-grandpa Trouble said after he took a battalion up Black Mountain and kicked a division off it. Just like Tom here learned from his grandma that there were always choices, you learned at your great-grandfathers' knees that there are no other choices."

"That's not true, sir. I can count on one hand the number of days I've seen Grampa Ray. And Grampa Trouble is my mother's least liked man in the universe. He hasn't been in our house since I was twelve." *And he saved my life.* "The whole reason I'm in the Navy is to get away from being one of *those* Longknifes. Sir." He wasn't being fair to her. He didn't know anything about her. And he probably didn't care, either. Kris put down her hardly touched mug of coffee, folded her hands, and prepared to ignore the rest of what Colonel Hancock of machine-gun-crowd-control fame had to say.

But the Colonel said nothing.

Instead, he leaned back into his seat and studied her for a long moment.

Outside, the rain was still coming down, making the truck's cab rattle like a drum. The driver and his mate carried on a conversation mainly of "There's a big rock." "Watch that hole!" "That mud looks too deep, go right."

Kris was tired . . . exhausted by the day and drained by the Colonel's critique. She just wanted Hancock to finish his say and let her get some sleep.

Then the Colonel smiled.

"Family is a strange thing. I remember visiting my old man when my son was seven or eight. I can count on one hand the number of days my dad spent with my son. But I kept having to swallow a smile that weekend. You see, my son had mannerisms just like my dad. Now, on a seven-year-old, they were cute, kind of rough and jerky, but looking at my dad push his hair back just so or tug at his ear just the way my son did tickled me. Funny thing was that, as I said, my son and dad hardly ever saw each other, so I kept wondering how they got the same mannerisms," the Colonel said, brushing his hair back with his right hand, then tugging at his ear. Almost Kris smiled.

"Your son got your dad's mannerisms from you," Tom said.

"Yeah, and, of course, I don't live in front of a mirror, so there was no way I could notice what I did. But my son did. And I guess I noticed what my dad did."

"But not consciously," Kris said.

"Never consciously."

And Kris unfolded her arms, ran a nervous hand through her hair, and started thinking out loud. "I remember Father telling parliament that they had no choice but to keep capital punishment on the books until Eddy's killers swung at the end of a rope. I can't count the number of times I heard him say, 'There *are* no other options.' That was the way he'd send me off to a soccer game. 'Win. There is nothing else.' "

"You couldn't lose?" Tommy asked, incredulously.

"Not as far as my father was concerned," Kris assured him. Then she frowned at the Colonel. "But sir, when I first saw the base, it was a mess. I knew we had to do something about it. I knew we had to clean up the mess hall, improve the chow. The alternative was just to wallow in the mud."

"Yes, and you did good. Thank God you did what you did. You've given me a second chance. You've got my command moving up, rather than lying on its back looking up. You've fed a lot of people. You chose right that time." The Colonel held Kris with his eyes. They were just as demanding, but somehow not as hard as they had been when he'd climbed in the rig.

"This time I chose wrong."

"Yes."

"But how do I know when I'm gonna be right and when I'm headed up a cliff?" Kris demanded.

The Colonel leaned back in his seat and snorted. "That's the question every ensign wants answered."

"And . . ." Kris insisted.

"With luck, you'll have a pretty good handle on it by the time you're a full lieutenant. You better know it damn good by the time they pin eagles on your collar."

That only added to Kris's confusion. "Sir, that doesn't answer the question, does it?"

"No. You've got to find the answer yourself. Better yet, the *answers*. There're a lot of answers you think you know that you don't."

"Sir?" That one really puzzled Kris.

"Who killed President Urm?" the Colonel asked Kris softly.

Kris blinked and said the first thing that came to mind. "My Great-grampa Ray."

"Right, it was in all the papers. Not a history book disagrees. How much have you read about that operation?"

"All the books, I think. The city library had a couple of bookshelves on that war that I went through when I was thirteen." *And drying out.*

"But you've never read the classified postaction report that Army Intelligence did, have you?"

"If it wasn't in the library, I guess not."

"You're cleared for it. It's old news now. Next time you get close to a secure station, call it up."

Kris didn't want to know later; she needed to know now. She was about to have Nelly get it any way she could, when Tommy leaned around her. "Colonel, what does it say?"

The Colonel chuckled at the unexpected source of the question, but he went on. "It says that Colonel Longknife and his wife Rita have got to be two of the gutsiest people in the universe. They flew halfway across human space with a bomb, then carried it through the tightest security devised by man up to that time. And they did it calm and cool as you please, never giving anyone a hint of what they were doing. Not the crew of the ship carrying them and not the security guards they walked through. Damn, that's guts."

"So they did kill President Urm," Kris said.

"It would seem so. But there's a few questions the poor intelligence weenies writing the report couldn't answer. As a visitor, the Colonel was seated about as far from the podium where Urm was presiding as the security guards could get him. Yet the autopsy report says the bomb went off right in the president's face. There were fléchettes that went in the front of his skull and were halfway out the back."

"How do you get a briefcase in someone's face?" Tommy asked.

"A good question." The Colonel chuckled. "A better question is, how do you get said briefcase in someone's face *and* live to tell about it?"

"But Grampa's given hundreds of interviews about the assassination. Are you saying he lied to all those reporters?"

"I've read a lot of those interviews, young woman, and I'll bet you money that your grampa has not told a single lie to any of those media meatheads. If you've never been out on the tip of the spear, Kris, you have no idea what goes on there. Those reporters ask the questions their

editors think the average Joe on the street wants to hear.
Figuring out the facts of what actually happened is as far
from them as"—he snorted—"this planet is from drying out.
No. Reporters may understand garden parties, and they think
they understand political campaigns. But understand what a
soldier does, a sailor? You might as well ask a pig to sing
opera."

Then the Colonel turned his full concentration on Kris.
"But you know what it's like. You've been the spear two or
three times. And if you're going to keep putting expectations on poor guys like Tom and those boatmen and your
warehouse department, you better have a damn sight better
understanding of just what the people did who made '*those*
damn Longknifes' into one word.

"Now get some sleep. We've got good people taking
care of things around here. The Fourth Highlanders will be
down tomorrow, and we can turn a lot of this stuff over to
them." The Colonel got a strange smile on his face. "And
maybe I can talk their Colonel into throwing a Dining In
before I ship you off planet."

Kris didn't like the look on the Colonel's face. There
was something about the Highlanders or the Dining In that
held a surprise for her. It couldn't be the Dining In; that
was just a meal. "The Highlanders, sir," she coaxed.

"LornaDo's Fourth Battalion, Highland Regiment.
I think Regimental Sergeant Major Rutherford is still
with them. His dad was with the Fourth and that platoon of
marines that your Great-grampa Trouble led up Black
Mountain. A battalion and a platoon out to evict a division
from a mountain they'd dug in on. Not just any division,
but one whose officers were indicted war criminals and
whose sergeants and men knew they were going to jail if
the newly elected government on Savannah wasn't run out
of town fast. You know the story."

Kris nodded; of course she knew the story. At least, she
knew the story the way the history books told it.

"Well, Sergeant Major Rutherford's dad was one of the
few Highlanders to walk off that mountain on his own two

feet. Gives him an interesting perspective on how the battalion won that particular battle honor." And with that, the Colonel turned to the window and, bumpy road or not, went to sleep.

Kris was maybe ten seconds behind him.

17

Kris missed the sonic booms of the incoming landers, what with the rattle of the wind-whipped rain on the side of the bus. She kept her eyes on the end of the runway; sooner or later they'd have to break out of the mist and scud. The weather folks had promised rain and warm for today. As usual, the rain was here, but warm was not. Kris wore a sweater and undress khakis.

Despite the injunction of the commander back on Wardhaven who'd briefed Kris for this operation, she'd brought along two sets of khakis and one set of dress whites. Upon return from her river trip, Colonel Hancock ordered her, effective immediately, only to wear them for the rest of her stay on Olympia. "Maybe you'll get in less trouble if you don't dress for it." He might be right; for the last thirty hours she hadn't caused or gotten into anything the Colonel didn't approve of.

Of course, the Colonel hadn't gone off base, and Kris was restricted to it. Well, maybe not restricted, more like grounded. When her parents grounded Kris, it wasn't an excuse to skip soccer or ballet or any of *their* stuff, only *her* stuff; same with Colonel Hancock. She could run the warehouse. Indeed, she was expected to get it in shape to turn over to the Highlanders. Tommy was still running the motor pool. He likewise was cleaning up the loose ends for a transition. It was just that neither one of them was supposed to take a step out of the warehouse or base or the direct line between them. And the Colonel had taken to dropping by at odd times to make sure. Five or six times a day.

It was as if he didn't trust Kris any more than her mother or father had when she was sixteen. Then, the Colonel had better cause for that certain lack of trust. Accompanying the rented buses and vans was Kris's first trip beyond her short leash. Kris had asked Tommy if he wanted to meet the Highland battalion; he'd jumped at the chance. Kris also asked the Colonel if he'd like to go. "Who's riding shotgun?" he asked without looking up from the reports on his desk.

"A couple of contract riflemen from the soup kitchens." Again today, just about the entire navy detachment was on the road delivering food.

"You going to start a war or do anything else that will increase the amount of paperwork on my desk?"

"No sir. Definitely not, sir. Straight boot ensign stuff, sir. No Ensign Longknife stuff either, sir," she grinned.

"Get lost," he grumbled. Then thought better. "But leave bread crumbs. I want you back here for supper."

"Yes, sir." She saluted. His return salute actually qualified as a military honor.

Both landers broke out of the scud at about the same time. Kris shook her head. This bunch were real hard cases; the landers were trying to set down side by side. On the collection of potholes Olympia called a duty runway, that was suicide.

Apparently, the pilot of the second lander took one look at the runway and came to the same conclusion. He added power and climbed into the overcast for a go-around. The first lander went long, missing the worst potholes, and did a reasonably smooth run out. It was taxiing toward the number-one parking slot when the second lander touched down. Unwilling to be soaked, Kris waited on the bus to see what happened next. Only when the second lander was at a full stop did both landers lower their aft loading hatch. Two men in plaid kilts and tall fuzzy hats marched smartly to either side of the hatch. Then the most . . . interesting . . . noises began.

"What are those women doing to those poor cats?" Tommy asked on net.

"Be careful who you're calling a woman," came from the Colonel, apparently monitoring the net.

"And that racket you're complaining about is bagpipes," Kris added.

"I thought all you Santa Marians were fake Celts," Hancock said. "Don't tell me you don't know what a bagpipe is."

"And didn't it not survive the hungry survival years?" Tommy answered in the thickest brogue she'd heard him manage. "And don't we thank Jesus, Mary, and Joseph every day for that small grace."

"And I thought I was shipping you off planet because you were too tied up with that Longknife person. Ensign Lien, you're not going to survive the night."

"And am I supposed to be afraid of men in skirts?"

"Ladies from Hell." Kris had read a bit of history. "Now Tommy, me lad, you can either start walking back to the base—" The heavy rain picked that moment to get heavier. —"or you can move your two buses around to Lander Number Two." Kris pointed to her driver, and she got in gear. "I'm bringing my three buses to Lander Number One. Don't worry, Colonel, we'll manage this evolution real smooth."

"And why have I come to doubt a Longknife's definition of *smooth?*" the Colonel asked in a brogue all his own. "Hancock out."

Kris ignored the last canard; her driver led the other two buses onto the apron and parked well behind the first lander.

Now troopers were filing off both landers, rifles on their shoulders. Under the influence of the pipers, their on-board route step quickly fell in sync as they marched, cutting each corner, to their places in formation under the watchful eyes of sergeants. Their kilts were mainly red, with a bit of green, black, and white in the mix. They wore bonnets of the same tartan and tan jackets that, in the rain, were quickly turning to a deep brown. As far as the sergeants and men were concerned, though, it might as well have been a balmy summer day back at the cantonment. Their heads were high; their steps were sure. They were on parade, and the devil take the wind and rain.

Officers dismounted from the forward hatch of Lander One. They also were smartly dressed, with no concession to the rain. Kris shrugged out of her poncho and opened the door. A gust promptly splattered her khakis, but she quick-marched for the rapidly forming command section. A tall, dark-skinned woman in full kilt came to meet her. Kris saluted as they met. "I'm Ensign Longknife, your liaison with Port Athens base."

"I'm Major Massingo, Battalion Adjutant," the other said, returning the salute. The major saw to Kris's introduction to Colonel Halverson, Battalion Commander. Kris had already checked; Halverson was six months junior to Hancock, so there shouldn't be any trouble on that account. Halverson seemed jovial and happy to be here. Kris suspected he'd never been anywhere he wasn't happy to be.

"Major, let's get the troops aboard the buses the good ensign has been so kind as to provide us. A few weeks ago when we got our orders, I feared we might have to march into town. Under arms, no less."

Kris brought the Colonel's briefing up to date while the major passed the order to the regimental sergeant major, who shouted the Colonel's orders to the company sergeants. It was a thing of beauty to watch the workings of a chain of command that had probably been in place when Bonny Prince Charles was learning escape and evasion in the original Highlands of Scotland.

"I understand that you require an officers' mess," Kris said as the troops marched in single file to their assigned buses. Hancock had informed Kris that the informal approach to meals that the detachment had been following would not meet the Highlanders' standards.

"Quite right, Ensign," the Colonel nodded. "Mixing officers and other ranks simply is not done."

"I've found a suitable facility only two blocks from the base," Kris assured him.

"Good. We are coming up on the anniversary of one of our proudest battle honors, Black Mountain on Savannah. Colonel Longknife sent us up that bit of real estate."

"I have the honor of being Colonel Longknife's great-granddaughter," Kris told him.

"We will be honored to have you as our guest at our Dining In, Ensign."

Kris nodded at the offer, then decided she'd better get it all off her chest. "General Tordon is also one of my great-grandfathers," she added.

"Good God, ma'am! Trouble and Ray both in your family tree."

"Quite an honor," she assured the Colonel.

"If it isn't a curse." He chuckled, leaving Kris to wonder if the two Colonels had already put their heads together. Once Kris got the troops back to the base and took Halverson to Hancock's office, the two rapidly made it clear that they had old-time ground-pounder talk unsuitable for an ensign's delicate ears, so Kris headed back to her office at the warehouse.

Jeb met her at the gate with Sam Anderson. "Longknife, you mind adding a couple of more foremen to the staff? Nights are getting kind of long for me."

"Sam, you want to work for me?"

"Kind of hard to run cows on a sunk ranch. Folks here around have found space for me and my people to squat, but we got to work, even if the food is free."

"Pay's not all that great," Kris pointed out. "A Wardhaven dollar a month."

"Beats nothing. After that miracle, we figure we owe you."

"Wasn't my miracle," Kris shook her head. "You folks were working as hard as us to climb that cliff."

"I don't mean the climb out, ma'am. The miracle was you even knowing we were in trouble. That radio we were hollering into. It was good for talking up and down the canyon, but what with the cliffs and all, we never talked to anyone more 'n say fifteen, twenty miles away. Had a repeater on the top of the canyon, a land line running along the bottom. Both got washed away six, seven months ago."

"Satellites?" Kris asked. The prime minister always said miracles were what lazy folks used to explain perfectly understandable happenings . . . once you applied logic to them.

"Too low on the horizon. So long as we had the repeater, it weren't a problem. Once it was gone, so were we. Can't tell you how surprised we were that you heard our call for help."

Not as surprised as Kris was fast becoming. She hired Sam and one of his foremen to work with Jeb overseeing the warehouse. Several of Sam's men were also available. Others were joining a road-building team that would work with the Highlanders' engineering platoon, putting things like the runway into better shape, knocking together bridges for the supply convoys and, in general, starting to put the planet's infrastructure back in order. Ester and Jeb saw real growth opportunities for the Ruth Edris Fund for Displaced Farmers. Kris would have to put the fund on a formal basis before leaving Olympia.

There were a lot of things to think about as Kris settled down to her new desk in her new office on the other side of the building from the burned-out wreckage of her old one. Spens was again at work, checking accounts and keeping her legal. Lots of things to worry about.

So why did her mind keep gnawing at the question of a radio signal that took a few extra bounces? No question, the atmospheric conditions on this planet had to be way beyond weird. So, no one had ever succeeded in getting a direct message out. Probably, no one had ever been so desperate, so unrelenting in their efforts. Right. A miracle put together by elbow grease and a volcanically hashed E layer or F layer or whatever radio waves bounced off. Easy explanation.

"Nelly, when did the Peterwald ship break orbit?" Might as well eliminate the first question Aunt Tru would ask.

"The yacht *Barbarossa* broke orbit Thursday, 11:37 A.M. local."

"When did you intercept the message from the Anderson Ranch?"

"Thursday, 9:42 A.M. local." Okay, so Auntie Tru would get to ask a second question.

"What time did I first activate the liquid metal boat?"

"Thursday, 10:12 A.M. local."

Kris gnawed on her lower lip. There was one more question Tru would ask. "Nelly, did the *Barbarossa* have a line of sight down into the canyon?"

"The yacht *Barbarossa* was in an unusually elliptical orbit that gave it a one hundred-percent probability of a line of sight on the bottom of the Little Willie Canyon three orbits a day, and better than fifty percent for four more orbits."

No use beating around the bush with her own computer. "Nelly, did the *Barbarossa* have a line of site on the canyon while we were intercepting the Anderson message?"

"Yes."

So there it was. That "miracle" could well have been someone on the Peterwald ship, maybe Hank, maybe not, sending her up a deadly river in a boat with a big potential hole in it. But just because Hank had the *potential* for killing her didn't mean that he *wanted* to kill her. She couldn't have been that bad of a first date. Kris tried and failed to laugh at her own joke. It made no sense. Why would Hank Peterwald or his dad or granddad want Kris Longknife dead?

One thing was clear: her mother or father wouldn't consider that question. "Nelly, search the net for similar instances of liquid metal boats failing."

"I have conducted that search. There are no instances of

similar failures in any of the 53,412 boats manufactured to date. Likewise, there have been no reports of similar failures by spaceships, either during their manufacture or operations."

"Thank you, Nelly, and thank you for thinking ahead of me," Kris told her AI. Tru must have passed along some real interesting upgrades last time.

"You are welcome. I will endeavor to do similar searches in the future."

Kris leaned back for a moment and stared at the ceiling. Once was chance. Twice was coincidence . . . maybe. Three times had to be enemy action. Question was, who was the enemy? Kris really didn't want to think a nice young guy like Hank already had an enemies list. Of course, Kris considered herself a nice young gal, and she sure was on someone's enemy list.

"Kris," Nelly said tentatively.

"Yes."

"Are you aware a five hundred thousand dollar, Wardhaven, donation has been made to the Edris Fund?"

"No, Nelly, I've been leaving the money handling to you. Who made the donation?"

"It is anonymous, but since it came in, I have been backtracking the money transfer. It is very likely that it came from Hank Peterwald."

"Before or after his ship broke orbit?"

"I cannot be sure, but it appears afterward."

Kris mulled that over. Hank would not be putting money in the bank account of a dead gal. Not likely. This planet was a major potential nexus for trade. Per Nelly's financial report, Wardhaven financed half of Olympia's start-up costs, the rest spread around liberally. How things were now that someone was stealing IDs and selling property off planet, Kris would check on later. But if Hank knew anything about what his papa was up to, he would not be giving Kris money to make things better.

Kris was surprised at how much better she felt, deciding that Hank was not out to kill her. But if Papa Peterwald wanted Olympia's jump points, just how far would he go? What more should she do before she left?

The rain pounded against the window of her new office. The windowsill showed caked dirt along with the streams of water running down it. Right, there was volcanic ash in the rain. What else? "Nelly, has anyone visited the volcano that blew up and caused this mess?"

"No."

Then, of course, why visit the volcano when it was coming to you? "Has anyone done an analysis on the ash?"

"There is no report in the public record of such a study."

Kris spotted an empty can next to the coffeemaker. Maybe she was crazy, but maybe it was time to be a bit paranoid. Outside, coffee can in hand, she studied the flow of water. There was a ditch behind her building; rusted pipes from the roof tried to keep up with the rain, dumping what fell into the ditch before the weight of the rain collapsed the roof of the warehouse. Jeb came up as Kris was staring into the ditch's muddy waters.

"Can I help you, ma'am?"

"How much volcanic ash was in the early rains?"

"Quite a bit."

"Think some of that original ash might be down in that ditch?"

"Wouldn't be surprised if some was. You want a souvenir?"

"Ought to have something. Might have it made into a vase or ceramic pretty. You know."

Jeb studied her for a moment, then got the attention of a youngster, no more than twelve. "Lady here wants some of the ash from our volcano. You mind getting a bit muddy?"

The kid looked like he'd been asked if he wanted to go to heaven. In no time he was up to his knees in water, using the coffee can to collect from the lowest part of the culvert.

"This what you want, ma'am?" he said, presenting Kris with a brimming can of mud surely as proud as any suitor handing a diamond ring to his girl.

"Certainly is," Kris said, slipping the top back on the

can. From her pocket, she pulled a dollar coin. "For you, thanks."

"My mum would never let me take it," the boy said, bobbing his head and not touching the money. "You been feeding us. She'd wallop me if I took it."

Kris pulled out a second coin. "This is for your mother for raising such a good boy. Now take both of them, and run along."

The kid did not look convinced, but a nod from Jeb did the trick. He grabbed both coins and ran for the gate, dripping muddy water all the way. "The least I could do for messing up his clothes," Kris chuckled.

"And for humoring a woman that's got to be as crazy as any two coots on this waterlogged planet," Jeb said.

Kris looked down at the coffee can in her hand, wiped some of the mud from it, and turned back to her office. "We'll see who's crazy," she muttered.

TWO evenings later, Kris followed Colonel Hancock into the officers' mess of the Fourth Highland Battalion, LornaDo Planetary Guard. Their invitation was as much due to what Kris and Tom had done for the battalion in the last forty-eight hours as for who Kris was. With the help of Kris's friends among the local craftsmen, a run-down and abandoned restaurant and lounge was now a spick-and-span officers' mess and club in the full and traditional meaning of the word. Overstuffed chairs were scattered around the room in tasteful conversational groupings. The walls now displayed photographs of past battalion commanders and groups of officers as well as the battalion's victorious soccer teams. One drop ship had actually delivered carefully packaged oil paintings of several battle scenes from the battalion's honor roll. The place was heated nicely, carpeted, and smelling of new paint, and Kris could hardly believe it was the abandoned dump they'd started with. Or that such a place could exist in the mildew and swamp that Olympia had become. The books

Kris read as a kid told of how a bit of England had been transplanted to India. She'd wondered how that could be. Wardhaven was no Earth and proud of it. Now she saw how . . . and why . . . a battalion might transplant LornaDo, or maybe England, to Olympia.

A new wall pierced by double French doors set off the club from the dining area and the bar. Still, as Colonel Halverson met Colonel Hancock, a young private in full dress blues and kilt hovered at his commander's elbow to take orders.

Commander Owing, Hancock's XO, was already in a corner, deep in an overstuffed chair with a scotch and immersed in a discussion with the battalion's medical and supply officers of the best single malt in human space. Lieutenant Pearson had passed on the offer with a sniff. Kris had heard her exclaim loudly to the duty section outside the Colonel's office about drunken debauchers. The Colonel's hearing must be going bad; though at Kris's elbow, he didn't seem to hear a word. Both the other ensigns drew the duty, leaving Kris, Tommy, the Colonel, and all the officers of the Highland battalion free to drink and/or debauch, so long as they dressed properly for the occasion.

The Marine Colonel and his Navy pair apparently were the last to arrive. Kris's white choker and pants had been an interesting fashion statement at the recognition reception on Wardhaven against all the bustiers and petticoats; here she was one of the few not showing off knees. But Colonel Halverson made sure that his visiting Marine Colonel in his dress blue and reds and the navy types in their whites were made right at home.

"What will you have?" the Colonel said, greeting them jovially, then turning to the private at his elbow. "Pass the word to all servers: these people's money is not good in the mess tonight. Yon woman's great-grandfather went up Black Mountain with the battalion. He was a Marine, but for someone ashamed of his knees, a damn good fighting man."

"Yes, sir," the boy said, looking at Kris as if she might have just stepped down from Mount Olympus.

"And pity be if their glasses go dry."

"Yes, sir. What are you drinking, ma'am?"

Kris had gotten comfortable ordering nonalcoholic drinks over the last ten years, but clearly, a soda would put her out of step with these men and women. The Colonel's scotch hadn't dragged her into a bottle. Grampa Trouble might be right. Maybe she wasn't an alki. With a swallow and a smile, Kris said, "A seltzer with a twist of lime, please."

Tom ordered Irish whiskey, neat; Colonel Hancock ordered what Colonel Halverson was drinking, and the boy marched for the other room. The new Colonel turned to the old.

"You said she had guts in a fight. Now I see she can be just as stalwart in the mess." The Highland Colonel turned back to Kris. "By the by, young woman, you'll not be the only one walking that line tonight. There's one or two others in the mess that know that beastie. Now, Colonel, I've a mind to show you a few things." And with that, the two senior officers left Kris and Tommy standing in the middle of the club.

Kris stood there for about two seconds before a young woman in full kilt was at her elbow. "I'm Captain Rutherford. I understand we share the same luck."

"I'm Ensign Longknife. What luck might that be?" Kris did not want to spend the evening comparing seven- and twelve-step programs and arguing which was better.

"Your great-grampa and mine both walked off Black Mountain with their balls still attached." The woman grinned. "Otherwise, we wouldn't be here. I'm Emma," she said, holding out her hand.

"I'm Kris," Kris said, shaking the offered hand. "This is Tom. He's from Santa Maria, but don't hold that against him."

"Ah, then you like our pipes."

"Love them, a wee bit of home so far from the old sod."

Kris almost choked on the first sip of her newly arrived drink.

"It can't be that strong," Emma said.

"Exactly the way I ordered it," Kris assured Emma and the young soldier who'd brought it, while eyeing Tommy like the rat he was.

"We always have choices," Tommy reminded her.

"Social coward," Kris whispered back.

"Politically astute. I thought, being a politician's daughter, you'd have more appreciation."

"Am I walking into the middle of something?" Emma asked.

"Only something that started at OCS when he stopped to tie his shoe in the middle of the obstacle course," Kris said, nudging Tommy in the ribs.

Emma studied them for a second longer, then smiled and shrugged as much as the heavy woolen doublet allowed. "Let me introduce you to some of the battalion's other junior officers."

Kris found herself trying to remember a blizzard of names made easier by a regimental tendency to give everyone a nickname. Chalky was Second Lieutenant Sutherland who had an unruly thatch of white hair. Tiny was, of course, well over two meters tall. In general, the junior portion of the officers' mess seemed comfortable with their place and delighted to meet Kris.

It was when Emma passed Kris to Major Massingo for introduction to the senior members of the mess that things got complicated. The corner with Commander Owing had acquired several more officers by the time Kris was pointed in their direction. Kris wasn't sure, but it seemed the mess server had made quite a few trips to this circle to refill empty glasses. The doctor looked unlikely to be vertical by the time supper was announced. After the obligatory round of names, Kris was prepared to bow out and return to the juniors when the supply officer, a major, blurted out, "And what does a Longknife think of devolution? You aren't going to stand with Earth, are you?"

A bit surprised, still, Kris found that an easy one. "I'm a serving officer, sir, I stand behind my commanding officer and in front of my troops," she said, deflecting the question.

"So you'll just do whatever you're told," the doc said, leaning forward in his chair and almost falling out of it. A friend helped steady him.

"I'm kind of new at this, just a boot ensign, but I understand that we're supposed to follow orders." Kris smiled and took a step back. It wasn't enough to get her clear of the conversation circle, however.

"But what if a greater good is involved?" put in a major with crossed muskets on his doublet. "If some idiot orders me to charge a heavily defended bunker, it's usually understood that I can use smoke and hunt for a flank." That got nods from his messmates. "So what's our duty to the greater good? It was a Longknife who killed President Urm. Was he following orders?"

"No," Kris agreed.

"So, when evil's rampant, the soldier, for the greater good, may have to act on his own?"

"The books I've read said Urm was pretty bad," Kris pointed out. "I don't see anybody around like him. Do you?" Kris wanted out of this discussion. It didn't look like anyone was taking notes, but you could never tell when someone might have their personal computer set to record. "Nelly," Kris said subvocally, "start recording." At least she'd have a transcript of this conversation if it did hit the Wardhaven media.

"Yes, evil as barefaced as Urm makes it easy to know a soldier's duty. But what if it's an insipid, tepid evil, wearing away the soul and psyche of humanity a little at a time? Evil that seeks to turn virtue into vice and pass vice off as virtue a bit today, a bit more tomorrow?" That didn't require an answer from Kris; she'd learned long ago to keep her mouth shut. No reporter ever got a sound bite from silence.

"Yeah," another officer filled the dead space. "When did you ever hear a civilian say anything good about duty? I don't even think honor's in their vocabulary. My kid's going to college, got her a new set of writing gear. Damn computer asked her how to spell honor. Wasn't in its database." That got snorts all around. Kris couldn't believe it was true, but it made a great story.

"Strange, it was in mine," Kris said before she knew her mouth was open. Damn, Judith said she had too much fight in her for her own good. And after all those therapy sessions, it was still there.

"Your father is rather high in the government. Your grandfather is running Nuu Enterprises. Some might see you . . ." A hand waved diffidently as if searching for words.

"As part of the evil," Kris supplied.

"More like allied with its sensibilities," the major countered. "Listen, we soldiers know the score. The game is rigged from the top. When common people don't like it, we're the ones that get called in to keep them placing their bets at the table. Look at your Colonel Hancock. Some farmers on Darkunder don't like the way the cards are falling, him and his battalion get called in. Dumb farmers don't know when to call it quits, so a lot of them die. Hancock did what he was told to do, and see what it got him. He had the power on that mud ball. When they ordered him off to face a court-martial, he should have marched his battalion down to that bunch of fat money men that passed for a parliament on Darkunder and sent them all scurrying for their rat holes. Then the media would have made him the farmers' bloody messiah rather than their murderer."

Kris couldn't say she was shocked. Back at the Scriptorum, there'd always been the right-winger, ready to call for war.

"What people need is fire and duty to purify them from the greasy money men and their cheap, easy ways." The vets on Wardhaven had said the same thing. Why was hearing it from a serving officer sending chills down Kris's spine?

Because these are the blokes that are supposed to stand between civilization and the rack of war, not the ones to bring it. The real question for Kris was, was this guy seri-

ous, or was it just the whiskey talking? Was he just pissed
that his battalion was stuck in the mud on do-gooder duty,
or might he really want to march down the street and take
over Olympia's government? Kris suppressed a smile.
He'd have a hard time finding any government to take
over. The exhibit barn the legislature shared every three
years with the weekly cattle auction had collapsed months
ago.

If this guy was for real, he wasn't Ensign Longknife's
problem. Colonel Hancock would have the job of facing
him down. And if it was only talk, whether drink- or anger-
inspired, it still wasn't Kris's problem. She'd faced kidnappers' guns and roving bands of heavily armed hungry.
She'd shown she had the stomach for a real fight. This kind
of O club bull session seemed rather tame now.

"Excuse me. Nature calls," she said and wound her way
out of the group to head for the ladies' room. Facing the
stalls, Kris concluded her heavily starched whites would
come away looking like an accordion, and wondered if
Wardhaven had any Highland units. A transfer might not be
a bad idea, except these guys charged machine guns when
they went into battle, and the Navy was smart enough to
take along a nice bunk and good chow when they went to a
fight. Kris splashed water on her face, told Nelly to quit
recording, and prepared to go public again. Major Massingo
and Captain Rutherford were waiting for her.

"That fellow is a blowhard," the major assured her.
"You did well to let it roll off your back."

Kris snorted. "I kept wondering if someone had a mike
recording. I learned long ago to be careful what I say."

"Must not have been easy, growing up a politician's
daughter," Emma said.

"Not many realize just what a pain it was," Kris agreed.
"Can I dodge Blowhard for the rest of the night?"

"Shouldn't be any trouble," the major assured her.

"We have a skiff racing team, one of the best on
LornaDo. The coach and pilots are dying to talk to you."
Emma said.

"Let's talk racing!" And that provided plenty to fill the time until dinner was announced, and announced in a most unusual way. One of the servers stopped to whisper in Major Massingo's ear. She rose, adjusted her tunic, and faced the door. "Pipe Sergeant, pipe us to dinner."

A sergeant in full regalia presented himself at the door, doing one of those strange double jumps that the Highlanders seemed to do as they came to a halt. "Ma'am," he shouted. After the most pregnant of pauses, he continued. "Pipes and drums, dinnerrrr paaa-rade."

With that, the sergeant marched forward, followed by two pipers and a drummer. At the spaceport, the sound of the pipes had carried. In the confines of the officers' mess, it threatened to crush skulls. Almost, Kris had Nelly do a double check on the structural integrity report they'd gotten on the building, but she was having too much fun watching Tommy.

His mouth hung open, his eyes were larger than dinner plates, and his ears were hanging on by a thread. "Take that, you liar," she mouthed at him. She could have shouted it, and no one would have heard her. But Kris could only relish Tommy's shock for so long. The officers were moving, some none too steadily, to form a parade behind their music. Major Massingo led off, as president of the mess, with the Colonels right behind her. Lieutenant Commander Owing and the majors were next, the battalion's company commanders, captains, right behind. Kris figured she and Tommy, as junior ensigns, would bring up the rear, but Emma gently took Kris's elbow and led her to join the company commanders and their first lieutenant execs. Tommy fell in somewhere with the platoon leaders.

And thus they marched into a dining room resplendent with linens and crystal, china and silver. The smell of roast beef almost knocked Kris off her feet, but a crescendo from the pipes carried her away. The walls were hung with battle flags. The Society flag held pride of place behind the head of the table with LornaDo's flag, but other flags the battalion had carried or captured hung along the wall as well.

Unity's red and black was there, along with several planetary flags that must have been captured in the wild days ninety years ago before Unity brought its brutal order to the Rim, then went down in defeat before the Society of Humanity's massed power. Did devolution mean a return to the days when every planet fought its neighbor for trade, for resources, for reparations that were little more than extortion by the more powerful from the weak? The battalion's battle flags were a visual reminder of humanity's history among the stars, and not the best part of it. Too bad something like that wasn't hung along the walls of the Scriptorum. Now, that would be a real education for the students.

Kris took the place Emma pointed her at. The chaplain offered grace, half thanks and half proud highlighting of battles won. The mess president followed the prayer with a toast, "To absent friends," that seemed as much a prayer as the chaplain's. Then, as the pipes paraded out, the soup was served.

"I understand you've had an exciting time of it," one of the captains said to Kris. With that opening, Kris provided all listening a quick overview of what she'd done and discovered about the local situation.

"So the fighting is pretty much over and done with," another captain summarized the most salient point of Kris's brief.

"Some of the farms still won't give the swamp runners the water off their septic tanks. You can spot them easily. They've got more bunkhouses than people in line to draw food. Others are just the opposite. Long lines of hungry, and you'll have no idea how they sleep them."

"How do you think it will shake out when this is all over?" a different captain asked.

"Your guess is as good as mine. I'm just glad that is not part of my mission. If you don't mind some advice, I'd suggest you don't let it creep into yours. There are some real nasty things at work here that you're not going to solve with a rifle."

That drew nods. "No surprise there," Emma added, "considering the strategic value of this system. You know you can reach almost fifty systems from here. Most of human space is less than three jumps away."

"I came across that when I was boning up on this place. It has great trade potential."

"Or military value," a captain added.

"Military value is nice, but it only pays when you're at war," Kris pointed out.

"You haven't been paying much attention to the media, have you?" the captain said.

"When you're up to your neck in snakes and wilde-beests, it doesn't leave much spare time," Kris replied.

"You might want to bone up on the news on your trip back," Emma suggested.

"What's happening?"

"There's a lot of unhappy people in the Society," a captain said.

"And getting unhappier," another one added.

"You know that little girl you rescued?" Emma said. Kris nodded. "Hardly a day goes by that she or the criminals that grabbed her aren't in the news."

"I thought that would have blown over."

"It's not blowing over," Emma assured Kris.

"Or isn't being allowed to blow over." Kris's comment was greeted by shrugs from her messmates.

The pipes were back, escorting the fish to the table. When it quieted to the dull roar of table conversation, Emma went on. "Several planets have already set up travel restrictions. Anyone born on Earth or the Seven Sisters has to request a visa to enter them. No visa, no entry. Some Earth business types are screaming its just a way to restrict trade, cut them out of business."

"Let me guess," Kris cut in. "Anyone serious about business writes ahead for a visa. The "One Flesh, One Galaxy" types or those more interested in media attention, don't."

"Got it in one." A captain grinned. "I always said

Longknifes did, too, have the brains God promised a billy goat."

Kris flashed a toothy smile at her supporter.

"Some planets already have taken ships back," Emma said, "painted on their flags, and declared their fleet not subject to Society orders. Earth is demanding the ships back or payment."

"A lot of those ships were built by the planets that manned them," Kris pointed out. "Wardhaven has several squadrons we paid for. Have we withdrawn them from Earth command?"

"No, your father has dodged the issue so far. But you're right about the problem. The planets that have taken ships back say they don't owe anything. They built them because Earth didn't provide enough to patrol the Rim. Earth says the ships were gifts in lieu of higher taxes and wants cash."

So it was back to the tax issue that had put Kris on the beach and the *Typhoon* in stand-down mode. In college, Kris had been surprised to discover that Earth's tax burden was about the same as Wardhaven's, 30 percent on average. But much of Earth's tax money went to social services. Earth investments were usually where there were cops on the beat. Wardhaven spent a much higher percent of her taxes on research and extra military ships, which were mainly used to patrol the new start-up worlds where much of Wardhaven's private investment capital went.

Earth and the Rim, even after eighty years, still had very different ways of looking at things and different ideas about what was important. Question was, could her grampas find enough shared interests to manage the change coming without it all coming apart with a big boom? Different officers at the table had different opinions. Kris kept her own to herself.

Sometime during this discussion, a piper had begun a tune. Several junior officers took claymores from the wall and began sword dances. Tommy was out of his chair, watching one dancer real close. There were shouts for Tommy to join in. Kris suspected the dancer had more to

do with Tommy's attention. That particular second lieutenant had a lightness to her step and a particularly broad
smile when her whirling brought Tommy in view.

Emma bent close to Kris's ear. "Your ensign seems to
have found a friend."

Kris shrugged. "Plenty of my friends have friends," she
assured her. *The story of my life.*

The dancing was interrupted as the beef was announced.
This particular animal got major honors. Sergeant, pipes,
and drums led the way as two servers carried a full roasted
carcass in on a pole. The mess cheered as the first slice
was cut and offered to the president of the mess. She
deferred to the Highlanders' Colonel, who in turn deferred
to his Marine guest. Hancock accepted it, cut a large portion off and, with his fork still in his left hand, bit into it.
Only after he declared it perfect did the servers begin to cut
and distribute choice cuts to the rest of the mess.

"You have a very interesting way of doing things," Kris
told Emma when the pipes marched out again.

"It's our tradition."

"When we are done with this fine beef, I have a question about your traditions." A thick slab of roast beef was
soon set before Kris. She discovered that Yorkshire pud-
ding looked more like a roll and that at least the English
tradition of stewing their vegetables had not survived. That
was one bit of merry old England that Kris would not
mourn. When the cheese and fruit were brought in with
much less fanfare, Kris turned to Emma.

"Was it traditions like these that took your battalion up
Black Mountain?" That got nods from all in hearing. "My
Colonel suggested I hear from Regimental Sergeant Major
Rutherford the story of Black Mountain, the way he told it to
you both before and after you put on the uniform. Colonel
Hancock thought he'd tell me about it during the Dining In."

"Oh, no," Emma shook her head. "The Regimental
Sergeant Major would never enter the officers' mess.
Certainly not during Dining In." Kris was beginning to
suspect there was the right way, the wrong way, the Navy

Way, and the Highlander Way. No wonder the Society of Humanity was having so much trouble keeping them all together.

One of the captains turned to Emma. "Why don't you tell her the story. I've heard you enlighten your new lieutenants. It wasn't just the nuggets that were spellbound in the mess those nights."

It took a bit more coaxing, but soon Emma turned from her selection of cheeses and fruit. She patted her lips with an immaculate white linen napkin, laid it down, then started. "If you paid attention in civics class, you know the situation on Savannah was bad. The old government had used its army to beat the civilians into submission. The soldiers spent more time on rape and murder than drill. More hours roaming the streets with knives and clubs than on the rifle range.

"Then Savannah had its first free elections, thanks in no small way to Kris's dear, if not yet departed, ancestors. The big players ran for the exits, taking with them their numbered bank accounts on Helvetica. That left just the little people, the ones who did the raping and the murdering, not the ones who ordered it. The army, such as it was, retreated back to its cantonment in the hills above the capital. Most folks were glad to be quit of them. Let them stay up there and starve was the mood of the man on the street. Unfortunately, the man in command knew there was a dam up there under First Corps control. Open those sluice gates, and the capital, with most of its people, would be washed away. They'd made Ray Longknife a general, but put few troops at his command. Those he had were professionals. And those he had included the Fourth Highlanders of proud LornaDo."

"Hear! Hear!" rang out up and down the table, and Kris discovered that the mess had grown very quiet. Glasses were raised in toast. Embarrassed to share this sacrament of her hosts with seltzer water, Kris followed their lead, then flagged down a server. "Whiskey, please." She'd be ready next time.

"There's a lot of gadgets in modern war, gizmos that can make a man think he's a soldier when he's not. The First Corps had them all, and if their people were none too sure how to work them, they could hold guns to the heads of technicians who would. There would be a bloody butcher bill for any and all who tried to invade their camp.

"Never trust an enemy to play fair, and never trust a Longknife, period," Emma said with a smile for Kris. "If he couldn't beat them with new soldiering, he figured to take the bastards down the hard, old-fashioned way. So he came to the Ladies from Hell, and the fancy Marines that held the line beside us. He offered us a night black as the devil's own heart, full of rain, thunder, and lightning. Then he added his own bolt from hades, an electromagnetic pulse that stripped a thousand years of contrivances from every soldier within fifty miles. Radar, radios, even night-vision goggles became just more dead weight for the poor booties to lug. With a will, Highlanders and Marines stripped their rifles of computers and vision gear. It was iron sights and cold steel for the rest of that night. So two hundred brave Highlanders and fifty dumb jarheads took off for a walk in Satan's rock garden."

"Hear! Hear!" again rang out. Kris's drink had just arrived. Glasses were raised all around. In proud blue and red, Colonel Hancock raised his glass high. "Dumb is right. Dumb as fence posts. Nobody smart would take the job."

Before the glasses were down, Colonel Halverson was on his feet. "To the bloody Marines. The only ones man enough to take the Ladies from Hell to that dance."

Kris raised her glass, and took no offense. Grampa Trouble had many a woman in his platoon on that hill. There were men, and then there were *men*.

"In the teeth of the storm, we went up Black Mountain. The first line hardly knew we were there before they had to choose: fight and die or surrender and take their chance with a jury. The second line was warned by the flash of our guns. Machine guns spat and mortars belched. Cannon spoke . . . all blind. Men lived and men died by the throw of a demon's dice. Here a platoon, there a squad moved forward across death's ground. They found their way into fighting holes and trenches. Men fought and men died while the fiends piped their own wild jig until the second line was ours."

"Hear! Hear!" again was answered with a toast. Kris drank, but the warmth in her stomach could not dispel the chill that made her shiver. Emma's words had transported her, the entire mess. They were there, in the lightning-streaked dark, in the shell-shattered rain. The troopers of the battalion that dark, distant night weren't men but gods.

"Our own cannon cockers applied themselves to their work with a will, lashing the second trench, then lifting for the third. Not a man of rifle and steel that night could help but bless the gunners who made the cowards duck and cry and throw their hands up at the first sight of steel or kilt.

"But as we closed on that final goal, the gunners did not lift their brimstone fire. Our Colonel fired the agreed-upon flare, but the enemy was waiting and drowned his proper color in a shower of lying hues. The gunners looked in despair to fathom the bayonet's intent. Runners were sent, but feet could not outfly bullets. Three men ran with the Colonel's words. Three men died.

"Then up stepped Color Sergeant McPherson, he whose twenty years were up, who carried his discharge papers in the pocket over his heart. 'I'll carry the message, Colonel. If an old fox like me can't cross that ground, no angel in God's heaven can.'

"The Color Sergeant slipped out of the trench like a ghost. Like a mist on the moors, he flitted from shell hole to shell hole. When flares turned stormy night to tempest-torn day, he froze like a rock. Shells flew at him, bullets reached for him, the enemy grabbed after him—and missed. No minion of hell could touch that messenger of our God.

"But fortune is not mocked, and the devil must be paid. A stone's throw from the first trench line, a rocket caught the brave Color Sergeant, picked him up, and flung him broken into the trench. With his dying breath, he passed the Colonel's message to Private Halverson. Now the torch was his. Without a backward glance, the private raced. Like a fearless hind he crossed the shattered field to where the gunners plied their trade.

"On the word of a private, the guns stood silent. At the word of the private, Black Mountain seemed split by quiet. And with a cheer we rose, each man and woman still able to slog through the mud. Those of the third trench who didn't run died where they stood or lived with their hands grasping for the clouds. We, the Highlanders of LornaDo, with a handful of brother Marines, took down a division that storm-racked night."

Once more the cry of "Hear! Hear!" was raised, and the glasses held high and drunk deeply. Emma seemed exhausted, as if she'd climbed Black Mountain herself. She certainly had taken the mess there. When she began again, she was subdued.

"In the morning, when those who boasted they led a corps saw our flag atop Black Mountain, they despaired. They say you could walk from one end of their cantonment to the other without touching the ground, the tossed-off uniforms were so thick. And those of you who know how mankind fought the long-tentacled Iteeche and know what a close-run thing it was, ask yourself if we could have held on until that last desperate battle if not for the weapons forged in the mills of Savannah? So when you gather for a drink, raise your mug with a thought to those fine Ladies from Hell who went dancing that night up Black Mountain."

The glasses were up and drained, and Kris immediately knew she'd made a mistake. There was no hearth in the mess to smash glasses that now were too sacred to ever be used for mere drinking. But as in so many things, the battalion would survive.

Colonel Hancock cleared his throat in the silence. "When did you first hear that tale, Captain?"

"At my grandfather's knee." She smiled. "I couldn't

have been as tall as his swagger stick. He was Regimental Sergeant Major, as my father is now after him."

"You took a commission."

"Yes, sir. Both Pa and Grandpa agreed the family had worked for a living long enough. This time they wanted an officer." That brought snickers from along the table, louder at the lower end where Kris suspected Emma's own platoon leaders found humor in the thought that they and she did not work for their pay. As silence returned, the Marine Colonel continued.

"The day you pinned lieutenant's bars on, I suspect your father had some advice for you. As misfortune would have it, there was no one there to perform that sacred duty for Ensign Longknife. Would you be kind enough to share with her what your father or grandfather gave to you?"

"Sir, that would be telling, and the Regimental Sergeant Major is not one I would choose to cross. He might not forgive me."

The sober looks exchanged among the officers at the table showed agreement. The RSM was one few officers would cross.

Colonel Halverson stood. "I think I can arrange the proper absolution for you from the Regimental Sergeant Major," he deadpanned. The mess broke up in gales of laughter but quickly fell back to silence when the Colonel did not join in but stood, his demeanor most serious. "If the ensign who bears the weight of a name like Longknife has neither had the blessing nor the admonitions appropriate to her calling, I can think of none better than the words the Regimental Sergeant Major shared with you."

Emma nodded. She stood and turned to Kris with a solemnity that brought water to Kris's eyes and a tremble that she had not felt at college graduation or Navy commissioning, or for that matter, even under fire. Kris found that to be the center of such intense attention made her skin burn. But that was not what made her tremble. To look into Emma's eyes was to face a goddess.

And there is nothing so frightening in the world as the face of absolute truth.

"These are the words of the Regimental Sergeant Major," Emma began softly. "The stories are true, I have not lied to you. Now you will command people, men and woman just as scared, hurt, tired, and confused as those in the stories. The difference between just anyone scared and tired and a soldier is you, the leader. It will be your duty now to help them find, deep within themselves, the courage and the will to go on, to do what you determine must be done.

"Never abuse that power. Waste that, and you waste not just the moment, but a life, and all that life could have held for some trooper.

"When that moment they have trained and lived for comes, you hold the power of life or death for your people. To earn that, you must be their servant. Are their feet dry? Is their food decent? Do they have a place to sleep? You answer for them before you seek an answer for yourself. You have been given authority over them. You waste it if you use it for anything that doesn't prepare the both of you for that critical day when death is at your side.

"You and they will live, or you and they may die. Despite all the care that you put into your training, chance may call the tune when the moment comes, but that is no excuse to leave anything more to chance than the laws of the universe demand.

"Despite all you've heard in the stories, there is no room for heros. You do not make yourself a hero. If you chase after glory, you waste your time and their lives. Glory will find you on its own. If you must spend time thinking of future glory, pray that you and yours will be ready for its heavy burden when it falls upon you in the heat of battle.

"And lastly, remember, we tell the stories not to entertain or bask in others' glory. We tell them because we must. We tell them to keep faith with the faces that haunt our nights and shadow our days. They gave up all they might ever have had—love, children, sunsets—not for a ribbon but for a faith. Not for a planet but for comrades. Not because they were ordered to but because they chose to.

"If you choose this uniform, you enter into that faith, lived and died for by so many before you. Break that faith, and though you breathe, there will be no life within you."

Done, Emma folded into her chair as if some spirit were going forth from her. Kris sat in a silence more sacred than she had ever touched. Somewhere the Colonel called for the pipes. They marched in, but their skirling did not break the silence in Kris's heart. Kris had gone through college graduation still in the heat of the words she'd passed with her mother and father over her Navy choice. She'd gone through OCS commissioning mad that her parents hadn't bothered to find time in their busy schedules to come. Her thoughts both moments had not been on what she was doing but rather on where she was from. Those moments she'd been wrapped up in being one of *those* Longknifes.

But here, these strangers with their traditions had kept alive something that brought her closer to what it meant to be a Longknife than she had ever touched. Yet, rather than making her smaller for it, it had grown her into something much more. Something was growing inside her, something she could not begin to fathom. Understanding would come with time. Time she had plenty of.

No longer hungry, Kris sat, hands folded into her lap. Around her, the mess went about its celebration. Pipes played. At some point, Tommy did try his hand, or rather feet, at the sword dance, and did it, if not with grace, at least competently enough not to bring opprobrium on the Navy. Kris's messmates left her in her silent bubble, like a child swimming in its mother's womb. And as with such a child, sounds, feelings, actions impinged on her and were taken into her, not so much by eyes and ears and fingers but somehow grasped whole.

When all was done and the pipes returned to march them from the mess and to brandy and cigars, Kris leaned close to Emma. "Thank you for sharing what you've treasured in your heart."

"I hold them there until it is time to pass them along to my daughter or son."

"I hope they won't mind the loan of them to me."

"There's something magical about them. Shared out, they're just as strong."

18

Colonel Hancock personally drove Kris and Tom to the spaceport next noon. "Not exactly the way I arrived," Kris said when he offered, thinking, *He really wants us gone*.

"And this place ain't anywhere near what it was when you showed up," the Colonel said. "Is it always this way with Longknifes? Their bosses either charge 'em with mutiny or give 'em a medal?"

"You tell me. I'm kind of new at this Longknife business," Kris said, and realized that it was true. Twenty-two years old, and she was only just discovering what she was really about.

The lander played the usual game of dodge potholes on its run out. As spacers and a handful of officers wound their way from shuttle to the buses Kris had hired, Colonel Hancock turned to her. "Give my compliments to Captain Thorpe. If he's anything like the fellow he was at the academy, he'll be happy to have a tiger like you on his boat."

"Hasn't shown much appreciation." Kris laughed. And if what the captain had been passing her way was his idea of happy, he was a very strange man.

"You have to remember that fellows like your captain put on the uniform to be war heros. Hasn't been much call for that out in space. I tried to talk him into joining the Corps, but he wanted to command his own ship. Wonder if he regrets that?"

"I'm not about to ask," Kris said.

"No, don't. It would ruin the effect of the fitness report I'll be forwarding. I suspect it may change the way he looks at you now that he knows he's got a tiger and not some debutante pussycat."

Kris could hope.

The trip back to Wardhaven was good for catching up on sleep and news . . . and what Kris had been putting off. She and Tommy studied the news feeds with scowls. As far as the media was concerned, what they'd been doing on Olympia didn't exist.

"And we could have been killed," Tommy snorted.

"Not a happy thought," Kris said, knowing that someone had been killed. How could she tell Willie Hunter's folks that he'd died for something important when the media ignored it? Kris had Nelly research all the final letters home recorded in literature. Feeling guilty, Kris cobbled some words together from the better ones and sent it off, telling herself it was better for the parents to have a good letter now than something better later.

But nothing in the media prepared Kris for what happened as she hiked though the crowded arrival hall at the bottom of the space elevator. A young woman walked up to Kris and Tommy, looked them up and down, then spat at them.

"You come to kidnap some little girl, you Earthy scum," she screamed even as she dodged back into the crowd before Kris could grab her arm, yell at her, *The Navy had rescued the last kidnapped little girl, and damn it, I did the rescuing.* While Kris was still shaking with unspent rage, Harvey appeared.

"Sorry. I thought after you rang off that I should have told you to wear civvies. There's a lot of bad blood around."

"And if I get my hands on that young woman, it will be flowing out her nose," Tommy growled.

Kris, surprised, gave Tommy a silent raised eyebrow.

"I mean it. I didn't go through losing your signal on that drop and chasing around in Olympia's mud with people shooting at me for that kind of treatment."

Unbidden, Kris saw again Willie lying in the mud, reddening the puddle with his blood, then the woman. Choking, she tried to find words to say to both. Maybe a poet could; she couldn't. "How bad is it?" she asked Harvey, willing him to talk, fill her head with anything but what was coursing through it.

"The PM's keeping Wardhaven in the Society, almost by his fingernails. It's going to break his heart when he finally has to give in. The opposition has demanded a vote. So far, he's managed to postpone it. Your pa wants Earth to call it quits first. That would give Wardhaven more leverage putting together some kind of follow-on organization out here on the Rim. There're fifty, sixty, maybe more planets that would join Wardhaven in some kind of confederacy. But so far, everybody's secceeding *from* the Society. Nobody's going *to* anything."

"Fifty, sixty planets," Kris said, doing the numbers in her head. There were over 600 planets in the Society. True, the newer colonies were only associates, but there were 500 voting members. "What are the rest up to?"

The old chauffeur shrugged. "Lot will just be happy to be rid of the Society. Greenfeld seems to be pulling a lot into some kind of federation, maybe forty, fifty, the ones they've colonized or hold the mortgages on. Wardhaven's got its own bunch; most were our colonies or places we helped. Savannah, Riddle. Pitts Hope is making noises like it might toss in with us. Big shock for Earth. They figured they could go back to the Society's original fifty and tell the rest of us to go to hell. Not that easy when some that fought Unity decide they like the Rim ways more than old Earth."

"Sounds confusing," Tommy put in.

"Ever tried juggling five, six hundred eggs?"

"Not eggs," Kris countered, remembering that Green-feld was run by the elder Peterwald. "Try six hundred hand grenades. And why do I suspect the pins are out of a few of them?"

"And aren't you starting to talk like me?" Tommy grinned.

"Only on a bad day. Harvey, I'm going to need to run some errands. You busy?"

"What do you have in mind?"

"I need to see Tru."

"Might be a problem. And speaking of eggs." The car was waiting where Kris expected. There was a new secret service agent riding shotgun. Kris remembered him from trailing brother Honovi at the reception. The agent was out, peeling a sticker off the side window. The windshield was spattered with eggs.

"Bunch of kids ran by," the agent explained as he slowly pulled off something declaring, Earth—Keep Your Hoods at Home.

Kris tried her hand at another sticker, Equal Taxation. Tommy pulled off one announcing, Humanity—No Limits. Harvey went around to the driver's side, growled, and pulled off a sticker saying, Remember Little Edith.

"Do I hear some jingoism jangling?" Tommy asked.

It wasn't a joke to Kris. "Looks like the opposition has discovered its slogans. Doc Meade said a good slogan could be more dangerous than an assassin at starting a war."

"Maybe." Harvey shrugged as he got the car into traffic, wipers struggling to clean the window of egg.

So now there were liabilities to licence plate PM-4. As the car pulled into traffic, she leaned forward. "I take it my problem meeting Tru isn't just that my father doesn't want me to."

"Right. Feelings are running high, daily protests against this or for that. Then there's the news snoopies looking for any scrap of trash to put on the media. They must get paid by the second. Anyway, our place is surrounded. So is Tru's. I had a bloody tail when I left to pick you up."

"It's still there," the agent said, turning around in his seat. "By the way, ma'am, I'm Jack. I'll be going with you whenever you leave the grounds."

"Not bloody likely, Jack," Kris snapped, pushing herself back into her seat.

"You might find me handy to have around."

"There've been three attempts to kill me in the last month. So far the score is me three, them nothing. I don't need help."

"They only have to get lucky once to make it them one, you nothing," Jack pointed out softly.

"You snooping for the prime minister?"

"I take it your father doesn't want you meeting this Tru person. You intend to, come hell or high water, and you consider meeting him or her more important than me keeping you safe."

"I consider me meeting her a damn sight more likely to keep me safe than you hanging around *and* telling the PM what I do."

"I'm a big girl now, so buzz off and leave me alone," he translated for her.

"Gosh, they actually assigned one that understands plain English," Kris marveled in pure sarcasm.

"Listen, my report only has to say you went out, you came back, I was with you. That's a Navy uniform you're wearing. You give orders and expect obedience. How much trouble do you want to make between me and the guy issuing my orders?"

Tommy snorted at that. "Nice try, Jack, but you haven't been around Longknifes long, have you? They don't care a whit for the problems they cause us lesser humans."

Kris shot Tommy a scowl. Then again, she guessed she did deserve it. With a sigh, she gave in. "I'll see what I can do to help you and your boss stay happy. What would you call it, Tommy, penance for how I treated Colonel Hancock?"

"More like how you treated me. And I'll believe it when

I see it," he said, settling deep into his seat and folding his arms across his chest.

Ten minutes later, Kris muttered, "I may need a little help breaking out of this place," to herself as the car drove into Nuu House. Marines stood at the gate, checking IDs; others walked the perimeter wall. They had to. There were five news trucks parked across the street. All sported satellite transmitters up and sending any and all feed from around the house. Kris spotted at least six news types following the progress of the car.

"They also have airborne cameras," Jack said before Kris asked. "But if you really want out of here unseen, I might be able to lend you a hand. You scratch my back, etcetera."

"I think I'll take you up on the etcetera. You got any running clothes?"

"I do, if you're willing to wear the Wardhaven U sweatshirt I give you," Jack said with a conspiratorial smile at Harvey.

"Uncle Harvey, have you been telling stories on me?"

"If it will get you a sweatshirt that will stop a three-millimeter dart at twenty paces, you're damn right I'll tell stories."

"You wouldn't happen to have an extra one of those?" Tommy gulped.

"From good old Santa Maria U." Jack smiled.

An hour later, Kris was wearing gym shorts and a sweatshirt with a bulletproof lining. She, Tommy, and Jack were jogging their second lap of the ivy-covered wall, approaching Kris's special section when Jack muttered, "Okay, guys, close them down," and led Kris through her very own private escape hole.

"How long have you guys known?" she demanded a minute later as they walked nonchalantly away from the stone perimeter wall.

"Probably before your great-grandmother paid to have it installed when she was a girl."

"The Nuus weren't political then," Kris shot back.

"They had money, and there's no such thing as money not being in politics," Jack reminded her, sounding very much like her Political Science 101 professor. Kris knew a losing argument when she stepped in one.

"Nelly, hail a cab."

Two minutes later, they were headed for the Scriptorum, the one place Kris had been able to tell Tru to meet them without actually saying the name. Tru seemed just as reluctant to trust the public net as Kris. Jack headed them for a dimly lit corner, usually reserved for the young and restless and in love types; it was early in the day and unoccupied. Kris and Jack got their backs to a wall. Tommy scowled and settled into the chair between Kris and the front door. "Don't like it?" she asked.

"Don't like having my back to whoever might be shooting at you," Tommy said with a glance over his shoulder.

"Don't fidget, and don't look around," Jack told Tom sharply. "Don't worry, I'll keep a lookout. Our biggest worry is a newsie shooting her with a camera. Heaven knows why."

"Heaven knows why they're not using a gun?" Kris asked.

"I doubt you have to worry about a shooter today. The prime minister's politics are not that divisive." Jack told her, apparently unaware that Kris had not been joking about three attempts on her life. Well, the prime minister had overseen Jack's briefing. Kris started to bring Jack up to date, but he was still talking background and he was interesting to listen to.

"Right now, folks aren't sure what's going to happen. Some big people with lots of money in the betting pool don't take well to that. They want to know which way to jump well before the time comes. But you learned that at your father's knee."

"And some of them like to get a thumb on the scales that decide which way we all will jump," Kris finished the statement.

"You're the expert on these things." The agent shrugged.

Kris ordered soft drinks all around when the waiter came. It was the same one who'd served them before, but with them in the student spring uniform of the day, he paid them no mind. Tru arrived when the drinks did and slipped into the vacant chair, backing it up against the wall so Jack's view was unhindered. In slacks and a sweatshirt that bore a university logo that was twenty years out of date, she looked the perfect old professor. "Good to see you," she said. "You having an interesting break?"

"Travel is a very broadening experience," Kris offered. "Good to be back where the sun shines."

"Right, I've been rather busy with local matters to keep my thumb on what you've been up to. Just why do we need to meet?"

Kris wanted to scream at Tru that Olympia and Willie's death and all the civilians she'd killed were worth people's time. Still, the fair part of her had to admit her personal struggle on that sodden planet hardly held a candle to all humanity choosing up sides and deciding whether to go their separate ways in peace or settle it with a long, bloody war. Kris pulled two vaccine bottles from her belly pouch and handed them across the table. Tru took them, held them up to the light, and frowned.

"What is it?" Kris asked Tru.

"Obviously not what the label claims."

"No. Fifty thousand liquid metal convertible boats have come off the assembly line. The six that ended up in my little sideshow are the only ones to date that developed a peculiar tendency to turn into liquid mercury the third time you change them. Those are small samples of what was a thousand-pound boat one moment, a bunch of metal droplets in puddles the next."

"Kind of leaves you up the river without a paddle or a boat," Tru said, unashamed at not passing up the opening.

"In the worst way at the worst time," Kris agreed dryly.

"Assassination attempt number two," Tru said, and Jack's head jerked around to look at Kris. Yep, dear Father had only told him what met the prime minister's elevated burden of proof.

"Nope, probably number three. A rocket took apart my desk the day before. I wasn't there, being at a long lunch with a friend of yours, Hank Smythe-Peterwald. Thirteenth of that name. He saved my life, Tru."

Tru raised a doubting eyebrow at that. "Any idea what earned you a rocket?"

"I took down some local warlords the day before."

"So the rocket was probably a local response to a local stimuli." Kris nodded. "And what was Hank doing on Olympia?"

"Delivering aid. Food supplies we needed. Thirty trucks we were desperate for."

"Any boats in the delivery?" Tru asked, rolling the vials between her hands.

"Six of them. Three went poof. Three will spend their lives permanently as bridges."

Tru pocketed the bottles. "Most labs probably couldn't tell you anything from these. I know a few that might. Would be nice to get a look at one that still thinks it's a bridge."

"Nelly," Kris said out loud, "buy a dozen liquid boats from different retail sources on Wardhaven. Ship them to Olympia. Ask Colonel Hancock to accept them as a trade for the three defective bridges. We want them for further analysis." Kris paused for a moment. "Want to bet the three somehow get activated for the third time before we can get them to a lab?"

"Hire a security team to escort the new ones out, be sure the old ones come back. I'll have Sam give Nelly the number of a reputable one."

"What I can't understand is, why?" Kris allowed herself to muse out loud on this attack for the first time. "I mean, trying to kill me while rescuing that little girl on Sequim, that would have gotten half the Rim worlds up in arms against Earth. But me drowning while on an emergency medical run? What political purpose would that serve?"

Tru just shook her head. "Sometimes I wonder what you Longknifes use for blood. Honey, your dad, your Grampa Trouble, your Grampa Ray are up to their receding hairlines trying to hold on to at least a part of the Society. You add grief to the load they're carrying, and they are bound to start making mistakes they wouldn't otherwise."

Kris listened to Tru, tried to picture her father broken up over her passing. The picture didn't fit. Then she thought of all the changes in the family after Eddy's death. It had cost Mother and Father. Would her death cost them as much?

Maybe.

"I'll think about that," she told Tru. "What's happening here? Are we going to war?"

Tru blinked at the sudden change in topic. She took a moment to rub her eyes with both fists. For the first time in Kris's life, she realized that her old auntie was old. Very old, probably over a hundred, and those years hadn't been gentle. "I hope not," Tru finally whispered. "It would do few any good."

"Who thinks it would do them some good?"

"Old farts who've fought one war and forgotten what it's like. Fresh-faced heros that are tired of doing a great job of nothing and have no idea what the real face of war is like." Kris winced, remembering her hero wanna-be. But he was just a kid . . . and now would never grow up to learn different.

Tru eyed Kris, seemed to measure the wince against some godlike scale, and shared with her a tired smile. "You've grown up since I last saw you."

"Aged," Kris offered in its stead.

Tru nodded. "Then, of course, there's the nutcases who want to be emperor of humanity, for reasons comprehendible only to shrinks. Included among them are your friend Hank's pappy and grandpappy. They're forming up their own alliance anchored on Greenfeld, fifty planets strong. Earth has forty or so that will hang with her. Your father has sixty to a hundred leaning toward whatever

Wardhaven does. Other folks are looking around, trying to figure out who they should join, better join, or have to join."

"Have to?" Kris asked.

"Peterwald's Greenfeld Group has the mortgage on lots of worlds and is squeezing them damn hard. His planet has a good collection of warships. They were the first to haul ships out of the Society fleet. Folks are looking at geography differently. Short trade routes might be fast invasion routes. Take that disaster you call Olympia. Forty-seven planets within one jump of there. Nearly one hundred and fifty within two. A quarter of human space could be defended by a fleet stationed there . . . or invaded. Why do you think Wardhaven was so quick to take an interest when it got in trouble?"

"Milk of human kindness?" Tommy offered.

"Right. Want to guess who bought up all those farms that suddenly came up for sale? Peterwald and associates."

"I was wondering about that. You saved me a search," Kris said. "Anything else new there?"

"Maybe. Seems one of Smythe-Peterwald's ships paid a visit to Olympia two years back. According to the automated control station in Olympia orbit, it left a week later. There's no record of that ship showing up anywhere for a solid year. Olympia has an asteroid belt. How long do you think it would take to usher one onto a collision course with Olympia? What kind of a volcanic explosion was it that wrecked Olympia's budding economy?"

"You can check it out," Kris said. "There's mud in with the liquid metal. See if it's got asteroid dust in it. If that's not enough, I've got a small can of the stuff in my duffel."

"Young woman, you are paranoid." Tru beamed.

"I contracted it from the people around me." Kris got to her feet. "Nelly, order a cab. I want to go see Grampa Alex."

Tru shook her head. "He's a harder man to see than the prime minister."

"I suspect so, but I need some answers, and old silent Al

is the only one that can even guess at them. Jack, you ready to protect me from high-paid private security guards?"

He made a face. "Overpaid, in my book."

"Kris, can I walk home from here?" Tommy squeaked. "Remember, I don't like guns. I don't like power lunches. I'm just a simple country boy from Santa Maria."

"Come on, Ensign, let's march," Kris started, then froze in place, remembering Colonel Hancock's little talk in the truck. "Tom, if you really want to sit this one out, it's okay by me."

Tom reached for her forehead, felt it. "You sick, woman?"

"No, but I'm remembering what Colonel Hancock said. Sometimes I think too quickly about what I want and too slowly about what others need."

"Good God," Tru drew herself up to her full height, turned her head to first stare at Kris with her right eye, then her left like some monstrous bird of prey. "Are you growing up, woman? You're actually starting to sound mature. Be careful about that. You can never follow in your father's footsteps if you start considering other people's needs. Come to think of it, I'm not sure any of your ancestors suffered from that affliction. Some of them did have the saving grace of putting their necks out a few millimeters more than the ones they were pushing."

Kris shrugged off the theatrics. "Maybe I acquired a little humility with all the mud on Olympia."

"No." Tru shook her head dourly. "More like wisdom. A horrible weight to bear for one of your disadvantaged upbringing. However"—Tru grinned, all teeth—"since you're headed off to meet your old grampa, I don't think you've acquired too much of it to dampen your fun. Now, excuse me, I've got a couple of holes to fill in on a very big jigsaw puzzle."

"The cab is at the door," Nelly reported.

"Well, Jack, you and me."

"And me," Tommy added.

"I thought you wanted out."

"Hey, a guy's got the right to at least say what's smart, even if he doesn't have the smarts to do what's smart. Okay?"

So, a half hour later they paid off the cabby at the door of the Longknife Towers. They'd had to pass through three checkpoints to get that far. Their IDs had gotten them past the first two, but only Kris's not insignificant holdings of Nuu Enterprises preferred stock had gotten them past the last.

The tower was really two skyscrapers linked at the bottom by food courts and other services for those who lived and worked there. Kris had heard that her grandfather had not been out of this building for ten years. She knew that was bum data; Grandpa regularly inspected his plants in orbit. Still, he moved at odd hours and kept his whereabouts as hard to follow as any spy. Kris had previously put that down to eccentricity and old age. Of late, she suspected the eccentricity might be responsible for that old age.

Under an information sign was a guard station with camera monitors and a half-dozen men in matching green blazers. One rose with a smile and a "May I help you," as Kris led the men through the automatic door.

Kris ignored both the smile and offered help and quick-marched for the bank of elevators. Several were open; Kris picked the far one. Marching in, she took station in the middle of it, leaving Jack and Tommy to arrange themselves to each side and behind her. "Floor two-four-two," she ordered.

"Thank you, ma'am," the elevator answered.

The guard was now running to get to the closing elevator. The doors quit closing.

"Your order has been overridden," Nelly said.

"Override the override," Kris ordered. The doors finished closing a second before a rather startled guard would have lost an arm. Kris turned to check out how her men were taking matters. Tommy's eyes were not quite as large as when he was introduced to the pipes up close and personal. Jack

seemed nonplussed as he removed his badge and ID from
the pocket of his running shorts and palmed it for ready use.
Good.

The elevator opened on the two hundred forty-second
floor. Kris marched out, followed by her tiny flying wedge.
Sweatshirt and gym shorts had helped them blend in on
campus. Among the three-piece suits, the effect was quite
the opposite. Talk stopped, people eyed them, but the
upside was that people in their way got out of it fast. Kris
went through double glass doors into a moderately huge
waiting room with chairs, couches, and small conference
rooms off to a side. The receptionist was heads up as Kris
entered. Eyes locked on each other, Kris marched for her
desk. "May I help you?" the woman said, a professional
nonsmile on her face.

"I'm Kris Longknife, here to see my grandfather," Kris
said without slowing.

"Do you have an appointment?" came right back.

"No," Kris said, and changed course from the desk to
the wooden double doors beside it.

"You can't go in there," the woman shouted, getting to
her feet, but she'd been outfaked on this one. Kris was at
the door before the receptionist could get away from her
desk.

"Yes I can," Kris said and pushed through the doors into
another foyer. The receptionist here was male, big, and
already on his feet.

"I require verification of who you say you are."

That was reasonable. Kris marched to his desk, planted
her hand on a glass, and glared at a camera behind the
desk. Done with that formality, she sidestepped to allow
each of the men following her to do the same. With all
three of the intruders stopped on the waiting side of his
desk, and work needed to verify the IDents provided, the
man settled into his chair.

Kris took the moment to lead her small invasion team
around his desk and through the door it guarded. "You
can't go in there until I finish your IDs," the man shouted.

"And probably not for a month after that," Kris said as the door closed behind her.

The next room was even more spacious than the two before it. The carpet was almost as deep as the mud on Olympia. The walls were wood paneled. Off to one side were a few chairs grouped around a holovid of a Japanese garden and waterfall—correction—around a real Japanese garden and waterfall. The room stank of wealth and power. Directly ahead of Kris was an older woman seated behind a desk made from a thick slab of stone. At either side of the desk stood two men in matching dark blue suits. Each held a gun out in the standard two hand stance, aimed at Kris.

"Don't take a step closer," the gunman on the right said. Kris decided that, for once, she would do what people holding guns aimed at her said. She halted.

"I am going to raise my left hand," Jack said slowly. His words were soft and hard in the deadly way hired killers have of saying the nastiest things in the nicest way. "It has my badge and ID in it."

"Do it slow," said left gunman. Kris tried to act unconcerned as her stomach did flip-flops. It was a whole lot easier to face armed men when she had her own M-6. But she wasn't here to shoot her way in. She waited, hoping she'd find the right words when this macho ritual was done.

"I am Agent John Montoya of Wardhaven Secret Service, assigned to the prime minister's family. This is Kris Longknife, his daughter. You are in violation of 2CFR, section 204.333 in that you are armed and in the presence of a primary Secret Service subject. I will ask you only once to put down your weapons."

"I am Senior Private Agent Richard Dresden, of the Pinkerton Agency, Wardhaven Division. You are in violation of Public Law 92-1324, dated 2318, revised 2422, to whit, trespassing on personal property. It has been legally posted that this property is protected with deadly force under subsection 2.6.12 of that statute. You have been warned; now remove yourselves."

"I guess this is why you don't have many family reunions," Tommy said.

"Yeah," Kris agreed, "by the time all our gumshoes have finish citing their legal authority, the potato salad's rancid and there's no daylight left for a friendly game of baseball."

"Why don't you drop in on the Liens next Santa Maria Landing Day. I'll show you how one of these is supposed to go."

"I may take you up on that." Kris noted that she and Tommy's effort at humor hadn't gotten even a flicker of a smile from the gunmen or the secretary. *There is such a thing as being too professional. Enough already.*

"Grandpa Al," Kris shouted, "this is your granddaughter. You know it's me, and if you weren't sure, that fellow at the last desk has had enough time to run a full genome on me. How long you going to make me wait out here?"

"And why do you suddenly have a need to talk to your grandfather, young woman?" the secretary asked.

"Grandpa, I don't think you want me shouting for all to hear just why a twenty-two-year-old woman suddenly feels the need to know a few things about what's going on in her family. Aren't there a few skeletons that you want kept in our closet?"

A door to the left of the secretary opened. A gray-haired man in a gray suit stepped out. The man was near two meters tall, explaining where Kris got her height. "Gentlemen, I think you can put away your guns." The guards quickly did. The man turned back to the room. "We can finish this later," he told a man and woman who quickly stepped around him and left by a door to Kris's left. "All right, young woman, you've interrupted my day. Come in and say your piece."

"Sir," Jack said politely, "I should examine any room she's going to be in alone with another individual."

"Who isn't vouched for by *your* system, young man. You honestly think my office isn't the safest place on this planet?"

"For you, yes sir, for her . . .?" Jack left the question hanging.

"Government!" Grandpa Al spat. "Do what you have to."

Jack trotted to the door, gadgets appearing in his hands that Kris had never suspected could be hidden by shorts and a bulletproof sweatshirt. The senior Pinkerton did a good imitation of joining at the hip as Jack went by. A minute later, both reappeared. "You have your personal workstation in your desk, as well as a recording device in all four corners of the room," he told Grandpa Al, but the report was for Kris.

"Shall I have my personal computer make a full transcript of our meeting?" Kris asked.

Grandpa scowled. "All security and recordings off, alpha, alpha, zed, forty-eleven. Happy, young woman?"

"You know Longknifes take more to make them happy than that, Grandpa." Kris smiled as she entered the room alone. It was vast. Glass on two sides offered a magnificent view of Wardhaven, better than Tru's penthouse. The room, however was gray: gray rug, gray walls, gray marble desk. Even the sofa and chairs around a gray slate coffee table were different shades of gray. The room smelled as gray as it looked. If air could be completely empty of odor, this room was it. Grandpa Al headed for his desk and only seemed happy when he had it between him and Kris. Nice way to treat family.

"So, what is it you want?"

"Grandpa, it's been what, ten, twelve years since we've seen each other. Don't you at least want to ask me how I am?"

"Computer, how is Kris Longknife?" he growled.

"Kristine Longknife is no longer in therapy. Her last doctor's visit involved a full physical checkup while applying to the Navy for a commission, which she passed. Her last medical issue involved an infected blister while in OCS."

"I know how you are, so that should cut the minor stuff. What do you want? And don't waste my time, young woman."

You don't know the half of me, Kris wanted to say. Instead, she opened with, "Who's trying to kill me?"

Grandpa Al actually blinked twice on that one. "Computer, have there been any attempts on Kris Longknife's life?"

"None, sir."

"Three, sir," Kris corrected the computer. "I have a pretty good handle on one of them. The other two puzzle me. Why would someone want to kill me?"

Grandpa swiveled in his chair to look out over Wardhaven. "You seem to have the matter under better control than I. What do the police tell you?"

Kris walked up to the desk and rested both hands on the cold marble. It could have been cut from Grandpa Al's heart for all the reaction she was getting from him. "The police are not involved."

That got Grandpa's attention. He swung around to face her. "Why?"

"Because there's no evidence that any of them took place. Father says if there's no evidence, they didn't happen."

"Your father is a horse's ass."

"He feels the same about you, sir."

Grandfather snorted at that, but he looked up at Kris with gray eyes intense and demanding. "What makes you think someone is trying to kill you, despite the lack of legal evidence?"

Kris settled into a chair and quickly described the rescue mission. As she talked, Grandpa's frowned deepened. "So a bum bit of equipment let you fly yourself right out of a trap."

"Yes. I keep meaning to talk to Father about the shoddy material in Navy issue, but since the only item I'm personally familiar with saved my life, I'm kind of on weak ground."

Grandfather barked a laugh at that but was all business the next second. "So what makes you so sure you were the target of that minefield?"

"I captured the ringleader's computer. Tru Seyd took it apart. She found a message saying the ship they wanted had drawn the mission and to prepare the 'welcome.'"

"How could they know where to put the welcome?"

"I did a check on the last seven rescue missions the Navy's done. All involved a night jump right into the bad guy's front yard. My captain was out to set some kind of record for shortest time from drop to last shot. I think the Navy's gotten a bit predictable during the long peace, and someone set me up."

"Reasonable conclusion. What's the second murder attempt?"

Kris described her trip up to the Anderson Ranch and the boat going poof. "Tru has the samples I got from the boat. She's sending it to a lab she trusts."

"It could have been an accident. This liquid metal thing is pretty new. My yards have only been making spaceships out of it for five years. Boats, what a waste of high tech."

"Of fifty thousand made, the six assigned to my project are the only ones with this little defect."

That got Grandpa sitting on the edge of his seat. "Who provided you with these boats?"

"Smythe-Peterwald."

"Smythe-Peterwald," Grandpa echoed.

"Smythe-Peterwald," Kris repeated. "The Anderson Ranch was out of radio contact with everyone. The Peterwald yacht was overhead when I mysteriously got the Anderson distress call. It didn't leave orbit until after I was on the river, had already modified the boat's configuration once."

"The next time you touched the controller of the boat . . .?"

"It would go poof." Kris snapped her fingers.

"Peterwalds," Grandpa roared as he shot from his chair.

"Who did you go to, to get money when Eddy was kidnaped?"

Kris's question stopped Grandpa in his tracks. He retreated back to his chair. With a wave of his hand that took in everything out the window, he said. "Why would I have to go to anyone for money?"

"Wealth is one thing, liquid assets another. I've gone

over our historical accounts. Father's and your money was in blind trusts. Your brother Ernie had the corporation pretty heavily invested in new planet developments, expansion, growth. I don't think he could have provided the money my father needed."

"Didn't matter. Edward was dead before we received the ransom note."

"But you and father didn't know that. I don't think the people who set up Eddy's kidnaping had any idea they'd gotten ahold of dumber and dumbest."

"Set up, not hired?"

"Grandpa, they wouldn't have gone to the gallows if they knew anything. Those kidnappers didn't need any upfront money. The guys on Sequim don't know anything, except for the honcho. He had a heart attack before he could start singing."

"Heart attack," Grandpa said slowly.

"Like the truck driver that killed Grandma Sarah," Kris threw across the desk.

Grandfather looked like he'd been hit by a truck. Or more correct, was seeing again the truck that hit him. "It was an accident," he whispered. "I saw the truck coming, but I couldn't get out of its way. I tried. Fifty years, I've been seeing that truck in my dreams. I always think I can get out of the way. I never do." He shook his head. "But they did an autopsy. There was nothing, no drugs, no beer, nothing in his blood."

"Grandpa, they didn't take the blood sample until two hours after the wreck. Even back then, they had illegal drugs that could vanish in that time."

"And Peterwalds always have known their way around the drug underworld." Grandpa sighed. "Smythe-Peterwald the Eleventh was visiting Wardhaven when your brother was kidnapped. You know his son went to school with your dad. Even dated your mother."

"She never lets us forget. Insists I get to know the son."

Grandfather winced at that. "Peterwald offered me the money. Said we could work the details out later. Then the police found the farm and the manure pile with a busted air pipe protruding from it. I didn't need the money after all.

"That's when I quit government. You're too big a target out there. I quit government and made sure I'd always have enough money to do what I need to do fast. Enough money to build a wall around me no one could get through. I told that son of mine to quit, too. So that idiot turns around and runs for my job."

"So you think the Peterwalds are behind it all?"

"There's enough bad blood between them and my dad. Ray may be a great general and a great president, but every time he turned around he was stepping on the Peterwalds. Closed down a couple of planets they'd invested in when they fell outside the sphere of development he set up with the Treaty of Wardhaven. Closed down their drug running if you believe the rumor mill."

"Do you believe it?"

"Ray believed he was closing down the Peterwalds. As your dad would point out, you couldn't prove it in a court of law, so some would say it didn't happen."

"I'm getting a bit tired of almost getting killed by what you can't prove in a court of law, Grandpa."

"Steer clear of the Peterwalds."

"Kind of hard to do. I go where the Navy sends me."

"Resign. Come work for me in this tower. Nothing moves within twenty kilometers that I don't know of and approve. I've made myself a fortress of people who believe in what I'm doing, are well paid, and would die for me. What have you got?"

"Jack out there, until I go back on duty."

"You'd be safe here. We don't even send our school-children out except on nonscheduled tours and with an armed escort. No better place to raise a child."

"Sounds good, but I don't have any children just now. When I do, I'll think about it."

"You should live so long."

"Grandpa, I intend to do just that."

The computer on Grandpa Al's desk began to buzz.

"Kris," Nelly announced softly, "I hope you will excuse my interruption, but Earth just announced that it is sending a large battle fleet to Wardhaven."

"What?" came from both sides of the desk. "Looks like it's a bit late for me to resign my commission." Kris swallowed.

"Good God, has Earth taken leave of its senses? An Earth fleet here on the Rim is just a *causi bellum* looking to happen."

"I thought business wanted a war, or at least a breakup," Kris goaded her grandfather, wondering what he'd say.

"Humph," Grampa Al glared at Kris like she'd just flunked first grade. "Earth is our biggest trading partner. Why would I want a customs house between us and that market? And a war just messes up all my business plans. No businessman in his right mind wants a war."

Nelly interrupted with, "The official report from Earth is that the fleet is coming to Wardhaven to participate with the Rim worlds in officially dissolving the Society of Humanity."

"You don't need a battle fleet to haul down the flag." He shook his head. "I know there are Earth types terrified of what our rim expansionists might wander into out in the galaxy. Have they got the upper hand back there? Is Earth willing to use force to keep us in the Society?" Grandpa wondered.

"But they're just a faction, like our unlimited expansionists. They couldn't be calling the shots. This fleet has to be what they say it is?"

Grandpa shook his head. "Whatever it is Earth wants to say, they're saying it all wrong."

"Excuse me for interrupting again," Nelly cut in. "All fleet personnel have been recalled to duty."

"Thank you, Nelly," Kris said, then looked at her Grandfather, "but to whose fleet?"

19

Three hours later, Kris had her duffel packed and led
Tom down the central stairs of Nuu House. A hastily contracted liner was scheduled to depart High Wardhaven
in three hours for a two-g run to High Cambria. If they
rushed, they could be back aboard the *Typhoon* in two days.

As Kris crossed the foyer, she found marine guards still
at the doors of the library, but the doors were thrown open
wide to facilitate the constant flow of officers and messen-
gers. She paused for a second. Yes, Grampas Trouble and
Ray were in there, surrounded by stars and eagles and
civilians that must have rated just as high. It looked like
Tru at a workstation in the back of the library, but Kris
wasn't sure. Trusting humanity was in good hands, Kris
turned for the main door.

"Wait a second there, Ensign," came through the library
doors in General Trouble's command voice. Kris kept
walking; she wasn't in his chain of command. Pity the poor
ensign who was, and made the old general shout.

"I mean you, Ensign Longknife. Halt."

Kris halted, set down her duffel, and waited. "I'll tell Harvey to wait for you," Tom said and left.

"Where you headed?" Grampa Trouble asked as he pulled in range of a normal voice.

"Back to my ship," Kris answered; then, because she couldn't suppress the question, she said what every spacer in the fleet was asking anyone handy. "Is there going to be war?"

"Your dad has me and Ray and a hell of a lot of good people doing our damnedest to see that there isn't," he said. They stood there, each measuring the hopes and fears in that statement; then Trouble started gnawing on his lower lip.

"Listen, Kris, we're putting together a staff here. They're also recommissioning anything that can hold air. I understand they're even trying to haul out my old ship, the *Patton.* You hang around the staff here for a week or so, we might be able to get you an XO slot on a destroyer or something. Same for Tom."

Kris forced her breathing to stay even. Was Grampa trying to get her and Tom out of harm's way? Was it that bad? "Is the Earth fleet really an invasion fleet?"

The old general gave her one of his patented shrugs. "God only knows, and she ain't talking, at least to the likes of me. No, we don't know any more about which Earth faction is calling the shots than you hear from the news' talking heads." He scowled at the lack of real information in all the noise.

Kris took a deep breath and shook her head. "General Grampa, the *Typhoon* may be small, but she's the best you have. When you send her where you need her most, you're going to need her the best she can be. I may be green, but I'm a hell of a lot better prepared than any shiny new nugget would be." Then she shrugged. "Besides, it's my turn in the barrel."

"Be careful, kid."

"You mean don't do anything you'd do?"

Grampa Trouble swallowed hard on that. "Don't do

anything stupid. Our families have all the medals gathering dust that we need. Remember, half of what you read about us in the history books were lies."

"Maybe poorly researched," Kris answered, "but not lies. Next time I'm home, why don't you and Grampa Ray walk me through a few of the more interesting stories?"

"It's a deal, Ensign. You come home, we'll have a long talk." And Kris discovered that ensigns could hug generals, and if the marines standing guard or anyone passing through thought different of it, well, they could just drop and give the old general fifty push-ups.

Kris got to the elevator to High Wardhaven on time. Only military traffic was going up or down; still, it was standing room only on the ride up. Kris was early enough to get the last seat. Then she gave it up when Commodore Sampson came through the door at the very last moment. Standing in the aisle, Kris remembered reading that it was illegal to have more people on an elevator pod than there were seats; the rule was forgotten today. That was when it hit her. The safe bets were off; someone really expected a war . . . and soon.

The *Happy Wanderer* had been hastily converted from a cruise liner to a troopship. Kris was lucky; she drew a one-person room with a single bed. The two ensigns across the hall were none too happy to be sharing one bed. Still, there was a cot in the corner of Kris's room; she waited to see who her travel mate was and couldn't suppress a grin when Chief Bo showed up at her door.

"Didn't know they were putting chiefs on the beach."

"Weren't," Bo said, dropping her duffel. "I was on leave, visiting my sister and her family." The chief glanced around, her nose twitching like she was smelling something foul. "Didn't anyone tell these people that chiefs and officers don't mix?"

"I suspect they're happy if they keep boys and girls out of the same staterooms. This is a kind of rush job."

"Yeah," the chief frowned at the cot. "Which bed you want, ma'am?"

"I'll take the cot. At two g's, a younger back can handle the cot better."

The chief gave Kris a canted scowl but didn't argue. As she stowed her gear, the chief asked over her shoulder, "What you hearing about the war, ma'am?"

"Some good people are doing their best to see it doesn't happen. What are you hearing?"

"I didn't have to pay for my beers last night. Lots of loudmouths saying it's time we show those Earthy flakes a thing or two. Course, none of them are on this transport."

"They flocking to the recruiters?"

"Doubt many would pass. Not tall enough for their tonnage," Bo chuckled, then got serious. "Saw where Ray Longknife and General Trouble were back on Wardhaven. They some of the good people you were talking about?"

"Wouldn't deny it to a friend, but wouldn't say it to a stranger," Kris dodged. She also didn't mention the staff offer.

"Your old man is doing the political two-step. I listened to him for five minutes last night. Couldn't tell if he was for or against us blasting that battle fleet out of space. Politicians," the chief spat.

"He's just trying to build a consensus," Kris explained.

"He better do it quick, 'cause I hear the Earth Battle Fleet is on its way."

Kris collapsed on her cot. "This is crazy. Yeah, Earth has a lot of big ships with big guns, but none of them have been up to speed since the Iteeche War, what, seventy years ago. In college, I knew this kid from Earth. His dad runs a steel mill in orbit. Once a year he and his mill workers man a squadron of old battleships, them and a thousand welfare types doing their annual active duty. As my friend described it, they go aboard, make sure there's still oxygen, then see if the boards show green lights on all the gear. God only knows what they'd do if they got a red one. Chief, this kid's dad gets to be a reserve vice admiral. Most of his plant foremen are captains. It's all a big show. If it came to a fight, the *Typhoon* could probably slag three or four of those battlewagons without breaking a sweat."

"But battlewagons like those slagged whole planets in the Iteeche War. I don't want them over Wardhaven, not with my sister and her kids on the ground under them."

"Prepare for two g's in five minutes," echoed down the former liner's halls from the public address system.

"I'll help you get that cot made up," Bo offered. "Not a hell of a lot to do for the next two days. Think I'll sleep. No use risking my back, not when the first live shoot of my too damn long career may be coming up. Besides, if I know Captain Thorpe, he's going to have all kinds of hairs up his ass. Doubt if we'll get an hour's sleep in twenty-five between reporting aboard and . . . whatever."

Kris followed the chief's lead, catching up on her sleep, following the news, and reviewing the manuals on her battle station. It had been a four-day trip, Cambria to Wardhaven. It took two days to get back. Still, it wasn't fast enough for the skipper.

"What took you so long?" was the captain's greeting as Kris and Tommy reported to the *Typhoon*'s bridge five minutes after coming aboard.

"Damn luxury liner didn't want to do more than two g's," Kris offered, while taking her place at defensive systems. "You know how civilians are, sir."

"How come you two didn't get out and push?" the XO asked. Kris suppressed a shake of the head. There were hard cases, and then there were very hard cases.

Captain Thorpe eyed Kris as she brought up her station. "I'm surprised you bothered to join us, Ensign Longknife. I figured you for a cushy staff job."

Kris turned. "I was offered one, sir. I turned it down."

The skipper raised an eyebrow a fraction and glanced at the XO. "So, you wanted to be on the best ship in the fleet when the shooting starts."

"I told a general that he'd want the best ship to be the best it could be when he needed it, sir."

"Okay," the captain said and actually seemed to be enjoying himself in Kris's presence for a change. "I liked the fitness report I got from Olympia."

"Colonel Hancock sends his compliments, sir."

"Good man. Got a bad rap. He says you handled yourself very well in some tough firefights."

"I did my best, sir."

"Ready to smash Earth battleships headed for Wardhaven?"

Kris took a deep breath. "Yes, sir," she said, giving the short, crisp answer the skipper wanted. Any prayer to avoid war was out of place on a fighting ship's bridge.

"Good. I want you and Ensign Lien to trade stations."

"I'm not trained on weapons, sir."

"No one on this ship is combat trained on any station as far as I'm concerned," the captain growled. "But you will be. Lien, out of there. Let's see how good Longknife is at a shoot."

So Kris moved forward to the offensive weapons station just in front of the skipper and beside the helm. Tommy didn't actually show relief as he moved to the defensive station behind and to Kris's right. Kris had never told Hancock about Tommy's problem with his weapon, but she doubted anything got past that Marine Colonel. And nothing got by the captain.

Thorpe synced weapons, helm, and defense together into a simulation; hostiles appeared just at the limit of the *Typhoon*'s sensor range. When Kris asked how they got there, the captain snapped, "It's my job to get you targets. It's your job to smash them." So Kris and Tommy and a new ensign with lightning reactions, Addison, went through the simulation, twisting and turning, dodging and charging, until the hostiles were dust in space and Kris's hands were knotted on the controls.

"Now do it again."

So they did. Off the bridge, Kris could hear the crew going through every possible drill, from hull breach to reactor containment failure. Only once did she hear abandon ship; that one must not be very popular with the skipper. On the bridge Kris went through problem after problem, gauging targets with hostile intentions and getting lasers out there to thwart them.

It was very late by the ship's clock when Kris went looking for her bunk.

And reveille was at oh five early the next morning. Kris showered, dressed, gulped down breakfast, and was on the bridge by 0600. And the simulations began again. "You're taking too long to blast those bogies. I want them dust in fifteen minutes from first contact. Addison, be more aggressive. Longknife, you're using too many ranging shots. Don't waste energy bracketing the target. Hit it."

Easier said than done, Kris could have said. Was the bogie closing or opening the range? But she kept her mouth shut and spent a bit more time evaluating the targets' behavior next sim. Yep, the skipper had them just as gung ho as he was. The next two sims all had the enemy closing fast. Kris was right on with her first shot the next time.

"Good going, Ensign. Think like they do."

"If you assume they're going for your throat, sir," Kris risked.

"If they aren't, Ensign, it's their funeral. There's only one rule in war. Hit them first. Hit them hard. Anything else just makes for more widows on our side."

"Yes, sir," Kris answered, the only answer he'd accept.

"When are we going after that Earthy battle fleet?" Addison asked.

"As soon as they give us orders, Ensign," the skipper assured him.

"Those old Earth tubs are taking long enough."

"I hear their engineering is lousy." The XO grinned. "Had to cut to half a g to keep all those clunkers together."

"But let one or two of them shoot their way into orbit, and there won't be any High Wardhaven, any space elevator, or many people left below," the captain pointed out.

Of course, Kris thought, Earth could have slowed her ships to half a g to give the politicians more time to sort this whole mess out. She kept that thought to herself; she was on a warship, and its job was to defend Wardhaven. The skipper was making this tip of the spear just as sharp as he could. Kris wasn't about to do anything to dull it.

At noon, while the crew was at mess, Thorpe ordered Tom to convert the *Typhoon* to battle configuration. "Longknife, look over his shoulder. I don't want to spend the next week finding the mop closet." The skipper eyed the XO when he said it, so Tommy didn't lose his usual grin. Still, he worked slowly and methodically as Kris joined him at his station. He went down the check sheet without a word from Kris. This was a standard reconfiguration; it had been done often enough that it should go flawlessly. Prework done, Tom reported, "We are ready, sir."

The skipper nodded to the yeoman of the watch. "All hands, stand by for reconfiguration," she announced. "Watch standers take your places."

"Make it so, Ensign," the captain ordered, and Tommy started tapping keys on his workstation. With most personnel at chow, the mess facilities were locked in place. Next, Engineering shrank. Then the outer berthing areas pulled in as spacers' double staterooms became berthing areas of eight, and the ship's diameter began to fall by half. All through the ship, spacious hallways became much more cramped passageways. Storage rooms with wide aisles became smaller. Lastly, the radiation bulkhead between the rest of the ship and engineering thickened, and the ship lost a good twenty meters in length.

"Now the *Typhoon*'s a real warship and a damn small target," the captain growled happily. "Yeoman, have all hands check for missing spaces and report them immediately to Ensign Lien. Ensign, don't waste time trying to get it right a second time. I like Longknife's solution. Empty any wayward spaces, delete them, then re-create them in the right place."

"Yes, sir." Tommy said with a wink for Kris. Maybe

she'd already been headed for the captain's good graces even before Hancock's fit rep.

Thorpe stood. "Bridge team, take thirty minutes for chow. You've handled those easy problems fairly well. Now let's see how you do on a few moderately complicated ones."

Wondering how the sims could get worse, Kris went to check her quarters. She quickly passed down narrow passageways to find her room was where it should be. Once she and Chief Bo were sure their own gear was straight, they took a quick walk through the enlisted women's quarters. There were no problems; even the usual complaints about being shoved back eight to a room were subdued. "They're scared it's for real this time," Bo muttered as they left.

So Kris arrived late for lunch. The shrunken ship had no wardroom; the officers now shared their meals with all personnel in the cafeteria. Most of the crew had already eaten, the exceptions being the bridge crew and, apparently, the engineering watch standers. The XO commanded one table far from the door and well away from the steam tables. Lieutenant Commander Paulus, the ship's engineering officer, was surrounded by his officers and crew at a table about as far from the XO as was possible. Tommy had joined the engineering staff and probably was deep into a discussion of nano or some other techno delight. Suppressing a sigh, Kris headed for an empty place next to the executive officer. This put her elbow to elbow with the communications officer and the ship's lieutenant, who, with the XO, stood eight-hour watches, seven days a week as officers of the deck or OOD. Kris and the other two ensigns should also be standing watches, one each, at their elbows as junior officers of the deck. That was what would have happened if the *Typhoon* had fifteen officers aboard. But it was peacetime. Right! On the last cruise, Kris had stood watches as the OOD and been relieved by chiefs and first-class petty officers. She wondered how things would change this cruise.

"So, things got exciting on Olympia," the XO started as Kris sat down.

"They had a bandit problem," Kris said simply.

"And don't have one anymore?" the communications officer added.

Kris measured her response carefully as she sampled the meat loaf, potatoes, and green beans. "We took out a few of the bad elements. Fed a lot of hungry elements. Problem solved."

"That's putting a fine twist on what I hear was a major firefight," the executive officer insisted.

"It got plenty hot for a while there," Kris agreed.

"So, looking forward to things getting plenty hot here?" The ship's lieutenant leered.

In the miniature chain of command on the *Typhoon*, he was the division chief of all the junior officers not in Engineering, and thus, Kris's boss. "I'd like to hope cooler heads prevail," she said to her string beans.

"God save us from cooler heads," the comm officer snapped.

"This has been coming for years," the XO said. "Earth bureaucrats have been leading us around on a chain. Telling us this. Telling us that. It's time we do what we want to do, not what those overpaid chair warmers back there say."

Kris didn't need to answer that, so she concentrated on eating. The XO filled the silence with every familiar argument for war. Rationally, to Kris, they added up to nothing. But hadn't Doc Meade warned her class that it was a rare war that had a solid basis in reality? "Emotions. Watch for the emotions that inflame," he'd said. Kris had dutifully taken notes, but she hadn't been one of his believers that day. Just now, it was starting to look like Doc knew what he was talking about, at least in this mess. Finished, she stood and picked up her tray.

"Ready to shoot Earthy antiques?" the XO demanded.

"I'll shoot whatever the skipper puts in range," Kris said.

"Good, Ensign. Very good," the XO said with a broad grin.

Captain Thorpe was on the bridge when Kris returned, having taken his meal in his cabin. And he had sims waiting that made this morning's seem easy. The afternoon went long.

When the captain finally released her, Kris quickly found her stateroom. Chief Bo was already snoring, giving Kris a reminder she didn't need that a warship was a cramped ship. At 0600 the next day, Kris was back at her board. The skipper was hunched over his own, apparently oblivious to his bridge team as they arrived, checked their stations, and awaited his pleasure.

Thorpe punched his own commlink without looking up. "This is the captain speaking. Fast Attack Squadron Six and the *Typhoon* have been ordered to the Paris system. There we will rendezvous with the rest of Wardhaven's fleet and ships from other planets that are ready to meet this threat from Earth. As of now, I consider this ship to be on a war footing."

"Nelly," Kris whispered subvocally.

"The media reports that the Earth fleet and nearly one hundred other planetary squadrons are to meet at the Paris system to officially mark their withdrawal from the Society of Humanity. The Paris system is a nearly uninhabited system with an unusual number of jump points created when two systems collided since the jump points were created by aliens."

"Cut the standard media pablum," Kris ordered, her gut knotting. "This is supposed to be a peaceful meeting, right?"

"Commentaries and news reports run the full spectrum, from war to peace to high-stakes gamble, usually reflecting established editorial positions and past commentaries."

"What does the prime minister say?"

"He hails this as peace in our time."

Kris remembered that quote from somewhere, searched her own memory, found it, and didn't like the taste of it.

"I have the conn," the captain announced. "I can get us away from the pier. Let's start you three on some really hard simulations." So Kris got down to business and stayed that way through the rest of the day. Arms and hands aching, she stumbled to her bed and was asleep before she even got her shoes off.

Next morning, Chief Bo was brushing her teeth as Kris awoke. "You slept right through reveille," the chief reported through the foam in her mouth. "Figured you could use a few extra winks. You know your hands were moving in your sleep?"

"I was dreaming battle scenarios," Kris admitted.

"Well, you were going through them full bore."

Kris stripped, stumbled to the shower, and was under the spray for a full half minute before what was missing dawned on her. Grabbing a towel, she asked the chief, "You remember us going through a jump last night?"

"Nope, they always wake me up. No matter how bushed I am, they wreck a night's sleep."

"Nelly, did they announce a jump during the night, or did I miss one yesterday?"

"This ship has not yet jumped out of the Cambria system."

Kris lifted her hand, estimated its weight. "One g, maybe a bit more."

"One point two-five g's, ma'am. Geeze, I thought you bridge types always got the word first."

"Skipper must have ordered that while I was deep in a sim. We should have been at any of the five standard jumps out of Cambria hours ago."

"Guess we aren't using them. I heard there's supposed to be a war on or something," the chief said, dryly. "Might account for brass doing the less expected."

"Yeah," Kris agreed. The skipper had put them on a war footing, and she should quit thinking peacetime drills. They'd packed them into the elevator pod, into the *Happy Wanderer*. Why not use the jump less traveled? "Nelly, keep track of the ship's acceleration, and let me know which jump we do use."

"Yes, ma'am."

Which was a good thing, because Kris's day rapidly

vanished, lost in simulations. Targets were moving faster, jinking and zigzagging. There were friendly ships now as well to keep track of. Space was more cluttered as planets and moons entered the exercises, warping maneuvers with their gravity. "Damn it, Addison, you accelerated us *into* that gravity well. We shot past those bastards so fast we'll never get turned around."

"Sorry, sir. I saw them, and I went for them."

"That's the right stuff when we're in deep space, but fights, real fights, take place where there's something worth fighting for. Nine out of ten battles with Unity and the Iteeche were within two hundred thousand klicks of a planet. Get used to working with gravity, Ensign, or I'll get someone who can."

"Yes, sir."

"And Longknife, why'd you miss them as we went by?"

"Rate of closure and rate of change on the defilade shot exceeded the capacity of the system, sir."

"I didn't ask why the computer didn't give you a shot, I asked why you didn't take a shot."

She didn't want to waste the laser energy, but that wasn't the answer the skipper wanted. "No excuse, sir."

"That answer may keep me from chewing your tail, Ensign, but it won't keep the enemy from cutting this ship open and spilling your shipmates into vacuum. You see a shot, you take a shot. Let me worry about my energy budget. You understand?"

"Yes, sir." Kris also noticed there were no euphemisms now. Earth ships were enemy, pure and simple. It was getting harder in her fatigue-fogged brain to remember that her Grampa Trouble said he was doing his damnedest to keep that from happening. Kris's hands were trained. They were fighting the ship's lasers all day; no wonder they were fighting the ship's lasers in her sleep. Like a well-trained automaton, she was reacting with little or no thought. That was what Thorpe wanted; that was what Kris gave him. The quick smiles he rationed her were worth it.

She didn't get that many smiles the rest of the afternoon as gravity wells swung the simulated *Typhoon* here and there, giving Kris damn poor shots. Kris was a zombie as she made her way to her stateroom that night. Surprisingly, Bo was still up.

"Crew's a bit edgy," the chief said as Kris stripped off her sweat-soaked uniform. Bo took it from her and ran it through the cleaner. "The skipper hasn't posted the ship's route on the mess room screen."

"That's peacetime practice," Kris mouthed, pulling on a nightshirt. "We're on a war footing."

"Yeah, but isn't that pushing it a bit?"

"You know Thorpe better than I do, but from where I'm sitting, I wouldn't put anything past him."

"We jumped early today. Did you notice it?"

"Went right past me. Nelly, what jump did we use?"

"Ninety-nine percent probability we used jump point India."

"India!" Kris struggled awake. Alpha, Beta, Gamma were the most frequently used, in that order, jump points of a system. India was never used. "What's India's safety factor?" Jump points wandered, understandable since they orbited two, three, or more stars. The more they wandered with respect to any one star, the more likely they were to send a starship on a sour jump in the bad old days. Still, even today, passenger liners only used levels A and B, and did it at a slow speed. The Navy was a bit more daring; they used C and D jumps.

"Cambria's jump point India is an F on the index."

"We *are* on a war footing," Chief Bo breathed.

"Nelly, project the shortest course from Cambria jump India to the Paris system. Display." A holivid shot from Kris's shoulder to dance in the air between Kris and Bo. Three long jumps took them far away from human space, which in and of itself violated the Wardhaven Treaty. Still, the last one brought them right back to where they wanted to go.

"We will arrive at Paris jump Kilo. It has not been used

recently. Assuming it is still within fifty thousand klicks of its last reported position, it will put us here," the holivid expanded on the Paris system. Five suns did a wild jig around each other and, in the case of the two smallest suns, through the orbits of several of the fifteen planets and the asteroids that marked the wreckage of two more. Two gas giants provided refueling stations to the six jump points that supported dozens of major shipping routes. If Olympia gave access to much of the Rim in four jumps, this train wreck of a system did the same in three . . . with Earth thrown in as well. A great transfer station for the last eighty years, was it about to become a great place to start a war?

"What's the nearest often-used jump point?" Kris asked.

"Alpha." A square in the system turned red. "It is on the main route between Earth and many of the Rim worlds."

"Wardhaven?"

"Yes. Traffic from Wardhaven used the Delta jump point." A second square halfway across the system turned green.

"We're going to be right next to the jump the Earth battle fleet is most likely to use." Bo frowned.

"And about as far from Wardhaven's as you can get," Kris finished. "Assuming, of course that we use this route. Nelly, estimate times required between these jumps. Report to me when I am not on the bridge if this ship's jumps match that course."

"Good thinking, ma'am. But even if this is our route, what does it mean?"

"I have no idea," Kris admitted. Kris also had to admit she was tired, wasn't going to get much sleep, and desperately wanted a lot more than she was likely to get. She would think about this in her spare time tomorrow. Right, like she'd been getting a lot lately. Kris drifted off within seconds of hitting the sack. Her dreams were vivid. No matter how hard she fought, the Earth ships were always there first with their lasers. No matter how fast she got her shots off, the Earth lasers were already slicing into the *Typhoon*. Time after time she watched Tommy and Bo and her marines' faces as they gasped for air in the vacuum.

Next morning, breakfast wolfed down, she was headed for the bridge but found Corporal Li facing her. "Ms. Longknife, the captain hasn't posted the course. These jumps don't fit any of our other trips out. Some of the marines are kind of worried."

"Trust me," Kris told the corporal who'd dropped with her to rescue the girl forever and just two months ago. "This ship is headed for the Paris system. Skipper's just taking a different route. Got to quit thinking like peacetime."

"Is it gonna be a war, ma'am?" The corporal's face was a mixture of emotions, leaving Kris to guess what answer he wanted.

"The prime minister and a lot of other good folks are doing everything they can to see that this all ends peacefully. But you know the old man. If it comes to a fight, he wants the *Typhoon* to be the best there is in the fleet."

"Yeah, that's the skipper. Thank you, ma'am." And the man was gone, and Kris was late for the bridge, but she suspected what she said would be through half the ship before lunch.

"So glad you could join us," Captain Thorpe said as Kris slipped into her seat at 0600 exactly. "Ensign Lien, you've been getting off too easy. Addison and Longknife haven't let the ship take enough hits. I'm putting you on your own set of sims. Addison, you're still not using gravity wells for all they're worth. The *Typhoon* is fast, and we operate independently. Forget about staying in formation with the rest of the squadron. Push it. Work it. Longknife, you're still waiting too long for the computer to offer you shots. Think ahead of the damn machine. I know you've got the killer instinct. Use it."

The captain drove them hard that day. He was none too pleased when Kris missed two shots; both when the *Typhoon* went through real jumps. "Ensign, you took three minutes to set the ship up for that shot, then you miss. Damn it, that should never have happened."

"Sorry, sir. The jump disoriented me for a second. It won't happen in battle."

"You bet it won't. Addison, Longknife, take a break. XO, Comm, meet me in my day cabin."

"Yes, sirs" answered him.

Kris and Addison dropped down to the mess room. Kris wrapped both her hands around the hot mug, willing the warmth to soften the knots in her fingers and the palms of her hands.

"Bet you can't wait to get some Earth ships in your sights. I'm so sick of steering the ship and not feeling her move under me. Let's get this thing on for real!" Addison crowed.

"We're not at war yet," Kris pointed out.

"What's the matter, you like Earth? They've been kicking us around for eighty years. It's about time we show Earth that space belongs to the Rim."

"So we show them the door and take off on our own. We don't need a war for that."

"You think they'll let us just walk? I hear they want payment for every ship we take. Full, brand-new price tag. Even the ones we bought ourselves. Earthies are brain dead."

"And a war is going to leave a lot of people real dead."

"What's the matter, Longknife, you afraid?"

"Addison, you ever faced a loaded weapon aimed at you?"

"No." That let some air out of him.

"When you've done it two or three times, I'll buy you a beer and we can compare notes. Until then, stow it." Kris cut off the debate and put down her cold coffee. "Let's get back."

The skipper cut them loose early that evening. "Take a long, hot shower. Get some rest. We jump into the Paris system at oh nine hundred tomorrow. Things may get exciting after that."

Kris headed for her room. "Nelly, what jump will an oh nine hundred arrival use to get us into Paris?"

"Kilo," the computer answered.

"Have you picked up any news?"

"No. We have been too far from human space."

The entire squadron was following each other through jump points without buoys. Of course, this far from human space, there should be no risk of running into another ship coming through the opposite way. No human ship. Right. This was way beyond weird.

"Kris," Nelly said slowly, "you asked me to conduct my own searches and let you know when I find something that does not match a pattern I am familiar with."

"Yes."

"Right after the comm officer met with the captain, he loaded some new systems that are not active and which I cannot discern the purpose of."

"Something that will put us on a war footing?" Kris said.

"I have a list of all systems to be loaded when a state of war is declared. These are not part of them. I also cannot in any way interface with this software."

"It's not running?"

"No, it is only sitting there."

"Let me know as soon as it starts doing something."

"I will."

Kris knuckled her eyes with both hands, trying to rub away exhaustion; her brain felt half dead. All this had to mean something. Why would Father or Grampa Ray order Attack Squadron Six to take this roundabout way to Paris? Why would they want their best ships jumping into that system right beside the Earth battle squadron? Beside or behind? Assuming the Earth ships arrived a while back, they should have cruised over to meet the Rim squadrons and done whatever they intended to do. How do you haul a flag down on a spaceship?

Kris got this mental image of admirals standing around at attention, saluting in space suits while some poor spacer scraped the blue and green flag emblem off a ship's bow.

Girl, you're punch drunk. A shower didn't help. She fell into bed and promptly went to sleep.

"Ma'am, you asleep?" Bo asked her a hundred years later.

"I was. Something wrong?"

"Nothing, I guess. What you told the corporal, it was nice. I think it dumped about ten tons of fear off this boat."

"That's nice," Kris said, pulling up the sheet.

"Word is we're going to get there tomorrow early."

"Yeah." Kris did not want to wake up anymore.

"You know which jump point we're going to use?"

"Looks like the one my computer expected. Kilo, I think."

"So we're going to jump right in on the Earth battle fleet. How do you think they're going to take it?"

"How should I know?" Kris barely kept her growing frustration out of her voice.

"I sure hope there aren't any jumpy gunner's mates over there. Those battlewagons have lasers good out to a hundred thousand klicks, and we're going to be well inside that."

Kris blinked and turned over. "We will be, won't we?"

"Fifty thousand klicks is almost in range for our twenty-four-inch pulse lasers, ma'am."

"Don't worry. What ship hangs out around a jump point? Those Earth battlewagons will probably be way to hell and gone over to meet the Rim ships. Figure some smart dude will have brought along a couple of barges of beer. Spacers from both fleets will be guzzling brew while their admirals talk nice."

"I sure hope so, ma'am."

"I thought you'd like a live shoot."

"Be nice to know that all this training was for something, but ma'am, a war between us and Earth. God help us all!"

"Get some sleep, Chief. We all have to be our best tomorrow." And Kris rolled back over and tried to go back to sleep. But tomorrow's tactical situation kept floating around in her head. What if some twitchy gunner in the Earth fleet took a potshot at AttackRon Six? Well, that was what the smart metal was for, to protect them. Commodore Sampson would sort that out. That was nothing for an ensign to worry about.

20

"Twenty seconds to jump," Addison announced.

"Longknife, I want a full target display with ranges and bearings fifteen seconds out of this jump," Thorpe ordered.

"Yes sir," Kris said and checked her board. All range finders were on-line: laser, optical, gravitational, and radar. They showed the rest of Attack Squadron Six in line ahead of the *Typhoon*. The flag, *Hurricane*, led *Cyclone*, *Tornado*, *Shamal*, *Monsoon*, *Scirocco*, and *Chinook*. Captain Thorpe was none too happy as tag-end Charlie. If the jump point moved suddenly, the *Typhoon* could miss it and have to make a go-around and hunt for it while the rest of the squadron was already on the other side.

"Are we on station?" the captain asked Addison again.

"Within a kilometer, sir," he reported.

"Keep us right there."

Kris watched the seconds until jump countdown . . . three, two, one. There was the usual disorientation in her inner ear. Her board went red as the receivers got no response to the various search signals they'd sent out only microseconds before. Kris blinked, and the board went back to green.

And reported more real targets than Kris had ever seen in any simulation.

Attack Squadron Six quickly deployed into a wedge attack formation. The *Hurricane,* as flag, held the middle with the second division's four corvettes echeloned out to the right, the flank closest to the Earth fleet, while three, with *Typhoon* at the end, swung out to the left. Kris took that in at a glance. It was the Earth Battle Fleet that made her fight to keep her mouth closed and her bladder under control.

Huge battleships, ice-armored three meters thick against lasers, were arranged in eight stately rows of sixteen, gleaming in the light of five distant suns. Without a moment of willed thought, Kris's hands went through the drill, establishing range and bearing, correlating that with her own ship's movement, seeking firing solutions. The Earth ships accelerated at a steady quarter g; they did not maneuver, did not stray from their line ahead. In ten seconds, Kris had them dialed in.

When orders came from the *Hurricane,* assigning the *Typhoon* four specific targets, it took Kris less than ten seconds to identify them, establish distance, and assign one to each of the *Typhoon*'s four pulse lasers.

The reactor of the small fast attack corvettes didn't have the capacity to recharge lasers like the big cruisers and battleships; however, storage capacity technology had come a long way since the Iteeche War. The *Typhoon* stored energy enough for nanosecond-bursts from her four massive twenty-four-inch pulse lasers. Again, because of the small size of the corvette, the laser was short. This didn't allow for the near-perfect concentration of the sixteen-inch lasers on the battleships, but for the 40,000 kilometers until the energy beam diverged, the pulse laser of a corvette was as good as any battlewagon's main battery. Better, as far as Captain Thorpe was concerned.

Behind Kris, the bridge hatch opened, and the marine platoon filed in, taking stations against the rear bulkhead. In full battle kit and armor, they looked as out of place as

Kris had been at Longknife Towers in shorts and a sweat-shirt. Captain Thorpe nodded at Gunny, then tapped his commlink.

"All hands, this is the captain. Today, we show Earth the mettle of Rim humanity. They have held us down for centuries. Here, today, we throw that yoke off. I have been informed that as of now a state of war exists between the Rim worlds and Earth and any other planet too decadent to stand against that tyranny. You have your orders. The *Typhoon* is the best in the fleet. Let's show them what we can do. Captain, out."

With a tight, proud grin, Thorpe turned to Addison. "Close with our assigned targets." Now it was Kris's turn to get the full power of her captain's attention. "Longknife, you may fire when the enemy is at twenty-five thousand klicks."

"Yes, sir," came automatically from the helm and Kris.

Without thought, Kris's hands went into motions, checking targets, verifying the rate and angle of closure. The Earth ships didn't alter speed or course in reaction to the arrival of Squadron Six. They were making it easy.

Easy? Too easy!

Kris's fingers raced over her board as her mind raced as well. War! We are going to war! What changed the prime minister's mind? What could make Grampa Ray or Trouble give up on a peaceful solution to this mess? Where was a news feed when you needed it? "Nelly, get me some news," she subvocaled. Hell, with all the ships here, there had to be a dozen news packets broadcasting in real time.

"All channels are jammed," Nelly reported.

"Jammed! Who's jamming?"

"The flag is jamming all traffic to and from the squadron."

"Even on Wardhaven command frequencies?" That wasn't standard procedure!

"On all," Nelly reported. Kris gnawed her lower lip. She was about to go to war. About to attack Earth's fleet! And for the first time in her life, she knew complete zip about what was happening. No, she knew the most important data there was. She knew her father and her grampas. Would they do this?

"Nelly, tap into the ship's message traffic, there's got to be some explanation to these orders." Kris had never been one to do what she was told, at least not until it was explained. This, of all things, needed explaining!

"Attempting."

"Sir," the communications officer's high-pitched voice got the skipper's attention real fast. "Someone is trying an unauthorized access to our communication logs."

"From where?"

"Inside the ship, sir."

"Track them down," Thorpe ordered. "I want to know who it is. Gunny."

"Nelly, stop," Kris snapped subvocally.

"Yes, sir," Gunny acknowledged, coming to attention.

"Prepare to dispatch a team to chase a saboteur. You may shoot on sight and shoot to kill," the captain growled.

"Sir. Corporal Li. You and two others." Li signaled two privates, who moved with him at the hatch, ready to respond.

"Comm," the captain demanded.

"Access was repelled, sir. Whoever it was dropped out immediately."

"Let me know the second it comes back."

"Nelly, what happened? I thought Tru gave you everything you needed to hack into anything Wardhaven has."

"She did, ma'am," Nelly sounded hurt by this rebuff. "But the *Typhoon*'s net is being monitored by Ironclad Software. I think that is the system I told you about last night."

"Never heard of that outfit."

"They're a small company on Greenfeld that never tried before to increase its market share outside that area."

Greenfeld. Peterwald's home! What was nonstandard Smythe-Peterwald software doing on a Wardhaven ship? A Wardhaven ship about to go to war!

"Range to targets?" the captain demanded.

"Forty-five thousand klicks," Kris reported with the part of her that was *Typhoon's* offensive weapons boss. Around the *Hurricane,* the other ships of the squadron spread out. Kris checked her targeting assignment. She had a column lead . . . that would be the squadron flagship . . . and the fifth, ninth, and thirteenth ships behind it. Those would be the division flags. Her shots would decapitate an entire squadron. She checked the other corvettes; each had a similar assignment. With four shots from eight ships, Fast Attack Squadron Six would render 128 battleships either wrecks or leaderless.

"Weapons. Status," the captain demanded.

"Four pulse lasers ready and dialed to full power," Kris reported automatically, her mouth almost too dry to talk. "Capacitor fully charged. We can reload one laser immediately. Three more in seven point five minutes, sir."

"Reload Laser One immediately. Target the last ship in our assigned column. We'll show them the *Typhoon* can get five battlewagons with four pulse lasers."

"Yes, sir." Kris said, fingers moving to obey.

Something is wrong here! a voice yelled in her head. *Those battleships aren't expecting an attack. Is my father ordering a sneak attack? Would Grampa Trouble do this?* Kris couldn't answer that. Did Grampa Ray give President Urm any chance at all? No. But those ships held troopers just like him, even if they were Earth conscripts!

"Nelly, can you pick up any communications?"

"Nothing."

Would Trouble who went up Black Mountain, Ray who fought Earth, then Urm, then the Iteeche, fight like this? Would her father? They were Longknifes. They would not give orders like these! *So what do you do, kid?*

Tommy says there are always options. She glanced over her shoulder; he was looking wide-eyed at her. *Colonel Hancock, I'm not seeing a lot of options here.* She checked the range, coming up on forty thousand klicks. Not much time to make an option. *So, Kristine Anne Longknife, what do you do?* We're here to keep a fleet from slagging Wardhaven.

This fleet is a threat. A threat . . . here! Hanging around its jump point!

"Sir," she said softly, "there's something wrong."

"What?" Captain Thorpe snapped.

Kris stood, fingers still resting lightly on her battle board. "This situation, sir."

"What situation?" Puzzle only slightly marred the captain's confidence.

"This is a sneak attack, sir."

"Of course it is. You want to give that massed firepower a shot at Wardhaven? Sit down, Ensign, you've got your orders."

"Yes, sir. But orders from where? The prime minister doesn't have an underhanded bone in his body. I know. He's my father. If he fights you, he does it up front and in your face. And these ships, sir. They're not making any effort to threaten our fleet. Our planet."

"Targets, forty thousand klicks," the helm said. Each moment put them closer to a shoot, closer to massacre.

"What's the matter, Longknife, don't have the guts for a fight? I should have known. Gunny, remove this coward from my bridge."

You just made a big mistake, Captain. You made this personal. Kris turned to the marines; not one had moved from the bulkhead. "Am I a coward? I jumped with you. Without me, half of you would have burned on reentry. Without me, all of you would have died on that minefield. I was the first in the door, and the first to the girl. Was that the act of a coward? Is standing here a coward's act? Captain, these orders did not come from the prime minister of Wardhaven. Where did they come from?"

"From the only people who have a right to give them, you spoiled brat," the captain snarled—and let his temper give her the only chance for legitimacy she could hope for.

"Those orders come from the people with the guts to take what you money-grabbing wimps have hoarded for yourselves. You have no use for duty, honor. You let power lie around, wasted. Well, some of us know how to use power. There's Earth's power, sitting fat and dumb. In one minute we're going to blast it to bits. How's that for power?" Thorpe raised his fist. "And if Earth comes back, we'll blast them again. We've had enough of being your bootlicking dogs, Longknife. Now we'll do what is right. Gunny, shoot that dog."

Gunny still stood against the bulkhead. He'd watched his commander with widening eyes. Slowly, his M-6 came down. Kris found herself facing into a loaded weapon . . . again. *Well, Emma, my Highlander friend, I guess this is where tradition brings a Longknife.*

"Is that what you want to be, Gunny?" she said, strength rising from her gut with each word. Was this what got Grampa Ray through the Presidential Guard? Was this what took Trouble and the Ladies from Hell up Black Mountain? She pointed at the captain. "That man says you've been the bootlicking dog of the rich and lazy. You ready now to be the bootlicking dog of the power mad and crazy? Because that's where you're headed.

"You may not like my father's politics, but people like you elected him. You figure the captain here and his friends can do a better job? Remember that minefield that some-how didn't get spotted before the jump? You'd think a guy so hot to trot to set the record for fastest rescue mission would notice a thing like mines. What else will he miss? Is this what you want?" She moved her gaze from the inactive Gunny to those around her.

"You want to follow the orders of whoever happens to be the biggest, meanest bastard around? Is that what you want for your kids and grandkids? Space ripped apart by whatever warlord can patch together enough power in the rubble? Because there's no question, men drunk on power who can't even run a good drop mission aren't going to know a thing about running a planet. Who gave the orders we're following? Communications. You have to be in on this. Who's calling the shots?"

The lieutenant at communications turned as red as one of his readouts. He nodded to the CO. "Sir?"

"None of your damn business, Longknife. People like you have been calling the shots for so long you can't believe that others know what our worlds need better than you. You've kept us under your thumbs, paid us pennies for risking our lives while you make trillions in your sleep. This is where your time ends. Gunny, shoot that mad bitch."

"Ma'am, I'm sorry," Gunny said, leveling his weapon.

"Gunny, don't move your finger," Corporal Li cut in, his weapon level. "You so much as twitch, Sarge, and I'll stitch you to that wall."

The Exec was out of his seat. As he turned on the marines, a pistol appeared in his hand. Tech Hanson was already bringing his rifle up. "Put it down, sir, or so help me, you'll be dead before you can bring it to bear."

The XO froze in midswing.

"Drop the weapon, sir," Corporal Li said. "I mean that, XO, and you, too, Gunny."

"You'll hang for this," the captain screamed.

"I'm not sure we wouldn't hang if we didn't, sir. Ma'am, I'm just a grunt, but I'd really like to know if I'm on the right side. I figure, if we've screwed up, we might be able to just put our guns down and let them do this attack thing and maybe it would turn out okay for us."

"Comm, open standard Wardhaven frequencies," Kris ordered.

The captain shook his head.

"Fuck you," the comm lieutenant said.

"Nelly, slave comm to Tom's station. Then hack it. Fast."

"Slaved, ma'am. Hacking in progress."

"Tom?" she asked, knowing once more she was assuming he'd follow her, demanding he follow her, give her the proof that would prove to the crew that they could follow her. Would he back her once more?

His hands were already flying across his board. "I'm working on it," he snapped. "Damn, the *Hurricane*'s putting out the jamming." He glanced around at the bridge crew. "Somebody sure doesn't want us getting anyone else's viewpoint."

"Push it," Kris ordered. "Narrow your beam. Limit search to the emergency command net. Tight beam it at the planet nearest jump point Delta," Kris guessed. She had to find the Wardhaven flag. If the Earth battle fleet hadn't moved away from its jump, she bet Wardhaven's was still somewhere around its.

Five seconds later, Tom shook his head. "We need more energy. I can't burn through the jamming."

"Drain the capacitor." She sure as blazes didn't want to use that juice on a fifth Earth ship. Tom tapped his board. Kris almost forgot how to breathe as his readouts went deep into the red. These people needed proof; she had to provide it.

"Thirty-five thousand klicks," Addison announced to whomever it mattered.

Then Tom got that lopsided grin again. "Done. I'm getting something."

". . . hell do you think you're doing. AttackRon Six, answer me, Goddamn it. What in God's mercy are you doing?"

"That's my Grampa Trouble," Kris breathed. "Last seen, he was working with the prime minister to find a peaceful way out of this crisis. Anyone still think we're supposed to be doing what we're doing?" Kris said, turning to face each of the bridge crew. Faces went from pale to determined as she searched them. In the background, Grampa Trouble tried, rather emphatically and in language she'd never heard him use, to raise the commander of Attack Squadron Six.

"Shall I send to him?" Tommy asked.

"No." Kris swallowed. "They're hell and gone across the system. If this attack is going to be stopped, we've got to do it ourselves. And it has to be a surprise."

"You can't do this," the captain screamed. "Don't you see you're blowing our last chance? You're giving rich bitches like her the galaxy. You're gonna let them keep running you around. They've had us by the balls, now they want our balls."

But no one was listening to Thorpe. Eyes were concentrated on screens, fingers tapped battle boards, the bridge crew was with Kris. "Gunny, you with us now?" she asked.

"Yes, ma'am. I got a grandkid coming. Be a hell of a world to give 'em."

"Gunny, Corporal, get these men off the bridge. We've got a battle to fight. And maybe one to stop."

"Yes ma'am. You heard the woman," Corporal Li ordered.

"When you first came on board," Thorpe spat, "I thought you had the makings of a fighter. Now I see you're just as full of chicken shit as the others."

"Sir," Gunny growled. "You either shut up and start moving, or, I swear to God, I'll shut you up," he raised his rifle butt, "and have the XO and Comm here carry you out."

Kris let Gunny handle Thorpe; she had other problems. "Addison, you all right with this?" she asked as the skipper finally fell silent and sullenly was led from the bridge.

"I guess so, ma'am. This isn't exactly the Navy my dad talked about."

"Or mine," Kris agreed. On her battle board the corvettes were spreading out. Still, the *Chinook* was a bare three hundred klicks from the *Typhoon*. "Okay, folks. Here's what we're going to do. The squadron needs a wake-up call that lets them know they've got big problems. Addison, prepare for evasive maneuvers on my orders."

"Yes ma'am," the helmsman said through a hard swallow. Kris settled into her seat, wrapped her hands around her controls, and aimed a twenty-four-inch pulse laser at the stern of the *Chinook*. She'd worked defensive on the *Typhoon* long enough to know its most vulnerable spot. Hit a Fast Attack right aft of the engineering control stations, and you sliced right through the reactor. There'd be one big explosion and one hell of a wild ride, but the crew would live to write home about it.

Kris took two deep breaths, waited for her hands to get rock solid on the controls, then set the crosshairs of her targeting computer carefully on the *Chinook*. A glance at her four ranging systems—radar, laser, gravitational, and optical—showed four different ranges. She dialed in a good compromise, reduced her twenty-four-inch laser's power setting to half strength, and squeezed.

On screen, a thin yellow line reached out from one corvette to the next. Radar showed an explosion of gases as Kris's laser slashed into the stern of her target. The *Chinook* took off in a wild gyrating spurt, then fell behind the rest of the formation as it lost acceleration.

"That's got to get their attention." Tom chuckled.

"Yep."

"Thorpe, what the hell happened?" came over the flag net.

Kris hit her commlink. "This is Ensign Longknife, now commanding *Typhoon*. Your attack orders are illegal. You are ordered by Commander, Wardhaven battle fleet, to break off your attack run. If you do not, I will stop you."

"Longknife? Where's Thorpe? Oh shit. *Scirocco*, and *Hurricane*, you will attack *Typhoon*. Division Two, continue your attack on the Earth fleet."

"Well, you wanted their attention," Tom said, raising an eyebrow in resignation to the new mess his Longknife friend had gotten them into.

"Addison, aim us at Division Two. Tom, get ready to put metal between us and the flag."

"Yes ma'ams" answered her. Kris hit her commlink again. "All hands, this is Ensign Longknife speaking. I have relieved Captain Thorpe. Our attack orders are illegal. Commander, Wardhaven fleet has ordered us to stop the attack on the Earth fleet. I have just damaged *Chinook*, and we are now attacking the rest of Squadron Six. Whether you were in on the attack conspiracy or stand with Wardhaven, I suggest we all stand with the *Typhoon*, because otherwise, we're all dead. Longknife out."

"Stirring words," Tom quipped.

Kris shrugged. "Have to do. Addison, start jinking ship, zigging and zagging like you've never done before."

"I'll ruin your firing solution," Addison pointed out.

"Ruin it. I'm more interested in us dodging their fire than us hitting them."

"Hostiles are coming around, ma'am," Tom reminded her. "They should be able to bear in five seconds." That was another limitation of the smaller ships. Cruisers and battleships had massive turrets that gave their lasers all-around bearings. The Fast Attack's twenty-four-inch lasers were limited to thirty degrees to either side of the bow. Kris used the time before attackers could touch the *Typhoon* to send four half-strength pulses at the four ships of the squadron's second division. She missed all, except maybe the *Shamal*. That didn't matter; getting their attention was more important. What was most interesting was the behavior of the *Cyclone* and *Tornado*. Both slowed, turned out of line and away from the Earth Battle Fleet. *Bet there are some interesting discussions taking place on their bridges.*

Kris's stomach jumped to her throat as Addison dropped the *Typhoon*. "Missed us," he crowed.

"Turn us bow on to the *Hurricane*," Kris ordered.

"Bow on, aye," he answered.

"Moving metal to bow," Tom reported, moving liquid metal to where it was needed. Kris tried to line up a shot at the flag, but every time she was about to squeeze off a laser, Addison jinked ship. She dialed the energy on her twenty-four-inchers down to one-quarter power and snapped off a few misses.

"Sorry if I'm lousing up your shots, ma'am," Addison said.

"Keep it up. If I can't hit him, he can't hit me."

Then the two attackers shot past the *Typhoon*, and Addison swung the ship to bring the bow back to face fire, but there was none. Both ships were headed for the jump point, accelerating for all they were worth. "He's running!" Tom shouted.

"Tom, get me a tight beam to the rest of Ron Six," Kris shouted as she mashed her commlink. "*Typhoon* to rest of

AttackRon Six. Please note that the flag is hightailing it for the jump point, and consider your own options."

"*Cyclone* here. Ensign Santiago acting commander. We're with you, Longknife."

"*Tornado* here, JG Harlan doing the temporary honors. Where do you want us?"

"Engage *Monsoon* and *Shamal*. Keep them away from the Earth fleet. I'll chase the flag." But *Hurricane* had gone to three g's on a zigzag course. The g's quickly stripped away her vector toward the Earth fleet and got her moving toward the jump point fast, while the zigzags did not offer Kris a good shot at the *Hurricane*'s vulnerable engines. For reasons known only to Thorpe, he had not rigged the *Typhoon* for high-g acceleration, nor did Kris remember any practice at higher than 1.5 g. For now, she held deceleration there and watched developments.

A couple of Earth battlewagons got one or two guns out of train. The *Shamal* and *Monsoon* found themselves the center of attention not only of their sister ships but also of a dozen Earth fourteen-, sixteen-, and eighteen-inch lasers. Had this slow reaction been spread over eight attackers, it would have been pathetic. It still was, but now it was concentrated on only two. The *Shamal* and *Monsoon* broke off and raced for the jump point, *Cyclone* and *Tornado* right behind them.

"Guess now would be a good time to report in," Kris said, tapping her commlink. "This is Ensign Longknife, commanding the *Typhoon* calling any fleet commander on circuit." Her screen split as two faces appeared, one familiar, one very familiar.

"This is General Ho, Chief of Staff, Earth forces. Do you want to tell me what I just saw?"

"This is General Ray Longknife."

"Mr. President," General Ho stiffened to attention.

"No, just General today, Howie, working with General McMorrison, Wardhaven's chief of staff. General, it looked to me like you just had your bacon saved by another Longknife."

"Kind of looks that way from here, too, Ray."

"Now General, you can sit over there and wait for another bunch of hotheads to do something stupid, maybe this time at us, or you can come over here and do what we both know must be done."

"Ray, you know my orders are to wait for Mac to come here."

"And Howie, you know Mac's orders are to sit right here for you. Now, just between us old warhorses, I'm getting tired of orbiting this worthless rock. There're asteroids whizzing around all over the place. I'm thinking of suggesting to Mac that he cruise his fleet over to Paris 8." Kris checked her board. Paris 8 was a gas planet about halfway between Alpha jump, where the Earth fleet was, and Delta jump with the Wardhaven fleet.

"I think I've used up enough fuel going in circles," General Ho said, looking off screen. "Paris 8 looks like the only planet around that isn't in an asteroid cloud. I think I'll inform Earth I intend to use that planet for a temporary fleet base."

"Pure coincidence." Grampa Ray grinned.

"Pure coincidence," the Earth general agreed.

"Now that we have that settled, Ensign, you have any problems?" Ray said, turning his attention to Kris.

"Just the normal ones of a mutineer, like what to do with the old captain and who on board is with me." She shrugged. "Do you want more prisoners?"

Grampa Ray pursed his lips at the hot potato she'd dropped in his lap. Was the battle only halfway over, or could she let the running dogs run and order beers all around? "Kris, as much as I hate to say it, I think the Earth fleet needs to see us in hot pursuit. Also, I want to talk to the bastards who set this up. What did they think they were doing?"

"I've got the skipper, XO, and comm officer of the *Typhoon* under guard. I'll see what I can do about getting you Commodore Sampson. If you'll excuse me, sir, I'm going to be busy."

"Understood, Longknife out."

"Longknife out," Kris repeated, liked the feeling—and switched gears immediately. "Helm, accelerate us smartly to one and a half g's. Make us a course for jump point Kilo."

"Aye aye, ma'am. One point five g's to jump point Kilo."

Kris tapped her commlink. "Chief Bo."

"Yes, ma'am," came instantly.

"Would you mind doing a walk-around. Reassure any scared kids that they are on the right side. Let me know if there's any trouble. You know, what I'd be doing if I wasn't kind of busy doing two jobs at once."

"Understand, Skipper. Glad to."

Skipper. That was a title Kris hadn't expected to earn for a long time. Well, she hadn't finished earning it today. She studied her board. At three g's, the vector symbol for the *Hurricane* and *Scirocco* had just about bled off all their motion toward the Earth fleet and would soon be making speed back toward the jump point. The *Typhoon*, now decelerating, was still making plenty of kilometers per second *away* from the jump. However, Kris didn't need to catch the flagship, only hit its engines, and as long as the flag was running, its engines were a prime target.

Kris dialed the power on her lasers down to one-tenth strength and started plunking away at *Hurricane*'s and *Scirocco*'s sterns as their zigs and zags offered opportunities. Her first shot was off to the left. Next was to the right. Third shot was again to the right as the flag altered course to the left. Kris tapped her commlink. "Commodore Sampson, I can keep this up all day. Sooner or later, I'll get you. If not now, I'll get you at the jump point. It's a losing proposition."

Two shots later, the commodore's two ships, instead of zigzagging around the course they needed for the Kilo jump point, took off on a long tack to the right that quickly took them out of reach of Kilo. "Where they headed?" Tom asked.

"I think they just picked another jump point, one they can outrun us to. Addison, any suggestions?"

The map of the star system appeared on the main screen. Four jump points were highlighted in red. "They could be making for any of those. Orders, ma'am."

Kris rubbed her eyes, trying to remember what a captain was supposed to think about at a time like this. She mashed her commlink. "Engineering, what's our fuel state?"

"Your shooting put a dent in it, but we've still around sixty percent."

"ComAttackRon Six is running, and the Wardhaven Chief of Staff would sure like a few words with him. Any suggestions?"

"We got a lot of green hands aboard, Skipper," that one word, coming from a lieutenant commander who might well have been in on the conspiracy, was good to hear. "You may not have noticed, the way Thorpe was keeping you deep in sims, but we never drilled at greater than 1.5 g's. I would suggest, ma'am, that you give all hands a half hour at 1.5 before going to two g's. If we don't find any problems, then take us to three. I know that's slow, but we've got a lot of green spacers who've never been in a high-g operation."

Which sounded good but could be an excuse to let *Hurricane* escape. But engineering and his snipes had tended to be their own clique. Hell, if he wanted to stop the pursuit, all he had to do was dump the reactor core. "Thanks, engineering, we'll follow that. Commander Paulus, in case you haven't noticed, you're the senior officer aboard. The spare chair here on the bridge is yours."

"If you'll excuse me, Ms. Longknife, I expect I'll be needed here if you put any kind of load on these engines. I know the yard's advertising says these liquid metal boats are supposed to switch to all configurations with no pain, but every time we shorten up the hull, my snipes and I go through the tortures of the damned to keep plasma flowing. You fought us fine, Ensign. Until you can get me a relief I trust as good as myself to keep these engines from blowing us to pieces, I'll stay here."

Which was the first Kris had heard about engineering having problems with the liquid metal. "How bad is it, Commander?"

"Nothing I can't handle. And if I can't, I'll holler."

Kris was rapidly discovering a captain's job was not all skittles and beer. "Yeoman, announce to all hands we go to two g's in thirty minutes and three g's as soon as we can."

It took the *Typhoon* almost three hours to work up to 3.25 g's. Among other things, the brig had bare metal for beds. Tempting as it was to let Thorpe take his g's the hard way, Kris had the marines scare up air mattresses. By the time Kris had the *Typhoon* up to full acceleration, the *Hurricane* and *Scirocco* were out of laser range.

Well behind Kris, the four ships of the second division fought their own battle, two experienced captains against jumped-up JOs who were getting their first taste of command in the middle of a fight. However, the decisions made by the designers of the fast attack corvettes came home to haunt the two rebels. Running, their weapons were pointed in the wrong direction, their engines fatally open to damage. It took Santiago and Harlan a while, but time was on their side and luck was against the *Monsoon* and *Shamal*. Long before they made it to the jump, their engines were nicked and their skippers replaced by subordinates who were not at all interested in fighting for a small group of officers who hadn't told them what they were fighting for.

That left Grampa Ray plenty of prisoners to interrogate, but Kris wouldn't bet that even Thorpe knew the whole story. If Attack Squadron Six had managed to decimate the Earth battle fleet, what did it do next? Ships might sail the stars, but they had to go somewhere for food, repairs, and refit. *Hurricane* was running. Where?

Once the *Typhoon* was up to speed, Kris got all the loyal officers on a hookup. "Engineering, how are we doing?"

"Lost power to laser three. Don't know why. With your permission, ma'am, I'd prefer not to send a repair crew nosing around it while we're on high boost. I've got my best ship maintainers down on the engines."

"Commander, engineering is your domain. You run it your way. Is our acceleration causing you any problems?

"No ma'am, not the way you put it on slowly, but if I was the skipper of the *Hurricane*, I'd be a bit worried about how fast the commodore put pedal to the damn liquid metal. Me, we're under control. It's them I'd worry about."

Which offered Kris a negotiating option. Why not make a friendly call to the commodore and suggest he review his engineering boards? That brought a chuckle to her, not a pleasant experience at 3.25 g's. "What else do I need to know?"

"Chief Bo, here, Skipper. The mess crew have never cooked a meal under high g. I suggest cold cuts until we slow down."

"Make it so, Chief. Any other problems?"

"None, ma'am. You got a good crew here, and we're rooting for you." That was good to hear.

The problem with a stern chase is that it is long and, at three and a quarter g's Kris weighed nearly four hundred pounds. Just breathing exhausted a person. Moreover, the peacetime staffing level for a fast attack corvette didn't make allowances for a battle running over normal work hours. The usual underway bridge watch was two. The engineering watch was a similar pair. At three and a quarter g's, Commander Paulus kept his entire watch and maintenance team on duty. On the bridge, there was no way Kris was leaving the attack board or relieving Tom from defenses. Addison was just as reluctant to go below. "Who knows when they're going to turn and fight. I'm here as long as you are."

So Kris scheduled Tom, then Addison, then herself for a two-hour doze at their stations and had the ship's officers and petty officers do the same for the entire crew, two-thirds alert at their posts, one-third resting. By the time Kris awoke from her nap, it was clear the *Hurricane* was headed for jump point Mike.

"It's never been used for anything," Nelly told Kris. "It's an F minus if there is such a thing."

"They've got to flip ship soon, start slowing down, or . . ." Tom swallowed the rest of that thought.

"They won't be able to adjust their course to account for the jump point's wandering," Addison finished, "or they'll hit that jump and end up somewhere in the next galaxy, if the points go that far." He turned to Kris, not easy under acceleration. "You Longknifes know more about that than I do."

Kris risked a snort. "Trust me. I don't know anything about jumps. Whatever you may have heard happened to Grampa Ray on Santa Maria, it's not hereditary. Let me make this decision early and make it clear. We are not going into a jump with this energy on the boat. Any questions? Any discussion?"

"Great by me," Tommy said.

"Engineering, what's your condition?"

"No change, ma'am. Three lasers fully charged. Capacitor full. Reactor is holding just outside the red. Everything looks stable."

So Kris ordered another six-hour nap rotation. As she was about to take her own, Tom frowned. "I'm getting action on jump point Juliet. That's not too far from Mike."

"What's it connect to?" Kris asked.

"Lots of Rim worlds. Just not so stable as to be one you want to use on a regular basis." And two minutes later, jump point Juliet coughed out six blips.

"This is Wardhaven corvette *Typhoon* to ships that just exited Paris jump Juliet. Identify yourselves," Kris demanded—and waited to see if the commodore had friends coming.

"This is Society cruiser *Patton*, out of Wardhaven," drawled a female voice; Kris exhaled the breath she was holding. "I hope the party's not over, and you folks haven't drunk all the beer. I'm leading Scout Squadron Fifty-four. It was no picnic getting these collections of junk and ice up to speed."

"*Patton*, this is Ensign Longknife, acting captain of the *Typhoon*. AttackRon Six launched an unauthorized attack on the Earth fleet. We are in pursuit of *Hurricane* and *Scirocco*."

"Good God, woman, I'll say you are. You're not going into a jump at that speed are you?"

"I'm not, but I'm not so sure about them. You game for trying to cut them off from jump Mike?"

"Good gravy, boys, they saved some of the fun for us. Scout Fifty-Four, follow me. General pursuit. Shoot 'em if you got 'em." And the *Patton* let off a long-ranging shot herself. During the Iteeche War, laser ranges had tripled. Still, the six inchers on the *Patton* were only good to 60,000 kilometers. By the time the residual beam hit the *Hurricane*, the energy level was no worse than a warm summer day at the lake on Wardhaven. Still, the *Patton*'s shot did reach straight and true to warm the *Hurricane*. Kris had her board check the vectors. With Squadron Fifty Four accelerating and the *Hurricane* locked into its course both by its hellacious speed and need to stay on a line to jump point Mike, the flag was in trouble.

Fifteen minutes later, that trouble was highlighted by a message intercept. "General McMorrison to ComAttackRon Six. Your situation is hopeless. You will be cut off long before you can jump. If you jump, it is suicide. Cease acceleration and prepare to be boarded."

"Yeah, right, in an hour or ten," Kris muttered.

"Holy Mother of God," Tom half prayed. "The *Hurricane*'s accelerating: 3.4, 3.8, a full 4 g's."

"He's going to come apart," Addison shook his head. "Ma'am, do you want me to accelerate?"

"Engineering, flag's gone to four g's. Any suggestions?"

"No ma'am. Just a fact. You order us to four g's, and I swear, I'll crawl up to the bridge and lead a mutiny personally. You want to spend the rest of this trip in the brig with Thorpe?"

"No, Commander. I just wanted your opinion. I have no intention of arguing with you." Kris flicked her commlink again. "*Hurricane, Scirocco,* this is Longknife. Be advised, the engines on these liquid metal boats can't hold four g's. You are risking catastrophic failure. You hit the jump at this energy level, and you don't know where it will take you. Do those of you not in on this conspiracy really want guys like the commodore deciding whether you live or die?"

"Think anyone is listening?" Tom asked.

"We'll know soon."

A minute later *Scirocco* cut power. "*Hurricane,* call it quits," Kris called. "You don't have any future. Don't let the commodore drag you down. Somebody over there put a stop to this before the ship blows out from under you."

No answer. Kris studied the track of the *Hurricane* on the screen, matched it against her refined estimate of the jump's actual location. With the *Patton* as a gravimetric arm, she got a much better reading than the *Hurricane* could. She tested for the location of the jump point one more time and smiled.

"*Hurricane,* you have misjudged the jump. It's to your right. I repeat, *Hurricane,* you are going to miss the jump entirely. Cut your acceleration and prepare to be boarded."

"She's zigging to the right," Addison said.

"And waving just a bit too much of her engines at me," Kris muttered. She dialed her three lasers into a loose pattern, put in the best estimate she had of range, and selected one-quarter power. Shooting a three-laser salvo, she got a good spread. All missed, but number four missed the least. Quickly, Kris tightened her pattern and re-formed it around number four. Again, she racked up three misses, but this time number two was closest. Reworking her solution, tightening her salvo spread, Kris moved her fingers over her battle board as quickly as three and a half g's allowed. She had juice for two more shots.

Again number four was closest. Kris adjusted her salvo for her final shot as she listened to Tommy praying fervently for the lives of the *Hurricane*'s crew. Kris had gotten three shots off without the corvette changing course. She paused for a second, her fingers on the fire buttons.

The flag began a zig to the left. Kris made a quick adjustment and fired.

For a long second she waited. She'd shot the *Typhoon* dry to wing the flag, slow her down, make her unstable, and just maybe help any sane person on board get a drop on the commodore.

Somewhere in the *Typhoon*, radar and laser pulses went out and came back. Somewhere gravitational and optical systems did their measuring. Somewhere a computer assessed all that feedback and reported it to Kris's battle board. It seemed like ages that the blip on her screen continued, unaffected, on its way. Then the blip wavered for a second and began a wild series of loops.

"By God, Kris, you winged 'em!" Tommy screamed.

"Just a second," Addison shouted. "Just a second. Yes. They're out of range of the jump. They can't make the jump."

Kris let her hand collapse on the commlink. "*Hurricane*, you are out of control. You cannot make the jump. For God's sake, cut your engines before they explode. Don't let that bastard kill you all," Kris pleaded. "Damn it, I fired a captain. You can sack that damn Sampson."

The *Hurricane* seemed to settle again on its course. Then all acceleration died.

"This is Captain Horicson. I am surrendering the ship to a junior officer. The commodore is unconscious. What do you want me to do?"

"Put one g deceleration on your boat," Kris ordered. "See that Sampson gets some medical attention. There are a lot of officers that want to have a word with him."

"They can have him," came back from the *Hurricane*. "He damn near killed us all."

So the strange tale of Attack Squadron Six ended. The celebration at Paris 8 was long finished and the fleets long gone to their respective homes before Kris got the *Typhoon*, *Hurricane*, and *Scirocco* down to a manageable speed. Most of Scout Squadron Fifty-four didn't miss the festivities, but *Patton* drew the duty of rendezvousing with the remnants of AttackRon Six to pass reaction mass. The *Typhoon* was bleeding sewage into the reactors before she fell in formation with the old cruiser. No sooner was a fuel line passed than Tom was tapping Kris's elbow. "We got a coded message coming in."

Kris ran the number groups through the decoder. It didn't seem all that secret to her. She tapped her commlink. "The *Typhoon, Hurricane,* and *Scirocco* are ordered to rendezvous with the battleship *Magnificent* still in orbit around Paris 8. All personnel suspected of being involved in the attack conspiracy will be transferred to the *Magnificent* and returned to Wardhaven under guard. All other officers are ordered to the *Magnificent* for debriefing and TDY to Wardhaven as material witnesses. The corvettes will draw new officers on temporary assignment to get them back to High Cambria."

That left the crew in a happy mood. Tommy eyed Kris when she didn't join in the smiles. "Anything in there about you?"

"Yes. Ensign Kris Longknife is detached from the *Typhoon,* with orders to report to Wardhaven."

"Detached?"

Kris knew they couldn't very well make her captain of the *Typhoon,* but to yank her off of it like this? She tried to look at the bright side. "At least I'm not under guard."

21

Kris paused at the top of the stairs. It was early morning; the sun shone through the crystal chandelier in the foyer of Nuu House sending tiny rainbows dancing on the spiral of black and white tiles below. On early mornings like this, a much younger Kris and Eddy had tried to catch the rainbows, hoping for the promised pot of gold. Was she any closer now to finding the end of her rainbow? A deep sigh drew in the smell of memories and morning, breakfast and wood . . . and the inevitable hint of electronics. Such was a grown woman's world.

The *Magnificent* had docked late last night; Kris and Tom were two of the few who left her. As expected, Harvey was waiting for Kris at the elevator exit. Surprisingly, two messages had quickly come in to Nelly. "So you made it back alive.—Al," was Grandfather's cryptic response, which also included Kris among the few people allowed to call him Al. The note from Mother had simply said, "We are expecting you for supper tomorrow." So, at least the family was not distancing itself from their mutineer.

As on a long ago morning, Grampa Trouble was downstairs. Today, Kris stood stiff in starched undress whites; Grampa Trouble wore civilian clothes. He stood with his back to Kris, talking with Grampa Ray. His voice low, his hands flew wildly as he remonstrated with the former president. Ray shook his head. He'd been shaking it since Kris first spotted him; he kept right on shaking it. Then he noticed her.

His eyes took on a sparkle, and his mouth morphed from frown to smile in the second he took to look up. Trouble paused his argument in mid-hand wave, turned to see what Ray was beaming at, and did his own version of proud great-grandfather. "Have we told you lately what a fine young woman you've turned out to be, Ensign?" Trouble smiled proudly.

Kris started down the stairs, feeling the scratch of the starched uniform on the back of her legs. "What got you two up so early?" she asked in a soft voice that filled the vast space.

"Meetings!" Ray spat. "You?"

"Another session with my inquisitor. He asks me the same questions. I give him the same answers. He likes oh eight hundred meetings."

"I survived that inquisition a few times," Ray assured her. "You will, too."

Kris nodded; she'd faced rifle fire and heavy lasers. Why worry about a little talk with an intelligence weenie? Or supper with Mother and Father, for that matter. Somehow tonight didn't hold nearly the terror it once had.

"What are you two doing for lunch?"

They exchanged a look. "I am not going to lunch with that bunch," Ray snorted.

"Before Kris shipped off last time," Trouble said, "she wanted to ask us a few questions."

"Questions?" Ray raised an eyebrow.

"One of my skippers, not Thorpe, said that if I intended to be another one of those damn Longknifes that I better get a solid handle on just what damn Longknifes really did and how they survived doing it. How come an autopsy showed a bomb went off in someone's face, but the bomber walked away?"

"Oh," Ray said, glancing at Trouble, who only raised an eyebrow in reply. Ray shook his head ruefully. "Should have known you'd be asking that one. Okay, Kris, tell you what, if you survive your little morning talk, and if I don't get lynched by the mob old Trouble here has matched me up with, we'll meet around ten-thirty for an early lunch."

"Ten-thirty!" Trouble protested. "That bunch of long-winded yappers and yammerers will just be getting started."

Ray gave Trouble a wide-mouthed, full-toothed grin. "Who do you want to spend time with, them or her?"

Trouble snorted. "Her."

The three of them turned for the door. Outside, Harvey had brought Kris's car around, but a huge black limo was ahead of him. A marine in Savannah greens held the door open for the two senior officers. Grampa Ray boarded the land dreadnought as if it were carrying him to a funeral . . . his own.

Kris headed for her car. Harvey was behind the wheel; Jack rode shotgun. Neither made a move to open her door. With one of Grampa Trouble's trademark shrugs, Kris opened her own door and slid into the backseat. She waved a hand at the monster ahead of them. "What's a gal got to do to get service like that?"

"Save the world a couple of dozen times," Jack grinned. "Until then, exercise is good for you."

Kris licked her finger, then drew three lines in the air. "Three down. How many to go?"

"Too many," Harvey grumbled and put the car in gear. "You know, an old grandfather like me could get used to a world that was nice and quiet. Maybe even boring. It's kind of pleasant for an old fart to have the kids come home every night."

Kris frowned a question at Jack. "His youngest grandson has a date with a recruiter for a swearing in this afternoon,"

Kris's Secret Service agent explained. "After whatever it was at Paris system, Wardhaven is expanding the Army and Navy."

Kris opened her mouth to say something to her old friend, then closed it. He'd cheered her when she joined up, but your adopted kid was one thing; the baby of your own flesh was another. She searched for words . . . and discarded *I'm sorry, I'm glad for you, and I hope he'll be a great soldier. I hope he'll come home after two very boring years* almost made it of out her mouth. "I'm sure you raised him right," Kris finally said.

"Yeah. Maybe too damn right." The driver checked his board, then turned to face Kris straight on. "Is all this messing around going to be worth it to us who just want to do our jobs and come home at night to enjoy our kids and grandkids?"

"I don't know what you heard about the Paris situation," Kris started slowly.

"Not much," Jack interrupted. "The media feed was cut off rather suddenly," he said, leaving Kris to suspect her agent knew a bit more than her driver. Once upon a time, she thought Harvey knew everything. The times were changing, leaving Kris sadder for it.

"Yeah," Harvey said. "We went a whole day without news. Longest news blackout ever. Then the cameras come back on, and the generals and admirals are smiling and spacers are guzzling beer. So why is your pa asking parliament to double the defense appropriation and my baby to give up a good job to be a spacer?"

Kris leaned back in her seat. She'd been so busy on the trip in, what with prisoners and debriefings that she'd had no time for news. She waved off the temptation to have Nelly give her a quick briefing. If the truth, the real truth, and what was actually happening were as confused as Harvey seemed to be, even Nelly would be hard put to separate the signal from the noise.

"I don't know," Kris finally said.

Harvey turned back to watching where the car was taking them. Jack gave Kris what might have been a nod of approval, but then again might have just been a bump in the road, and turned back to being a lookout.

When Kris got out in front of Main Navy, Jack joined her. "You coming to my meeting?" she asked.

"I understand your last cruise got a bit exciting."

Kris smiled. "People *were* pointing guns at me. You volunteering for ship duty?"

"Maybe you ought to avoid duty where I can't provide my services."

That sounded like a line. "And what kind of service are you providing?"

"I take your bullet," he said simply, eyeing the hallway ahead of them. "Other grief you earn is your problem."

"I'm sorry," Kris said and found she meant it. She'd been so concentrated on her own job, she'd forgotten the jobs others had. And after the reaming out Colonel Hancock had given her!

Jack opened the door signed OP-5.1. "Ensign, you have your job. I understand you're getting rather good at it. I have my job. You concentrate on yours, and I'll take care of mine."

Kris identified herself to a civilian receptionist who pointed her at a conference room. Its door was closed; a sign flashed In Use—Top Secret beside it. Jack raised an eyebrow as he settled into a chair and picked up a magazine.

Inside, Kris found the lieutenant who had been questioning her twice a day since she came aboard the *Magnificent*, as well as a new commander, forty-something, black hair just starting to gray. He wore neither name tag nor ribbons on his khakis. The lieutenant began with his usual questions. What was Kris's job on the *Typhoon*? What did she know of its voyage? What happened on the bridge that morning?

Kris gave her usual answers. That took the usual hour. Then the commander leaned forward. "Who helped you plan your mutiny, Ensign Longknife?"

"Huh," Kris bridled at this new line of questioning. "No one."

"How long had you been planning your mutiny?" he shot back.

"I did not plan it." But the rapid-fire questions kept coming. After five minutes of who, what, when, where, and how questions all ending in that nasty word *mutiny,* Kris's temper snapped. "Commander, Captain Thorpe's and Commodore Sampson's actions didn't leave me a lot of options. What was I supposed to do? Follow orders and shoot up the Earth fleet?"

"No, no, Kris," the lieutenant jumped in. "Still, you must admit that the smooth way you took over the ship leaves people wondering if you hadn't planned something on your own and just got lucky when their illegal actions gave a fiction of legality to your previously planned course of action."

"Horse shit," Kris spat. Then she spent the next hour explaining to the commander why armed marines chose to follow her lead rather than obey the orders of the ship's captain. That she'd been right didn't matter one bit.

Kris was drained by the time they let her go. Leaving Jack to follow in her steaming wake, Kris stomped for the nearest exit. Outside, she found a day too damn beautiful for how she felt. She spotted a small attempt at a garden. Someone had arranged three trees and a half-dozen bushes around a stone bench. She collapsed onto it.

"How'd it go?" Jack asked, taking station behind her.

"Haven't hung me yet," Kris growled. She was mad; she wanted to hang a few folks herself, starting with a nameless commander. What did he expect her to do? Follow orders, slag the Earth fleet, and when the war was over, tell the newsies from the winning side, "Well, I was just following orders"? No way!

Kris took a deep breath; it carried a faint hint of evergreens and turpentine, but the smell of rubber and concrete was not held at bay by the wilted greenery. "Hell of an end to the rainbow," she muttered.

Jack kept up his quiet surveillance as Kris tried to organize herself for what was left of a miserable day. Several deep breaths brought in only the stink of warming concrete. She ought to do something. What was on the schedule? Right, a meeting with Grampas. *Wouldn't that look great, they accuse me of mutiny, and I run off to tell my Grampas.* Have to cancel that.

Why? They were wrong about her mutiny, and they'd be wrong about her and her Grampas. *Damn it. Here I am just getting to know them, and I'll be damned if I'll let that commander stop me.* Kris stood; she'd never find the end of any rainbow if she let people like the commander call her shots.

After two steps, she paused. She'd planned to include Tommy in her meeting with her Grampas, let him get a look at what "those Longknifes" were really like. *No way was she going to change that.* "Nelly, call Tom."

"How'd the meeting go?" came a second later in Tom's voice.

"Not too bad," Kris said. "Want to get together?"

"I'm not due for another beating by my inquisitor until 1400 hours." Tom laughed. "Where you want to meet?"

"I'll have Nelly call you back in a second," Kris said and rang off. "Nelly, get ahold of either Grampa Trouble or Ray."

"How'd your meeting go?" came back a second later in Trouble's voice.

"Nothing I couldn't survive. How's yours going?"

"I think we've done all the damage here we can," was followed by a laugh that from anyone else would sound evil. Grampa Trouble didn't have an evil bone in his body. Or did he?

"Where are you?" Kris asked.

Grampa rattled off an address; Nelly brought up a map for Kris. "You're in my old stamping ground around the university."

"Yep, some folks thought it would be easier to dodge the newsies. Seems to have worked. Know any good place to eat?"

"There's the Scriptorum. Shouldn't be anything but students there. Nelly, flash a map to Grampa."

"See you there as soon as we close this down, say in about fifteen minutes," was Trouble's closing remark.

That didn't go too badly. Kris smiled to herself. "Nelly, tell Tom to meet me at the Scriptorum."

Jack coughed. "You're not warning him who he's meeting?"

"Why ruin his morning?" Kris laughed, feeling a big chunk of the morning's misery sloughing off her.

Harvey didn't have any trouble finding a place to park. Jack preceded Kris into the student dive. Even this early in the morning there were students here, dodging class, cramming for tests, just hanging. Jack stepped aside, giving Kris her first view of the quiet corner where she met Auntie Tru last. The woman sat there, smiling sunnily and holding down two tables.

"What are you doing here?" Kris demanded.

"You keep asking Nelly to take updates from my Sammie, you got to expect that your old auntie can at least get a calendar out of your computer."

"Nelly, we've got to talk," Kris growled through a smile.

"I don't know how she did it." Nelly sounded startled, with more than a tinge of hurt, if an AI was capable of such.

"What will you have?" the student server asked, taking in Kris's undress whites without so much as a blink. Apparently the Navy wasn't unwelcome today. How things change.

"Coffee," Kris ordered.

"Coffee," the others repeated.

As the server turned for the drinks, Tommy passed him. He slid into the chair next to Kris. "How'd the morning go?"

Kris considered warning him of what lay ahead but decided she wanted to be able to say under oath that she had not coordinated any of her testimony with Tom. "Worse than some, not as bad as facing Captain Thorpe."

The waiter returned with a pot of coffee and cups.

Grampas Ray and Trouble came through the door as the coffee was poured. As they stopped across from Kris, the waiter took them in with a glance. "What do you want?" he said, then frowned, worried his lower lip for a second, then his eyes got very big. "Sir."

Trouble seemed used to the reaction. He glanced around the table and ordered. "Beer, dark, fresh brewed, one," he said, pointing at himself. "Two," he pointed at Ray. "Three," as his moving finger took in Harvey and he got a return nod. "Four" was Tru; "five" was a very bug-eyed Tom. Poor guy seemed torn between falling through the floor or taking the beer. Jack and Kris shook off the offer. "Five then." As the waiter headed for the bar, Trouble took the last chair.

In a second, Jack was up and offering his chair to Ray. "Mr. President," he said.

"Not president today," Trouble said in supreme gloat as Ray clouded up. Ignoring him, Trouble turned to Kris. "Who are these good-looking guys?"

"I think you met Tom at the reception, if he wasn't too busy hiding." Tom tried to nod at her grampas and glower at Kris, all at the same time. "He also was my right arm when the *Typhoon* took on the rest of the squadron."

"Well done, son," came from both older men. And the rest of Tom's face turned as red as his freckles.

Kris figured Tom had about as much concentrated Longknife attention as he could survive. "This other fellow is my new Secret Service agent. Jack, meet Trouble. He's supposed to be my great-grandpa, but to Mother, he's just trouble."

"Still?"

"She hasn't forgiven you for introducing me to orbital skiffs."

"Woman has too long a memory."

"Excuse me, I'll be over by the door," Jack said, backing away while still trying to keep his attention fully on the people talking to him as well as do the required search sweeps. Almost Kris laughed, but she remembered too well whose job it was to take her bullet.

Trouble grabbed the agent's elbow. "No way. You hang around us, you might as well know the seamy side. Besides, this old codger sitting next to me needs special protection."

Jack eyed Ray. "From whom?"

"Himself," Trouble chortled.

"I may slit my throat," Ray grumbled.

"Don't let him fool you," Trouble cut in, grabbing a chair from the next table and pulling it over for Jack to settle into. "Ray's tickled pink."

"It's a lousy idea," Ray spat. "It's half-baked. They don't know what they really want, and this whole lash-up is a poor way to fix whatever problem they want solved."

Still unenlightened, they paused while the drinks arrived. Trouble raised his mug. Automatically, the others followed suit with beer or coffee. "To His Majesty, King Raymond the First of that name," Trouble intoned.

Kris clanked her mug with the rest, mainly because Trouble was busy making sure there was a loud enough clink to drown out Ray's raspberry response to the toast. "King who of what?" she said after a sip of her coffee.

Glowering at Trouble, Ray explained. "Some jokers who are old enough to know better think they'd have an easier time keeping sixty or eighty planets together in some kind of federation if they had a king sitting in the middle of all their politicking. By tomorrow they'll have thought it through and realized what a crappy idea it is." Ray raised his glass. "To peace and quiet in a well-earned old age."

"Hear! Hear!" Harvey said, joining the toast. Kris raised her mug with a heartfelt "Hear! Hear!" of her own.

Ignoring them, Trouble leaned back and took a long pull from his beer. "In your dreams," he muttered.

"They want an ombudsman," Ray snapped. "Well, I can be a fine ombudsman. I don't need a crown on my head to listen to a lot of whining losers."

"Without a crown, you won't last a week. You'll tell them to stuff their bitching and take off for Santa Maria."

"Well, at least there, I'm doing something worth doing."

Trouble just shook his head. "Not like you'd be doing here? Ray, old boy, everything we built eighty years ago is coming apart. They want you to help keep a chunk of it together." Kris nodded; glancing around the Scriptorum, she saw students whose lives were being decided for them by a lot of old men and women. Her own life among them. She, and all these kids would be a lot better off with the likes of Grampa Ray in the mix.

"Damn it, Trouble, we served our time. In any decent world we'd be dead and pushing up flowers, and kids like Kris here would be having all the fun. It's not fair." Involuntarily, Kris leaned back in her chair, counting the different emotions racing through her gut. She was glad her grampas were still around for her to get to know when she needed them. Yes, it was her world out there, but she didn't mind sharing it.

Trouble reached across the table to rest a hand on his friend's elbow. "You still miss Rita."

"Every day, but that's not what I mean. They really should be Kris's worlds."

Now Kris leaned forward to touch a man who was more an icon than a person to her. "Grampa, they are my worlds. But that doesn't mean there's not room in them for you, too. They belong to me and the kids at the other tables . . . and they're yours, too. It looks like we're all in trouble. And if we need someone that we all remember as a good guy to have around to hold it together, well, did they say, 'Buck up and soldier,' back in your day?"

"Probably more often than in yours," Ray grumbled.

"And next he'll be telling you about walking twenty miles to school, uphill and in the snow, summer, winter, spring, and fall." Trouble grinned. "Weren't you the one saying a minute ago how we ought to respect them and let them have their world?"

"Let them have it, yes. Respect them, never."

That got a laugh. Still, it was Ray who sobered first. "I still say this king idea hasn't been thought through. Like not letting anyone in the king's family sit in their parliament, what did they call it, 'House of Commons.' "

Kris, the political science student, sat up straight. She and her friends had come up with some really far-out ideas during their bull sessions at the Scriptorum. This was a new one on her. "What are they trying to do?

"They want to cut down on the money in politics," Trouble explained. "For the twenty years Ray's king, none of his kin can run for the House or donate money to any political party or campaign. They think that will keep big money out of politics. We noticed that your dad, Prime Minister Billy, wasn't there."

Kris knew that money was the fuel and bane of politics. This approach had the advantage, if nothing else, of never being tried before. However, the mention of Father meant this scheme was going to stretch out to a certain Kris as well.

"Hold it, Grampa. I think you'd make a great king. But that doesn't mean you're going to make me a princess, does it? 'Cause I've got to tell you, I've had all the problems a growing girl can handle just being the prime minister's brat."

Trouble barked a laugh, but Grampa Ray just stared across the table at Kris. Then he smiled. Kris had the feeling that fleets of Iteeche had died after such a smile. "Trouble, what if I make someone a duke or count?"

"Didn't know they were going to let you." Trouble stroked his jaw. "They didn't say anything about more royalty."

"There's a lot of things they didn't say anything about."

Kris shook her head. "Why do I think I should have kept my mouth shut?"

"No, Princess," Trouble said with an evil grin as Kris winced, "that's just the kind of talk your grampas like. Gives us old coots great ideas."

"No, bad ideas. Very bad ideas," Kris insisted to a grinning table.

Grampa Ray sat there eyeing them with a tight smile for a moment, looking very much like Kris thought a king should. Maybe the human race could use a king just now. Before she finished the thought, Ray got to his feet. All followed him. He raised his mug, and five rose with his. "To us, and those like us. May there always be enough of the few to keep the worlds turning for the many."

Kris shivered and answered, "Hear! Hear!" with the rest. So this was what it felt like to be "us" to the likes of Trouble and Ray. This was what it meant to be "the few." She took a deep pull from her coffee.

And Nelly gave her polite equivalent of a cough. "Kris, you are wanted in General McMorrison's office at one o'clock."

"Oh, oh," Tru said. "One of those Friday afternoon talks with the boss."

"Want us to put in a good word for you?" Trouble offered.

Kris straightened her shoulders. "No sir. This is my problem. I'll handle it." *It's my career. I better be able to handle it.*

"Wouldn't have expected any other answer," Ray said. "What a Longknife gets into, we get ourselves out of."

"Probably 'cause no one else could get themselves in so much, so fast, so deep," Trouble grumbled through a smile.

Kris laughed with them, realizing that they were giving her all they had to give. A joke and a laugh and a light-hearted confidence that she could handle her own problem.

With that she took her leave of them.

As he had this morning, Jack walked her into Main Navy. This trip covered several halls and an elevator before Jack announced unnecessarily, "Here's Mac's office." He opened the door, and Kris presented herself to the general's secretary. "Ensign Longknife reporting for a thirteen hundred meeting." The clock behind the woman showed Kris to be thirty seconds early.

"The general is waiting for you."

Kris squared her shoulders and marched forward. How

hard could this be? She'd rescued a little girl . . . and got shipped off to a mud hole. She'd fed a lot of people . . . and damn near drowned for the honor. She'd gone hell for leather into her first live firefight . . . only to discover she needed to refine her targeting for her second. Now she'd led a mutiny and fought a small naval battle to prevent a bigger one. Explaining to the Chief of Staff of her father's military just why and how she'd mutinied shouldn't be too painful.

The door slid open. General McMorrison was behind his desk, deep in reports, but he glanced up as she entered. She marched for the proper place in front of his desk, but as she did so, he was already out of his chair. A thin, graying man, he looked more like an accountant than a general, but he moved with quick, smooth steps around his desk. She ended up saluting a moving target. He answered with a wave in the general direction of his forehead that moved easily into an offered hand. As she shook it, he said, "Well done, Ensign. Very well done."

That was a good start. "Thank you, sir."

"Might as well get comfortable," he motioned her in the direction of a couch. She settled onto one end as he took the chair next to it. Just as Grandfather Alex's office was gray, this one was beige: tan walls, tan carpet, tan furniture. Even the general was wearing khakis. Kris crossed her ankles, folded her hands in her lap, and prepared for whatever was to come.

The general cleared his throat. "I guess I should start by thanking you for saving my neck. All I could think of as AttackRon Six spread out was that after they'd made their run, they'd lead the survivors of a very mad Earth's battle line right into Wardhaven's fleet."

"Is that what Commodore Sampson intended?"

"Yes, but that's not for publication. The politicians are still trying to find a way to smooth this over."

"They're going to have a hard time of it," Kris said. "Where was Sampson planning on running? Who paid him?"

"We've checked his banking records. I don't think anyone paid him," the general said wearily. "I think he was doing something he believed in."

Kris considered all the talk she'd heard from those in uniform and decided that was quite likely true. "Still, he'd have to take our ships somewhere. This wasn't the start of an internal revolt on Wardhaven, was it?"

"No, he apparently acted alone. He refused to tell us where he planned to take the squadron."

"Refused." Kris didn't like the finality of that word.

"Commodore Sampson died of a heart attack last night."

That knocked Kris back. "A real one or . . ."

"One of the other type." The general scowled. "We were able to follow the money on that one. The fellow who brought him his supper last night had a strangely excessive bank account."

"You wouldn't be willing to tell me where that money led?"

"I suspect if I don't, Tru will worm it out of our database soon enough for you." He almost smiled. "A small businessman on Greenfeld. Runs a software firm."

"Makes Ironclad Software," Kris finished.

"Yes. We already noticed that unauthorized software on your ships, so this provides us no new leads," the general said, settling deeper into his seat. "There is one bit of information that you might have a personal interest in. Commodore Sampson did select the *Typhoon* for that little girl's rescue mission. He was quite angry that you disrupted his entire plan after surviving what he'd set you up for during the kidnapping." McMorrison looked puzzled. "What did he do?"

"I and my squad of marines were ordered to do a night drop . . . onto a minefield," Kris said, both glad to have one mystery answered and frustrated that Sampson wasn't around to answer more about it. There was no use following that one any further. "Are you getting anything out of the other people, like Thorpe?"

"Painfully little. They claim that Commodore Sampson hadn't told them what his battle plan was. They were just following orders." The general made a sour face at that.

"And what will you do with them?" The answer to that would pretty much tell her what was in store for a certain mutineer.

"Hang them from the highest yardarm, even if I have to build it myself, is what I want to do. Nothing is what I'll probably settle for."

"Nothing?" was out of Kris's mouth before she knew it. *Damn it, girl, you have to do something about yapping first, thinking second.*

"Nothing," Mac repeated. "Oh, we'll cashier them, though most are eligible for retirement. But a court-martial would only provide them the public forum they want. And I'll be damned if I want either my officers wondering if they can trust their orders or the citizens of Wardhaven wondering if they can trust my officers." It was hard to disagree with that. It also told Kris what awaited her.

Mac reached over to the table beside his chair to pick up two small boxes. Opening one, he handed it across to Kris. She eyed its contents: the Legion of Merit. Nice medal. The second one contained the Navy Cross. Very nice medal. She held them in her lap for a moment, then closed the boxes and handed them back. She'd learned at Father's knee to let silence grow until the other fellow fills it. General McMorrison took back the medals but set them on the table in front of her.

"I've read Colonel Hancock's full report. You did well on Olympia. Very good for a junior officer." The emphasis was on *junior.* Kris ignored that and said, "Thank you," softly so as not to interrupt or let the general off the hook for filling the silence.

"You earned the Legion of Merit on Olympia," Mac said. Kris nodded but refused to ask why the Navy Cross was on the table. Mac eyed her as the silence stretched, thinned out, and started to twang like an out-of-tune violin. "You are a problem, Ensign," he finally growled. This time from the table he pulled a plastic flimsy and handed it to her. It was her resignation all filled out with today's date.

Kris locked her face down even as her stomach went into free fall. This was just another fight. Unlike the last one, the incoming was plastic and could not kill her. She finished reading and looked up. "You want me to sign this?"

"Resign from the Navy today, and I'll give you the Navy Cross for your part in whatever didn't happen at Paris."

The general is politicking. "This my father's idea?"

He snorted. "If your father so much as peeps publicly he wants this, I'd be fighting him tooth and nail, just as publicly. Half my officer corps would have my head if I gave in to him."

Kris considered herself politically savvy; this clearly was a political hot potato in her hand. She glanced again at the resignation. "So why are you asking me to quit?"

"You relieved your last CO, and his superior tried to kill you. Ensign Longknife, who should I assign you to next?"

Kris tried to see herself from Mac's perspective. Well, Hancock would have her back. Or would he? It had been a learning experience . . . for both of them. But it was not an experience either needed to repeat. Ship duty was her first choice. But what skipper would want to see her on his bridge? "Hi, sir, I'm the prime minister's brat, maybe even a princess. I hope we get along fine. I relieved my last CO." Right. No way they could give her her own command. Ensigns do not command. Besides, every command position was subordinated to someone. Mac here reported to her father, and Kris knew well that Father considered every voter on Wardhaven as his boss.

"I don't know who would take me, sir. But certainly there has to be some place in the Navy for me," she said, setting the resignation on the table between them. "I won't resign."

"Why?" Now it was the general who seemed content to wait until space boiled for her answer.

"Because I want to stay in the Navy, sir."

"Why?" he shot right back.

Kris paused for a moment; Chief Bo's late-night counseling session came to mind. "Sir, an old chief once asked me why I joined the Navy. She wasn't much impressed with my answer." The general smiled, leaving Kris to wonder if he'd once had the same counseling session.

"A Highland captain shared her family story of how her grampa and mine survived Black Mountain, and what it means, now, to be an officer in their shadow." That seemed to surprise the general. Kris leaned forward; her answer must be short. She poured all the passion she could into its few words. "Sir. I am Navy. This is my home." She handed him back her unsigned resignation. "I will not walk away."

Mac glanced at the form, sighed, then slowly tore it in two. Its static charge broken, the words vanished from the plastic as if they'd never been written. "That settles that. A word of advice to you, woman. Half of the officer corps is cheering you. Half think you're a mutineer who should be cashiered with the others. Good luck telling the two apart."

He reached for the medals on the coffee table. First he picked up the Legion of Merit. "You earned this one on Olympia." He tossed it to her. "There will be no formal ceremony. Wear it in good health." Kris looked at the box; this wasn't the way it was supposed to be. Her crew on Olympia, people like Willie, deserved better. But because of her, there would be no official recognition. Would all her joys be so mixed?

The general picked up the Navy Cross, opened the box, studied it thoughtfully, then closed it again. Standing, he muttered. "We'll think about this one for a while. Might wait to see what Earth does about your role in that Paris thing."

Kris started to stand, but he waved her back down. From his desk he retrieved another flimsy. "Present emergency is botching up all kinds of things. We'll be commissioning a flock of new ensigns. BuPer is promoting all ensigns with four months in grade to lieutenant, JG. It seems you are exactly one day into that window. So, instead of keelhauling you, I'm promoting you." He glanced back at her. "Purely by the numbers, you know."

"Luck of the commissioning date." She assured him of her understanding but couldn't suppress her grin. He went around his desk and retrieved something from a drawer. It took her a moment to identify what he held. What was an army general doing with a set of JG shoulder boards? She stood as he walked toward her.

"My father was Navy," he said. "I don't think he ever forgave me for going Army. These were his shoulder boards. I'd appreciate it if you'd wear them."

Kris blinked. This was not at all what she expected when she was summoned here. "I'd be honored, sir."

General McMorrison removed the ones on her shoulders and replaced them with his gift. "I'm actually returning these," he told her as he worked the fasteners. "They were given to my dad by your late Great-grandmother Rita Nuu Longknife. He got news of his promotion when on the *Oasis* taking her and Ray to their rendevous with President Urm."

Kris shivered; Grandma Rita had died in the Iteeche War. Not all Longknifes survived to listen to the media folks get it wrong. Standing tall, Kris waited while General McMorrison finished. It wasn't the extra half stripe that made them heavy. "I will try to wear them as honorably as your father and my great grandmother did," she said when he was done.

"I am sure that you will," he said simply in dismissal.

She saluted; he returned it. She marched slowly from his office. Jack fell in step beside her as she headed once more for the exit. Coming in, she expected to leave a civilian. Instead, she was leaving promoted. Promoted! For the first time, maybe in her whole life, she knew what she wanted. She'd demanded it. She'd refused to give it up . . . and it was hers. She smiled as she came into the bright daylight. The deep blue of the sky held no rainbow, but Kris now knew what lay at the end of one.

"I see they didn't hang you," Jack said.

Kris bounced lightly on her heels, looked around at the buildings of Navy, Army, government, and smiled. "Nope, they missed their chance. The Navy still has a Longknife."

"Why do I feel like saying, 'God help us all'?" Jack said.

"'Cause it just may be true," Kris said and waved for Harvey.

About the Author

Mike Shepherd grew up Navy. It taught him early about change and the chain of command. He's worked as a bartender and cabdriver, personnel adviser and labor negotiator. Now retired from building databases about the endangered critters of the Northwest, he's looking forward to some fun reading and writing.

Mike lives in Vancouver, Washington, with his wife, Ellen, and her mother. He enjoys reading, writing, dreaming, watching grandchildren for story ideas, and upgrading his computer—all are never-ending pursuits.

His website is www.mikeshepherd.org, or you may reach him at Mike_Shepherd@comcast.net.